How to Find a Missing Girl

VICTORIA WLOSOK

LITTLE, BROWN AND COMPANY
New York Boston

Copyright © 2023 by Victoria Wlosok

Cover photos copyright © by Indeed/GettyImages.com.
Cover design by Karina Granda.
Cover copyright © 2023 by Hachette Book Group, Inc.
Interior design by Michelle Gengaro.

Little, Brown and Company
Hachette Book Group
1290 Avenue of the Americas, New York, NY 10104
Visit us at LBYR.com

First Edition: September 2023

Little, Brown and Company is a division of Hachette Book Group, Inc. The Little, Brown name and logo are trademarks of Hachette Book Group, Inc.

The publisher is not responsible for websites (or their content) that are not owned by the publisher.

Little, Brown and Company books may be purchased in bulk for business, educational, or promotional use. For information, please contact your local bookseller or the Hachette Book Group Special Markets Department at special.markets@hbgusa.com.

Library of Congress Cataloging-in-Publication Data

Names: Wlosok, Victoria, author.
Title: How to find a missing girl / Victoria Wlosok.
Description: First edition. | New York : Little, Brown and Company, 2023. | Summary: Seventeen-year-old amateur sleuth Iris and her sapphic detective agency investigate the disappearance of Iris's cheerleader ex-girlfriend, who also happens to be the creator of a notorious true-crime podcast about Iris's missing older sister.
Identifiers: LCCN 2022057300 (print) | LCCN 2022057301 (ebook) | ISBN 9780316511506 (hardcover) | ISBN 9780316511827 (ebook)
Subjects: CYAC: Missing persons—Fiction. | Detectives—Fiction. | Podcasts—Fiction. | Lesbians—Fiction. | LGBTQ+ people—Fiction. | Mystery and detective stories. | LCGFT: Detective and mystery fiction. | Novels.
Classification: LCC PZ7.1.W617 Ho 2023 (print) | LCC PZ7.1.W617 (ebook) | DDC [Fic]—dc23
LC record available at https://lccn.loc.gov/2022057300
LC ebook record available at https://lccn.loc.gov/2022057301

ISBNs: 978-0-316-51150-6 (hardcover), 978-0-316-51182-7 (ebook)

Printed in the United States of America

LSC-C

Printing 1, 2023

To my parents, for always believing in me—this first one's for you.

HOW TO FIND A MISSING GIRL PODCAST

Trailer

HEATHER NASATO: If you take a good long look at Hillwood, Louisiana—a sleepy, small Southern community nestled in the heart of the Lafourche Parish—you'll quickly realize one thing: This is not a ghost town.

MAN #1: It may be a rural area, but we've got Deveraux Industries. We're part of the Acadiana Sugar Belt. A lot of fishermen still make a living off the Bayou Lafourche, and even with hurricanes, tropical storm damage, and way too many flash floods to count, we're all safe here. We look out for our own.

HEATHER NASATO: And yet, six months after an eighteen-year-old star cheerleader first vanished into thin air, a ghost town is exactly what it's become. One haunted not by abandoned buildings, but a single question: What happened to Stella Blackthorn on the night she disappeared?

[THEME MUSIC PLAYS]

WOMAN #1: Her little sister...was the last one to see her.

GIRL #1: A runaway? Please. You don't plan to skip town on the night of the homecoming dance, especially if you were just crowned queen. Especially if it's your senior year.

MAN #2: She was a cornerstone of our community. A shining example of what it means to achieve excellence through persistence and hard work, and we all suffer from her absence.

[THEME MUSIC FADES]

HEATHER NASATO: It is this very question that I'll be attempting to answer in my new local true-crime podcast, *How to Find a Missing Girl*, as I look into the circumstances behind Stella Blackthorn's disappearance last September, and why the police have since opted to pull back from investigating her case. You can tune in with Spotify, Apple Podcasts, or your favorite podcaster; I plan on releasing new episodes on the first Monday of every month starting this March.

[OUTRO MUSIC PLAYS]

HEATHER NASATO: Teenage cheerleader Stella Blackthorn is still gone. Her family is still searching for answers. And while I know some people may only see me as a junior at Hillwood High, I'm not going to stop until I find them . . . until I learn how to find a missing girl, and bring her home. Because when people talk, I listen. And in the past few weeks that I've been listening? Well, Hillwood . . . let's just say I've learned a lot.

Part One

Chapter One

Everyone knows you wear black to a stakeout. It's common knowledge, right up there with *wlw listen to girl in red* and *having mental breakdowns at school dances nearly lands you in shitty mental hospitals.* Sammy Valdez-Taylor, hacker extraordinaire and one-third of my sapphic amateur detective agency, nods along as I explain this, my gloved fingers irritatedly resting on—but not quite rubbing—the bridge of my nose.

I glance at her neon-yellow Hatsune Miku shirt, short checkered skirt, and holographic jumbo pink platform boots. "So why," I ask her with my teeth clenched in what I'm guessing is decidedly *not* my most charming smile, "are you wearing *every other color*?"

Next to me, Imani—the other third of the agency—snickers and leans back against their car. They parked right in front of the Valdez-Taylors', which would be more of a problem if Sammy's parents didn't love the two of us. But as long as Sammy keeps her grades up, her family doesn't care where she goes at night—or what she looks like doing it.

"Is it really that bad?" Sammy asks, tugging at the space buns she's managed to wrangle her thick brown curls into. I sigh, and my fingers start rubbing.

The thing is, Heather Nasato would never forgive us if we screwed up this job. She's currently our agency's best client, but that's only because she's been a paranoid mess ever since she started dating her douchebag boyfriend Nathan Deveraux last month. Which is exactly why the three of us are out tonight, about to conduct surveillance of said douchebag boyfriend, and not at home working on the soul-crushing process of applying to college. Turns out a customer is a customer, even when she happens to be your last (and only) ex-girlfriend.

"You know the good thing about being a cynic?" Imani asks as they pop open the trunk of their car with a smile. Out of the three of us, Imani's the only one who can drive—Sammy hasn't applied for her learner's permit yet, and I'm pansexual. It goes against my nature.

Sammy shrugs as Imani emerges from the trunk of the Homicide Honda with a stack of neatly folded clothes—black, I note approvingly—and holds it out to her. "You're always prepared."

A large grin finds its way onto Sammy's face. "You finished them already?"

"Last night," Imani confirms, their smile softening. "I spent way more time on them than on the Pink Ladies' jacket alterations for *Grease*, though, so don't tell Mrs. Landry."

"This is amazing. Give me, like, two seconds to change!" Sammy says, and then she darts back into her house. Imani and I exchange dubious glances as the door rattles shut, and I shake my head. We're going to be here a while.

At least the weather is nice. It's a crisp, cloudless October night in Hillwood, filled with the tantalizing promise of falling leaves and blustery winds that even my favorite black longcoat can't completely stave off. It doesn't matter, though, because my blood is electric under my skin. This is my first agency job since my fiasco at the homecoming dance last month—since the one-year anniversary of my older sister Stella's disappearance—and I'm determined to do it right. To make it through this day, just like I made it through that one, and keep my feelings tamped down and my agency on track.

Sammy emerges ten minutes later, newly changed and beaming. The turtleneck and flared pants Imani made her fit her perfectly, and she's even wearing a black knit beanie pulled low over her forehead. Except the hat's rim is studded with at least twenty star-shaped stick-on jewels, and she's wearing plastic earrings shaped like tiny babies.

I level her with a look. "Sam, we need you to take this seriously."

Her smile drops off her face. "I am," she insists. "Look, just because I don't entirely dress the part doesn't mean I'm not a valuable part of this team. I developed a GPS-based app and synced it with a highly illegal tracking device on Nathan's car. I can hack into any database. I inject some much-needed levity into our group dynamic, and I also made a really kickass stakeout playlist for our ride to Bellevue Estates, so you really shouldn't judge me for choosing to bedazzle my wardrobe a little." She tugs a stray curl out of her beanie. "It has all the hits: 'Every Breath You Take' by the Police, 'People Watching' by Conan Gray, 'Paparazzi' by Lady Gaga—"

"Enough talking," Imani interrupts, thankfully sparing me from having to listen to more of Sammy's song choices. "Both of you, get in the car."

I open the door of Imani's sleek black Honda and slide into the back seat, letting Sammy take shotgun so she can keep an eye on our position relative to Nathan's. If he makes it to Bellevue Estates before us, we'll have to call the whole night off.

Imani starts the engine, and their speakers roar to life with a jarring guitar riff. I catch their eyes—and Sammy's self-satisfied smirk—in the rearview. "'One Way or Another'? Really?"

Imani grins. "Blondie or bust, baby," they say, and then they shift gears and expertly speed out of Sammy's driveway.

I curl a protective hand around the strap of my camera bag as we roar away from the Valdez-Taylors'. The Nikon DSLR within it is one of my most prized possessions: It has a high-res adjustable lens and a quiet shutter, it performs well in low light, and it's come in handy for the slew of clients our agency has amassed since the three of us became friends and started doing detective work together after my sister went missing last fall. It was a gift from Imani and Sammy when we officially decided to launch the agency in mid-January—a decision that pulled me out of one of

8

the lowest points of my life—and it serves as a tangible reminder that the three of us are a unit. A team.

And that none of that shows better than when we're about to execute a job.

"It looks like he's taking a back road," Sammy says, scrutinizing her phone. "If we hurry, we can cut him off."

"Why would we cut him off?" Imani asks as we fly past beaten-down houses, magnolia trees growing half-heartedly out of dusty red dirt, and a big sign for JOAN'S DINER: THE BEST CAJUN & CREOLE BREAKFAST IN TOWN! "We're supposed to be on a *stakeout*. Right now, we need to focus on getting to Bellevue Estates before Deveraux, because *someone*"—Imani takes a sharp right turn, their dark brown hands flexing against the steering wheel—"threw off our entire schedule by blatantly disregarding our dress code."

I grin. Imani's really serious about clothes.

Bellevue Estates is our town's sole gated community. It's filled with huge houses that all look the same, about one species of grass, and a whole lot of rich white people. The Nasatos live there, but the Deveraux don't—and last Thursday at 10:00 PM, Heather thought she saw Nathan's pickup pull into the cul-de-sac even though he wasn't coming to visit her.

Hence the stakeout.

"All I'm saying is, he turned onto Nouvelle Lane," Sammy insists. "We can beat him if we drive right up to the gate, but we'll need a keycard to get through."

"I have a keycard."

It's meant to be an offhand remark, but Sammy's wide eyes

meet mine in the rearview mirror as her mouth falls open anyway. "You did not."

"What?" I ask innocently, pulling out my phone and sliding off the WORLD'S OKAYEST PANSEXUAL plastic case. Underneath, Heather Nasato's golden ticket to Bellevue Estates blinks up at me. "She won't miss it—I took it from her half a year ago."

Six months, two weeks, and five days ago, in fact.

Imani smirks. "That sounds like the Iris Blackthorn we all know and love," they say, turning onto a freshly paved road and coasting to a tall metal gate. The large sign in front of it proclaims the area beyond as BELLEVUE ESTATES: RESIDENTIAL GATED COMMUNITY; I can practically smell the privilege and see the ugly, bug-eyed white dogs already.

A single swipe later, we're winding through a neighborhood of luxury homes while Nathan Deveraux is still inching his way along Nouvelle Lane. It's funny that Bellevue Estates boasts so many, especially since Hillwood was just a poor Cajun Country fishing town before the Deveraux came in and set up their chemical plant along the Bayou Lafourche, but the place Heather lives in might as well belong to an entirely different world.

Hillwood sounds like it's filled with lush trees and wooded forests, but most of it—the part that isn't swallowed by twenty miles of sprawling swampland, at least—is run-down trailer parks, cracked pavement, and gray skies. But in Bellevue Estates? The grass is perpetually green even in the middle of fall, the artificial lake contains families of ducks that get fed instead of hunted, and the homogenous houses are as pristine as the Francophiles who live in them.

It's a paradise. And a little bit of hell, too.

Sammy frowns. "I just texted Heather to let her know where we're at, but I don't think she'll respond in time. She's kind of been ignoring my texts lately."

"Then it's a good thing we're already here," I say, tipping my chin to Heather's boring gray-shuttered two-story. It's dark enough outside that no one should notice the Homicide Honda idling in front of the residential pool three houses down the street, but also light enough to get plenty of close-ups to satisfy Heather if her boyfriend isn't paying her a visit. Which I kind of hope is the case.

Sammy nods, and Imani lowers the volume on the stakeout playlist just as an engine roars behind us. And yeah, maybe it isn't ethical for us to have a tracker on Nathan Deveraux's car. Maybe his parents, the revered Edward and Elizabeth of Deveraux Industries, would take the three of us to court and sue us to high hell if they knew the kind of shit we get up to after hours, and maybe not even Mayor Nasato's influence would be enough to save us from the wrath of the family that *truly* runs Hillwood if that were to ever happen.

But even knowing everything I do about the precarious position Imani, Sammy, and I hold as under-the-table high school detectives, nothing beats the exhilaration I feel as Nathan's white pickup ambles into view.

Right on schedule.

"We have a visual," Sammy whispers, pressing record on her phone just as Heather's boyfriend gets out of his car and I take a silent photo. Nathan Deveraux, heir to his family's industrial plant empire: tousled hair, broad shoulders, terrible ego, dark brown eyes. I have no idea what Heather sees in him, but then again, I put a lot more weight behind personality than most people do. I know enough to gauge that Nathan's is shit, though, no matter how many times he runs his fingers through his amber curls.

My lens zeroes in on the black plastic bag in his other hand. I can't see through it, but it looks sketchy as hell. Is it for him and Heather? Is she still doing drugs?

Imani catches my eye, and I know they've spotted what Nathan's carrying, too. They shake their head a fraction of an inch, their face a warning. *Finish the job, Iris. That's all we're here for.*

I grit my teeth. There won't be a job to finish if Nathan's just going to his girlfriend's—they'll smoke together, we'll lose the money from tonight, and Aunt Megan will get onto me about applying for a real job instead of spending my free time playing detective. We'll have to have The Conversation again.

But then, just as I think Nathan's going to turn into Heather's driveway, he keeps walking. Frantically, I adjust my lens.

Blurry.

Out of focus.

Not in the shot.

Damn it!

Knowing exactly what I risk for me—for all of us—if I get caught, I lean forward and change the settings of my camera. Those few seconds of adjusting make me lose sight of Nathan, and I panic until I see him again. There.

I watch it all through my lens: Nathan turning. Nathan bounding up the steps of another bland two-story. Nathan knocking once. Twice.

I almost miss the shot. Almost, because a year of practice forces my finger to click the button instead.

"Holy shit," Imani breathes.

The door of the house closes, echoing down the street just as the last photograph I took loads: one of Nathan Deveraux pulling a blonde girl into a passionate kiss, the two of them perfectly in frame.

A girl who isn't Heather Nasato.

Chapter Two

I stare at the crumpled wikiHow article in my lap, angling myself over my desk so my AP Chemistry teacher can't see I'm not actually doing my atomic theory worksheet.

HOW TO TELL A FRIEND THEY'RE BEING CHEATED ON (WITH PICTURES)

So you think you saw your friend's partner cheating on them. What should you do? First, know that the decision to tell your friend can be a difficult one to make. Always think of the potential emotional, psychological, and physical fallout from disclosing what you saw. Next, decide whether your information will—

"Miss Blackthorn."

Shit.

I cram the wikiHow article I printed out before class between my thighs and lift my head, making eye contact with Ms. Eastwick. She adjusts her horn-rimmed glasses and glares at me, her hawklike eyes locking on mine. "Are you already finished?"

One of the girls sitting next to me smirks, and I can feel the tips of my ears burn. "Yeah," I lie, forcing myself to keep looking at my chemistry teacher.

"Excellent," she says, turning back to her digital whiteboard. I'm hoping that's the end of it, but Eastwick pulls up a blank copy of the worksheet and taps it with the end of her pen instead. "So then you'll be able to give us your answers."

She holds the pen out and inclines her head to the board. I narrow my eyes, stuff the wikiHow pages back into my pocket, and pull the edge of my beige sweater over it. Eastwick knows I haven't done shit, and she's testing me. But this is nothing. I can do this.

I stand up and walk to the front of the classroom, taking the pen from her and scrutinizing the questions in front of me. They're all multiple choice, thank God, so I hastily circle some letters at random and shove the pen back into Eastwick's hand. The bell rings, and Eastwick glances from the board to me. Ridiculously, hope swells in my chest. Have I actually done it?

She smiles a wolf's grin. "See me after class, Iris."

Guess not.

Fuming, I grab my messenger bag and wait for the classroom to clear. It takes a couple of seconds, but then it's just me, Eastwick, and the four Galileo thermometers sitting on her desk. *Let's get this over with.*

"I'm concerned about your work ethic, Iris," Eastwick begins, the same way she always does, and I let my eyes glaze over until she needs me to nod or go "uh-huh" so it sounds like I'm listening. It's the same lecture every time with her: *You're a bright student, but you need to try harder. Your effort drops off considerably in my class. Your grades are slipping.*

You're not Stella, and I can't stop judging you.

I'm used to this by now; no one in Hillwood knows how to see me for myself anymore. Apart from the agency, everyone knows me only as Iris Blackthorn, Stella Blackthorn's little sister. I constantly live in her shadow: She was the star student, the varsity cheerleader, the girl who'd give you her left arm if you asked. I'm the useless one. I'm the one she left behind.

I glance up at the clock. My older sister's favorite teacher is still talking, but I'm supposed to be meeting the agency for our debriefing with Heather right now. Before I can interrupt Eastwick with an excuse to leave, though, the door bursts open and Delphine Fontenot walks in.

Sharp-faced, pale-skinned, and with white-blonde hair that falls to her mid-back in the kind of ringlets you might expect to find on a porcelain doll, Delphine Fontenot dominates almost every room she enters. She's the captain of the cheerleading team, the president of our National Honor Society chapter, and the resident mean girl of Hillwood High. I don't know what she's here for, but she couldn't have come at a better time. She comes to a stop beside me, entitlement practically radiating out of her high cheekbones, and I don't hesitate to take advantage of the clear distraction her presence creates.

"Are we done here?" I interrupt Eastwick, finished playing nice. "Because I actually have things to do, so…"

My chemistry teacher frowns. "Yes," she says, her gaze flicking to Delphine warningly. She probably doesn't want her to ask for extra credit or whatever the hell she's here for in front of me, but I couldn't care less. "We're done here. For now."

I barely suppress an eye roll as I collect my phone from the front bin next to Delphine and leave Eastwick's classroom, letting her door bang behind me. So much for her concern.

"Where have you been?" Sammy demands when I stop in front of Mr. Cooper's physics classroom a few minutes later. She's wearing an oversize pink raincoat with knee-high yellow go-go boots; Imani, by contrast, is dressed in a faded *Wicked* shirt, a black-and-white flannel, and a pair of cuffed black jeans. For someone whose life revolves around designing outrageous theater clothes, it's ironic Imani's so casual about their own. It makes sense, though. They'd much rather be backstage collecting gossip and fixing wardrobe malfunctions than parading around in the spotlight—a factor that will eventually win them a Tony for Best

Costume Design in a Musical, and currently makes them a vital asset to the agency.

I grimace. "Eastwick kept me after class."

"Again? God, you'd think that woman would let you catch a break."

"Well, we're glad you're here now." Imani appraises me and hands me a brand-new flash drive. "Have you decided how you're going to break the news?"

Last night, the three of us decided I should be the one to tell Heather what we found out about Nathan. The depth of our information regarding her stupid cheating boyfriend is limited, especially since a Bellevue Estates security guard noticed us before we could get the identity of Nathan's mystery girl and the gated community's online registry is firewalled to perfection, but we have the photos. And while we don't know the people who live at 343 La Belle Lane, Heather might.

"Yeah," I tell Imani, forcing myself to believe it.

"Good," they reply, glancing down the hallway. "Because here she comes."

I turn my head as Heather Nasato walks toward us—slim, tall, dark-haired, and dressed to the nines in Hillwood High's signature green-and-gold cheerleading uniform. She's clutching a glittery diary to her chest, and confidence—the real kind—rolls out from her in waves.

Our school's current golden girl, I think as she comes to a stop in front of us. The mayor's daughter. My ex-girlfriend.

"Hey," Heather says. She doesn't look so golden up close.

Something tugs at my chest as I look at her, an opening

floodgate of memories that somehow feel both real and half-imagined: sharing slushies on the bleachers at cheer practice. Pretending it was nothing when her leg brushed mine. Asking for her Instagram under the guise of comparing homework answers and then texting constantly, sending song recommendations and long vent-rants and stupid memes about AP Environmental Science long into the night. Making her a playlist. Having her make me one back.

"Um, hi," Sammy says, her large brown eyes darting to me. Willing me to stop staring. But I can't. Now that there's less space between us, it's easy to see that the girl in front of me isn't the one I remember. She's not the one I used to kiss for hours, the one who called me Butterfly, the one I once cared so much about. And even though she hasn't been for a while, I've never seen her look like *this*: dark eyes bloodshot, sleek black hair snaking out of her high ponytail in strands, pleated skirt wrinkled and dirty. She looks over her shoulder for a half second before turning back to me, and my thoughts from last night come back in a haunted whisper: *She's a paranoid mess.*

Heather smiles, but the motion is tired. "Want a picture?"

I shake my head and hold out the flash drive. "Here."

She doesn't move to take it. Instead, she readjusts her grip on her purple diary and glances around the hallway like she's looking for someone. "Just tell me," she says. "Tell me what you found."

I bite my lip as more students rush down the halls, chatting and laughing with one another on their way to our thirty-minute club meetings between first and second period. This is it. The moment of truth.

"It's Nathan," I say softly, forcing myself to meet my ex-girlfriend's eyes. "He's cheating on you, Heaths."

I don't know what I expected from Heather—denial, numb shock, tears maybe—but her face doesn't change. She just keeps standing there, hugging her glittery notebook to her chest, looking tired. "Is that all?"

My friends nod, and Heather mirrors them. "Okay. Thanks." She takes the flash drive and turns on her heel, her shiny black ponytail swinging as she drifts to where Delphine Fontenot and Arden Blake—wearing the exact same cheer uniforms—are waiting. The two slide apart to make room for her, Heather slotting perfectly into place beside them both, and then they turn around together. The notorious cheerleader trifecta, my ex-girlfriend floating in the middle like a phantom. An enigma.

A ghost.

"Huh," Imani says, watching her leave. "That was…interesting."

Sammy shrugs. "Maybe she already knew? She must have suspected something. There's no reason she would hire us otherwise."

"Who knows?" I tell the agency lightly as the three of us walk into Mr. Cooper's classroom, trying to mask the sick feeling in the pit of my stomach. "Either way, it's out of our hands now. We've done our jobs."

Except this time, I can't fully force myself to accept the words as I say them.

"Right. So, what's next?" Sammy asks with a grin as we slide into our usual desks. Although Mr. Cooper is a Very Serious Physics Teacher, he's also a massive nerd who's barely out of college. He runs the Media Appreciation Club, which basically means he plays anime for thirty minutes every day while occasionally mediating arguments between FIRST Robotics nerds avoiding their fundraising duties, and he doesn't mind if we text—or in our case, furtively whisper—throughout episodes. It's the ideal club to be a part of if you also happen to run an underground detective agency. Or if, like Sammy, you happen to fall in love with every anime girl who's come on screen thus far.

"We're going to the game tonight," I remind her, taking my honey-brown hair out of its signature bun so I can put it back up tighter. "Luz Lorres-Torres is late on her payment from last month, and I don't think we're ever going to see the money she owes us unless we corner her in person."

I've been eyeing a forensics kit for months now. It would be the perfect upgrade to our agency gear—which currently consists of a couple of disguises Imani designed to bolster their fashion school portfolio, my Nikon, and a pocketknife I got from my mom on my twelfth birthday—so it would be great if our paying customers could actually start, you know, paying.

Mr. Cooper hits PLAY on the latest episode just as the last few stragglers file in, and then the three of us lapse into silence. Sammy focuses intently on the show, Imani flips their sketchbook to a new design for *Grease*, and I wait until the OP before I pull out my phone and start scrolling through the posts on Reddit's r/WithoutATrace.

A pang shoots through me each time I read a new title:

Nala Riós, 23, Missing Since 10/11.

46yo 6'3" Steven Andrews, last seen Tuesday in West Point, Virginia.

On September 7th, my dear friend Lara P. Hannigan disappeared. I am asking…

As I keep scrolling, though, the pangs turn into an all-too-familiar aching hurt. Because there's nothing here about Stella. There's nothing new about my sister.

I put down my phone, unable to look through the subreddit any longer. I'm not sure why I expected to find anything—Stella went missing over a year ago. But still, there's a part of me that holds out hope. I know it well; it's the part of me that started the agency after her case went cold in early January. The part of me that believes in justice. The part of me that wants, more than anything, for the sister who raised me to be found.

It's funny: After word spread about how invested I was in Stella's case—after I made myself notorious by getting detained for looking into my sister's disappearance last December—Luz Lorres-Torres unofficially kickstarted the agency when she cornered me in Media Appreciation Club to ask if I could identify a catfisher who was using her photos on dating apps within thirty miles of Hillwood. I wouldn't have agreed to do it if the quiet short girl who always wrote code at the back of the classroom hadn't volunteered to help me, or if she hadn't commissioned her friend to design us outfits for a sting operation that would have put MTV's *Catfish* to shame. But the three of us did it. We finished that first job. And things have just taken off from there; now Luz is one of our most frequent clients, and Imani and Sammy have become my best friends.

"Anything new?" Imani asks, glancing up from their sketch.

Except even with all the investigating we do, I still have no idea what happened to my sister on the night she disappeared.

I shake my head, but my mind is still buzzing by the time the bell rings and we leave for our second-period classes. I'm thinking about Stella when I go to lunch and force myself to eat Hillwood's cafeteria food. I'm thinking about Stella when I walk into AP US History and see a photograph of a girl with crystal-blue eyes in a practice DBQ. I'm thinking about her when I meet up with Imani and Sammy after the final bell rings and the three of us head out to the football field, and I'm thinking about her when the two of them get into a heated debate about the anime episode I didn't pay any attention to while I absently rub the star charm on her old necklace between my fingers for strength.

We pay for our tickets, and then we find a grassy spot near the concession stand and cycle through as many card games as we can think of with the Sanrio-themed pack Sammy has—President, Rummy, War, Go Fish—until a crowd begins to trickle in and the sky above us fades to a hazy blue. The game will be starting soon.

"Look," Imani says, pointing to a cluster of girls in green-and-gold cheer uniforms whispering furiously in the back of the line for nachos. "There's Luz."

We each lay down our cards. Imani wins our pool of bobby pins, three crumpled one-dollar bills, and a long-expired coupon for Lucille's General Store, and then we make our way through the concession crowd until we're standing directly behind Hillwood's star flyer. Sammy taps her on the shoulder, and the cheerleader's dark expression instantly melts into annoyance as she turns.

I fight the urge to roll my eyes.

"One sec," Luz says to her friends, and then she follows us until we're in the hidden alcove between the concession stand and the stadium bathrooms. We all know the drill.

"The three of us need you to pay up," I say flatly.

Luz puts her hands on her hips, and I try my best to filter out the smell of lemon-scented cleaner as the bathroom door opens behind us. "I don't have my wallet on me."

"Really?"

She shifts uncomfortably, and my eyes narrow. "Um," she says. "Just...hang on until after the game, okay? Coach Hannequart doesn't want any of us leaving right now, but I can pay you once it's over."

"Pay them for what?" a smooth voice interrupts, and this time I do nothing to stop myself from glaring into the back of my own skull as my ex-best-friend steps into our half circle.

Lea Li Zhang glances between the four of us, her stupid HWHS PRESS pass flashing under the stadium floodlights. She's wearing a pristine knit sweater and clutching a very battered school camera in one of her six-fingered hands—clearly eager to snap whatever incriminating photos she can get to ensure the *Magnolia* has a juicy new front-page story ready to run next week—and something about the half smirk that ghosts her face as her eyes meet mine pisses me off more than anything. I can practically see the headline now: "Iris Blackthorn—Amateur Drug Dealer?"

Yeah. That's not going to happen.

"Don't you have a childhood friendship that needs destroying?" I ask Lea lightly, watching for just a second too long as she

24

brushes her snow-white bangs out of her face. She raises an eyebrow in response to my lingering gaze, and I tear my eyes away from her to glance back at Luz, ignoring the way heat rises to my cheeks. "We'll talk later."

"After the game," Imani adds, and Luz nods as the three of us whirl on our heels and leave her and Lea Li Zhang, Hillwood High's most notorious amateur journalist, behind.

Sammy sighs as we weave our way through the concession stand line and head back down the bleachers. "I guess this means we're staying, huh?"

"Indeed," Imani says sagely. "But don't sound so dejected—Senior Night is basically the Lafourche Parish equivalent of New York Fashion Week. I mean, you've got your shoulder pads. You've got your dramatic under-eye makeup. You've got your statement gloves, your giant helmets, your tight pants...." Sammy snickers. "The list goes on."

I grin as we wedge ourselves in between two girls waving green noisemakers in the packed student section. Sammy wanders off ten minutes after kickoff to buy popcorn, Imani pulls out their sketchbook and starts drawing poodle skirts after fifteen, and I keep sneaking glances at the cheerleaders. Heather isn't with them.

I frown. "Hey, Imani?"

"Hm?" they say, scribbling an appliqué near a hemline with their pencil. The referee blows his whistle, and the parents above us immediately start booing. It seems like Nathan got tackled—I know he's number 19 only against my will—but he gets up and shakes it off.

My frown deepens. "Never mind."

Halftime is officially called. Since tonight is Senior Night, the announcer takes turns waxing poetic about each player leaving for college in the spring, and the student section—led by the Fighting Gators cheerleaders, sans Heather—goes wild as their parents walk them across the football field. When Nathan Deveraux, son of Edward and Elizabeth Deveraux, is called, he walks across the brightly lit grass alone.

"Sorry," Lea says, not sounding sorry at all as she materializes next to me and knocks into my elbow with her camera. She leans forward, adjusting her lens for what will undoubtedly be a perfect shot of the Hillwood senior football players, and Sammy offers me a consolatory handful of popcorn. The game, according to the giant LED boards on either side of the field, is meant to resume in five more minutes.

But it doesn't happen that way.

Something happens near the edge of the artificial grass as Nathan joins the lineup alongside the rest of his team. The announcer is still talking, but my blood runs cold as a single Hillwood police car quietly pulls up beyond the chain-link fence that separates the road from the stadium and two tall officers step out of it. They stride toward the sidelines, and as the men come to a stop in front of the Fighting Gators football coach, Imani stills. So do I.

For the first time all night, I deliberately scan my surroundings for things out of place: a nervous-looking Arden Blake whispering to Delphine Fontenot and stealing glances at Coach Hannequart even though they're both supposed to be hyping up the stands. Luz Lorres-Torres fiddling with her pom-poms as the girl next to her bounces on her feet. The stony-faced football players themselves, no longer posing for their moment of recognition and instead advancing as a pack toward the cops and Coach Louviere.

I think about what Luz said when the agency and I tried to question her earlier: *Coach Hannequart doesn't want any of us leaving right now.*

Next to me, Sammy stops eating her popcorn.

"Iris, I don't think…," she says softly, but it's too late. I can't stop the sinking feeling in the pit of my stomach, the sick questions swimming through my head as I stare at the field.

What if it's Stella?

What if they've finally found her?

The policemen say something else to Coach Louviere, and there's a sudden uproar from the Hillwood High football team. The cool night air is tense and silent. The stadium floodlights are warm and too bright. The student section jostles me, and the spiral of obsessive thoughts I often trap myself in starts tightening around me like a noose: *Stella was found. Stella is here. They're talking about Stella.*

Nathan nods, and the officers nod back. He steps away from the team, looking angry, and then he's escorted away.

They're trying to do this quietly. To not make a fuss, to pass this moment off as nothing. But Nathan's teammates are following him and jeering at the officers, and everyone is seeing this. *I'm* seeing this.

The cheerleaders aren't even pretending to cheer anymore.

"Hey," a sharp voice demands, drawing my attention away from the field. "What's happening? What's going on?"

And I don't know what it is about Lea Li Zhang. But when she asks questions, people answer.

A wide-eyed junior in front of us glances up from his phone, his green-and-gold-dotted face drained of color. "The cops want to question Nathan Deveraux," he tells us softly. "Heather Nasato's been reported missing."

Chapter Three

The world drops out from under me.

"What?" Lea whispers. And then her face changes. "Wait, who are you? How do you know that?"

The junior shakes his head. "My dad's a police officer. He just texted me, see?" He holds up his phone, and Lea, the agency, and I all lean forward to read the screen. Sure enough, a text from a contact saved as "all cops are dad" reads *I'll be home late. Someone filed a missing persons report for a girl at your school.*

The junior sent back: *who?*

And the response after that: *Heather Nasato. We're going to speak to her boyfriend just as a precaution, but don't worry. You know these things usually clear up fast.*

Unless they don't, I think coldly.

"When was she reported missing?" Lea demands. "Who filed the report? Do you know anything else?"

The junior shakes his head, an apologetic look on his face as he pockets his phone. On the field in front of us, the rest of the Hillwood High football team doesn't rejoin their coach as Nathan gets in the police car—one of the officers holds the door open for him—but instead they all storm out of the Alfred J. Deveraux Stadium. In solidarity, maybe? Coach Louviere's face purples, and another coach breaks off from the sidelines and starts jogging toward the announcer box. "I'm sorry," the junior says, and my gaze flicks back to him. "These texts are all I have."

The announcer's voice crackles back to life. "Attention, folks. I'm sorry to have to do this to y'all, but in light of recent events, tonight's Senior Night game against North Lafourche High has been canceled. Be sure to hold on to your tickets—they'll be valid for the rescheduled game—but for the time being, please leave the stadium. Thank you for your cooperation, and have a great night. Y'all stay safe out there."

There's a groan from the North Lafourche bleachers, and the assembled cheerleaders who are still on the football field look collectively stunned as a lone firework explodes behind them. I guess the pyrotechnician didn't get the memo.

"Oh my god," Sammy says as everyone in the student section exchanges whispers and furtive glances. "We have to go."

"What do you mean?" Imani whispers. "We should stay. If Heather's missing, then we need to—"

They stop talking as soon as I give them a warning glance, but it's not fast enough. Lea swivels toward us. "Then you need to what?"

I grit my teeth. It's not like our agency is a total secret, but we're off the books and operate on a strict need-to-know basis. And Lea Li Zhang doesn't need to know anything about my life. Not anymore.

I ignore her scathing question, but her tone is as icy as the air around us as she follows it up. "You're not really planning to go looking for her, are you, Iris? Especially after what happened last time?"

The bleachers tilt sideways, and my throat tightens as I register Lea's words. *What happened last time. Flashing red and blue lights, and sirens slicing through the air like knives, and the tapping of my combat boots against speckled linoleum. Fighting to keep the bile from rising.*

I reach out a hand to steady myself, my fingers curling around the cold metal of the guardrail in front of me. I'm here. I'm in this moment. I'm not the same person I was a year ago, and Heather isn't Stella.

"Leave me alone, Lea," I say softly, forcing the memories of homecoming night out of my mind. Her condescending expression drops off her face, and I turn to face the agency.

"Come on," I tell Imani and Sammy, already tilting my head to the stairs to our right. No more slipping. No more breakdowns. I'm keeping my feelings tamped down, and everything is going to go right this time. "We're not going anywhere until we get some leads."

Here's a little-known fact about missing persons cases: You can report someone missing at any time. There's a common misconception that you have to wait twenty-four hours before you can file an official police report, but you don't have to. If you have reasonable cause to believe someone has disappeared, you can make that known immediately. It's actually better to do so, because here's another thing about hours and missing persons cases: Most of them are resolved within forty-eight.

Some people—many people, a lot more than one would think—return voluntarily. If they don't, they're easy enough to find: They're often with a parent or guardian, and each year most reports of missing children are filed over disputes between custodial and noncustodial parents. But then there are cases that aren't so easy. Cases where the person who's gone isn't at a relative's or a friend's, cases where they're deemed runaways. Cases like Stella's.

I hope Heather's is like the former. But if someone reported her missing within twelve hours of her last sighting, they must be convinced something is seriously wrong. And if the police are so desperate that they're interrupting the last home game of the season to quietly whisk away Nathan Deveraux, then my hopes aren't very high.

Dread starts to trickle into my stomach.

"What's our plan of attack?" Imani asks, blowing into their hands to warm them from the cold. The three of us are back in the same alcove where we first talked to Luz after canvassing the football bleachers, but the sickly lemon smell from the stadium bathrooms is making it hard to think. It's been about thirty minutes since the game got called off and the rest of the football team started posting Snapchats with captions like #AllOfUs-OrNoneOfUs and #FreeNathanDeveraux, but no one else we talked to knew anything about what's going on with Heather. We're losing precious time.

"We should go to Joan's Diner," Sammy says, looking up from where she's been scrutinizing Snap Map. "It seems like everyone's congregating there, and it's the perfect place to overhear gossip since we can't exactly ask the police what's going on."

I take it all in: my friends, the heavy scent of cleaner, the floodlight shadows flickering across their faces. I think about Heather. Her paranoia, her hollowness, her tired eyes. Somehow, in the darkest part of my mind, I already know she won't be found at a relative's or friend's house. I nod. "The diner sounds great."

"Okay, then," Imani says, jingling their car keys. "Let's go."

As soon as we step through the silver chrome door of Joan's Diner, my mouth waters like I'm one of Pavlov's classically conditioned dogs. But then I spot Joan's twin sons carrying two plates of sweet, puffy blueberry beignets across the checkered linoleum, and my stomach grumbles for real.

Sammy was right: The booths are absolutely packed with people from the game. Andre and Damon are practically tripping over themselves in their rush to deliver everyone's orders and top off their coffee, and sizzling po'boys keep coming out of the kitchen. I shake my head and push my hunger out of my mind. Right now, we're here for information. That's more important than ordering everything off the menu, even if the food is absolutely fantastic.

Behind the counter, a woman with skin a few shades of brown lighter than Imani's spots the three of us and grins. "Well, well, well, look what the cat dragged in," Joan says cheerfully, wiping her hands on the front of her apron as she makes her way around the counter and pulls us into a warm hug. Her retro-themed small-town diner has vintage red leather booths, black-and-white diamond floors, miniature jukeboxes that play oldies for twenty-five cents a pop, and the best home cookin' you can find south of the Big Easy. It's the agency's go-to hangout spot, and my favorite place in all of Hillwood.

"Hey, Joan," Sammy says, pulling back from the woman's embrace. "Did you hear Heather Nasato's missing?"

Joan nods, her smile dimming. "I hope they find her soon," she says, glancing for a moment at a couple whispering at the bar before turning back to us. "Is it true they're investigating her boyfriend?"

Imani's face is grim. "We think so."

"Well," Joan says again, and I find myself marveling at just how much contempt she can inject into a single sugarcoated syllable. "Isn't that something?" She shakes her black curls, her smile fixed back in place. "Have a seat, and I'll fix y'all up some milkshakes. You want your regulars?"

Imani nods. "Thanks, Joan."

The three of us move farther into the diner, past the framed photographs of Louis Armstrong and James Booker, a blown-up article about the New Orleans Saints winning Super Bowl XLIV, and a big sign that reads GEAUX TO HELL OLE MISS (a new addition after Andre and Damon's older brother, Patrick, committed to LSU last spring). We're just walking past my favorite section of the wall décor—a set of seven photographs that show Joan with her husband and her sons throughout the years at the annual Lafourche Parish Oyster Festival—when my eye lands on Arden Blake at the bar. She's crying, her heart-shaped face stained with mascara and crusted snot, and there's a small crowd gathered around her that murmurs reassurances every time she reaches for a brown paper napkin from the middle dispenser and blows her perfect freckled nose. Bingo.

Sammy and Imani follow my gaze, and we change course to melt into the crowd just in time to hear the tail end of what Arden's saying. "...didn't know she wouldn't go to class afterward. We just wanted to have l-lunch here. And now she's... she's..." Her voice catches on the last word, and someone pats her on the back as she tearfully reaches for another napkin.

My mouth draws itself into a thin line. I don't particularly like Arden Blake—she has the most forgettable personality in the trifecta composed of her, Heather, and Delphine Fontenot, though that might be because she moved to Hillwood a month after Stella had already disappeared—but I don't hate her, either. The only thing she's ever done to me that I feel like I actually have a right to be upset about was volunteer as one of the first guests on the notorious investigative podcast my ex-girlfriend

35

started back in March that completely sensationalized my sister's disappearance. The entire thing was probably one of the many reasons I never got past the first minute of episode one—and why I now purposely avoid everything about *How to Find a Missing Girl*.

Even now, I think the podcast was the most audacious thing Heather ever did. She broke up with me a few months before she actually started it—our relationship officially ended in December, after I was detained by the police for scaring off the only key witness in Stella's case—but our split definitely didn't stop her from capitalizing on my personal pain. From what I can tell, my ex-girlfriend made five episodes of her podcast in total before she got bored following her old cheer captain's trail. Then she started acting like a typical resident of Bellevue Estates, solidified her friendship with Delphine and Arden, and also managed to lose every bit of the personality that attracted us to each other in the first place. Heather getting together with Nathan Deveraux last month was just the final nail in the coffin.

And now no one knows where she is.

"It's not your fault," Delphine says from where she's standing next to Arden, clasping a balled mass of napkins tighter in her carefully manicured hands. "You didn't do anything wrong."

"I kn-know," Arden hiccups. "But what if something really b-bad happened? The police are probably going to q-question us after Nathan, s-since we were the last two people to s-see her."

I can't help myself. "You were?"

Arden looks up at me, her crystal-blue eyes framed by clumpy wet lashes, and nods. "We came here for l-lunch. Got back to school about five minutes before third p-period. Delphine and I went to class, and no one's seen Heather s-since."

Carrie, one of the waitresses, chooses that particular moment to breeze by. "Do you three want anything?" she asks the agency, her triple eyebrow piercings catching the light filtering through the glass block behind Arden and Delphine. Among all of Joan's employees, Carrie's always been one of my favorites—her heavy eye makeup, dark green hair, and swampland sleeve tattoo may not exude the homiest air, but she's definitely badass.

"Joan's getting us milkshakes," Sammy whispers back, and Carrie nods before moving to whisk away a tower of dirty plates from the bar.

Imani frowns at the cheerleaders. "But you both have alibis, right? You were at school. You'll be fine."

Arden sniffles miserably. "So w-was Nathan," she says. "And the police have already t-taken him in, haven't they?"

"He hasn't been arrested," Delphine snaps, passing her another napkin. "They're just ruling him out. I mean, Heather *is* the mayor's daughter—her parents might think he did it."

Arden takes it, blows her nose in a loud honk, and shakes her head. "But th-they don't even know she's g-gone yet, remember? Heather told us yesterday—they're hiking the Southern Alps for their a-anniversary."

That's the most Arden manages to get out, though, because then she breaks down completely and Delphine glances around the diner and says she's driving her home.

Sammy's and Imani's expressions drop into identical frowns. So does mine. Heather's parents didn't file the report.

My thoughts whirr as Heather's two best friends leave Joan's Diner and the crowd clustered around us slowly starts to dissipate. Arden and Delphine were the last people to see Heather, at around 12:25 PM. Heather's parents are out of the country. The police have taken in Nathan Deveraux for questioning.

I lift my head, staring into the distance to let my mind finish running through all the new information it's just been given, and then I make eye contact with *her*. She's in plain clothes, still sipping from a mug of black coffee, but her calculating brown eyes are locked on my face. She wants me to know she's seen me.

Before I can decide if I should turn away or not, she inclines her head to the empty seat across from her.

"Hey, guys?" I tell Sammy and Imani, forcing myself to swallow past the lump in my throat. "Go ahead and find a booth without me. I'll just...be a second."

"You sure?" Imani asks, but all it takes from me is a single nod of confirmation before they turn around. "All right. We'll see if we can grab our usual corner," they add, and then the agency disappears into the throng.

Detective de Rosa doesn't flinch when I sit down across from her. The wrinkles at the corners of her dark brown eyes are deeper, her hooked nose is slightly more crooked, and her shoulder-length black hair isn't as sleek as it used to be—but everything else about her is just as it was when I last saw her a year ago. "Hello, Iris."

"Detective," I greet her, like the two of us are old friends. Partners, even. "You should go back to your old shampoo."

She doesn't smile. That's the same, too.

"One of the students that attends your high school has been

reported missing," Detective de Rosa says, clearly not interested in wasting any time now that we've gotten our designated pleasantries out of the way. "Her name is Heather Nasato. Do you know her?"

Images flash through my mind on rapid-fire: Heather's dark eyes meeting mine from across the gym during sophomore cheerleader tryouts. Watching her shiny ponytail swing at practice and games and drills. Stella's smile as she officially introduced us: *This is my sister.* And the two of us dancing around each other for months, me falling harder with every bleacher conversation while telling myself Heather couldn't be queer because I just didn't have that kind of luck, until she finally kissed me in the locker room at the end of sophomore year, her lips soft and warm, my fingers curling under the hem of her dark green HILLWOOD HIGH FIGHTING GATORS sweatshirt.

I blink. "I know her," I tell de Rosa.

The detective nods. "I'm sure you're already aware of this, Iris, but I'm not here to exchange the details of her case with you. If we can find her, we will."

My mind spins. Already, it's not enough.

The detective seems to take my silence as complacency. "But," she continues, and her tone is decidedly less sympathetic now, "I need you to hear me when I tell you that if we are unable to locate Heather in forty-eight hours, you will stay out of her case. Do you hear me?"

I nod. If I speak, I might say something I'll regret.

"You're not a child anymore," Detective de Rosa says. "You're… what, a senior in high school? Almost eighteen?"

Nod. Just nod, Iris. Don't lash out. Don't say anything that gives her reason to suspect you more than she already does.

"Right. And if I find out you're sabotaging my investigation again," Detective de Rosa says, "I will not hesitate to have you— or anyone assisting you, for that matter—arrested for criminal obstruction. The charge will stay on your permanent record. You will never receive your private investigator license in Louisiana or in any other state. Do you understand?"

But I don't understand, because I stopped listening after "sabotaging my investigation again." Sabotaging my investigation *again.*

"She was my sister," I whisper, and this time my voice really does break. Hot tears fill my eyes and spill over my cheeks, and the version of myself reflected in the fleur-de-lis wall mirror behind the detective doesn't move to wipe them away. "My *sister.*"

Detective de Rosa almost looks sorry. Except she doesn't apologize. "Actually, Iris," she says instead, pulling out her sleek black phone, "that's part of what I wanted to talk to you about."

I blink at what she's showing me. The thought of de Rosa listening to this, the thought of her even knowing what it is, is so bizarre that it takes me a second to register what I'm even looking at. But then I do.

"This is Heather's podcast," the detective says, tapping a single fingernail against the cool glass of her phone screen, and my throat constricts. "*How to Find a Missing Girl.* Where she investigated Stella Blackthorn's disappearance. Your *sister's* disappearance."

"Yeah," I whisper.

"She started it in March and uploaded one new episode every

month until July, when she stopped." De Rosa takes the phone and scrolls to something before sliding it back to me. "Until two days ago," she finishes, "when Heather uploaded her sixth episode."

My world shatters as I stare at the screen. I'd heard rumors floating around Hillwood in the past week, and snippets of whispered conversations between cheerleaders in the halls—but I hadn't realized it was because of *this*. It almost doesn't seem real, but there it is regardless: a new episode of Heather's podcast, right on de Rosa's phone. "What...what does it say?" I ask, flicking my eyes up to meet the detective's.

"You haven't listened to it?"

"No." My voice is hoarse. "I haven't listened to any of it."

De Rosa makes a small noise that I can't possibly hope to decipher. "Well, the podcast is public. You can listen to it on your own time. But it's something my department is looking into as a potential reason for Heather's disappearance. It's certainly a link between Stella and Heather."

Everything in Joan's Diner suddenly seems too bright and too loud. "But Stella's case isn't currently being investigated," I tell de Rosa, placing my hand on the sticky chrome tabletop to stop the world from dropping out from under me. "You—your department—declared her a runaway."

De Rosa's lips purse. "We did," she says.

Here is what I hear: *Maybe we were wrong.*

"This is a warning, Iris," de Rosa says as she stands. "I will be watching you."

Breathe. Don't give anything away. Go back to the agency. You can do this.

41

My mouth refuses to cooperate with my brain, though, because what I end up saying to Detective de Rosa, the woman who couldn't find out what happened to my sister any more than I could, is, "Maybe you should focus on looking for Heather instead."

I stand without waiting for her answer and stalk to the bathroom, barely managing to lift up the bright red seat of its lone toilet before I lean over it and empty the contents of my stomach into the bowl. It happened again.

Another girl I know has disappeared.

I take a few seconds to breathe, and then I methodically get to my feet and flush the remains of my thrown-up popcorn. I don't have any time to waste—the agency is all-in, which means I have to be at the top of my game. Because this is my second chance.

Because I failed my sister, and I won't fail Heather, too.

Outside, a tabletop jukebox starts playing a tinny version of an old rock song, and I wipe my cheeks. Splash some water on my face. Grip the edge of the sink until my knuckles turn white.

My ex-girlfriend is missing. Hillwood is crawling with officers. The police will be watching me, and if they find out I'm investigating with the agency, de Rosa will take every opportunity to make sure I land in jail again.

But if de Rosa's here, I think as I scrutinize the Iris Blackthorn who peers back at me, *it's also a good thing*.

I square my shoulders and set my jaw as I push open the bathroom door and step back into the neon glow of the diner.

Because it means that the two of us—the police and my agency—are starting off with the same leads.

HOW TO FIND A
MISSING GIRL PODCAST

Episode One

HEATHER NASATO: Hey-o, Hillwood. This is Heather Nasato, and I'm here because I'm angry. I'm angry because the police haven't done their job. I'm angry because they've taken the easiest way out even though their explanations don't make sense, and because none of this is fair. In case you're living under a rock, I'm talking about the disappearance of eighteen-year-old Stella Blackthorn, a senior and varsity cheer captain at Hillwood High. Back in early January, three months after her disappearance, the Hillwood PD put out a statement that strongly indicates they believe Stella to be a runaway. But I don't think that's what really happened. If you know Stella, which I did, then you know she was one of the best students at Hillwood High. She was set to become the valedictorian of her senior class, she was a National Merit Scholar, and she was planning on applying early decision to an Ivy League school. Her life in Hillwood was perfect, and even if she wanted to get out, her academic performance was her golden ticket. Which brings me to why I started this podcast: to figure out the truth. So. With that being said, welcome to our first episode, which will focus on who Stella Blackthorn was and her alleged reason for leaving her old life behind. Once again, I'm Heather Nasato. And this is episode one of *How to Find a Missing Girl.*

GIRL #1: Everyone wanted to be Stella Blackthorn.

GIRL #2: She was, like, the most popular student ever. There's no reason she could have had to run away.

BOY #1: It feels like there's no justice. Like, you would think she would have told someone if she was planning on skipping town, right? But she never brought it up. At least, not with me.

HEATHER NASATO: Although not everyone in Hillwood, Louisiana, is familiar with everyone else, most of our locals were at least somewhat aware of eighteen-year-old Stella Blackthorn even before her disappearance. Tall, slim, with striking blue eyes and long, tumbling brown hair, the Hillwood varsity cheerleading captain made it a point to stand out. She had a 4.62 GPA, scored a 1560 on her SAT, and planned to major in biology on the premed track at UPenn, which she was getting ready to apply to. She had what seemed like a perfect life before she vanished in late September. She studied, spent her free time volunteering at the local animal shelter, and tried her best to juggle her obligations to her extracurriculars with her obligations to her family.

GIRL #1: She basically raised her younger sister. There's a special type of confidence you get from doing something like that. It forced her to mature quickly. It made her grow up faster.

HEATHER NASATO: That's Noémie Charmant, Stella's best friend and a fellow Hillwood High varsity cheerleader. I spoke to her over the phone about what kind of person Stella was, and whether she agrees with the assessment of the Hillwood police.

NOÉMIE CHARMANT: Not at all. The fact they're even calling her a runaway is laughable. It's ridiculous. Stella would never do that. I mean, she was basically a modern Renaissance girl. Everyone wanted to be Stella Blackthorn—she was class president, and varsity cheer captain, and on track to graduate as valedictorian in June. Someone like that doesn't just decide to skip town one day, you know? Besides, Stella has her younger sister to take care of. She's the older daughter and her dad's out of the picture, so she always kind of felt like picking up her mom's slack was her burden to bear. She wouldn't...she wouldn't leave Iris. Not like that.

HEATHER NASATO: Noémie's sentiment seems to be shared by many of Stella's classmates. I asked Arden Blake, a junior cheerleader at Hillwood High, if she could think of any possible reasons for Stella to voluntarily disappear.

ARDEN BLAKE: I mean...Coach Hannequart runs difficult cheerleading practices. She's tough on us, and some of the drills we run are awful. We're under a lot of pressure, constantly. So...I don't know. Maybe Stella snapped one day? Maybe she felt like getting away from it all.

HEATHER NASATO: Coach Catherine Hannequart is the cheerleading coach and health and PE teacher at Hillwood High.

ARDEN BLAKE: I don't think it's that much of a stretch. Sometimes people just...need a break. And there's a lot of evidence that suggests Stella's gone, right? Like, her car isn't here anymore. And there was that person up north who reported her plates, things like that. But at the same time, it's really weird. I moved to Hillwood a month after Stella disappeared, but everyone kept telling me I looked like her. Teachers would get our names mixed up, and people would show me pictures of her—we both have brown hair, blue eyes, pale skin, and freckles—and I ended up hearing a lot about Stella because of it. She was, like, the most popular student ever, and also cheer captain, so I'm sure she handled Hannequart just fine. I don't know. I feel like there's no reason she could have had to run away, really. But, you know. Maybe she did.

HEATHER NASATO: A lot of people in Hillwood speculate on this very question, even if the police haven't been desperately searching for answers: The initial momentum spurred by Stella's disappearance fizzled out within the Hillwood PD after just three months of active investigation. Although Stella Blackthorn's case technically remains open—missing persons cases are not closed in the United States until the missing person is found—no one at the Hillwood Police Department is actively working on her case. And since running away is perfectly legal for someone who was eighteen at the time they went missing, the police don't seem very eager to keep looking.

BOY #1: They're not doing [BEEP].

HEATHER NASATO: This is Franklin Brown, one of Stella's coworkers from Lucille's General Store and a fellow classmate. Franklin says he and Stella were close, although they never had a romantic relationship; when he confessed his feelings for her in late August, she let him down gently with an assurance they could still be friends.

FRANKLIN BROWN: The cops said they launched a full investigation, but we all know that's [BEEP]. Sorry, can I swear on the podcast? I don't know if I can swear. It's just...they're treating her like an adult and not a minor, which yeah, she is one...legally. But her birthday was just before homecoming—and if it was after, this entire thing would be treated totally different. So it's [BEEP]. It feels like there's no justice. Like, we're just supposed to believe that she left? That the cops want anything other than the ability to wash their hands of this entire situation as quickly as possible? No. It's such a [BEEP] conclusion to come to. Like, you would think she would have told someone if she was planning on skipping town, right? But she never brought it up. Not ever. At least, not with me.

HEATHER NASATO: In fact, although I reached out to multiple people who knew Stella best in the years, months, and even weeks before she vanished, there wasn't a single person who told me they had any prior knowledge of Stella planning to run away. So. Either Stella Blackthorn is amazing at keeping secrets, or her decision to leave Hillwood—if she did indeed decide—wasn't a rational one. The evidence—and the interviews, at the very least—certainly seem to be pointing that way.

[OUTRO MUSIC PLAYS]

HEATHER NASATO: For now, this is where I'll be ending the first episode. Thank you so much for tuning in, and please know I hope to come out with new episodes of this podcast as I receive more updates about Stella. That being said, if you have information you'd like to share with me or even just want the chance to offer your perspective on her case, please send me an email at howtofindamissinggirlpodcast@gmail.com. Until next time, I'm Heather Nasato. And this has been the first episode of *How to Find a Missing Girl*.

Chapter Four

I get home late. Aunt Megan is waiting for me on the living room couch as soon as I enter, her black hair still wet from her nightly shower and her expression equal parts tired and stony. I'm not really in the mood for a lecture right now, but I grab a granola bar and a can of seltzer from the kitchen and plop down next to her anyway. If she doesn't yell at me right now, her anger will just build up until it explodes all over me like a sixth-grade science project. Might as well get it over with.

"Where were you?" Megan starts, and I pop the tab of the can and take a swig.

"Out."

"I called you, Iris. I texted you, too. That's why you have a phone. You could have at least let me know—"

"My phone died," I tell Megan. This, at least, is true. I forgot to charge it before I went to school this morning, and it was hanging on by a thread through most of the day—though I have a vague recollection of noticing a few messages from my aunt before it ran out of battery at the diner. "I'm sorry I didn't let you know where I was."

"A girl is missing," Megan hisses, turning to me. "Do you know what I—do you know how much you *scared me*?"

And suddenly I feel like the World's Biggest Asshole, because of course that's why she's mad. Heather is gone. Stella is gone. When I don't come home right after school, or forget to tell her about my impromptu plans to attend football games, Megan's going to assume the worst. And she has every right to.

"I'm sorry," I tell her, my voice suddenly as flat as the warm seltzer I'm holding. "I wasn't thinking."

"No," Megan says coldly. "You weren't."

My fingers drift back to my sister's necklace. After Stella's disappearance—after my mother lost her lifelong battle with alcohol addiction in a drunk driving accident last winter, leaving me as the local girl who took the traumatic one-two punch of missing sister *and* dead mom in the span of only three months—Aunt Megan took me in. I would have ended up in the foster care system if she hadn't, seeing as my mom never married my dad and he's totally AWOL, so I'm grateful to her. But Megan never wanted kids. She's not even a Blackthorn—she's my aunt by marriage only, a second-generation Mexican American widow who I'd met only a handful of times before my mom's brother passed away. And even though she does her best to take care of me, I know she never meant to stay in Louisiana. I know she misses the Pasadena sun and her family, and that she feels unappreciated as the head nurse of the Hillwood Assisted Living Community, where she works long hours for little pay.

She's stuck in Hillwood now, though. Stuck with me.

I glance at my granola bar, but my appetite is suddenly gone. An uncomfortable silence descends over Megan and me, one that I would try to fill if I cared more than I actually do, if I was more of a people-pleaser than I actually am. I think my MBTI type is more suited to burning bridges than building them, though, so instead I keep quiet.

Aunt Megan exhales, and suddenly all the fight in her is gone. "You knew her, didn't you?"

"I know her."

"Know, right."

I fidget with my half-full seltzer can, trying to figure out how much to tell her. How much she already knows.

I didn't tell the rest of the agency about my run-in with the detective at the diner. I'd met up with them at our usual booth after getting out of the bathroom, and Sammy had taken one look at my face and asked me if everything was okay, and I'd lied. I'd thought about de Rosa's words (*I will not hesitate to have you—or anyone assisting you, for that matter—arrested for criminal obstruction*), and I'd kept my breathing even. *Yeah, everything's fine.*

I think I'm just trying to keep my friends safe. Like if they don't know the detective from my sister's case is out to get me, they won't get in trouble if she succeeds.

"I saw Detective de Rosa tonight," I offer, glancing up at Megs as I say it. The piece of information is meant to be placating, but then I realize it'll be easier if I lie to my aunt, too. One lie is easier to keep track of. One lie makes sure nothing gets out that shouldn't. "She told me to leave her investigation alone."

There—a half-truth.

Megan wraps her fluffy gray bathrobe tighter around herself. "Are you going to?"

I flash back to the diner. Back to how, after Joan had brought us our milkshakes, Imani and Sammy had asked me where we should begin. How I'd told them we'd start off slow, how I'd told myself I would let them know about de Rosa's threat if we started unraveling clues we couldn't handle. How Sammy had put up her lion's mane of curls with a glittery pink elastic band and Imani had twirled the stem of a red maraschino cherry while I drafted a persons-of-interest list in my Notes app: Nathan Deveraux. Delphine Fontenot. Arden Blake. Whoever Reported Heather Missing. Nathan's Mystery Girl.

I snap back to the present, to Megan waiting in front of me. *Lie. Lie. Lie.*

"No."

It's the wrong thing to say, and I know it as soon as I hear Aunt Megan's sharp inhale. "Are you serious, Iris?" she asks, rising off the couch. "This isn't a game. You can't just run off and meddle with the police every time that—"

"A girl goes missing?" I ask, meeting Megan's eyes. "Right. My bad."

She blows out a breath. "That's not what I meant."

I remain silent, and Megan's lips purse in the signature way that means I've hurt her feelings. Part of me wants to apologize, to say I didn't really mean it. But that would be lying, too.

After a beat, my aunt sighs. "You're not a detective, Iris," she finally says, her voice soft. It doesn't keep the words from stinging. "At least charge your phone next time."

I nod. Megan heads upstairs, and I retreat down the hall a few minutes after she's gone.

I slip into my neutral-toned room, letting the familiarity of its contents—my bookshelves, my desk full of plants, the full-length mirror I sit in front of to do my makeup in the mornings I have time—wash over me. When I first moved in, Megan wanted to help me set things up exactly the way they were in the Chevalier Trailer Park, where I lived with my mom and Stella before everything went wrong. But I wanted something completely different. A fresh start.

Now that I have it, though, I don't know if it's enough.

I sigh and drop into my desk chair. If the Hillwood police are taking *How to Find a Missing Girl* seriously enough that de Rosa's warning me to stay away from her investigation because it could be linked to my sister, then I have to listen to the entire podcast. No more chickening out. I take out my phone and scroll through an open tab for local news stories: Edward and Elizabeth Deveraux are unveiling a new wing for Deveraux Industries next month; one of the guys on the football team who walked out earlier tonight seems to have gotten an interview about the

53

importance of standing with their star quarterback; the police are expected to put out an official statement about the Heather case on Saturday—wait.

I scroll back to the last headline and tap on the article. Sure enough, the police have already issued a statement about Heather, some stupid PR garbage that the *Hillwood Herald* already boosted on Twitter. But tomorrow they're going to update the public on the investigation and their role in it as part of Hillwood's "ongoing commitment to police transparency." *Channel Six News* is expecting to cover the story, which means their favorite bubbly blonde reporter, Claudia Garrett, is going to be on television screens across the parish for more than a few days, but I won't be able to find out any more information about it right now.

On to the podcast, then.

It doesn't take me long to navigate to it, and it takes even less time to plug in my earbuds and hit play. Heather's voice floods my ears, and I grit my teeth.

I make it through ten seconds before undiluted panic rises in the back of my throat and my eyes fill with tears.

I can't do it. I can't listen to Heather, can't bear to hear her voice, can't pretend I'm okay with her dissecting the life of my sister—my life—and not break down. Whatever clues are in these podcast episodes, I don't think I'm strong enough to hear them.

At least, not alone.

Before I can navigate to the agency group chat, though, my phone pings with another notification from the *Hillwood Herald* Twitter account. I open the article and swallow, wanting to see. Not wanting to see.

And then my heart drops. Because it's about her. About Heather. My mouth goes dry, and I begin to read.

THE HILLWOOD HERALD

<u>Home > Top Stories</u>
By Jean J. Dupre

The Hillwood Police Department is asking for help in finding 17-year-old Heather Rose Nasato, who was last seen on Friday, October 15 in the Hillwood area. Heather is white, five-foot-eight, and weighs 120 pounds. She has brown eyes, black hair, and a slender build.

"We're desperate to get our daughter back home safe," wrote Hillwood Mayor Robert Nasato in a statement to Hillwood Police this evening; the 52-year-old Lafourche Parish native is currently in New Zealand with his wife for their 25th anniversary. "Of course we're cutting our trip short and flying back as soon as we are able.... Heather is a bright young woman with a promising future ahead of her, and my wife and I are deeply distraught by her absence."

Heather Nasato is not the only person from the Hillwood area to go missing in recent memory. In the months before her disappearance, Miss Nasato ran her own true-crime podcast, called *How to Find a Missing Girl*, which focused on the disappearance of 18-year-old Stella Blackthorn last September.

"We are currently investigating multiple different avenues, but anyone with information regarding Miss

Nasato's whereabouts is encouraged to contact the Hillwood Police Department at (985) 555-0189 or dial 911," said Detective Maria de Rosa, the lead detective on the Heather Nasato case.

"We expect to be approved for a search warrant for the Nasato residence shortly," added Assistant Detective Mason Hunt, who is also working on the Heather Nasato case, in a phone interview.

Mayor Nasato is expected to arrive in Hillwood with his wife on Monday morning.

I shake my head, unable to contain the grim expression spreading over my face. It seems like the police update came early—even the *Hillwood Herald* can't help themselves when it comes to speculating on missing girls. But as long as the Nasatos aren't here in Hillwood, we have to take advantage. And if the agency and I want to stay in the game, if we want to figure out what happened to Heather, there's only one option, no matter how dangerous it may seem.

We have to break into Heather's house.

Chapter Five

On Saturday morning, I grab my phone to text the agency with an update about Heather's case as soon as I wake up.

be gay solve crime
8:34 AM

guys

i have an idea

wedoalittlehacking:
go away i'm still asleep <3

imaniturnnerr:

> Does this idea of yours involve doing anything highly illegal?

no

well, maybe

imani, do you still have those old fake girl scout uniforms you made us

imaniturnnerr:

> I already don't like where this is going. But yes

cool

in that case, do you all want to come check out bellevue estates with me today

for absolutely legal purposes, of course

while we're there i also want to check out mystery girl's house again

just to see if we can get any more clues on her identity

you know, since the white pages are scrubbed clean

imaniturnnerr:

> Wish I could. But I have play rehearsal all day today so I can't drive you or commit federal crimes, sorry

> Mrs. Landry is really stressed about selling enough tickets. I'll be free tomorrow though. We can check things out then

The hope in my chest pops like a balloon. I can't wait until Sunday—I need to keep moving, to keep going. I can't stop. I can't *afford* to stop.

Maybe I don't have to.

I close out of Instagram and swipe to the news, scanning for the new police update on Heather's case. The official statement isn't much different from what the department put out yesterday, but it does look like the cops are taking her disappearance seriously. Part of me is relieved, but there's a smaller part that's resentful. After all, Heather isn't an eighteen-year-old girl from the Chevalier Trailer Park—she's the mayor's daughter. The police will come under more fire if they don't put their all into the investigation this time.

I shake my head and change into my clothes for the day, careful not to make much noise. Aunt Megan's still asleep after her long shift at the nursing home, and her car's in the driveway. *I don't need Imani to take me to Bellevue Estates after all*, I think as I slip on my black combat boots. *I can drive there myself.*

I find Megan's keys in the kitchen and stride outside into the warm, bright morning, unlocking her silver Impala with the fob. I slide into the driver's seat, check all my mirrors, and inhale. I may not have my license, but I used to practice three-point turns and navigating through Hillwood's dusty red back roads with Stella before she disappeared. This is nothing. I can do this.

But I thought I could do homecoming, too, and look how that turned out.

The panic sets in almost as soon as I shift gears, the overwhelming pressure on my chest building until my breath comes in short gasps and I have to ground myself: things I can see.

Things I can smell. Things I can touch. But it's hopeless. I can't power through the way I'm feeling, can't stop my eyes from feeling like a dam about to burst, can't keep myself from visualizing myself crashing. I can't drive.

I'm completely useless.

Fuming, I get out of the car and take my bike out of the garage. As I strap on my helmet, I think about how not every Reddit thread posted after my sister went missing was filled with respectful speculation. About how the media picked apart my family, reduced us to nothing, and entertained conspiracy theories poorly disguised as town gossip: *Their mom had something to do with it. Stella left to find her dad. Diane Blackthorn's grief was so palpable it drove her back to alcoholism and right off the Le Pont de Fer Bridge.*

I don't want the same thing to happen to me.

I push back the kickstand and start to pedal, forcing myself to leave the memories behind. My emotions are tamped down. I am going to get through this day. And even if I'm almost a legal adult and still don't have my license, at least when I have no other options I can reasonably bike through the flat land of Hillwood to do the only thing that matters right now: find Heather, before it's too late.

My heart starts racing the second I turn down Nouvelle Lane. I pump my legs faster, soaring toward Bellevue Estates, and I feel almost jubilant by the time I reach the residential gate. But then my hand strays for the phone in my pocket, and my mood instantly sours. Damn. I left it in Megan's car, which means I don't have Heather's keycard, either.

"Scoping out the scene of the crime?" a voice asks behind me, and I almost leap a foot into the air.

I curse as I turn around, coming face-to-face with Lea Li Zhang. "Didn't your moms ever tell you not to sneak up on people?" I tell her, eyeing her laminated HWHS PRESS pass with disdain. "It's rude. And it could get you murdered."

Lea doesn't even bat an eye. "Is that a threat?"

"Depends. Do you want it to be?"

My ex-best-friend shoulders her camera, ignoring me. "I've been trying to get in all morning. Gate's locked."

"Yeah," I seethe as she tips her chin to the scanner. "I know."

"Okay," Lea says as I turn my bike back around. "Nice talk. Thanks for that, Iris."

I don't respond as I pedal away.

Lea and I haven't really spoken to each other since my sister went missing. Since I overheard her whispering to the editor in chief of the *Magnolia* about covering Stella's disappearance for the school paper last October and she lost my trust forever. Since she stopped being my best friend, even though I still have memories of those slow, sticky summer days when we were thirteen and she was the closest person in my life.

Of course, that all changed after I cut her out of it and she retaliated by tipping off the police about my investigation. She knew I'd gotten into the Hillwood Police database and obtained my sister's files, and she also knew I was planning to interrogate the only witness involved in Stella's case. She was the only person with that information, because I had trusted her back then.

That was a mistake.

As I turn back down Nouvelle Lane, my fingers tighten around my handlebars. I don't like remembering the night Lea sold me out. I don't like thinking about de Rosa intercepting me before I could talk to the Deveraux Industries worker who potentially had information regarding Stella's disappearance, or about how I was detained after the detective blew my cover and the guy bolted, or about how Heather broke up with me shortly afterward because she thought the entire situation was bad for her image. I don't like being reminded that even though I'm the reason my sister's case fizzled out in early January, Lea Li Zhang is the one who backstabbed me.

The autumn wind stings my eyes as I whip past a grove of gnarled trees that grow out and upward like they're reaching for more. I'm heading to town, nearing the end of the winding red-dust road that will eventually take me to Sugar Boulevard, but I can't stop thinking about the press pass on Lea's oversize jacket and the large camera slung around her neck. I don't love the fact she's sniffing around Bellevue Estates—but if she's looking for another great exposé, she's free to try and get it.

Except this time, I'm not going to stick around long enough to give her any dirt on me.

By the time I get to Sugar Boulevard and lock my bike in front of Lucille's General Store, sweat is pouring down the back of my neck. It helps that my hair's up in its perpetual bun, but I still feel gross as I walk inside the cool, air-conditioned mom-and-pop shop and stride over to one of their saltwater taffy displays.

I decided on the way over here that if I'm going to be serious about this investigation, if I'm really going to find Heather, then I need a visual reminder of my commitment. Something that will push me. Something that reminds me that my time with this case—that the agency's time with this case—is not unlimited.

I pick up a bag of taffy, a kitten calendar, and a thick red marker. There's only one cashier at the register and the elderly lady in front of me has a ton of coupons, so I flip through pictures of tiny calicos wrestling with balls of yarn while I wait. November 14, the day I legally turn eighteen, is just under thirty days away.

The front bell jingles, and my gaze idly flicks over the entering person before I freeze. It's Arden Blake.

"Sorry," she mumbles, her downcast eyes red-rimmed and puffy as she steps around me. And I should leave her alone. It's clear she doesn't want to be disturbed, and she's probably going through a lot right now. But then again…

"Hey, Arden."

She looks over her shoulder and slowly blinks. "Iris," she says.

"Do you have a minute?"

"Oh," she says, her unfocused eyes darting to a spot over my shoulder. Her dull hair is pulled back in a sloppy ponytail, and her breath smells faintly of alcohol. "Um, I already told Lea I'm not interested in being featured in the *Magnolia*."

"It's not for the school paper," I say, shifting my weight. Talking with Arden has always made me a little uncomfortable.

Even though she's never been anything but nice to me since she moved here late last year, it doesn't change the fact she bears an uncanny resemblance to my missing sister. "I actually just wanted to check up on you? I know it's not the same, but I kind of know what you're going through. If you want to talk about it, I can help."

Arden's eyes soften. "Because of Stella," she says. "Of course."

The woman in front of me finally finishes paying, and I hand the cashier the kitten calendar, the taffy, and the marker. He picks up the items without comment and scans them, and I keep my breathing even as I turn back to Arden and let her assess me.

"Yeah," she eventually says. "Yeah, that sounds good." She glances around Lucille's General like she's not entirely sure what she came here for in the first place and wipes her nose with the back of her lightly freckled hand. "Just…can you give me a second? I have to…"

I nod, and Arden disappears behind the nearest shelf. She comes back with two cheap bottles of strawberry vodka just as the cashier hands me back my change, and I don't comment when she shows him her fake ID and slips them into a reusable HWHS VARSITY CHEER tote bag.

The two of us head outside, and I sit next to Arden when she plops down on a bench right next to my locked bike. She unscrews the top of one of her vodka bottles and tries to pass it to me, but I shake my head. I don't drink, and I definitely don't drink when I'm about to interrogate a suspect. Arden shrugs, then takes a swig, and that's when I pounce.

"I'm sorry about being pushy at Joan's Diner yesterday," I say, opening with a measured apologetic look. "I'm sure this whole thing has been exceptionally hard on you."

Arden bobs her head and drinks some more of her vodka. "I just can't believe she's really missing, you know?" she says. "That no one knows where she is, that the last time I saw her..." Her lower lip trembles. "I don't know. Heather was the first person to actually make me feel welcome when I moved here. It's always difficult being the new girl, but it's even more challenging when your face reminds everyone of Stella Blackthorn."

I manage a wry smile. "I can imagine that."

Arden sniffs. "Everyone kept staring. Whispering, gossiping, refusing to talk to me. It was so hard to make friends. But then Heather introduced herself to me and clued me in to what was going on with Stella, and I felt like I finally had someone in my corner." Arden swallows. "And now I'm signing up for search parties with my stepdad to go look for her, so yeah. It's surreal."

I scour Arden's expression carefully as she talks, but nothing she's saying feels unwarranted or out of the ordinary. There's a slight pang in my chest as a truck drifts by on the street in front of us, sending a warm breeze our way. It doesn't feel like October. It doesn't feel like the day after a girl went missing.

"Some people are saying Heather ran away just like Stella," Arden continues softly, "but I don't know if I believe that. Del and I gave her a ride to school on the day she went missing, and she seemed so... normal. But I could have missed something, you know? I keep playing that conversation over in my head, looking for signs, and…if she did disappear…" Heather's best friend takes a shuddering breath. "I'm w-worried it's my fault."

All my sympathy for Arden suddenly disappears. *Why?* the detective in me asks, cold and assessing. *What did you do?*

"Is there any particular reason you feel that way?" I ask lightly instead.

Arden bites her lip and glances away, and I instantly know I've overdone it. "I…sorry, I just realized I should go," she says, screwing the cap of her bottle back on and getting to her feet. "But thanks for talking to me, Iris. I appreciate it."

"No problem," I force out, taking extra care to keep my body language relaxed and open as she leaves.

When I get home, I grab my phone out of Meg's car and pull up Instagram. Someone's designed a missing poster—I saw a few stapled up around town on my way back from Lucille's General—and every other story post I tap through that isn't something hashtagged with #FreeNathanDeveraux has Heather's smiling face staring back at me. So at least they're trying to get the word out, and the search parties are starting. That's good.

I move to tap on another story post, but a loud ringing noise stops me. It's an alarm I set last night. For 12:25 PM.

My stomach drops. It's officially been twenty-four hours since Heather Nasato was last seen.

Chapter Six

Bellevue Estates looks different during the day, especially when the three of us are dressed like members of the Girl Scouts Louisiana East and touting boxes of Peanut Butter Patties that Imani bought secondhand. The costumes and ancient cookies are both from a more involved job we did over the summer, though they've come in handy with getting us through Bellevue's gate today, too. So far, we haven't even run into the meddling security guard from Thursday.

But even our expertly crafted, fashion-school-portfolio-worthy disguises won't protect us if someone catches us breaking down the Nasatos' front door.

I suppress a yawn as the three of us crunch through the dewy grass of the Nasatos' monoculture lawn—I didn't get a lot of sleep last night, because I spent most of it poring through my old DMs with Heather. I don't exactly know what I expected to find, but there were a lot of messages to sift through; all those *hey butterfly* and *meet me in the locker room?* texts from the days when we talked constantly. I'm currently running on four cups of hazelnut iced coffee and pure adrenaline, but I think that's probably pretty normal for a Girl Scout. At any rate, I definitely don't look as suspicious as Sammy, who got into the Homicide Honda wearing heart-shaped sunglasses and literal cat's-ear headphones on top of her khaki uniform and flat-out refused to change. So.

"It's all on you, Iris," Sammy whispers, trying and failing to blend in from where the three of us are positioned in front of the Nasatos' doorway. We decided earlier that I'd be the one to actually do the breaking in, since Sammy's nails are too long and Imani is strongly opposed to orange jumpsuits, so now I'm adding burglary to my rapidly growing list of serious crimes.

I take a deep breath and slip two pre-straightened bobby pins out of my pocket as the agency strategically steps to either side of me, their cookie boxes blocking every Bellevue Estates resident's view of my hands. I can do this. This is nothing.

"Ready?" Imani asks, eyeing a woman walking her (ugly, bug-eyed, white) dog as she rounds the cul-de-sac and disappears past the hedges surrounding the artificial lake. "Now."

I carefully insert the pins and jiggle the knob, feeling for the right positions. Miraculously, the door clicks open after only a few panic-infused seconds. "Ha," I breathe as the three of us step inside. "Thank God for wikiHow."

Imani laughs, and I almost manage a smile as I close the door and Sammy moves to disable the beeping house alarm. It's lucky I still remember the code from the last time I was here—Heather tried to keep it from me, but being observant (and nosy) has always been my strong suit.

Paws skitter on the mahogany flooring, and Imani stiffens as a giant dog with curly brown fur skids to a stop in front of us. He barks once, wagging his tail, and I reach forward to scratch him behind the ears. "Hey, Gumbeaux." I glance back at the rest of the agency. "Don't worry. He's friendly."

"Has he been in here alone this whole time?" Sammy asks as she presses a final button and the device stops beeping.

I nudge the full twin kibble and water bowls by the door with the toe of my combat boot. "Nah, the Nasatos have a pet sitter."

Good thing she's not here right now.

Gumbeaux sniffs Imani, gives my hand one last half-hearted lick, and then pads off, satisfied. Sammy turns from the disabled alarm system. "I'm glad Heather's dog is okay, but I can't say the same for her family's taste. Everything here is so...soulless."

She's right. The only décor in the foyer is a very official-looking wall portrait of the mayor and his family—which could either be a high-quality photograph or a hyperrealistic oil painting, I genuinely can't tell—and a tall, winding staircase made of dark mahogany.

"Is the mayor a *Phantom* fan?" Imani asks. Sammy snickers, and I shrug.

"Heather's room is on the second floor. Follow me."

When Heather first moved to Bellevue Estates, the two of us

69

had already been broken up for a couple of months. She invited me over exactly once in March, which is when I got my favorite longcoat back and stole her keycard, and that's also when she told me she was planning to release a podcast about my missing sister. It's a little ironic that our only client from Bellevue since then has been Heather herself, since I bet she'd be more than happy to turn over a keycard voluntarily if it meant aiding our investigation into her boyfriend.

But then again, with everything going on right now, I'm not so sure anymore.

We ascend the stairs, and at the top I turn down a vaguely familiar hallway. "Down here," I call, gesturing to the door that leads to Heather's room. I put my hand on the knob, ready to turn it, and then I stop. I can't open the door.

"Iris," a grounding voice says behind me. Imani puts their hand on my shoulder, calmly but firmly pulling me away. "I can do it."

I swallow past the lump in my throat as they twist the knob instead. The hinges creak as the door opens, and my breath catches.

Heather's room looks the same, with dark purple walls adorned with fairy lights and a large queen bed. The flooring is a plush sort of puce carpeting, and different exotic plants with intricate curling vines spill out from Heather's various off-white bookshelves. Light streams through the half-open window, showing us the greenery beyond Bellevue Estates and the railing of the house's balcony. Above her expensive-looking desk, Heather's put up photos: her and Delphine, her and Arden, her and Nathan, her alone. I'm notably absent from the pictures, but that's to be expected. She probably threw away all the ones depicting the two of us.

"Jackpot," Sammy whispers, gravitating toward the desk and the pristine computer that sits on top of it. "Heather, thank you for having a notoriously hackable Windows PC."

She moves for my missing ex-girlfriend's desk chair, but Imani stops her before her hand can make contact. "Wait," they say sharply. "The police don't have a warrant to search Heather's room yet."

"And neither do we," I finish, taking three pairs of latex gloves out of the hidden pocket stitched into my Girl Scouts sash. Imani never misses. "Which is exactly why we're going to be careful about this." I pass out the gloves to Imani and Sammy and snap on my own pair. "Don't take off the gloves, and put everything you take out of place back after you examine it. We don't know exactly what we're looking for, so spread out and be as efficient as you can without compromising our safety."

Sammy nods, and then she slides into Heather's chair, takes off her ridiculous cat's-ear headphones, and gets to work.

"I'll take the room," Imani says, watching Sammy fiddle with the locked computer. "Iris, the closet?"

I nod, biting back a smile as I pull open the door. Even though I've seen it briefly before, I'm still struck by the sheer magnitude of my ex-girlfriend's wardrobe. Heather has a rotating rack of over twenty pairs of shoes, a floor-to-ceiling shelf filled with perfumes and sprays and body glitter, and enough miniskirts to fill my entire room back at Megan's.

"I got her computer password!" Sammy calls from the main room. "Her desktop picture is a cat surrounded by knives."

I stick my head out of the door. "You're a lesbian icon," I tell Sammy—I have to keep up team morale somehow—and she shoots finger guns in my direction before sticking a cookie-shaped USB into Heather's computer. I guess she decided to really commit to the theme today.

I duck back into Heather's closet, and then I check pairs of boots, rifle through pockets, and slide apart sweaters, stopping only when I find a dark green sweatshirt. A bittersweet smile finds its way onto my face, and I trail one finger along the soft underside of the cuff. HILLWOOD HIGH FIGHTING GATORS.

I'm almost ready to conclude the closet as a bust. But just as I'm sliding the sweatshirt to the side, a crumpled cardboard box labeled BEDDING catches my eye. On a whim, I take out my pocketknife and lift the lid. And when I come face-to-face with Heather's old butterfly comforters, the plush carpeting of her closet drops out from underneath me.

"It's all so fucked up, Butterfly," my ex-girlfriend says softly. "The investigation. The way the cops are handling it. All of it." She turns to look at me, her eyes dark, and my hands fist the sheets of her bed.

She's so real, I feel like I can almost reach out and touch her. But I can't.

Heather takes another drag of her sparkly pod, the one studded with pink rhinestones, and exhales slowly. "And I know how you feel. I mean, I love Stella. I want her back, too. But you ... you need to pull it together, okay? Because this teenage detective act? It's honestly beginning to freak me out, Iris."

I swallow, and Heather's feathery lashes flutter against her cheeks as she mirrors me.

"I'm sorry. I am. It's just...getting detained is a big deal. And like it or not, I am the mayor's daughter...." She scrunches her nose. "You know what? Let's talk about this later. Right now, I kind of just want to lie back and forget everything."

Heather turns to the spider plant on her windowsill and lifts it up by the stem with one manicured hand—taking a slightly smaller, newly exposed second pot with it. One that leaves just enough space for all my ex-girlfriend's secrets.

I gasp, snapping myself back to the present. We need to find the plant.

I poke my head out of the closet and scan the room for it, but it's not on Heather's windowsill anymore. Imani frowns. "What are you looking for?"

"A scraggly spider plant." I carefully put the bedding box back in place, and then I close the closet door. "It's double-potted, and Heather has a hiding space at the bottom she used for weed and vape juice."

Imani frowns. "I don't see a spider plant here."

"Check the balcony," I say, already moving into the hall. "I've got the bathroom. She could have put it somewhere else after the move."

Imani still looks doubtful, but they head for the balcony anyway. I pull open the door of my ex-girlfriend's bathroom and frown. There are plants here, but they're all either too fake or too small to be hiding anything. I'm about to turn around when my gaze skips across the bathroom mirror and lands on its hinges. It's a medicine cabinet.

Maybe Heather's house is hiding more than one secret.

I pull open the cabinet, revealing a neat row of pill bottles. It's standard stuff—Advil, Tylenol, Tums—other than the orange prescription bottle at the very edge. I take it out and scrutinize it. It's Zoloft, prescribed to Heather and last filled a little over a week ago. All in all, totally normal, except the bottle is nearly empty when it should be almost full.

My mind, so prone to spinning out of control, slows entirely. Was Heather abusing her antidepressants before she went missing? And if she was, what could that mean?

You know what it could mean.

"Hey, Iris?" Imani's voice calls from behind me. "I think I found it."

Stop. Don't think about that. This is nothing.

It's nothing.

"Coming," I call. I snap a quick picture, put the bottle back into place, and step back into the main room.

"It was on the balcony," Imani says, holding up the spider plant. They set it down with a barely perceptible smirk, and I wedge my fingers between the two pots and pull upward. Inside the inner recess, a plastic bag glints up at me.

My breath catches. I pull out the bag with trembling fingers, set the first pot back inside the second, and hold up the transparent gallon bag. It's filled with seven small multicolored objects—flash drives. And on the front, scrawled with gold Sharpie in what is unmistakably Heather's handwriting, are the words FOR IRIS.

"Shit," Imani says softly as Sammy turns away from the computer. "What do you think's on them?"

The third member of our trio cocks her head. "Only one way to find out, isn't there?" she says, tipping her head to Heather's PC. "I've been downloading her files, but I can pause it for a sec. Hang on. Let me..." She adjusts the screen, clicking away at a few things before taking her own flash drive out. I hand her one at random from the USB bag, and she plugs it in. We wait.

"Damn," Sammy says, pushing her heart-shaped sunglasses farther up her nose. "I can't access the drive—it's encrypted."

"But you can decrypt it, right?" Imani asks.

"Think so. Now that we have access to her computer, just give me a second to—"

Below us, the front door creaks open before Sammy can finish her sentence. Gumbeaux's paws skid on the hardwood floor, and the three of us freeze.

Hide, Imani mouths.

I glance around Heather's room, my heart beating too fast and too loud as Sammy pulls the drive out of the computer and hastily logs out of Heather's account. She hands me the USB stick, I shove it back in the bag with the others, and Imani gestures to the balcony just as voices float up the stairs. The three of us rush outside and close the door behind us, ducking right as Heather's doorknob turns.

Imani, Sammy, and I press ourselves against the shuttered outside wall, hardly daring to breathe. "Are you sure it's here?" a sharp voice asks. Someone garbles something in response, but the first voice cuts over it. "Yeah, that's what you said last time, and you know what I found? Nothing. God, I can't believe I'm doing this again."

There's a loud rustling as the person inside Heather's room searches through papers, drawers, cabinets. "It's useless. There's nothing here, all right? I already told you, I know her better than anyone. If she really was hiding—"

The voice cuts itself off, and my blood runs cold. Whatever made them pause can't be good for us.

"Oh my god," the voice whispers, and I know.

Sammy's headphones. They're still on Heather's desk.

Next to me, Imani stiffens. They've realized it, too. Sammy's eyes widen, and I shake my head a fraction of an inch. A few seconds of agonizing stillness pass as the whole house holds its breath. Then the voice comes back, quiet and low: "Someone was in here."

Heather's floorboards creak, and I can picture the person in Heather's room sniffing us out. Not under the bed. Not in the closet. The floorboards stop creaking, and I want to scream.

They're looking at the open window.

The intruder takes a step forward. Two steps. Three. If they come any closer, they'll see us. It'll all be over.

In the distance, another dog barks. An engine revs, and there's the distinct sound of tires on pavement. Someone is heading toward the cul-de-sac.

The voice swears. "I'm getting out—her parents must be back." There's more banging and shuffling as the person moves around the room. "Listen, I already told you it isn't here, okay? And the next time you want me to do your damn dirty work for you, maybe consider giving me what the hell I want first. No, don't hang up." There's a pause, and the voice curses again. "Asshole."

The engine rumbles again, and then a door slams as the person leaves Heather's room. I press my head against the gray shutters of the Nasatos' house and breathe, forcing my heart rate to slow. We're okay. We survived.

·And, I think, glancing at the bag clenched in my hand, we got what the person on the phone couldn't.

I only have one question, really, I think as the three of us slip back into my ex-girlfriend's freshly vacated room.

What the hell was Delphine Fontenot doing breaking into Heather's house?

HOW TO FIND A MISSING GIRL PODCAST

Episode Two

HEATHER NASATO: Hey-o, lovely people of Hillwood. My name is Heather Nasato, and this is the second episode of my new podcast, *How to Find a Missing Girl.* If you missed last month's episode, go back and listen to that one first. I'll be waiting.

WOMAN #1: You can only trust what you've seen with your own eyes... what you know. The things you believe.

MAN #1: She was an incredible student. Why would she disappear?

GIRL #1: It's been hard. Everything's different now.

HEATHER NASATO: Today, I'm back with a few more interviews from those who knew eighteen-year-old star senior Stella Blackthorn best—as well as those who didn't. The varsity cheer captain vanished from Hillwood, Louisiana, just over five months ago; the police believe her to be a runaway, but that means Stella might still be out there. And that, listeners, is where you come in. If anyone has any information relating to Stella that they believe should be shared, from alleged sightings to descriptions of her behavior in the weeks leading up to her disappearance, they can phone or text the anonymous tip hotline I've set up specifically to coincide with the upcoming episodes of this podcast, or send an email to howtofindamissinggirlpodcast@gmail.com. More information about the former in a minute. But for now, let's get on with the episode.

[THEME MUSIC PLAYS]

HEATHER NASATO: In our first installment, I focused on who Stella Blackthorn was before leaving Hillwood. I talked with others about her personal life and whether they think the police's conclusion that she was a runaway has merit. But in today's episode, I'll be looking into alternate theories of what people think really happened on the night she disappeared, as well as the circumstances behind the conclusion of the Hillwood police. Welcome to episode two of *How to Find a Missing Girl.*

[THEME MUSIC FADES]

HEATHER NASATO: So. We know Stella Blackthorn was a star student and successful athlete—because yes, cheerleading is a sport. We know she was eighteen when she disappeared, which prompted the Hillwood police to handle her case as that of an adult instead of a minor. We know she went missing in September of last year, leaving behind her mom and a younger sibling. But let's focus on that for a second, shall we? Stella's situation at home.

WOMAN #1: Well, it wasn't good, I can tell you that much. I don't want to speak ill of the dead, but Diane wasn't always completely...maternal. She just wouldn't act like a mother. There was this instance once, back when Stella had just made junior varsity cheer, where I had to drive her back home after practice because Diane had forgotten to pick her up. She was like that....Always erratic in the few instances I spoke with her. And what she did after Stella went missing...I don't know. I mean, you know what everyone was saying about her back when it all first happened.

HEATHER NASATO: I'm not sure what you mean. As Stella's old cheer coach and the current cheer coach at Hillwood High, can you elaborate? For our listeners, this is Coach Catherine Hannequart speaking.

COACH HANNEQUART: What? Oh, no. I don't want to speculate on her case. Quite the opposite, in fact. That's why I wanted to come onto this...?

HEATHER NASATO: True-crime podcast.

COACH HANNEQUART: Right, exactly. Because the police seem very sure that Stella was running away from parental neglect—maybe even domestic abuse, whether it be physical or emotional—and I wanted to personally say that I understand where they're coming from. I can see...I think it's the only possible conclusion.

HEATHER NASATO: But if that's the case, why would Stella leave Iris, her vulnerable younger sibling, behind?

COACH HANNEQUART: Once again, I don't want to speculate. I think facts...Well, you can only trust what you've seen with your own eyes, right? What you know. The things you believe. But I can tell you with full honesty, I know Diane resented Stella because she looked like her father. I know Stella's mother hated looking at her daughter and seeing his face.

HEATHER NASATO: And how do you know that?

COACH HANNEQUART: Diane told me herself, right after Stella went missing. I think it was at the funeral. Which, if you want to talk [BEEP] up...that's the definition of it. What kind of mother has a funeral for her missing daughter before her body's even been found? While community members are still holding out hope? When the police think she might be somewhere out there? It's like she was trying to make herself look guilty.

HEATHER NASATO: Did you go to the police about what Diane said?

COACH HANNEQUART: I didn't have to. They came to me.

HEATHER NASATO: With Coach Hannequart's testimony, it's easy to side with the prevailing theory of the Hillwood police. If Stella *was* in fact being emotionally abused by her mother at home simply because of how she looked, it would make sense for Stella to leave once she became a legal adult. The theory certainly tracks when other well-known facts of Stella Blackthorn's missing persons case are taken into consideration: Her car is gone, her plates were allegedly sighted in Kentucky three months ago, and she's cut off all contact with everyone she knew in Hillwood. But it doesn't quite all fit together, because Stella also left the house without taking her wallet or any identification besides her driver's license. She didn't pack any of her items. In fact, when she left her house on that September night, Stella wasn't wearing anything except for a sparkly blue prom dress. That's right: Stella Blackthorn went missing on homecoming night.

MAN #1: I don't know what happened, and I think that's the scariest part for most people. We just don't know.

HEATHER NASATO: This is Collin Cooper, Stella's AP Physics teacher and the head of the Media Appreciation Club at Hillwood High.

MR. COOPER: She could have run away. She could have gotten into a car accident. She could have stopped somewhere along the way and gotten herself hurt and had her car stolen. It's terrifying to think about the possibilities, especially considering the state of the world today. And the fact she was such an incredible student... It was highly unexpected, especially for most of the Hillwood faculty. We all kept asking ourselves, *Why would she disappear?* But she never arrived at that homecoming dance.

HEATHER NASATO: Mr. Cooper, who was a chaperone at the dance last fall, certainly noticed Stella's absence. She was on the homecoming court and had just been crowned homecoming queen during halftime at the football game the night before, so when she didn't show up, the situation struck him as odd.

MR. COOPER: I ended up writing it off. I thought maybe she was just too cool for the dance, you know? We have a lot of students like that. Hell, I was like that in high school. But I wish I'd paid more attention. Maybe then she would still be here.

GIRL #1: It's honestly complicated. You hear about something, and you think, *Oh, that's not real. That could never happen to someone I know.* And then it does and everything else kind of just…shatters. It's like, *Do I really know this girl as well as I thought I did? Do I really know anyone?* It's like… yeah. Everything's different now.

HEATHER NASATO: The voice you're hearing here is that of Penelope Chiasson, the junior who was crowned homecoming princess alongside Stella last September.

PENELOPE CHIASSON: It's been hard. I can't say I have any theories about what happened. I don't know if I believe what the police said, though. I honestly think they should be looking closer into her mom, but I guess that's kind of difficult now that she's dead.

HEATHER NASATO: Do you believe that Stella's mother, Diane Blackthorn, had something to do with Stella's disappearance?

PENELOPE CHIASSON: I don't know. I really don't know anything at this point. But she must have hated her a lot, right? Especially to have that funeral for her when people were still out there searching.

HEATHER NASATO: Here, Penelope references what Coach Hannequart brought up earlier—that is, the fact that only a month after Stella went missing, Diane Blackthorn had a funeral for her eldest daughter even though many still believed her to be alive. You can visit Stella Blackthorn's gravestone at the Hillwood cemetery; however, local opinions are divided on whether the funeral was something Diane needed to do in order to move on, or an indicator of her own guilt.

GIRL #2: I always thought she killed her daughter.

HEATHER NASATO: This is Lucille Thomas, the great-granddaughter of the founder of Lucille's General Store.

LUCILLE THOMAS: I mean, I listen to a lot of true-crime podcasts. I love this kind of stuff—obviously not the fact that something happened in Hillwood to warrant one, but you know what I mean—and nine times out of ten, the perpetrator is someone who was close to the victim. They always attend the funeral, and they cry and give a big speech about how sad it all is, and the whole time they're the one who put the body in the coffin. So what does it say about you if you host one?

[OUTRO MUSIC PLAYS]

HEATHER NASATO: For now, this is where I'll be ending the second episode of my new podcast. Once again, I'm Heather

Nasato, and this has been *How to Find a Missing Girl.* Please text or call the number linked in the description with any tips you may have about the whereabouts of Stella Blackthorn—or email howtofindamissinggirlpodcast@gmail.com—and I'll see you in the next episode. Thanks for tuning in, Hillwood, and until next time.

Chapter Seven

Sunday, October 17, 10:42 AM

The three of us have just gotten off Heather's balcony when a door bangs shut downstairs. Delphine must have left.

We, however, are still trapped inside the Nasatos' house. And unless we figure out a way to get out ASAP, we're about to be in trouble for more than just selling expired Girl Scout cookies.

"How can Heather's parents be back so soon?" I hiss as we dart into the hallway and another door creaks open somewhere below us. "Aren't the Southern Alps all the way in New Zealand?"

But then voices float up from downstairs, and I realize the new people in Heather's house aren't her parents at all.

"Can't believe it took us this long to get a warrant," an arrogant voice grumbles. "It's like they don't want their kid to be found." A pause. "Can you hurry up with the alarm, Norrington?"

"I don't think the system's activated."

"The company must have disabled it on the way over." A scoff. "We don't have time for this. Come on—the girl's room is upstairs."

It's the police.

Sammy's eyes widen. "Shit!" she whispers, her grip on her newly retrieved headphones tightening. "What do we do?"

"Bathroom," I whisper, but Imani shakes their head.

"Too small. We're exposed up here."

They're right. We need to get downstairs as quickly as we can so we can leave before the detectives notice anything's amiss. But they're coming up the stairs. They're going to see us any second. They're going to—

Ding-dong!

I startle as the doorbell rings. The footsteps of the police still, and then the arrogant one swears. The door flies open after a few seconds, and I hold my breath for whoever's on the other side.

"Hi, I'm Lea Li Zhang. I'm a reporter with the *Hillwood Herald*, and I was wondering if I could have a minute of your time?"

There's a gruff response from one of the detectives that I can't quite make out, but I hear Lea push her way inside before they can slam the door in her face.

Imani raises an eyebrow in my direction, and the corners of my lips twitch against my will. Classic mistake: The cops should have closed it while they still had the chance.

"As a journalist, I'm committed to encouraging police transparency, addressing social inequality, and bridging the gap between public knowledge and private information," Lea says, her voice carrying as she walks farther into the foyer. "Now, I understand the two of you are currently conducting a search of Heather Nasato's house…but given the mysterious circumstances of her disappearance, is there anything in particular you're hoping to find?"

I dare to peek around the banister. Both of the cops are fully engaged with Lea now, though they seem to care more about getting her to leave than anything else, and neither of them notices when Lea's eyes flick up to meet mine for half a second before she glances back at the shorter blond detective with a light smirk on her face.

She knows we're here. And she's buying us the time we need to get out.

I tilt my head to the back staircase just as the taller detective starts arguing with my ex-best-friend about the freedom of the press. As long as Lea keeps the police occupied, there's a chance we can slip out of here the same way Delphine did: undetected.

Imani and Sammy follow my lead, and the three of us touch down on the first floor just as Gumbeaux comes careening around a corner. He sniffs Imani happily, and their expression freezes with panic and fear.

One of the detectives sneezes. Twice. Thrice. Suddenly, there's an enormous crashing sound, a gasp from Lea, and then Gumbeaux wags his tail and trots around to the other side of the staircase just as the arrogant detective says, "Jesus, Norrington, pull it…together."

I glance at my friends. The back door is just a few feet ahead of us. Lea has successfully distracted the cops. We can leave.

But still, there's a part of me that desperately needs to see what's going on.

I motion for Imani and Sammy to go on without me. They nod and successfully slip out the doorway, and my heart feels like it's going to explode as I peer around the staircase. I have to know what made that crash, what made Lea gasp, what made the arrogant-sounding detective trail off like that.

Farther, farther, farther...

My heart stutters.

Behind the space where the Nasato family photograph-slash-oil-painting used to hang is a gun cabinet.

And the spot for the pistol is empty.

"Oh my god," Imani says once we've successfully regrouped by the artificial lake. "That was horrible. I need to go home and lie down as soon as my hands stop shaking—I thought we were gonna get caught for sure."

"Yeah," I say, my gaze flicking back over to Heather's house. "Me too."

"I know we hate her for everything she did to you last year," Sammy says, drawing my attention back to the agency, "but Lea was incredible back there. Also, can I take the flash drives? I can keep trying to crack them at home."

"Sure," I say, handing the plastic bag to her. FOR IRIS. "We should stop by Hillwood Electronics tomorrow to ask about encrypted USBs, but it would be awesome if you could hack into them before then."

"I think I'm gonna head out," Imani says, looking back at the cop car in Heather's driveway. "I don't want to be around when the detectives come out, and I have some poodle skirts that need appliquéing anyway." They frown. "I already know I'm taking Sammy back, but do you need a ride?"

I should nod my head, because Imani drove me here and my aunt's house is too far away from Bellevue Estates to walk, but instead I shake it. "I'll be fine. You two get out of here."

They do, and then I hold my breath and wait. A green anole skitters across the pristine pavement in front of me and darts into the even-greener grass, and a few moments later Lea comes out of Heather's doorway. She spots me and instantly pivots, and for a moment I entertain the thought of pushing her into the reservoir to join the bathing ducks. But then the cops glance at me right before they disappear back into the Nasatos' house, and I think better of it.

Though that doesn't stop my blood from boiling as Lea stops in front of me with one perfect eyebrow quirked.

"Hey," she says casually, tucking a strand of short snow-white hair behind her ear as her other six-fingered hand drops to the camera around her neck. "Fancy seeing you here."

"Cut the bullshit," I snap. "Police transparency, Lea? Really?"

My ex-best-friend grins. "You like that? I thought you might."

I shake my head. "Why are you in Bellevue Estates? And be honest—I can tell when people lie to me."

It's true, for the most part. I don't have psychic powers or anything, but I'm good at recognizing physical tics and reading nonverbal cues. It was a necessary skill to have growing up, though it came in handy once I started the agency, too. But I've never been able to read Lea. Not that she needs to know that.

She appraises me coolly. "Oh yeah?" she asks, taking a step closer to me. I can smell the familiar green tea scent of her shampoo, and I clench my fists. "Well, someone let me through the gate today. Which you should be incredibly grateful for, considering the fact I just saved your ass." She gives my disguise a thorough once-over before meeting my eyes again. "Now it's my turn to ask a question. What the *hell* were you doing inside Heather's house?"

I stare right back. "I wasn't the only one in it."

Lea nods and adjusts the strap of her camera. "I have crystal-clear shots of both you and Delphine. Are you in on it—on whatever happened to Heather—together?"

I can't stop myself from rolling my eyes. "Oh, give me a break."

Lea's face hardens. "No, really. Because Heather is gone, Iris, and you were her ex-girlfriend. I doubt the police know that yet, but if they did, and if they had these photos…"

"What?" I sneer. "Are you going to turn me in? Go ahead." I set my jaw. "We both know how well that worked out for you last time."

Lea bristles. "I still don't know why you think I did that. I already told you it wasn't me who tipped off de Rosa last year, all right?"

I cross my arms. "There's literally no one else who knew I was going to be there that night. You set me up." My eyes narrow. "And you just threatened to do it again."

Lea glares at me, and this time my eyes drop to her midnight-blue sweater. It has white star patches sewn onto it, and it's the kind of thing I would find cute if my childhood-friend-turned-mortal-enemy weren't wearing it. "Because you were breaking into a missing girl's house!"

"And?"

"And I'm trying to figure out what happened to her, and right now you look like the biggest suspect!"

"Join the club," I tell Lea, and then the rest of her sentence registers. "Wait. What?"

She looks exasperated beyond words. "Have you listened to Heather's latest podcast episode?" When I don't respond, she shakes her head. "Well, it doesn't look good for you. You should, by the way." She gives me a meaningful look. "It might...clear the air between us."

I dig my fingernails deeper into my palms.

It seems like everyone who's heard the latest episode—everyone who doesn't start having a panic attack the second they hear Heather start talking about my missing sister, at least—suspects it's related to why she's gone. It sounds plausible: something about my ex-girlfriend's public investigation into Stella rubbed the wrong person the wrong way, and they made her vanish because of it. But what could Heather possibly know about me and Lea?

"I'm trying to break the story on Heather's disappearance," Lea continues. "But—"

"You?" I say. "What the hell makes you think *you* can break the story?"

Lea gazes back at me evenly. "What the hell makes you think *you* can solve the case?"

Touché.

"I dated Heather." I scuff at the perfect concrete of the sidewalk with the heel of my combat boot. "So I know her."

Lea scoffs. "So do I," she retorts. "I helped her produce *How to Find a Missing Girl*. The first five episodes, at least. It turns out knowing audio-editing software is useful for journalism *and* pseudo-true-crime podcasts."

A car door slams somewhere behind me, and I fight the urge to push Lea into the duck pond for real this time. Logically, I know I can't lunge at her in broad daylight—especially with the cops in a house only a few feet away—but that doesn't mean I won't. I can't believe she worked on my ex-girlfriend's podcast, too. Is there anyone in Hillwood who hasn't been on it?

"Besides, what I said back in Heather's house wasn't a lie— I really do work for the *Hillwood Herald*," Lea adds, answering my earlier question and stopping me from doing something stupid. "I have an internship there, which I do in conjunction with running the *Magnolia* for school, and my editor said if I write an article worth publishing about the Heather case, he'll put it in."

Now it's my turn to scoff. "That seems like a long shot."

My ex-best-friend's nostrils flare, and in that moment, I remember how much of a chronic overachiever Lea Li Zhang is. If there's even a minuscule chance she'll be able to accomplish something, she'll go for it. But even though that mentality and ambition is how she ruined my life last year, she also technically saved me from spending the rest of it in even more trouble with the police a few minutes ago. So the least I can do is try not to wince too much when I say, "Though I guess it's not any more of a long shot than my agency figuring out what happened to Heather."

There's a beat of silence, and then Lea cocks her head. "Are you admitting you run a detective agency?" she asks, her dark eyes holding my gaze. A seventeen-year-old investigative journalist staring at an almost-eighteen amateur detective. "Fine," she says when I don't respond. "New question: Did you have anything to do with Heather's disappearance?"

"No," I tell her truthfully.

"Okay," she says, tapping her camera. "Then here's the deal, Iris. I won't leak the photos of you committing criminal trespass to the police, and in exchange you'll agree to help me with something... time sensitive. I know you see me as more of a nuisance than a proper newshawk, but I happen to be sitting on a lot of evidence right now. I could use your eyes."

And I don't want to smile. Not at Lea Li Zhang. But the corners of my lips seem to have a mind of their own.

"What kind of evidence?" I ask, and Lea almost smiles back.

Lea's moms were surprised to see me, considering I haven't set foot inside the Li Zhang house for over a year. After the initial shock wore off, though, they didn't miss a beat—I've already been invited to stay for dinner, and I currently have more Hot Kid Shelly Senbei rice crackers in my Girl Scouts sash pocket than I know what to do with.

Overall, though, it's surreal to be back. Not much has tangibly changed since the last time I was here—there are still the same faded red-and-gold scrolls hanging by the doorway, the same dusty oboe and clarinet cases leaning against the battered piano in the corner of the living room, and the same off-white walls boasting the same framed baby photos (Lea pouting at the camera in a cheap Cinderella costume, Lea grinning maniacally in a boat on the Bayou Lafourche with a singular tuft of thick black hair and no front teeth, Lea attempting to feed hand-pulled noodles to a stuffed Mickey Mouse plushie)—and seeing everything like this, it's almost like I never left. Like the blip in our friendship meant nothing, because everything here is exactly the same. The couch is still piled high with clothes. Mrs. Zhang is still attempting to coax the mint plant on the kitchen windowsill into growing. Mrs. Li is still cooking something that smells like warmth and love and home, and the whole house is thick with emotion. Or maybe that's just the back of my throat.

"Thinking about how much you missed being here?" Lea quips as we finally escape her moms for long enough to stomp up the carpeted stairs.

"Hardly," I retort, and her lips do that strange little half-twist almost-smile again as she pushes open the door to her room.

Immediately, the overpowering scent of old paper and mildew hits me. I wrinkle my nose, and Lea notices my expression. "Yep. That'll be the collage wall," she says, nodding to the collection of newspaper clippings, postcards, and magazine cutouts caked onto the plaster directly in front of us. "The rest is all these ancient newspapers, though. Like I said." A wicked grin flits over her face, her expression smug as she surveys the maelstrom. "Evidence."

My gaze tracks over the collage wall and lingers on the bisexual flag hanging in the top left corner. Lea catches me looking and raises an eyebrow. "What?"

"I...uh..." I clear my throat. "Are you holding on to that for a friend?"

She rolls her eyes. "No, it's mine."

Huh. That's actually...new.

"Anyways," the girl who's unofficially blackmailing me says, "as part of my internship, I scan old newspapers and upload them to the *Herald*'s online database. Jim only started building it late last year, so it's a ton of work, but it also lets me have access to information you can't find anywhere else."

"Really?" I ask, eyeing the precariously balanced stack of articles near the edge of Lea's desk as she hoists herself on top of it. "Don't most places normally, like, archive these or something? Have a file cabinet of microfilm by a machine at a library somewhere?"

Lea tilts her head again, and I straighten. So I paid attention when she used to lecture me about journalism during our sophomore year. Sue me.

"Yeah. In fact, most of these"—she sweeps an arm around the room—"are currently at LSU. You have to jump through some hoops to obtain them, though, so I think I have some time before the rest of the media catches up."

"Right. I'm sorry—catches up on what, exactly?"

Lea considers me for a beat. "Finding out what happened to Heather."

A ball of fluffy orange fur chooses that moment to come streaking through the open door, and Lea remains unfazed as it careens into the nearest newspaper stack. Pages go flying, and the ball uncurls to blink its giant green eyes innocently, as if it didn't just topple dozens of ancient newspapers as easily as a toddler demolishes dominoes.

"That's Sin, our local menace," Lea says by way of introduction, pointing at the cat with one socked foot. "Short for Upton Sinclair. He hates everyone."

Sin blinks and takes a tentative step toward me, picking through the wreckage to sniff the cuff of my khaki pants. He purrs, curling around my legs as he rubs his forehead against me, and I lift my eyes to Lea. "Really?"

"Don't read too much into it. He's a terrible judge of character," she says, and then she grabs the nearest stack of perilously high newspapers and brings them over to me. "Here. This is the first pile we're going to go through—it's everything that ever ran in the *Herald* concerning the Deveraux, the Fontenots, or the Nasatos."

"Nathan, Delphine, and Heather's families? That's…a lot," I say, staring at the mountain of yellowed pages. "How long did it take you to even pull this together?"

"Oh, forever," Lea says breezily. "But this is my job. Investigating potential leads, running the *Hillwood Herald* Twitter,

coercing my ex-best-friends into doing all my work for me…"
She smiles, cutting the stack in half. The papers wobble threaten-ingly, and Upton Sinclair mewls at our feet.

I ignore her extortion-related jab in favor of taking the top half of the stack. "Why?" I ask. "What are you hoping to find?"

Lea settles on her floor, her back against the foot of her bed. "Anything suspicious," she says simply. "Sketchy business deals, family scandals, big bold ransom notes for kidnapped teens…if you find something strange, flag it." Lea hands me a row of sticky neon index tabs, I nod as Sin settles into my lap, and then we get to work.

We spend the next hour reading, cross-referencing, and scan-ning old articles for…well, I don't know exactly what. I note a few things that seem interesting—a downright tabloidesque piece on the rise of Deveraux Industries, a section outlining Mayor Nasato's political campaign, an article on Delphine's grand-parents donating money to help renovate Hillwood High after a hurricane took out most of the original building—but nothing substantial. Unless the love child of Edward Deveraux's alleged affair can tell us where Heather is, we're wasting our time.

"I've got nothing," Lea says dejectedly, tossing the last paper in her stack to the side and flopping down on her carpeted floor. Sin purrs and eagerly leaps from my lap to her chest.

"Me either," I say, exchanging the latest letter to the editor I just finished reading for a persimmon slice from the bowl of freshly cut fruit Mrs. Li brought up for us a few minutes ago. "Some of the stuff in here is actual garbage. Makes the *Magnolia*'s piece from last week about potential doping on the football team shine by comparison, though."

The ghost of a smile settles onto Lea's face. "I didn't know you read the paper. But just for the record, most of our sensationalized articles have Jasmine de Costa written all over them. Seriously." She shakes her head. "That girl is a modern-day William Randolph Hearst."

"Lucky for Jasmine, I have absolutely no idea who that is."

Lea sighs as Sin starts kneading her sweater. "And you were doing so well with the microfilm."

I snort. Lea's almost-smile starts edging into smirk territory, and something about the way she's looking at me makes me want to volley another snarky comment back at her. Or maybe even look up who the hell William Randolph Hearst is. Or possibly rent a documentary about his entire life, just so I have something to poke fun at with Lea the next time I come ov—

No. This is bad. I can't let myself be swept up in this—I can't let myself start bonding with my ex-best-friend. Even if this is the first time we've interacted like actual people since my sister disappeared, I haven't forgotten how she threw our friendship away to exploit Stella—and me—for her own personal gain last year.

And I haven't forgiven her, either.

I look away, deliberately breaking the moment between us. Lea isn't someone I can let my guard down around—I'm here so she doesn't get me arrested for criminal trespass. And I no longer get close to people.

I need to remember that.

Out of the corner of my eye, I can see her open her mouth,

but the alarm on my phone goes off again before she can say whatever she was going to. It's 12:25 PM, which means Heather Nasato's been missing for more than forty-eight hours.

We just passed the time threshold for when most missing people are successfully found.

Chapter Eight

I'm supposed to meet up with Lea after school tomorrow to continue helping her sift through old newspapers so she doesn't leak incriminating photos of the agency to the police, so it looks like I have to officially set our grudge aside. Despite everything that happened between us in the past, she's right—the two of us can help each other. She has information no one else has access to, and so do I. Everything I've learned in the past two days churns through my head as I walk through the hallway, my hands firmly clutching the strap of my messenger bag: the missing gun, Heather's almost-empty prescription bottle, the fact de Rosa went out of her way to warn me about meddling in her investigation.

The agency still doesn't know about that last part, but I plan to keep it that way. It keeps them safe.

As I make my way to Mr. Cooper's classroom, snatches of conversations jump out at me in the hallway:

"I bet her boyfriend killed her."

"How does someone even go missing from *school*? At this rate, Principal Phillips won't make it to November."

"That bitch really chose the best day to disappear, huh? God, I'm never going to get Hannequart to approve our cheer routine now."

At that last comment, I whip around and scan the hallway. My gaze lands on Delphine, and my stomach churns as I remember her using the same cold, indifferent tone while she was going through Heather's room on Sunday.

Since then Imani, Sammy, and I have theorized to death why Delphine was at Bellevue Estates and what she could have possibly been looking for. Our best guess for now, though, is that she knew about the flash drives.

And that someone else wanted her to find them.

Delphine catches me staring and holds my gaze, her icy green eyes piercing mine. "Something the matter, Iris?"

Beside her, one of the other cheerleaders laughs, and I turn around and stalk down the rest of the hallway.

In Media Appreciation Club, the buzz about Heather is much more subdued. A few acne-ridden boys wearing graphic tees are quietly discussing how Heather's disappearance might impact their FIRST Robotics practice, but it's not until Mr. Cooper closes the door and clears his throat, fiddling with his galaxy-patterned tie as he stands in front of us, that any HWHS staff member besides Principal Phillips (who made a very awkward speech about Heather over the intercom this morning) mentions her.

"Just before we get started today, I wanted to acknowledge the recent situation with Heather Nasato," Mr. Cooper says. "I know her disappearance marks a difficult time for us all." His gray eyes flick to me for a second, and I wish I could make myself invisible. I don't want anybody's sympathy. "But my door is always open, and if you're in my physics or astronomy classes, I'll be pushing back our upcoming tests a week in an effort to give you time to process everything that's going on."

There's murmuring from the robotics boys, and I look down at my desk to avoid meeting Mr. Cooper's eyes. He's the first teacher to even acknowledge the fact that Heather is gone, but he might not be the last. And I don't know how I'll be able to get through the day if everyone is looking at me and thinking of Stella.

Eventually, our Media Appreciation Club teacher starts the next anime episode and Sammy scoots the edge of her desk to touch mine. "Hey," she whispers, her worm-on-a-string earrings comically jingling as she leans forward, her hair today cascading to her shoulders in loose ringlets. "I looked through all the files I managed to download from Heather's computer last night, but I haven't cracked the flash drives." She makes a face. "Heather's computer password was basically the same as her password hint—Heath1225—but that didn't unlock any of the USBs. They're numbered, though—the one with pink rhinestones has a small 'one' on the bottom, and the yellow one says 'seven.' So we know they're supposed to be looked at in order, at least."

"But," Imani says quietly, pushing aside the pile of fabric on their desk, "we've kept our eyes and ears open this morning." They nod to Sammy, who takes out her phone and slides it to me right on cue.

I skim the note Sammy's phone is open to.

what we know about heather's disappearance so far:

- heather posted a new podcast episode two days before she disappeared
- the police have made no arrests in her case
- there were search parties over the weekend throughout lafourche parish organized by arden's stepdad, dan blake
- delphine fontenot broke into heather's house
- delphine and arden were both in their third-period classes from 12:30 to 1:00 on the day she went missing (confirmed by luz lorres-torres, kevin wu, and others)
- nathan was cheating on heather
- mystery girl doesn't go to hillwood high

"Wow," I say, glancing back up at the agency with equal parts admiration and jealousy. "You two got all of this just from first period?"

"And the library," Sammy adds. "I got here early this morning to look for matches to the girl we saw kissing Nathan in the school yearbooks—you won't believe how many blonde, thin, white women go to this school, by the way—but there were none." Sammy shrugs. "Whoever Not-Heather is, she's not a student here."

"Okay," I say, gearing up to ask more questions. Before I can, though, something new and guarded flickers to life in Imani's face.

"Actually, Iris, there's something else we wanted to talk to you about," they say, just as Mr. Cooper's door opens and Arden Blake storms into Media Appreciation Club.

She doesn't look like Stella today. Her normally sleek brown waves are disheveled, and her heart-shaped face crumples as she approaches Mr. Cooper's desk. There's a piece of paper in her hand—a study guide, maybe?—and even though their conversation is too quiet for me to hear over the blaring episode, it's not a long one; Arden leaves the room almost thirty seconds after she entered it, her expression like that of a kicked puppy.

"Iris," Imani says, drawing my focus back to them. "That thing Sammy and I wanted to tell you? It's Deveraux. Some people are saying he doesn't have an alibi."

I blink. "What?"

Sammy's eyebrows crease. "It might just be gossip, but Nathan doesn't have a third period. And there's no one that's been able to account for his whereabouts from 12:20 to 1:15."

I glance back over the second bullet point Sammy made: *the police have made no arrests in her case.*

"We know," Imani says preemptively, lowering their voice as Mr. Cooper glances over at us. "If the police haven't arrested him yet, there isn't enough evidence. But you have to admit, Iris, he has the best motive out of anyone on our persons-of-interest list.

He was Heather's boyfriend, and he was cheating on her. Besides, the way she talked about him in the last podcast episode…"

Cold dread slithers into my stomach at the mention of *How to Find a Missing Girl*, and the agency notices.

I didn't listen to Heather's podcast when it first came out. I flat-out refused to, because I knew it would be filled with speculative garbage and gossip about my family. Heather broke up with me shortly after Detective de Rosa detained me in December and she realized that my obsession with finding my missing sister—the girl who took care of me, who was there for me, who looked out for me even when everything around us was falling apart—was bad for her cheerleading, mayoral daughter image, so the fact my ex-girlfriend decided to start her own public investigation into Stella's case just a few months after our split always felt incredibly performative to me. But she didn't stop. Monthly update after monthly update, each one accompanied by side-eyes in the hallway and the sensation being picked apart, being watched.

And now Heather is missing, just like Stella, and I want nothing more than to avoid the podcast—and its contents—at all costs.

"It's okay if you still haven't listened to it, Iris," Imani says softly, and gratitude wells up in my throat. "We understand."

Sammy bobs her head. "You might want to take a look at the newest episode, though, because Heather claims to have evidence in it."

My heart rate picks up. "What kind of evidence?"

"We don't really know," Sammy says. "It seems like she was being vague on purpose, but she does mention planning to go wide with whatever information she had." She points to the first bullet point on her Notes app list, her expression grim. "And two days later, she disappears."

Imani's phone buzzes, and they pick it up and scan their messages. "Arden just got an early dismissal pass from the front office, and Nathan is notably absent today, so we should corner Delphine at lunch. She might not talk, but it wouldn't hurt to try—especially since rumors about her are already swirling. Maybe she'll give us something we can use, try to clear herself while she's alone."

"Sounds like a plan," I say, trying to push the podcast—and Heather's flash drives—to the back of my mind as I stare at Imani's WORLD'S OKAYEST LESBIAN phone case. The three of us all have matching ones from when we went to NOLA for Pride, and they're one of my favorite reminders of our friendship. Our camaraderie. "As long as after fourth period we're still going to Hillwood Electronics to see if we can do anything about the encryption on those flash drives." I raise an eyebrow at Sammy. "You did bring them with you, right?"

She grins, tilting her head to her holographic backpack. "Locked and loaded."

The bell rings, signifying the end of our short club period, and I take out my own phone. "Okay. Keep listening to what the student body is saying, but don't interrogate anyone directly until lunch," I tell the agency, already swiping to r/WithoutATrace to scan for any updates that might have something to do with either Heather or Stella. "And write down any gossip you overhear, no matter how far-fetched it seems. It'll help to know what other people's theories are."

Imani gives me a look as they collect their fabric pile and tuck their sketchbook back into their own tote bag. "I know my whisper network can be helpful, Iris, but gossip isn't very conducive to investigative work."

"No," I reply seriously, my eyes locking onto theirs as the three of us stand up near the back of Mr. Cooper's classroom. He gives us a small wave as we leave, which Sammy returns with a bright smile. "But we have to start somewhere."

After my second-period AP Human Geography class, I pay for my lunch and follow the agency out to our regular spot in the courtyard. It's nice we have the option of eating outside, especially since the smell in the cafeteria makes me want to hurl all my food rather than consume it, but also because our table is in the center of the quad.

Meaning we have a clear view of everyone else.

I catch Imani's eye just as Sammy grabs one of their cheese dippers and tilt my head to a picnic table a few feet away from ours, where Delphine stabs at a salad with all the vengeance of the senators who murdered Julius Caesar. Right now, we need information. And since this entire operation sprouted from Imani's intel, they're the one I need for this job.

"Hey, Delphine," Imani says as the two of us approach the angry blonde. The corners of their lips turn up. "Know anything you could tell us about Heather's disappearance?"

"No," Delphine snaps, punctuating her sentence with a

particularly brutal blow to a cherry tomato. I figured this conversation might get off to a better start than this, especially since Delphine's had a soft spot for Imani ever since they swooped in to save her with a series of expert emergency alterations when the dress she ordered for homecoming court last month didn't fit, but I guess you can't win every battle.

I lean forward, giving up the pretense of making small talk. "Listen, Del. You were one of the last people to see Heather. Surely—"

"*You* listen," Delphine interrupts, setting down her fork, "and do it carefully, Iris. You shouldn't be asking me questions. You shouldn't be looking for Heather. And you definitely shouldn't be standing here, sticking your unfortunately freckled nose into an active missing persons case"—she moves toward me slightly, like she's sharing a secret only the two of us are in on—"*especially* since everyone here remembers exactly what happened the last time you did."

Against my will, I glance over my shoulder at the rest of the courtyard as her words sink in. And at every table, people are staring at us. Whispering.

Damn it.

"I'll tell you three things," Delphine says as she straightens smugly, and I turn back to look at her. "Three things, and then you're going to leave me alone. Understood?" When Imani and I don't say anything, she smiles. "One: Heather's parents were out of the country when she went missing. Two: Heather was obsessed with Stella Blackthorn. Three: Heather's phone was fully charged when Arden and I took her out to lunch at Joan's Diner on the day she disappeared, but the police haven't been able to trace it or reach her since." She snaps her salad container shut and gives me a chilling look. "Now, I'm no detective, but I feel like those three things all point to a very obvious conclusion. Don't you?"

Imani's face is impassive. "You think she ran away."

Delphine shrugs. "I mean, why else do you think Heather started her little podcast? It's because she wanted to do the exact same thing as your sister, Iris. Ditch Cajun Country, cause a scene, and cement her name in local legend forever."

"That's not what Stella did," I snap, but something cold twists in my gut at Delphine's words anyway. Something that knows about the missing pistol and the almost-empty Zoloft bottle. Something that understands Hillwood is a town you pass through, not one you live in. A town you're born into. A town you're meant to escape.

"You can't think it's that easy to wrap up," Imani says evenly. "What about the football players? Senior Night? #AllOfUsOr-NoneOfUs? *Nathan?*"

Delphine flips her curly white-blonde hair out behind her. "Nathan would never hurt Heather. Use your brain—he's a Deveraux. He has everything he could possibly want. And arguments are normal—"

She freezes a second later, but it's too late.

"Nathan and Heather had a fight?" Imani asks sharply. "Before she went missing?" They glance at me, and alarm bells go off in my head. "Was it because of Heather's new podcast episode? Was it because of *How to Find a Missing Girl?*"

Delphine's icy green eyes glitter dangerously. "I think it's time for you to leave," she says.

The Hillwood Electronics store clerk carefully assesses the three of us, his gaze ping-ponging from Sammy, Imani, and me to the photo of Heather on my phone. The agency and I came here right after fourth period, and it didn't take long to find the easiest target to question.

"Well?" I press.

"Yeah, I know her," the clerk finally relents. "Not too closely or anything, but she came in here a few times. I don't remember a lot of customers, but I remember her."

Sammy looks at his greasy hair and downcast eyes and rolls her own. "Yeah, I bet," she mutters. Imani elbows her in the ribs.

"Anything you could tell us?"

"Not really," the clerk says, blushing as he glances at Sammy. "She seemed a little on edge the few times she was here. Always came to my register. Nice girl." The clerk frowns, his gaze suddenly a little more suspicious than I would have hoped as it drifts back to me. "Why? Are the three of you detectives or something?"

I smile. "Or something," I supply, plopping the bag of flash drives on the register in front of him. "These are encrypted USBs. Were they bought here?"

The store clerk barely looks at the bag before nodding. "Not a lot of places sell drives like those in Hillwood."

My smile widens. "Great. Can you crack them?"

The clerk frowns, and Imani elbows Sammy again. She huffs and bites out something under her breath before stepping up beside me. "Hey. We *really* need to access those drives, so your help would be, like, super appreciated." She flashes him a cat-like grin, and the clerk visibly swallows. Too bad Sammy's not attracted to men in any capacity.

"S-sorry," he says, fidgeting with the collar of his shirt. "It's against store policy to tamper with purchased equipment. But even if I was willing to break into them for you," he rushes at the sight of our fallen expressions, "it's basically impossible to unlock encrypted USBs of this kind without their recovery keys."

Sammy's eyes spark with recognition, but Imani and I frown. "Recovery keys?"

"A drive-specific, forty-eight-digit number that allows you to bypass the input of a USB's password," the clerk says. "They can be stored in a variety of formats, but the most common variations are text files or strings attached to an online account. There's also a possibility it was p-printed, though."

My heart sinks as soon as I hear the word. I think about Heather's paranoia. About her purple diary. If she went to all the trouble of leaving encrypted drives for me to find, she must have left the printed papers somewhere, too. But it's useless. The three of us can't go back to Heather's after our near run-in with the police, and there's no guarantee we'd be able to find the keys even if we did go back. Unless Sammy magically downloaded all seven recovery key .txt files from Heather's computer onto her own flash drive, which we already know she didn't, brute-forcing the drives is the only way we can open them.

The three of us thank the clerk, and then we leave the store. My gaze flicks over to Sammy. "What's the verdict?"

"I don't know." She sighs as we walk through the parking lot, expertly weaving past potholes and suspicious oil stains alike. "I mean, most people make their passwords by using important things from their lives. Their birthdays, their names, their phone numbers...something like that would be easy to crack, just like Heather's computer account." She tilts her head, and her worm-on-a-string earrings shake. "But for a heptad of flash drives, with potentially seven different passwords? Our best bet is finding the actual keys."

Imani shakes their head. "Heptad," they mutter.

"What?" Sammy says defensively. "That's what it's called. A group of seven USBs. A heptad."

"And you just knew that?"

We get to the Homicide Honda, and I'm just about to open the rear side door when Delphine's words from yesterday echo in my head.

Are you sure it's here? Yeah, that's what you said last time, and you know what I found? Nothing. God, I can't believe I'm doing this again.

Doing this *again.*

What if that wasn't Delphine's first time breaking into Heather's house? What if she found something on her first sweep that made her come back?

Sammy waves her hand in front of my face. "Earth to Iris. Are you going to get in the car or what?" I shake my head and look up at her, and her expression changes. "Iris?"

"It's Delphine," I tell her. "Delphine has the recovery keys."

Chapter Nine

TUESDAY, OCTOBER 19, 6:27 PM

Lea blinks at me, and then she laughs. I wait patiently for her to stop, and when she does, she fixes me with a fierce stare. "No," she says. "No way."

We're sitting in her bedroom, once again poring through old newspapers in search of potential reasons for Heather's disappearance—a common theme, now that Lea and I have spent hours reading alongside each other while exchanging increasingly creative insults and keeping Upton Sinclair from devouring evidence. By now, the two of us have settled into a routine: After school, Lea drives me to her house. We take turns putting on the most horrible songs we can find on the way over, and after we steal a few Chinese snacks from the kitchen and stomp up to her room, we scan AIs while we listen to YouTube playlists with titles like "pov: you're investigating a mystery in a secretive small town" until we're both falling asleep and Lea eventually blinks herself awake for long enough to take me home.

The whole thing has been oddly comforting. Lea's moms have been bringing us bowls of sliced persimmons, placated by the idea we're working together on a big research project for an English class we don't share, and Sin has taken to settling into my lap and purring loudly while I'm slogging my way through more articles about the Deveraux and their secret children.

But when Lea won't even take two seconds to consider me when I ask for a favor, it makes me question—her threat of turning me in to the cops aside—why I'm reading all these ancient articles for her in the first place.

"At least act like you're thinking about it," I complain, sullenly petting Sin with one hand as I finish tabbing another column and set it into our *maybe* pile. "I need to figure out who Delphine was talking to on the phone at Heather's, and there's no way for me to do that unless someone helps me distract her while I go through her call history. She already knows about the agency, but she'd never suspect you."

"You have a death wish," Lea comments, and I make a face at her as I pick up another issue of the *Herald.*

Even though the agency and I are operating on the theory that Delphine has the recovery keys, there's no way she'll hand them over voluntarily. The three of us are supposed to meet later tonight at the diner to brainstorm potential passwords for the drives, but part of me still desperately wants to hack into Delphine's phone.

We're missing a vital piece of the puzzle—who she was calling when she was looking for the USBs—and until we have it, my mind won't let me rest.

"You're right," I tell Lea as I open the newest newspaper. "You should just blackmail her with the photo you took of her breaking into Heather's instead."

"Vetoed," she responds, sticking a neon tab onto her own newspaper. "I only have enough energy to blackmail one person at a time." She grins. "Seriously, though, stop worrying about Delphine. If Sammy's as good a hacker as you claim, she should be able to crack the flash drives on her own. You might not even need the recovery keys."

"I guess we'll see tonight," I say, scanning a puff piece about a food drive organized by the Rotary Club of Hillwood.

"We?"

I glance up from the paper. "Aren't you coming with me? Think about it—you know Heather. You worked on the podcast together." I glance at the car keys sitting next to Lea's phone. "You could give me a ride."

"I don't know," my ex-best-friend says, turning a page. "I don't think your friends like me very much, seeing how they believe I'm the one who ratted you out to de Rosa a year ago."

"You *did* rat me out to de Rosa a year ago," I inform her. "But we could always use another brain. You might just be the new perspective we need to figure out the passwords to the flash drives."

"What do you think's on them?" Lea asks, finally setting down her newspaper to look at me. "Evidence? Something that pins everything on Nathan?"

I frown. Deveraux wasn't at school today, either, and Imani's backstage crew rumor mill is churning with whispers about how his entire family is busy doing damage control with their big-shot New York City lawyer. It's a little too late, though—despite the backup from his football teammates, Nathan's public image is already tarnished. And the police haven't even figured out he was cheating on Heather yet.

"Maybe," I tell Lea. I reach over Upton Sinclair, who's napping on top of my *no* stack, and grab my phone. "Ugh, I'm supposed to be at Joan's already."

"I can take you." Lea pauses the YouTube playlist and stands up to stretch, her fingertips brushing the top of her bisexual flag. "As long as you guarantee Sammy and Imani won't kill me for crashing your hackathon."

I hold up my hand in a three-finger salute. "Scout's honor," I tell Lea, and my ex-best-friend actually laughs as she grabs her car keys and we walk out the door.

It's pouring outside, which means the diner is much more crowded than usual. People are crammed into every red leather booth and barstool around us, their faces lit up by jukebox lights and window signs, and the air is thick with the smell of frying shrimp, greasy fries, and the sweat of countless bodies. It's sweltering, but I'm thankful for the crowd. With so many people in here at once—slurping down gumbo made with the Cajun Holy Trinity and chowing down on perfect muffulettas—no one should even spare us a second glance as we try to crack Heather's flash drives.

Sammy's laser-focused on the computer in front of her, the blue glare from her screen amplified in the reflection of her prescription glasses. She only wears them when she really needs to concentrate, although she's still sporting a pastel crop top, long fake eyelashes, and several pieces of chunky resin jewelry. "I'm in," she announces, looking up from her keyboard conspiratorially.

Imani glances over at her computer and rolls their eyes. "You literally just logged into your own user account."

"So?" Sammy says, popping a fry from Imani's plate into her mouth. "That still counts."

Next to me, Lea shifts uncomfortably. She's been fidgeting for the past five minutes, and I'm almost certain it's because she's nervous to be here.

Part of me wants to take her hand in mine and squeeze it to reassure her, but instead I slide the napkin I've been scribbling on across the sticky chrome tabletop. There's a ton of numbers on the paper: Heather's birthday, her address, her phone number, and the birth years of her parents are just the start. "Try these," I tell Sammy, decidedly ignoring the fact I just wanted to comfort the girl who is literally blackmailing me.

Earlier today, Sammy told us Heather's drives are double-encrypted with both a PIN and a password—but because she managed to download some kind of hash value off the computer in Heather's house, we now have an indefinite number of attempts to figure out both.

Sammy glances up at me. "None of these work."

"You finished trying them all already?" Imani asks incredulously, handing her another fry.

"Don't knock my WPM, Turner," Sammy says, taking it. She chews and swallows, adjusts her glasses, and fixes me with her most serious stare. "Iris, are there any other dates you can think of that might be important to Heather? The day she started dating you, maybe?"

I scoff. "May twenty-third?"

Two seconds later, Sammy's eyes widen. "Oh my god," she whispers. "No way that actually worked."

Lea blinks. "What?"

"It worked," Sammy repeats softly. "I got it. I have the PIN."

The diner fades in and out of focus. Heather made the day we started dating the first USB's PIN. FOR IRIS.

"So what's next?" Imani asks.

"Well, now we try to crack the password," Sammy continues, already back to furiously typing.

"Are you taking suggestions?" Lea asks. She slides her phone across the table, and Sammy glances over it for only a second before pushing it back to her.

"The password isn't going to be *admin*."

"How do you know? Try it."

"Already did," Sammy responds, idly adjusting the glittery pink USB sticking out of her laptop. "And it's not 1234, either." She flashes Lea a grin. "Come on. Give us lesbian coders some credit."

The bell of the diner chimes, and I do a double take as Nathan closes the silver chrome door behind him. It's the first time I've seen him since Friday, and he looks like a complete mess. His eyes are red-rimmed and puffy, his ridiculous blazer is askew, and his greasy hair makes it look like he hasn't showered since last week's game.

But I don't even have time to dwell on Nathan before he moves out of my field of vision and the bell chimes again. This time, though, the only person entering is Mr. Cooper, who shakes out an umbrella with a sheepish smile on his face. We make eye contact, and he glances at us for a few seconds, his eyes traveling over Sammy, Lea, Imani, and me, before he waves and makes his way to the bar.

I've lost Deveraux, though. Great.

"I got another order of fries here for the princess," a voice croons before I can move to go after him. Andre sets down a basket of glistening sweet potatoes in front of Lea, and irritation floods my body as I look up at the twins.

"We didn't order anything else."

Andre winks. "You got me. It's on the house." He smiles, but the expression slides off his face just as quickly. "You know, since we needed an excuse to come over here and talk to y'all."

"Really?" Sammy asks without looking up from her computer. "About what?"

"Damon and I were thinking, you know?" Andre continues, glancing around the diner before leaning in toward us. "About how you're all looking into the Heather case."

I glare at them. "How do you know that?"

Damon scoffs. "I told you," he says, turning to his taller brother. "This is a waste of time."

Andre shakes his head, refusing to be deterred. "We mean no disrespect, Iris," he says, drawing my focus back to him. "You and your friends are here all the time, and we notice things, you know? But we're also just trying to help. Because we might know something. About Heather."

I narrow my eyes. "What?"

"It'll be easier if we show you," Andre says, glancing at the crowded bar. "Can y'all come with us?"

The four of us exchange looks, silently debating. "Sure," Sammy finally says, pulling Heather's USB out of her laptop and shoving it into her backpack with the rest of the drives. "Lead the way."

The four of us slide out of our regular corner booth and follow the twins as they take us through the cacophony of Joan's Diner and through a back door marked EMPLOYEES ONLY.

"Do y'all remember how there was that break-in at Lucille's General Store last year?" Andre asks us as we enter. "Well, Moms decided to get some surveillance cameras around then. We didn't think anything of it. Haven't had any break-ins, and the footage clears itself out after about a week."

Joan's shorter twin son gives us a dark look as he stops in front of a computer surrounded by boxes of packaged food. "Except we checked it today." He pauses, pressing a few buttons on the computer until a grainy image pulls up on the monitor. "And we thought you should see this."

Damon hits PLAY, and my eyebrows furrow.

The footage shows the outside of Joan's, catching a brief

stretch of the main road and about a quarter of the parking lot. As we watch, a minivan roars by, and then another.

"What are we looking at here?" Sammy asks, but then she stops. Because there's movement inside one of the cars parked in the bottom left of the screen. A white pickup.

Nathan Deveraux's truck.

Damon skips the video forward, and then he stops. "Go back," I direct, my voice cold. He does, already knowing exactly where I want the footage to pause. "There."

"Can you zoom in?" Lea asks, and I know she sees it, too. The pixelated scene enlarges, catching the side window, and my stomach lurches at the profile of the girl sitting in the passenger seat, her face radiating fury.

It's Heather.

"Is this time-stamped?" Imani asks sharply.

Andre nods. "It's from last Wednesday, at 4:53 PM. You can see it right there." He points to the bottom of the screen.

My mind whirls. Last Wednesday, on October 13. This had to be right after Heather uploaded her final podcast episode. The one where she threatened to go to the police with significant information. The one she uploaded before she disappeared.

I wish the clip quality weren't so low-grade, but it confirms Delphine was right—Heather and Nathan did have an argument before she went missing.

But they had it in the diner parking lot. And Andre and Damon caught it on camera.

"It runs for, like, twenty minutes," Andre says, as Damon

skips the video backward and then forward again. "You can't hear them, and you can't see them the entire time, but they're both there." His voice drops, and I can hear the accusing undercurrent in his tone before he even finishes his next word. *"Arguing."*

"This is big," Lea says softly, staring at the screen. "Have you two told anyone else about this?"

"Not yet," Damon says, with an irritated look at his brother. "We're showing the police, but Andre figured we might as well show y'all the footage, too."

Andre nods, giving me a vulnerable look I'm not sure I deserve. "Moms really believes in you, you know. Says if anyone can figure out what really happened to that girl, it's you."

Thankfully, Sammy spares me from having to think of an adequate response. "Would you mind if I emailed this video to myself?" she says, already situating herself in front of the monitor.

"Go ahead," Damon says, giving up his seat. "If you can figure out how to do it, it's all yours."

Sammy gets to work, and Imani nods at the brothers. "Thanks so much for showing this to us. We can't promise anything will come of it, but it definitely helps."

Joan's sons say something in response, but I'm not listening anymore. My mind is working in overdrive, rapidly scrambling to slot all the new pieces into place. We have evidence of the fight. This is good—even with no audio and subpar footage, it's still a concrete lead.

Out of habit, I glance down at my phone to note the current time, but it buzzes before I can. At first, I think it's just another one of my Heather case timers, but then I catch a glimpse of the banner at the top of my phone and inhale.

It's a notification. A text from a blocked number.

GIVE UP THE SEARCH, IRIS.
YOU'RE NEVER GOING TO FIND HER.

Part Two

HOW TO FIND A
MISSING GIRL PODCAST

Episode Three

HEATHER NASATO: Hey-o, lovely Hillwood residents. I'm Heather
Nasato, and this is the third installment of my serialized
investigative podcast, *How to Find a Missing Girl*. In case
you missed the first two episodes, go ahead and listen
to those first. Today, I'm going to do something slightly
different.... In today's episode, I'm not going to be speaking
to eighteen-year-old Stella Blackthorn's best friends,
teachers, or fellow cheerleaders about the plausibility—or
implausibility—of her being a runaway. Instead, I'm going to
be switching tactics to the circumstances behind the senior
cheer captain's disappearance last fall. That's right: In
today's episode, I'm going to delve into what happened on
the night that Stella Blackthorn disappeared.

[THEME MUSIC PLAYS]

PENELOPE CHIASSON: It was homecoming, obviously. There were
a lot of people there. But Stella wasn't one of them.

NOÉMIE CHARMANT: I texted her about ten or twenty times. None of the messages ever delivered, and my calls went straight to voice mail. I figured her phone was dead....I never thought she was running away.

[THEME MUSIC FADES]

HEATHER NASATO: Let me set the scene: It's September nineteenth in Hillwood, Louisiana. Lucille's General Store is selling homemade pumpkin spice chai lattes for $2.75 a cup, parishioners are stocking up on TV dinners to watch the New Orleans Saints face off against the Carolina Panthers on Sunday night, and families across Acadiana are making sure they have a working generator—or know a friendly neighbor who does—in case they lose power when Tropical Storm Nolan makes landfall at 3:45 AM. But for the students of Hillwood High, their first major dance of the school year is set to go off without a hitch. The Prom Committee has decked out the gymnasium with streamers, balloons, and fairy lights. All that's missing are the students...except twenty minutes away from the home of the Fighting Gators, a mobile home at the edge of the Chevalier Trailer Park tells a very different story.

NOÉMIE CHARMANT: Yeah, I remember what it looked like.

HEATHER NASATO: This is Noémie Charmant, Stella's best friend. She previously appeared on episode one of *How to Find a Missing Girl.*

NOÉMIE CHARMANT: I'd say it was one of the nicer trailers in Chevalier. Cream shiplap, lots of windows, finished hardwood interior...the whole thing was propped up by

128

cinder blocks, but it wasn't bad for $450 a month. The stairs were rickety, and the shutters were painted with this dark green paint that was prone to peeling, but their spot was just off of Saint Roux Drive across from the Bayou Lafourche. A riverside view.

HEATHER NASATO: Did Stella see it that way?

NOÉMIE CHARMANT: No. She hated living in Chevalier, and she avoided her house as much as possible. Growing up, I was probably the only one she ever had over at the park.

HEATHER NASATO: It was this very mobile home that Stella drove away from on homecoming night, at around 7:30 PM, according to her sister's statement to the police. In her white Honda Accord, it should have taken Stella around twenty minutes to get to the dance, which started at 8:00 PM.

PENELOPE CHIASSON: Except she never showed.

HEATHER NASATO: This is Penelope Chiasson again. She was previously interviewed during episode two.

PENELOPE CHIASSON: I mean, it was the night of the homecoming dance, obviously. There were a lot of people there, either messing around with the photo booth or crying in the bathroom or having a great time with their girlfriends. But I was watching out for Stella because I knew her and because we were both on court together, and she just never showed.

HEATHER NASATO: Odd, considering Stella left her house so early. I asked Penelope Chiasson what time she arrived.

PENELOPE CHIASSON: Oh, I think I came around 9:30 PM or something. It was pretty late.... Yep, 9:32 PM, according to this heinously blurry selfie I just found in my camera roll.

But you're not really supposed to be early to these things. Even if you're on the court, there's no rush.

HEATHER NASATO: Since Penelope came to the dance later, I thought Stella might have arrived before she got there. When I asked around, however, others quickly ruled this possibility out.

MR. COOPER: I actually had car trouble that night, which was embarrassing, especially since I've been driving around the same beat-up Ford since *I* was in high school, so I definitely should have seen it coming. But I managed to get to the gymnasium at 8:20 PM, and I didn't see Ms. Blackthorn at all.

GIRL #1: No, Stella wasn't there.

HEATHER NASATO: This is Delphine Fontenot, a rising senior at HWHS.

DELPHINE FONTENOT: I came to the gym around 7:00 PM to help the Prom Committee put up decorations for the dance. Stella never showed.

HEATHER NASATO: And with that, Delphine rules out Stella stopping by the dance earlier and leaving before Penelope got there. That means that, after 7:30 PM, Stella Blackthorn's whereabouts are unaccounted for.

PENELOPE CHIASSON: It sounds sinister, but it's true. No one knows where she went that night after she left Chevalier.

BOY #1: I mean, I don't really remember anything. Some shouting, maybe.

HEATHER NASATO: This is Jackson Criswell, another student at Hillwood High. He still lives in Chevalier—and before Stella Blackthorn went missing, he was her neighbor.

JACKSON CRISWELL: Homecoming isn't really my thing. You used to be able to have more fun at these kinds of events, but now the entire PD shows up the second someone even catches a whiff of weed. The cops break up the grind circles, turn on the lights, and hold everyone in the sweaty gym until they catch the perp. Not really my scene, if you catch my drift.

HEATHER NASATO: Which means you were at home during the night Stella disappeared.

JACKSON CRISWELL: Yeah. I was actually on a walk—not gonna lie, I was kind of buzzed. But I remember people, like, screaming at each other. And any other time, I'd say that's just a typical Saturday night in Chevalier. But the Blackthorns were always real quiet, so I thought it was strange. I saw Stella storm out of their trailer, looking pissed as hell, and then she just got in her car and drove off.

HEATHER NASATO: She could have been visiting someone else. She could have gotten herself injured. Or she could have been running away. Of course, the 7:30 PM time is only a rough estimate, provided by Stella's younger sister, Iris. I reached out to Iris before recording this podcast episode in case she wanted to give her take on that night, but she declined to comment. Here's Noémie Charmant again.

NOÉMIE CHARMANT: Stella didn't have a date to homecoming. I think that's important because she had an abundance of guys asking her.... She turned them all down, though, so she was alone when she was coming to the dance, and she was driving herself. I don't know if that means anything, but it could be the only piece that shows her actions were premeditated if she really was running away. Or maybe it's just a coincidence. I don't know.

HEATHER NASATO: There's just one last thing I want to touch on before I wrap up this month's installment. In our last episode, I spoke with Coach Catherine Hannequart, who told me she believed Stella might have been suffering from emotional abuse at the hands of her mother, simply for how she looked. I thought about that for a while after I talked to Coach Hannequart, because something about our conversation didn't quite feel right to me. And then it finally hit me: If Stella really did run away because she had a purportedly difficult home life, wouldn't it make sense for her to return to that same home after the person who was making it difficult passed away? Especially if before she disappeared, Stella was raising her younger sister? I spoke to Dr. Brenda Miller, a licensed psychologist here in Hillwood, to find out more. Hi, Dr. Miller. Thank you so much for agreeing to speak with me over the phone.

DR. MILLER: Of course.

HEATHER NASATO: So, Dr. Miller. Would it be normal for Stella to stay away from her hometown after her mother, the woman who was allegedly abusing her, passed away?

DR. MILLER: Well, I think that's a question I can't answer, Heather. Obviously, everyone's situation and circumstances are different, and I don't want to speculate on Stella's case. But speaking very broadly, it's possible for people who run away from home to stay away even after their abusers pass.

They can associate their abuse with their hometown, for example, and make the conscious—or subconscious—choice to stay away. And then there's the fact that a lot of people seek a fresh start when running away.... They often want a completely clean slate. And to come back to a place where you were in a toxic situation after you've managed to take yourself out of survival mode...Well, I would say I can absolutely understand why a person may not want to return after they've started to make a new life for themselves.

HEATHER NASATO: But to not return in the midst of an ongoing missing persons case? Knowing you left behind your family...your little sister?

DR. MILLER: Well, with Stella's case specifically, there are a lot of factors at play. We don't know all of them, obviously, so it's hard to be able to tell what truly happened. But think about it this way—if you uprooted your entire life to break free from your family, if you risked that much to leave them behind, if you knew that some of them maybe even grew to resent you for your decision—would you come back later if you had the choice?

HEATHER NASATO: No. I guess I wouldn't.

DR. MILLER: Then I think there's your answer.

HEATHER NASATO: So there you have it, Hillwood. I don't know. I started this podcast to look for answers. To find the truth. But the more I dig into Stella's case, the more it seems like the police weren't wrong to let it go cold. Though some of the evidence for Stella running away is a little shaky, it could have been a spontaneous decision. She could have

chosen to leave that night. And she could have chosen to
stay away, too.

[OUTRO MUSIC PLAYS]

HEATHER NASATO: That's all I have for now. Thank you for
tuning in to the third episode of *How to Find a Missing Girl*.
Until next time, I'm Heather Nasato. And, Stella, if you're
out there—please come back. We miss you.

Chapter Ten

Lea glances over at me as she drives. "You're being awfully quiet."

"Hm?" I say, tearing my attention away from the raindrops racing down my passenger window and to her pretty profile instead. I focus on the familiar bridge of her nose, on the way her lashes curl up and outward, on the blunt cut of her chin-length white hair. Anything but the swirling fear in my gut. Anything except the growing unease in the pit of my stomach or the goose bumps brushing against the wool of my collared coat.

"I'm fine," I say quietly, rubbing the cool metal of my sister's necklace between my fingers. "Just thinking."

GIVE UP THE SEARCH, IRIS.

YOU'RE NEVER GOING TO FIND HER.

"Just thinking, huh?" Lea says as she pulls into my street. The route guidance of her GPS ends, and I force myself to let go of Stella's star charm as she parks her car.

"Yeah," I lie, reaching for the door handle. It's pitch-black outside, but I can see a light coming from the kitchen, which means Megs is home. "Thanks for the ride. I'll catch up with you tomorrow."

"Iris," she says.

I let my trembling hand drop in the darkness.

I don't like this. I don't like how Lea can see right through me. I don't like that she can hear the lies in my voice, or that I can't hear them in hers. I don't like how when I meet her eyes, they blaze in a way that's fury and kindness all at once.

She's the only person who's ever been able to fool me, but the reverse doesn't apply.

The two of us sit in silence for a moment, and I focus on what's around me. The smell of Lea's shampoo. The soft indie song playing from her speakers. Rain.

"Are you worried about the video?" she asks, and I exhale. Of course. The video.

I can blame my anxious silence on that.

After Sammy exported the footage, Imani took the four of us to the Valdez-Taylors' so we could analyze it. I was skeptical about how much information we would be able to glean from it, but Imani took one look at my face and scoffed.

"Please, Iris," they'd said after I asked if they could lip-read. "I'm a thespian."

As admirable as Imani's skills were, though, there's nothing they could do to interpret the parts of the conversation where Heather's and Nathan's mouths weren't visible. Which was most of it. So far, we don't have a lot to go off of—the only thing Imani's certain about is that the two of them said the words *Arden*, *brother*, and *Deveraux* frequently. At one point, Imani also thinks Nathan said, "You're insane," but that's about it.

It's proof of turmoil in Heather's life, though. And it makes Nathan look very, very bad.

Lea bites her lip. "Iris," she starts, and then stops. Swallows. Starts again. "I know you have . . . reservations about me. I know you don't think I'm a good person, and I know you're only working with me because you think I'll betray you if you don't."

A small smile finds its way onto my face as I turn to look at her, but it doesn't reach my eyes. "Won't you?"

"No," Lea says seriously, her dark eyes searching mine. "I won't."

Something strange twists in my heart. The roof of my mouth goes dry, but I don't move as Lea keeps looking at me. And I don't look away.

"I know you think I put myself above everything else," my ex-best-friend continues softly. "My reputation, my future career . . . and I used to." Lea frowns, her gaze flicking to the raindrops sliding down her front windshield. "But then I lost my best friend. I lost you, Iris. For an entire year. And honestly? I'm kind of grateful I did, because that was enough to wake me up.

To make me realize I don't want to be the kind of journalist that hurts people." Her eyes flit back to me. "The kind that hurt you."

I inhale.

"You have no idea how much I regret wanting to run that article on Stella in the *Magnolia* after she disappeared. I would have never done it without your consent, but I shouldn't even have been thinking about it. You were grieving, and it was wrong, and I'm sorry." Lea frowns. "And you don't have to accept my apology, but I wanted you to hear it from me."

I don't know what to say.

Emotion wells up in my throat, and I swallow. I don't do this anymore. I keep people at an arm's length, and I don't let them in, and I definitely don't dole out second chances. But Lea looks so genuine. So honest. She tilts her head, and something flips in my stomach.

I need to get out of here.

"Okay," I mumble, purposefully breaking eye contact with my ex-best-friend for the second time. "I have to go."

I don't look at her as I turn away. I don't try to assess the expression on her face as I fumble with the car door and manage to wrench it open. I don't dare to begin untangling the feelings in my chest as I stumble out into the downpour, leaving Lea Li Zhang behind, because she just apologized. And I just forgave her.

Which means I still care.

I push the thought out of my mind as I maneuver my way around puddles of muddy water, putting distance between the two of us until I'm far away from Lea and in front of Aunt Megan's house. My house.

I take a deep breath as I steady myself in the refreshing coolness of the rain, forcing myself not to look back as Lea's headlights flick back on. I have to be careful with her. Even now, even with her apology, she's still not someone I can trust. I know that, and yet...

I curse under my breath as I glance over my shoulder, hoping for just one more glimpse of her face. And then mine pales.

Lea's brights aren't on.

Farther down the street, there's another car. I can't see the driver, but an ice-cold sensation that has nothing to do with the storm I'm caught in trickles down my spine anyway. Someone's watching me.

I turn and fumble with my keys, my sweaty hands shaking until I unlock the door and shut it firmly. What the fuck?

"Hey," a voice says behind me, and I whirl around. Megan looks up from her plate of almost-finished muffulettas—instantly recognizable leftovers from Joan's Diner two nights ago—and I desperately try to still my rabbiting heart. "You're home late."

"Yeah," I say, trying my best not to look suspicious as I slide off my combat boots and step into the kitchen. "Yeah, sorry, I just...had some studying to do. With a...friend."

Megan lifts an eyebrow. "Oh yeah?" she asks. I can feel my pulse in my temples, can hear blood roaring in my ears. "Which friend?"

I need to calm down—the car was probably nothing. No one's

following me. I'm overreacting. I take out the elastic band holding up my bun and snap it taut against my wrist. "Do you remember Lea Li Zhang?" I ask my aunt, forcing myself to sound relaxed as I run a hand through my wet hair.

A series of memories flashes through my mind: Lea and me inhaling dreamsicle sno-balls at the Sno Shack in the summer, and skinning our knees in the backwoods bayou, and spitting straw wrappers at each other during milkshake study sessions at Joan's Diner while Stella memorized derivative rules. The two of us sneaking around the Chevalier Trailer Park at night, trying to guess what the people in each mobile home were like based on their shiplap siding. Friendship bracelets and secrets and moments in between where we almost felt like something more.

Megan's eyes soften. "I do," she says. "I'm glad you're reconnecting, but please text me next time your plans change, okay? I worry."

I nod. My aunt must sense that I'm not in the mood to elaborate, though, because she picks up her plate and stands up from the kitchen table. "Your muffulettas are in the fridge if you want them," she adds, but my stomach practically curls into itself as she washes the dish and retreats upstairs. I'm not hungry. I only have one thing on my mind:

GIVE UP THE SEARCH, IRIS.
YOU'RE NEVER GOING TO FIND HER.

I don't want to think about what those words could actually mean, or who they could possibly be from. I don't want to think about the indiscernible car that might have followed me home. I don't want to think about anything.

But as I walk into my room and stare at the kitten calendar that's now pinned above my desk, its string of mocking red Xs marking each additional day I've failed to figure out what happened to my ex-girlfriend, I know I can no longer push away the undeniable.

Heather's disappearance wasn't an accident. Someone wanted her gone.

At school the next day, Eastwick's chemistry class feels like it takes twice as long as usual. I'm too fucking anxious to even look at my titration lab sheet, let alone answer a single question, because I can't stop hyper-focusing on evidence: the video from the parking lot, the missing gun, Heather's antidepressants. The *HTFAMG* podcast. Delphine's phone call. The police, who have to know about the footage from Joan's Diner by now.

The fact there might be someone out to get me. Someone watching, lying in wait.

"That's time," Eastwick announces with a wry smile, snapping me out of my spiral. I look back at my unfinished table and wince. I'm definitely getting a failing grade on this one.

Eastwick tells everyone to pass up their papers, and then I pack my bag and stand up.

"Miss Blackthorn?" Ms. Eastwick says before I leave. "A word?"

Fucking splendid.

I hang behind as the rest of the class files out, and then Ms. Eastwick's hawklike eyes are on mine again. I'm in for another lecture.

"Your grades are dropping," Eastwick says flatly, and I bite the inside of my cheek to keep myself from saying something stupid. I've been neglecting my chemistry homework, but that's to be expected. I have more important things going on in my life right now. But it's not like I can explain that to Eastwick, or that she'd even care if I did, so I keep my head down instead as she continues. "Is there anything I can do to make sure you stay on track academically?"

I continue staring at the speckled linoleum floor, hoping I don't look as surprised as I feel. There's no way Eastwick just said something... considerate to me.

When I don't respond, she sighs. "I know this is a difficult time for you. It's hard for the majority of the student body, but..." She frowns, and it suddenly clicks: Stella was her favorite student before she disappeared.

"I'm fine," I say softly, and Eastwick takes off her horn-rimmed glasses.

"I don't usually share this with students," she says, "but I almost lost my father a few years ago. He was diagnosed with lung cancer, which was treatable, but the treatments themselves were so expensive, I thought he wouldn't be able to survive." She blinks. "All the stress made me a worse teacher, but after I took some time away, I was able to do my job again." My chemistry teacher puts her glasses back on. "I'm willing to make accommodations for you, Miss Blackthorn, but I need you to communicate with me. It's not a crime to ask for help if you need it—or to let me know if there's anything I can do for you while you're struggling."

I nod, not trusting myself to speak. The only thing Eastwick can do for me is let me catch enough of a break so I can do *my* job—which is to do the police's job, but better. Because the fact they haven't found anything of note in over four days—not to mention their mishandling of my sister's case last year—makes me doubt they'll prove adept at finding my ex-girlfriend.

I leave Eastwick's classroom as quickly as I can, but a flash of amber hair in the hallway stops me from continuing to Media Appreciation Club. Nathan Deveraux is finally at school.

There are so many things I want to ask him. Whether he's been following me. What he fought with Heather about two days before she disappeared. Where he was on the day she went missing, and why the police felt the need to quietly interrupt Senior Night to question him. But when I sidle up to his locker, he slams it shut before I can see inside it and scowls. "Leave."

"It's nice to see you, too, Deveraux. Hey, so, totally random question, but did you make your girlfriend disappear after she put out her latest podcast episode?"

Nathan snaps his combination lock shut and sneers at me. "I already talked to the police, Blackthorn. You really think I'm going to talk to you, too?"

I glance at the dial. Thanks to Hillwood switching to paperless e-textbooks a few years ago, the only people who still use their lockers are mathletes and Nathan Deveraux. He's definitely doing something shady, but I have to focus on the big picture.

"Heather's gone," I tell him, and his eyes meet mine. "If you know where she is, you should cooperate. Whether that's with the police or with me—"

"You think I don't want her back just as much as you do?" Nathan asks vehemently, banging his hand against the hollow metal next to him. "You think I'm not tearing my hair out each night thinking about what could have happened to her? Because I am, Blackthorn. I'm sick and I'm scared and I'm *exhausted*, and I want her back more than anything."

The show of genuine emotion catches me off-guard, and I frown as Nathan runs a hand through his curls. But then I remember last Thursday. Watching the same motion as he walked down Bellevue Estates, right before he kissed someone other than his own girlfriend.

My voice is cold. *"I don't believe you."*

Before I can say anything else, though, a familiar voice calls my name. Reluctantly, I take a few steps back from Nathan as Mr. Cooper comes into view. His gray gaze sweeps between the two of us, taking us in, and I don't know if it's my imagination or a trick of the light, but Deveraux seems almost nervous in his presence.

"Iris," Mr. Cooper says again, pretending to be oblivious to the fact I was seconds away from tearing into Hillwood's golden boy and the prime suspect in Heather's case, "I'm glad I caught you on my way back from the faculty lounge. We're about to start the best arc of the entire anime back in my classroom, if you'd like to join us."

And I know Mr. Cooper's giving me a way out. So even though I don't want to, I take it.

"Yeah," I say coolly, my eyes locked onto the cheater in front of me, "I'd love to, since we're done here."

But there are words left unspoken in the air between us as I turn on my heel and give Nathan's locker one final glance, words both Deveraux and I hear as clearly as if they were.

We're not.

I should be in my fourth-period class right now. I know that, but instead I'm on my way to the gym. The cheerleaders have been in there running drills all week, and I'm desperate. I need to find a way to get into Delphine's phone and figure out who she was talking to at Heather's.

I clear the hallway and push through the doors to Building C, my forged hall pass (one of Sammy's best) clutched firmly in my left hand. There's a tantalizing display case to my right, filled with old school trophies and team photos—including one of Stella front and center next to her best friend, Noémie Charmant, for varsity cheer—but I don't stop to stare at it today. I don't have the time.

Past a gold-and-green mural of our school crest, Hillwood's motto etched in the ribbon around it—*poursuivre la connaissance.* Through another set of windowed doors. And then, finally, I round the corner and see the entrance to the school gym. Bingo.

One of the double doors is propped open, and I immediately spot the pale blonde girl stretching against one of the bleachers inside. Delphine Fontenot. Perfect.

I pivot before Coach Hannequart or any of the cheerleaders can see me, taking the nearest staircase down to the Fighting Gators locker room. From sitting in on Stella's old practices, I know none of the girls keep their belongings locked during drills, and I also know Coach Hannequart doesn't allow phones inside the gymnasium. Which means Delphine's has to be down here somewhere. If I'm lucky enough to find it.

I slip inside the locker room for the first time since Heather and I broke up, thinking of stolen kisses and soft sweatshirts and loaded glances in the moments I trailed behind my sister like a shadow. But even if this place feels delicately haunted, it's just another musty area of Hillwood High. And I have a phone to find.

I start with the locker closest to the door and work my way clockwise, going through bags and gym clothes until I find a pristine white backpack hanging from the hook of Locker Number Twelve. A grin spreads across my face. It's Delphine's.

I unzip the bag and rifle through it with gloved hands, searching for Delphine's expensive phone among its contents. But instead, my fingers connect with something else. Something bulky and smaller and all black, tucked away and hidden in a cloth compartment at the bottom.

It's a burner.

I take it out and turn it on, my pulse quickening as I scan the burner's lock screen. It looks like it only unlocks with a PIN, but I can see two visible text notifications without needing the code: *Don't call me again*, dated from 10:58 AM on Sunday, and *Stop by later. I have something new for you*, from thirty minutes ago today.

I snap pictures of the texts and type the number—*970-555-0141*—into my own phone. And then I set my jaw, click a button, and wait while I dial it.

"I thought I made myself clear," a sharp voice says behind me, and I spin around to face Delphine Fontenot—along with her entire posse of cheerleaders—just as my phone starts ringing.

Shit.

"And yet, here you are," the blonde cheer captain muses, tilting her head. "Iris Blackthorn, amateur detective." She smiles, and I swiftly end the call and tuck my phone back into my coat. "Snooping through my things."

Behind her, Arden nods, her crystal-blue eyes downcast. Luz Lorres-Torres snickers.

Delphine takes a small step forward. "You don't belong here, Iris," she says softly. "You're not a cheerleader. And you don't have any friends among us, because no matter how hard you try, you are *never* going to be anything like your sister."

I meet Delphine's gaze dead-on as she comes to a stop in front of me. "I'm not the one who's trying to replace her."

A dark look flashes across Delphine's porcelain face, and she reaches out and snatches her burner phone back with a viciousness that chills me. "Get the fuck out of here, Iris," she hisses. "And don't ever let me catch you messing with my shit again."

I swallow and slide past her, and Luz deliberately jostles me as I move to open the door and leave the locker room behind.

I'm leaving all of it—kisses and cherry lip balm and wearing Heather's scrunchies on my wrists. Knowing I'll honor Delphine's request, because next time she's not going to catch me.

It's not until I'm out of Building C that my heart rate slows down enough for me to finally register the incessant buzzing coming from my phone. Instagram notifications.

be gay solve crime
2:49 PM

imaniturnnerr:

Iris. Please tell me you still don't have Snapchat.

wedoalittlehacking:

hello what are we talking about

omfg i just saw it. what the hell delphine

IMG_9913.PNG

did she really just out our agency on her freaking SNAPCHAT STORY

imaniturnnerr:

Yep.

wedoalittlehacking:

i hate her <3

WAIT OMG

IMG_9914.PNG

HOW DID IT GET WORSE

I stare at the two screenshots Sammy sent as I'm turning down the hallway that leads to my AP Literature class—there's no name linked to the story, but it's obviously Delphine's.

great news, everyone! forget the real cops trying to figure out what happened to heather—there's an amateur teenage detective agency in hillwood, the first caption reads. Delphine's punctuated it with a grainy picture of Sammy, Imani, and me hunched over a phone in the back booth of Joan's Diner, and my stomach twists.

But the second one is worse.

There's no accompanying photograph this time; the blurry background image is murky and unfamiliar. But the ten-digit sequence following the text—*a little birdie was even kind enough to pass along their tip line to me, so make sure you send them ALL your best info!*—isn't. Because it's mine.

Delphine leaked my phone number to the entire school.

Chapter Eleven

It's officially been a week since Heather disappeared. My compromised phone is filled with voice mails and texts telling me to fuck off and die, but there's not much I can do about it unless I go to the police. And that's not going to happen.

No. What I can do—what I have been doing—is keep focusing on Heather's case. And with me turning eighteen in three weeks, it's more imperative than ever that I solve it fast. We have a few good leads so far: the flash drives, Mystery Girl, 970-555-0141, and the argument from Joan's Diner. But we're also missing things: the recovery keys, who exactly lives in 343 La Belle Lane, and who the phone number belongs to. Part of me wants to bang my head against Imani's cushioned headrest—nothing is leading anywhere, and we're stacking up more questions than answers.

I'm not a quitter, though. So here the four of us are, sitting in the Homicide Honda outside of school at seven o'clock in the morning, trying to come up with a plan to connect at least a few of the dots we've collected. It's a long shot, but we're running out of options.

Time, too.

"It's weird, isn't it?" Sammy asks, pulling her straw in and out of her diner milkshake. "How people are just...moving on." She tips her chin to the school marquee ahead of us, which now reads RESCHEDULED SENIOR NIGHT FOOTBALL GAME TONIGHT @ 7 PM—GO, FIGHTING GATORS!

"Not everyone, though," Lea adds, eyeing the news vans parked near the edge of the school. She's been hanging out with the agency more ever since Andre and Damon showed us the footage of Heather and Nathan arguing, seeing as Imani and Sammy both really gel with her quote-unquote "distinguished bi energy," and even though the two of us haven't spoken directly about her apology—or me running off after accepting it—we're not exactly mortal enemies anymore.

She's right, too. Ever since the Nasatos got back, they've constantly been giving televised speeches imploring the public for Heather's return. One of their interviews on *Channel Six News* went viral a few days ago, and now our town's crawling with journalists looking to profile Hillwood as a town notorious for its missing girls. They haven't been bold enough to venture into the senior parking lot, though. Yet.

"Okay," Imani says, tearing a piece of paper out of their sketchpad and ripping it into four separate strips before handing one to Sammy. "Done."

Sammy stops fidgeting with her straw and takes the paper. "What are these?"

"Delineated roles," Imani answers, passing two more slips back to Lea and me. "We all agree there are too many things related to Heather's case we need to know more about right now, so I've decided to divide the main four between us. Hell Week for *Grease* will be here before we know it, and I want to find Heather as soon as possible anyway."

I glance at the piece of paper Imani's handed me. Mine says MYSTERY GIRL.

"Later today, I'm going back over the Joan's Diner footage to see if I can figure out any more words Heather and Nathan exchanged in their argument before she went missing," Imani continues, holding up their own CAR FIGHT slip. "Sammy, you're going to keep working on the flash drives, at least until we can figure out if Delphine really has the recovery keys and how to get them from her if she does. Lea, you're on duty to try and find out who the burner phone number belongs to, so see if you can pull some strings at the *Herald*. And Iris—"

"I'm Mystery Girl," I say, giving my paper a little wave just as my phone vibrates with another random call. "I got it. Thanks."

"I still can't believe Delphine doxxed you," Lea says as I hit DECLINE. "Though I guess that's kind of her MO."

"Yeah, well, it's my fault for being reckless enough to dial that number," I say as I silence my ringer, even though my leaked phone number bothers me a lot less than the GIVE UP THE SEARCH text. Not that I've told anyone about the latter. As far as I can tell, I'm the only one in the agency who got a cryptically threatening message, and I intend to keep it that way. I don't need to make my friends nervous over nothing.

Imani's eyes flick to Lea in the rearview mirror. "Her MO?" they ask. "Who else did she doxx?"

"Jackson Criswell," Lea answers. Our local amateur drug dealer. "Apparently Delphine had some sort of fling with him this summer, but things ended badly and she leaked his number *and* his address. No one could prove it was her, but Criswell got so many harassing calls from her friends that he had to get a totally new SIM card. Jasmine wanted to do an article about the whole thing for the *Magnolia*."

"What?" Sammy asks, twisting around in her seat. "Did Jackson ever report her?"

Lea raises an eyebrow. "To who? The police?" She smirks. "No. I doubt he wanted to get more cops involved in his personal life."

"We have that in common," I say dryly, taking a long sip of my hazelnut iced coffee.

Back when I still lived in Chevalier, Jackson Criswell was my neighbor. I never interacted with him, mostly since his hobbies included scalping vape pens to freshmen and selling weed and pills to Hillwood's rich kids, but all that got shut down after he was arrested and put on probation late last year. Now he mostly keeps his head down, shuffling through classes while allegedly using up the rest of his stash in his trailer with his friends.

I drain the rest of my coffee, and then I glance at the agency.

"Let's keep moving. Is everyone good with the roles they've been assigned?"

They nod.

"Great," I say. "Then let's get to work."

The four of us get out of the Homicide Honda, and Imani and Sammy walk ahead of Lea and me as we all make our way to school. "Be honest," I tell my ex-best-friend, shouldering my messenger bag. "Do you think we've bitten off more than we can chew this time?"

"Probably. But it'll be worth it if we find something important to Heather's case."

I cast her a sideways glance. "Or something good for your groundbreaking piece for the *Herald*, I bet."

Lea won't look at me as we cross the road. "Actually, Iris... I've been meaning to talk to you about that," she says, and dread slithers into my stomach. "Before you freak out, though, just hear me out. Okay?"

When I don't say anything, she bites her lip. "Okay. Well... basically, I think the general public is having a hard time figuring out what to believe regarding Heather's case. A lot of people love the Deveraux, and though *How to Find a Missing Girl* may have made Heather famous, it didn't exactly make her well-liked." Lea tucks a strand of hair behind her ear with one of her six-fingered hands. "But if more people knew about Nathan cheating, or the fight in the Joan's Diner parking lot, or even Heather's flash drives, there would be more pressure to find her. And if I could write about those things... *inform* people..."

Lea's determined eyes flick up to mine, and the dread turns to a visceral churning. I think I'm going to be sick.

"You can't, El. I mean... first of all, you can't publish anything I told you. The agency is an underground operation, and none of our information was obtained legally—"

"I know," she says, cutting me off. "But, Iris, I'm not like you or Imani or Sammy. I can't break into missing girls' houses, or design killer disguises, or hack into flash drives. I take photos and I go through old articles and I write pieces for the school paper. And now I have a chance to actually get the word out at a time when it really matters—"

"So what's the plan?" I ask Lea sharply. "Write a tell-all exclusive about Mystery Girl? Crowdsource potential passwords for the USBs no one is even supposed to know about? Start Milkshakegate?" I shake my head. "You don't even have any evidence."

Lea assesses me. "I have evidence," she says, and my blood runs cold.

"What?" I take a step back from her—I need to put physical space between us. "I thought... Oh my god. This whole time, you were only using me to get close to the agency. So you could gain access to our information for your piece."

Lea's expression hardens. "Iris, people don't pay attention unless there's a narrative. You know that better than anyone. And there's a narrative here—one that will help Heather if I can tell it." Her blazing eyes lock on mine, searching my face. "Think about it—all this information will get out eventually, but if it comes from me, I can keep you—and Imani and Sammy—safe. I can protect you. You'll all be anonymous, and no one will have to know—"

But I should have. I should have seen this coming, because of course Lea is exploiting me. She's trying to get a piece in the *Herald*, she's blackmailing me to get an in with the agency, and she's only looking into what happened to Heather so she can get her big break. Her apology in the car, all those words from earlier—*I know you think I put myself above everything else. My reputation, my future career... and I used to*—mean nothing.

She hasn't changed.

I want to smack myself for how naive I was. For being stupid enough to let my guard down around Lea even though I promised to keep it up; for letting myself believe, however briefly, that we were falling back into our old patterns; for starting to trust her like we were friends again. For actually thinking we could be friends again.

I blink, and it's only when my lashes clump together that I realize they're wet with angry tears. I inhale, desperately trying to keep myself from spiraling further. *The dark patches sewn onto Lea's knit sweater. Exhaust and motor oil. The crumpled slip of paper in my palm.*

"Anything to get your name on that A1 story, right?"

"Iris," my ex-best-friend says. Her tone is torn between emotions: grief, anger, exasperation.

Fear.

"No," I bite out. "You still want your exposé. Like always. Like last time." I spin on my heel, only catching the tail end of the hurt on her face. "Good luck with your inquisition, then. Just stay far away from me."

When I step into Ms. Eastwick's classroom, it only takes a few seconds before she rounds on me.

"You're late."

"Sorry," I say, knowing I don't sound sorry at all as I drop my phone into her plastic bin and find my seat at the back of the classroom. I swipe my fingers under my eyes, hoping I don't look like I was just crying in a parking lot, and Eastwick glares at me before redirecting her attention to her ancient PowerPoint presentation. Fuck. We're prepping for our field trip to Deveraux Industries today. As if this morning couldn't get any worse.

My mom used to work at Deveraux Industries before she died. She hated it there, but in Hillwood it's either the plant or selling drugs, and Diane Blackthorn wasn't really a people person. She was more of a high-functioning alcoholic who never got over the fact my dad left, but that was always our family's private business. At least it was, until Heather decided to air it out on *HTFAMG*.

Eastwick continues to the next slide, and I return my attention to the PowerPoint just as the door to the classroom opens and a perky woman from the front desk sticks her head in.

"Iris Blackthorn?" the woman says, and every head in the class swivels to me. "You're needed in the office."

Some asshole *oohs* as I stand up and sling my messenger bag over my shoulder, walking past Eastwick with a sinking feeling in the pit of my stomach. The door closes behind us, and then it's just me and the office assistant in the hallway.

I give her a look. "What's going on?"

She frowns, and my stomach sinks deeper. "It's the police. It appears they want to speak with you."

My blood runs cold as I follow the office assistant down the hall-way. I try to slow my heart rate by focusing on things I can see, smell, and touch around me, but it doesn't do much good. I can't believe the police are already here.

I can't believe Lea leaked the photos.

As we turn past the west locker wing, I try to understand how my ex-best-friend did it so quickly. Maybe she sent the pictures to Jim, the editor at the *Herald*, and he notified the cops. Maybe she scheduled a meeting with Principal Phillips right after our argu-ment. Or maybe it doesn't even matter, because this is the only pattern the two of us can really fall into regardless—one where we're always using each other. Except this time, Lea is going to be the reason Detective de Rosa finds out I'm interfering in Heath-er's case. She's going to be the reason I never get my private inves-tigator license. If things really work out for her, she might even get to have me detained again.

The agency, too. Depending on which photos Lea chose to leak.

There's only one cop waiting for me in the front office. He's in uniform, making polite small talk about the humid weather with the secretary, and slithering unease tightens my throat as I catch sight of his arrogant expression. I've seen him before: at Heather's house. But since the rest of the agency isn't here, and neither is Delphine, I guess Lea singled me out for committing criminal trespass.

The detective turns, and my mouth goes dry. *Act normal, for the love of God.*

"Hello. You wanted to see me?"

"Yes," the cop says briskly, his eyes flicking down to meet mine. There's no recognition in his face as he looks at me. Good. "I'm Assistant Detective Hunt, and I'm working alongside Detective de Rosa on the Heather Nasato case. The two of us have a few questions for you."

I swallow. His voice is blunt and haughty, just like it was when he was chastising his partner right before they found the pistol missing from the Nasatos' hidden gun cabinet. Which I can't know about.

"Couldn't this wait until I got out of school?" I ask, failing to keep the slight wobble out of my voice. *Damn it, Iris, pull it together.*

"We'd like to take you to the station now," the assistant detective says. "Do you consent to come with me?"

I nod. I can't make it seem like I have anything to hide. Not when I don't know what I need to be hiding, anyway. "I consent."

The inside of the station is the same dark beige that I remember, with small glass-block windows and even smaller chairs that make the interior seem like it's collapsing in on itself. I follow Hunt through the metal detectors and down a hallway, feeling vaguely claustrophobic, before he ushers me into a cramped gray room with a metal table, three chairs, and a very tired Detective de Rosa.

Ah. Nothing like a good old-fashioned interrogation room.

I slide into an empty chair. Assistant Detective Hunt takes the other one, and then the three of us stare at one another for a long moment. My lips twitch. "I'm pretty sure I'm not supposed to answer anything without a lawyer," I tell them.

Detective de Rosa doesn't laugh, but a vein pulses in Hunt's jaw. "If you won't cooperate," he says, "things are going to go very poorly for you, Miss Blackthorn."

I lean forward. "Is that a threat?"

Hunt glowers. "You've been withholding information from the police."

Withholding information? A frown flickers over my face for a millisecond, and Detective de Rosa clears her throat. "Thank you, Assistant Detective Hunt. I'll take it from here."

Hunt shrugs and leans back in his chair, and Detective de Rosa turns her steely gaze to me. "Iris, you're free to leave this room at any time. You don't have to answer any of our questions, and you are not being held in custody. Do you understand that?"

I cross my arms and tuck my feet in firmly under me, trying to forget what it felt like to be detained here last year. The panic sliding up the back of my neck, the jittery tapping of my combat boots against speckled linoleum. Trying to fight back the bile rising in my throat. "Yes," I say, feeling the same anxiety coil in my stomach. I don't want to be in this room. I don't need to be detained again.

Detective de Rosa nods. "Recently, my department came across something we believe you'd be interested in seeing."

I force myself to hold my breath. This is it—they know I was in the house. My investigation into Heather is over.

Detective de Rosa slides something small and rectangular in front of me, and my mind struggles to comprehend the object for a moment. The thing the police found, the thing they think I'd be interested to see, is…a Polaroid picture?

The detective appraises me coolly. "You're Heather Nasato's ex-girlfriend."

I exhale. Thank God—the police don't know anything. In fact, they're about ten steps behind, as usual. Which means I'm not here because I'm about to get in trouble for trespassing. I'm here because the police think I have a *motive*.

Oh shit.

Upon closer inspection, I can see how the Polaroid did me in. It's not exactly subtle—it's a selfie Heather took of the two of us around the beginning of our junior year, mid-kiss on her bedroom floor, dark and honey-brown hair tangled together, with Heather's own loopy script captioning the bottom: *<3 u butterfly.* The memory flashes into my mind: the bright flash and whirr of the instant camera, the taste of Heather's cherry lip balm, the press of her soft skin against mine. A frozen moment before we were a detective and a true-crime podcast host. Before Stella went missing. Before my mom died.

Heather must have shoved the photo into a drawer or

something and forgotten about it—it certainly wasn't displayed on her wall when the agency and I were there the other day. But de Rosa doesn't know that, and I shouldn't, either. I keep my face neutral.

"I am," I tell the detective calmly. Hunt shifts in his seat, and I narrow my eyes as my gaze flicks to him. "Does that make you uncomfortable, Assistant Detective?"

"Iris," de Rosa says, ignoring him. "Where were you on the night of October fourteenth?"

"October fourteenth?" I ask. "That's the day before Heather went missing. She was last seen a day after, on the fifteenth."

"Answer the question," Hunt says.

I scoff. "In Heather's neighborhood. With my...friends."

Sapphic detective agency. Same difference.

"And what were you doing there?"

"I was following Nathan Deveraux," I say, and Hunt sits up.

"Because you were jealous."

"What? No," I say, starting to get an idea of their angle here. "Because Heather thought Nathan was cheating on her, and he was. The three of us saw him kiss the blonde girl who lives in the house at the very end of Bellevue Estates that night. 343 La Belle Lane. I even have the time-stamped photographs to prove it, if you want to confirm my alibi."

"That can be faked."

Detective de Rosa's brows crease. "Nathan was cheating on Heather?" she asks, once again ignoring the AD. "And you have photographic evidence of this?"

"On private property."

"It was the middle of the street," I snap, glowering at Hunt. I turn my focus back to de Rosa. "There's more, too, if you want to know it. Heather took pills for depression. Her computer password is Heath1225. *How to Find a Missing Girl* is—"

"Look, kid," Hunt interrupts, his voice dripping with condescension. "You're not the one investigating this case. We didn't ask for your opinions on the girl's podcast, or any of the other things she did for attention. All we want you to do is answer our questions, all right?"

"*You* look," I say, slamming my hand on the table, hoping I'm not incriminating myself with every second I continue to spend in this room. "I don't know how you got that picture, but I didn't have anything to do with Heather's disappearance." I turn to de Rosa, my voice tinged with desperation. "You know that. You *know* it, Detective."

Hunt opens his mouth again. "That's hardly—"

De Rosa holds up her hand to cut him off. "Enough. I think you've both said enough." She rubs the bridge of her nose. "If you can get us a copy of that photo, Iris, I can see if it leads anywhere."

I nod.

"As for everything else..." De Rosa scrutinizes me.

"My alibi is solid. My friends can confirm the time, but the three of us were there from ten o'clock to about eleven. One of the security guards saw us, too. Before and after that, I was at home with my legal guardian, and during the *actual time Heather went missing*, I was in AP US History, doing a DBQ about tension in the 1920s." I cross my arms and level my gaze at both of the adults sitting across from me. "I didn't do anything to Heather. I wasn't jealous of her boyfriend. And, yes, I used to have feelings for her—romantic ones," I add, glaring at Hunt, "but not anymore. Heaths makes her own choices. She's also missing. And you should make sure you find her, because the last time I checked, your department's rate of successfully recovered vanished Hillwood girls is currently sitting at zero."

The detective exhales sharply. "Fine," she says, nodding to Hunt. "That'll be all, Iris."

But even as I'm escorted out of the room by the assistant detective, I know the fire in de Rosa's eyes means only one thing:

This is far from being over.

Chapter Twelve

"So," Imani says, their judgmental gaze lingering on my kitten calendar. They're draped over my chair, I'm sitting cross-legged on the floor, and Sammy's splayed out on my bed, because none of us ever sit anywhere properly. "We need to go back over our POI list. Heather's still gone, and the police took Iris in for questioning yesterday, so we should work on motives. Figure out why each person on it would potentially want Heather out of the picture."

Sammy sits up abruptly, sending her plastic baby earrings swaying. "Wait. So we're operating under the assumption that she was kidnapped or something?"

Imani's eyes flick over to me, and coldness seeps through my veins. GIVE UP THE SEARCH, IRIS.

"Yes," they say, almost as if they can read my mind. "For now, at least."

I swallow and pull out my phone, navigating to the list the three of us made at Joan's Diner on the night Heather disappeared. There aren't many people on it:

PERSONS OF INTEREST

Nathan Deveraux
Delphine Fontenot
Arden Blake
Whoever Reported Heather Missing
Mystery Girl

And now 970-555-0141.

I suck my teeth and glance up from the glowing screen. "Did we ever figure out who filed the report for Heather?"

Imani nods. "I heard some things when I was at rehearsal last night—apparently, it was Coach Hannequart. Heather didn't show up to practice before the game, and Coach was pissed until Delphine and Arden said they hadn't seen her since lunch." Their face is grim. "Hannequart made some calls, and when no one else said they'd seen her, she notified the police. Déjà vu, you know?"

I blink back tears. I know.

"Why didn't you bring this up earlier?" I ask Imani, focusing instead on what I can control. Out of the three of us, Imani's definitely the most well-connected—between their in-demand tailoring skills among the upper echelons of Hillwood High, their involvement with the fall and spring musicals, and their willingness to drive around gay licenseless theater kids for money, they accumulate a lot of knowledge. Unfortunately for Sammy and me, however, Imani habitually forgets to share it.

They give me an apologetic look. "Sorry, Iris. You've just been so busy with Lea lately...."

"Yeah, well, I won't be anymore," I mutter. Imani raises an eyebrow, and I scowl. "Don't look at me like that. You know she's the one who turned me in to the police."

"Maybe last time," Imani concedes, glancing at Sammy. "But you don't have proof she turned in the Polaroid. It would make a lot more sense for that to be Delphine, especially given the doxxing."

Sammy bobs her head. "And before you can bring up the article again," she adds, "Imani and I both think you were too hasty in turning her down. If Lea says she can keep us anonymous and help get the word out about crucial details in Heather's case, why shouldn't we trust her? We shouldn't be the only people searching for justice."

"Lea's proven she isn't someone to be trusted," I say quietly. "All she cares about is making a name for herself. She's sold me out to de Rosa before, and she keeps dangerous grudges—I mean, just look at the Wu Incident."

Last month, Lea keyed *CHEATER* into Kevin Wu's brand-new car in the senior parking lot three days before homecoming, because he had been her boyfriend up until he hooked up behind her back with Arden Blake. Photos of the damage spread like wildfire all over Snapchat and Instagram, but because there are no cameras in the Hillwood parking lot—not even now—Wu, Principal Phillips, and the rest of the HWHS admin couldn't do anything about it. Lea came to school the next day with her head held defiantly high—perfectly showing off her new chin-length snow-white hair in the process—and no one mentioned it to her again.

Sammy scoffs. "The Wu Incident was incredibly badass," she counters. "I mean, come on. Lea's *cool*. She has awesome hair and sick sweaters, and her articles for the *Magnolia* are always filled with these eloquent calls to action—you know she's, like, ninety percent of the reason there are free menstrual products in the Building B bathrooms now?"

I uncross my legs. "Are you saying you *want* her to expose us?"

Sammy sighs, twisting one of her tiny plastic baby earrings out of her mane of curls. "You're impossible, Iris. All I'm saying is maybe you should give her an actual chance. After all, the worst thing Lea can do to you if things go south is...hm, I don't know. Spray-paint your bike, maybe."

Imani snorts.

"Fine," I say, redirecting my attention back to my phone. I change "Whoever Reported Heather Missing" on the POI list to "Coach Hannequart," since her reasoning doesn't make her any less suspicious, and then I share the note with both members of the agency. "Tabling Lea's constant theme of betrayal for a moment and going back to motives: I still think Nathan has the biggest one. He was cheating on Heather—maybe he wanted her out of the way."

"But why?" Sammy counters, getting to work on detangling

her other earring. "Cheating is a motive, sure, but Nathan was perfectly content with sneaking around behind Heather's back in Bellevue Estates the literal day before. What would have had to change for him to make her go missing?"

Imani picks up Benoit Blanc, my only cactus, from my desk. "Both of you are looking at it from the wrong angle," they say thoughtfully, spinning him around. "The Deveraux care about their reputation more than any other family in Hillwood, and Nathan wasn't just cheating on Heather—he was a target in her last podcast episode." They shake their head, their expression dark. "I doubt he appreciated that."

Sammy frowns. "That's a better motive for Nathan, but we still don't have one for Arden. She could have just been in the wrong place at the wrong time."

"And so could have Delphine," I add, reading through the list again. "In fact, the person with the most motive to want Heather gone is Mystery Girl, because she could have wanted Nathan all to herself."

"So she kidnapped Heather from a high school she doesn't even go to?" Sammy asks. "Try again, Iris."

I lapse into silence, looking out over my collection of plants. My room is all neutral tones and natural light, and there's not much color in it apart from the vibrant greens of my monsteras and succulents. Most of the larger ones have names—Holmes, C. Auguste Dupin, Columbo, and Velma alone make up a significant portion of my desk décor—but none of the fictional detectives I idolize are going to help me now.

"Actually, Arden has a motive," Imani muses quietly.

My head snaps toward them so quickly that I pull a muscle in my neck. "What?"

"Arden has a motive," Imani repeats. They stop fidgeting with Benoit Blanc and turn to look at me. "Heather put her on blast for going to homecoming with Kevin Wu in the last episode of her podcast, and I doubt Arden was happy about her best friend calling her out to the tune of over two thousand monthly listeners."

"But everyone knew about that way before Heather's new episode," Sammy muses. "You don't take revenge over old news. And besides, Arden looks like she's actually taking Heather's disappearance the hardest."

"That's true," Imani concedes. "I know someone in tech crew who's on Arden's private story—apparently, she's going to parties and getting blackout drunk almost every school night."

"But is it because of Heather?" I ask. "Or something else?"

The three of us lapse into silence again, but this one is even more short-lived. "Hang on," Imani says. "Sammy, do you remember what you were telling me yesterday about Assistant Detective Hunt from de Rosa's force?"

"Oh shit," Sammy says, swinging her legs over the side of my bed. "I totally forgot about that."

"Forgot about what?" I ask, suddenly light-headed. But Sammy is already pushing Imani out of my chair and opening up my laptop, her fingers flying across the keys.

"You know how I have that fake Facebook account where I pretend I'm a middle-aged white Republican mom?" she asks. When I blink in response, she shakes her head. "It started as a joke, but I'm in way too deep now. There's a divorced lady who keeps messaging me to ask when I'm going to come to her church." Sammy hits a few buttons and glances my way. "I honestly think she's a closeted lesbian. Comphet really is a bitch."

My brows knit together. "And you do this in your free time?"

"It's easy," Sammy says, waving me off. "All I do is send them a link to the Lesbian Masterdoc disguised as my favorite lemon shortbread recipe, and...ah, here it is." She spins the computer toward me, and I get up to stare at the screen. "A while back, someone accepted me—or rather, accepted Gertrude Powell— to a Facebook group that's basically a fan page for the Hillwood Police Department. I figured I should stay in it in case it ever came in handy, and I went back through it after you told us you were taken into the station. Turns out"—Sammy smiles smugly— "it absolutely did."

I scan the screen. It's a post from a woman with badly bleached hair that's cropped to her ears, a too-wide smile, and unflattering bright-pink lipstick. *Very saddened to learn about the missing girl podcast that SLANDERS the police!* the text reads. *The girl who runs it should be LOCKED UP...That'll show her to put some REAL RESPECT on the cops who keep Hillwood safe!*

Sammy watches me as I finish reading the post, and then she tips her chin to the comment under it. *Thank you, Linda*, AD Mason Hunt's response reads. He manages to exude haughty arrogance even through his own profile photo, though most of that can be attributed to his orange-and-blue mirrored sunglasses. *If only there was a way to shut her up. ;)*

My pulse quickens. "This is one of the detectives who interrogated me yesterday. The arrogant one at Heather's house." I bite my lip, trying to find a date on the message. "When did he post this?"

Sammy squints at the screen. "Uh, about a day after Heather's second podcast episode came out. I had to scroll down *really far* to get to this."

"Okay," I say, taking a deep breath and closing my eyes. Clearing my mind. I take down my bun and immediately pull my hair into a tighter one, which always helps me think, and try to visualize our next course of action. Arden. Nathan. Mason Hunt. Recovery keys. Missing gun. 970-555-0141.

YOU'RE NEVER GOING TO FIND HER.

My eyes snap open. "We're going to send an anonymous tip about Hunt to de Rosa," I tell the agency. "It's too risky to investigate him ourselves, but she deserves to see what he said."

Imani snorts. "You think she's going to take that seriously?"

I think about the detective's steely brown eyes. About her fierce warning for me to stay out of her investigation. About her promise: *If we can find her, we will.*

"I hope so," I tell the agency. A second beats between us, one that seems like the perfect opportunity to warn them about the ticking clock over my head. About Detective de Rosa's threat. About the text message I got at Joan's Diner.

But even if Sammy, Imani, and I are a team, there are things I can do to protect them. Secrets I can keep. And I've already worried them enough lately—by telling them about the police questioning, and sending the photograph of Nathan and Mystery Girl to de Rosa, and making them come with me to Heather's house.

So as Sammy swivels back to my laptop and the moment passes, I choose to keep my mouth shut.

I can't fall asleep.

Every time I close my eyes, I see the persons-of-interest list emblazoned behind my eyelids. Motive. Heather. Missing. Gone.

I know I'm obsessed with finding out what happened to her. With finding her alive. And I also know she's not my girlfriend anymore, but that doesn't change the fact I'd still do a lot of things for her. That even though we're no longer dating, I still care a lot about her. And that, more than anything, I want her to be found safe.

I miss the sound of her voice.

I stare up at my ceiling for a few more seconds, waiting to see if the glowing list of names will disappear when I blink, if the hollow, gut-wrenching ache in my chest will go away. And when they don't, I fumble in the dark for the phone sitting on my nightstand.

I still haven't changed my mind about the contents of Heather's podcast. But right now, I care more about making the hurt disappear.

All pretense of sleep forgotten, I grit my teeth, pull up episode one of *How to Find a Missing Girl*, and finally hit play.

HOW TO FIND A
MISSING GIRL PODCAST

Episode Four

HEATHER NASATO: Hey-o, Hillwood, and all its lovely
inhabitants. I'm your host, Heather Nasato. If you're here,
that means you've stumbled across my podcast, *How to Find
a Missing Girl*, where I investigate the circumstances behind
the disappearance of teenage varsity cheer captain Stella
Blackthorn and speculate on where she might be now. This
is the fourth installment of my serialized podcast, so if you
missed the first three episodes, go back and give those a
listen first. Today, we're going to continue where we left
off, as I once again tackle the question on all of our minds:
Where did Stella go?

[THEME MUSIC PLAYS]

HEATHER NASATO: As you all should already know, Stella
Blackthorn went missing almost ten months ago from
Hillwood, Louisiana. She disappeared on homecoming
night, September nineteenth, and was last reported to be
seen around 7:30 PM. She was eighteen years old. Back in
January, Stella's case went cold after the police declared her
a runaway, but the consensus in her hometown is split on
whether Stella left voluntarily—if she ever left at all.

FRANKLIN BROWN: I don't believe that runaway [BEEP].

HEATHER NASATO: There is evidence in favor of this theory:
Jackson Criswell's eyewitness account testimony regarding

Stella having a blowout fight the night of homecoming before storming out of her mobile home and driving off from the Chevalier Trailer Park, the alleged abuse Stella endured from her mother, and the fact someone in Kentucky reported seeing her plates in Lexington earlier this year. But according to others, the evidence on the other hand—Stella's meager paycheck from Lucille's General Store; the fact she left without any credit cards, identification, or packed clothes; the way she disappeared before she received her high school diploma despite wanting to major in biology at the University of Pennsylvania—suggests otherwise.

[THEME MUSIC FADES]

HEATHER NASATO: What's the truth? Why did Stella Blackthorn really leave Hillwood, and where could she be now? These questions are the reason I started the podcast—but honestly, Hillwood, I don't have much for this month's update. Don't get me wrong—I still want to find out what happened to Hillwood High's homecoming queen. I still want to find out the truth. But people are starting to move on, and I am, too. Most of Stella's friends are heading off to college, and the teachers I managed to get onto *HTFAMG* in the past have been ... dissuaded from continuing to speak to me, thanks to a very strong reprimand—and a lovely threat of disciplinary action—from our own Principal Phillips. All of that means I don't have very many interviews for you today. And without interviews ... well, everyone around me is determined that I let this podcast thing go. So I probably will. Soon. Just a heads-up.

WOMAN #1: Hello, Heather. This is Detective Maria de Rosa over at the Hillwood Police Department. I'm calling in response to the dozens of emails you've sent my department over the course of the past few months. Although I can't tell you what you should and should not post on the internet as long as you aren't violating Louisiana state law, I would like to remind you that Stella Blackthorn's case is not currently being investigated. I believe it's disrespectful to her family to disregard that, and I also believe it's in your best interest to stop creating your podcast. Additionally, I ask that you stop messaging my department. We have enough work to do as is.

HEATHER NASATO: What you just heard is the voice mail I woke up to after uploading my third episode of *How to Find a Missing Girl* last month. Detective Maria de Rosa, the lead detective in Stella Blackthorn's case, came under fire last year for the way her department handled their investigation after Stella went missing. In fact, de Rosa almost lost her job because the only lead in Stella's case skipped town before he could be properly investigated; rumor has it the man was a worker from Deveraux Industries, but I couldn't find any sources willing to confirm this for me.

MAN #1: I don't know about all that. What I do know is things have been fishy with that company ever since those Deveraux snakes first slithered into town. They run their own little corner of the parish, and they just get richer while we do all their work for 'em.

HEATHER NASATO: This is a worker from Deveraux Industries who wished to remain anonymous.

MAN #1: If you take a look around, most people here don't wanna work at the chemical plant. We'd rather be trappin' or fishin' off the Bayou Lafourche, but most times, we ain't got any other choice. If you're not from an old-money family, you gotta sell your soul to the Deveraux. They practically own the town anyway—you might as well join 'em and make an honest livin'.

HEATHER NASATO: Aren't there other ways to make an...honest living in Hillwood? If this witness was, say, someone who remained in the Hillwood area, wouldn't they be able to find another well-paying job?

MAN #1: Well-paying? Ha. You could find another place to work, sure, but the mom-and-pop shops on Sugar Boulevard are filled with college kids and high schoolers who want a little spendin' cash, not a proper paycheck. Same with the schools. If you're dirt-poor in Hillwood, you stay dirt-poor in Hillwood. You live in Chevalier or another white-trash trailer park, and you get mixed up in drugs tryin' to get out, and then you realize that's not steady money. So it's really just the plant that's a viable option. And the snakes control it all.

GIRL #1: Dealing isn't a big deal.

HEATHER NASATO: Again, I can't tell you who's speaking. She agreed to this interview only under the condition that she remain anonymous, but she's a Hillwood local who reached out to me through my tip line after the third episode to talk about the underground drug scene at Hillwood High. Once again, if you have any information that you think should appear on the podcast, you can text or call the same tip line, or email me at howtofindamissinggirlpodcast@gmail.com.

GIRL #1: It only starts to get dangerous when you get into the harder stuff, the things you need to get people to buy if you're trying to get money fast. Weed isn't a problem, but pills, generally anything that comes in a powder...that can come back to bite you, especially if you're desperate enough. I've seen it happen before.

HEATHER NASATO: Can you tell me who you've seen it happen to?

GIRL #1: I mean, a lot of people. It's high school. Kids do drugs. They drink. They experiment. Not all of them, and less than you would think, but enough for business. I would know—I used to deal to Hillwood kids all the time.

HEATHER NASATO: And was it good money?

GIRL #1: [*laughs*] Oh yeah. It was addictive. I was making so much, it was like dealing became its own drug. If someone was struggling with money, if someone wanted to run away, I can absolutely see them trying to save up that way. It would be easy, especially if they needed cash fast, to get caught up in something like that.

HEATHER NASATO: Are you saying Stella sold drugs?

GIRL #1: I'm saying there's a market. I'm saying if someone wanted to connect with a supplier, it probably wouldn't be too hard to do that. Especially in this town. Especially if you know enough people who fit the bill.

HEATHER NASATO: Of course, this is all just speculation. It doesn't prove anything or provide any new concrete details on Stella's case. All you're saying is that if Stella wanted a large amount of money quickly, perhaps to fund her escape from her hometown in a way that wouldn't rely on her paycheck from Lucille's General Store, a mom-and-pop shop on Sugar Boulevard, it would be easy to get it.

GIRL #1: Yeah, but I'm also saying that kind of shit comes at a price. It's like what that teacher said in one of your earlier episodes: She could have stopped somewhere on the way to the dance and gotten jumped. Her car could have been stolen. You get mixed up with the wrong kinds of people, you make a mistake, and you can find yourself dead the next day.

HEATHER NASATO: Though it's certainly a chilling insight and one we can't entirely discount, there's absolutely no proof of Stella being a drug runner. She was—

GIRL #1: A desperate golden girl. Which is exactly why no one would suspect her of being one.

[OUTRO MUSIC PLAYS]

HEATHER NASATO: Well, Hillwood, there you have it. This has been the fourth episode of *How to Find a Missing Girl*. I'm sorry I don't have better news to share, but I hope this update will suffice for now. As always, I'm Heather Nasato, and until next time—whenever that'll be—thanks for tuning in.

Chapter Thirteen

SUNDAY, OCTOBER 24, 2:28 PM

I drag my plastic knife against the bottom of the container in front of me, drawing nonsensical lines in the malleable foam. Megan and I are eating takeout for lunch again—and even though I love muffulettas from Joan's Diner, I can only eat them so many times in a given week before I start thinking about how Stella used to cook homemade meals for us and the tight seal I keep all my sister-related memories locked up with starts threatening to break.

It doesn't help that I can't stop thinking about Heather's podcast. I don't know what came over me last night, but I managed to make it through four episodes of *How to Find a Missing Girl* before I finally passed out. I'm not sure when I'll be able to listen to the remaining two, though, because I'm pretty sure all the stress from hearing Heather talk about Stella made me crack a tooth in my sleep. Still, I'm proud of myself. I did it without throwing up.

Although that doesn't mean I don't want to.

The podcast is just as bad as I thought it would be. Heather has no idea what she's doing in each episode, even though the accusations she makes are clearly without regard for anyone else. Implying my sister dealt drugs? Continuing to interview people after Detective de Rosa asked her not to? It's ridiculous, and it makes me wonder—not for the first time—why Heather even started it in the first place.

I would think it was for attention, just like Assistant Detective Hunt, but my ex-girlfriend had more than enough of that even before she went missing. Maybe it wasn't as much as she wanted. Maybe she orchestrated her own disappearance just to get more of it. I don't know anymore.

I scoff and force myself to take a bite out of my sandwich. Listening to the podcast isn't good for me. Reliving the past isn't good for me. Thinking about how Stella left that night, about how she screamed at me on the last night I ever saw her, isn't good for me.

"Are you seriously wearing that to the dance?"

"Oh my god, can you just let me fucking live? It's a dress, Mom."

"It's hideous. You look like a hooker."

Jackson Criswell was right: There was an argument right before Stella was supposed to leave for the homecoming dance. Mom had picked a fight over her outfit—it was too revealing, how had she been able to afford it, why was she putting so much effort into her appearance for a bullshit school dance anyway—and Stella snapped. Told her she was a horrible mom, that we could have been out of Chevalier already if she paid the bills as often as she paid to fund her alcohol habit, that she was lashing out because we'd been managing despite her negligence...and it was all true, but I didn't say that. I couldn't. I'd just stood in the kitchen, too paralyzed to intervene, and when Stella's crystal-blue eyes caught mine and she asked me to back her up, I stayed silent instead.

The memory haunts me. Stella did so much for me growing up: She bought groceries, she took odd jobs so we could go to Joan's Diner on weekends, she stayed up until the wee hours of the morning helping me with essays and papers and posters on historical figures while *Scooby-Doo* played silently in the background on our small TV. But when it came down to it, when she asked me for *one thing* in return, I couldn't give it to her.

I still remember how she'd looked at me after I said nothing, the furious way she'd held my gaze right before she slammed our trailer door. I remember what she'd said to me on the last night I ever saw her, the words clinging to my body like a second skin for every moment afterward: *You're so fucking useless.*

When she didn't come back, in the beginning, I really did think she had run away. I thought she'd saved herself. I thought she had chosen to forget about me. But then my mom swept it all under the rug, and the police didn't pay enough attention to the holes in the story. Stella had left without her credit card. She hadn't packed any clothes. She hadn't finished high school.

I figured it out after a while. That if the Hillwood PD wasn't going to handle my sister's investigation properly, I would need to open my own. Because I cared about Stella, and even if her last words to me were awful, she wasn't. She was kind and good and real.

And I wanted the full picture. I needed the full story. So I decided to make myself useful.

"Iris," Megan says, and I glance up from my picked-at bread to meet her eyes. She knows I'm looking into Heather's case, but she hasn't given me any grief about it since our first conversation over a week ago. It's not because she understands the deep hunger I have inside of me for justice, though. It's because she hasn't been around.

The Hillwood Assisted Living Community sees more of Megan than I do, but that's fine. I know she's working hard to pay for our life, and I've always been okay with being on my own. But now that she *is* here, I know I'm about to get lectured. Again.

"Yeah?" I ask lightly, stabbing at a fry with my plastic fork so hard that the foam underneath cracks.

My aunt purses her lips. "We need to talk."

I drop my fork, and my fingers curl around the charm on Stella's old necklace for protection. For strength.

I try to anticipate what she'll open with. *I'm worried about you* seems like it would be too on the nose, but so does *some stones are better left unturned*, and that's what she actually said to me after she picked me up from the police station last year. Maybe it'll be *you don't need to know everything*, which is one of her favorites. Or maybe—

"Detective de Rosa stopped by earlier," Megan says, lifting her coffee cup, and my breath hitches in my throat. "She said she talked to you a couple of days ago and asked me how often I'm home. Mentioned something about wanting me to make sure you'll stay out of her investigation." She takes a sip and raises one cool, thick eyebrow in my direction. A warning.

"And?"

"I told her I'll do my best."

I nod, keeping my expression neutral as I think about the anonymous tip I sent to the Hillwood Police Department this morning about Mason Hunt. Sammy emailed me a screenshot of the Facebook post while she was still here yesterday, and once I'd attached it to a message from a shiny new burner email account and sent it off, I'd gotten an auto reply from the police department telling me to come in person if my request was urgent.

So that's going great.

As Megan keeps talking, something about *the seriousness of more police charges* and my *obsessive tendencies*, I'm reminded of the fact I'm still withholding de Rosa's threat from the agency. I'm not completely sure that was the right choice, but I want Imani and Sammy to be protected if things go sideways with Heather's case. To have the ability to claim plausible deniability if de Rosa actually manages to prove I'm meddling again.

"Hey," Megan says, snapping me out of it. "Are you even listening to me?"

"Sorry," I say instinctively. "Thanks for talking to de Rosa, Megs. I'm being safe, though. I promise."

Except I'm not. I'm being sent threatening texts, and someone tried to frame me with the Polaroid tip to de Rosa, and I can't shake the sense that I'm being followed. Stalked. Watched.

But Heather is gone. And if I want to find her—which I do—I have to lie to the people I love. I have to protect them, even if I'm unsure of how to protect myself.

I have to promise things that aren't actually true.

Megan sighs. "I'd feel better if you had a job," she says, and then, when I open my mouth, she adds, "A real job, Iris." Another sigh. Another placating look. "You could apply to work at the diner...." She frowns, probably because of the stony look on my face. I can't help it, though.

We're having The Conversation again.

"Sorry," I repeat, this time in a completely different tone as I push back my chair, "but I actually just realized how swamped I am." I throw my broken foam container away without meeting Megan's eyes and swallow. "Lots of assignments I need to get started on."

This, at least, isn't a lie—I do have a lot of work due. Ever since Heather went missing, I've fallen behind in every single one of my classes, especially AP Chemistry, but I don't intend to start catching up now. Not when I have to pick up Lea's slack now that I know the true intent behind her *Herald* story. Not when I feel like the agency and I are closer than ever to uncovering the truth.

And Megan and I are different. She may never understand me, and I'll never get her dedication to the patients at the nursing home, at the way she manages to be gentle and stern all at once. At the fact she's the kind of person who can take in a kid without a second thought despite never wanting one.

But even after all these months, the two of us are still learning to live with each other. So when I retreat to my room without taking my messenger bag with me, Megan lets me go.

PERSONS OF INTEREST

Nathan Deveraux
Delphine Fontenot
Arden Blake
Coach Hannequart
Mystery Girl
970-555-0141
Assistant Detective Mason Hunt

I chew my lip, reviewing the list of names on my phone as I spritz Jacques Clouseau, my largest monstera, with water. Nathan wasn't arrested, but I still think he's hiding something. Delphine probably has the recovery keys for Heather's USBs, as well as a definite connection to 970-555-0141, but Mystery Girl remains an enigma. The assistant detective is probably just an arrogant asshole.

But I know almost nothing about Arden Blake, except that she looks like my sister and has been partying a little too hard lately.

And her social media handle. Which is definitely a start.

I finish watering Jacques and put down my spray bottle, swapping it for my phone so I can navigate to Instagram. I find Arden

Blake's profile, tap the button to message her, and only take a few seconds to compose two innocuous texts.

ardennn.blakeee

3:34 PM

> hey arden! you haven't been at school in a while, so i just wanted to check in.

> you okay?

I chew my lip and send a follow-up.

> if you ever need someone to talk to, i'm here for you

Especially if you want to tell me what you didn't back at Lucille's General Store, I think but don't add.

While I wait for a response, my gaze flits back over to my calendar. I'm marking off more and more days as time goes on, and my mid-November birthday is rapidly approaching. I need Arden to text me back. I need to find a lead I can actually follow.

My phone buzzes, and my heart rate picks up as I scan the screen. But it's not a reply to my Instagram DM. It's one from my actual Messages app.

> Iris, it's Lea

> Sorry to reach out to you through your leaked phone number but you've blocked me literally everywhere else.

> Can we talk?

And I plan on ignoring the messages. But before I know it, my fingers are hitting send on a text.

> nothing to talk about. and even if there was,

> how do i know this is really you?

A few seconds later, my phone chimes with a photo of Lea smushing her face into Upton Sinclair. They're both sitting on the floor of her room, surrounded by newspapers.

Damn it.

I sigh.

> what do you want?

Another ping, this time from a screenshot of an online article. "Journalistic Integrity and You," the headline reads. "How to Write Credible News Articles Using Anonymous Sources."

> I know you don't really trust me, but I always keep my word, Iris

> I promise I won't use your name in my piece for Jim. And I won't exploit you, either.

I have to stop myself from rolling my eyes.

> de rosa will still know your evidence ties back to me even if you keep my name out of it

> and besides, you lied to me. multiple times.

i don't honestly even know why you're texting me right now. don't you have everything you need to publish your article already?

if you're going to sell me out, then do it. but don't try to act like you're doing this with my permission. letting you meet the agency, working with you...

this entire thing was a mistake, lea. we aren't friends.

But Lea is prepared. "Suing in a Court of Law," the next article she sends me reads. "Confidentiality Pledges and John Doe Lawsuits: Are You Really Protected as an Anonymous Source?"

where are you even finding all of these

you know i'm not going to read anything i have to physically click on, right

You're literally the worst. You know what? Just block me again.

I can't help it—a smile creeps its way onto my face.

Fine. TLDR: they can't touch you, Iris. Not as long as what I print—which will only be what you approve—is true.

And I'm sorry we fought. I would never actually sell you out. I hope you know that.

I don't respond. After a few seconds, Lea's typing bubble pops back up, and then another message comes through.

> Look—I know you want to find Heather. And I want to bring public awareness to this case. I want to help. You know I can help.

I'm still mulling over my response when Lea's next text delivers.

> So please, Iris. Let me.

I let out another sigh, something deeper and longer this time. I look at Jacques Clouseau, who stares back at me blankly because he is a plant, and then down at my phone.

> fine, as long as you can pick me up.

> i don't want to bike all the way to your house.

> (also i'm sorry too.)

Lea's response is immediate.

> I'll be there in ten.

A beat.

> Oh, and Iris?

> I do think we're friends.

I blink at the screen. I'm not going to let Lea publish everything—the flash drives are definitely out of the question, at least until the agency and I can ascertain exactly what's on them—but if she's going to be writing an article about Heather regardless, I'll feel better if I'm there to screen it before it goes to print.

But when I reread her last message, something soft floods me. Something that feels a lot like old newspapers and smells like green tea shampoo and tastes like dreamsicle sno-balls.

I shake my head and close out of my messages before I can think too much about it. Plans successfully made—and for better or worse, partnership tentatively reinstated—I navigate back to my DM with Arden. But something's wrong with the page.

Frowning, I open her profile and furrow my eyebrows. I can't see any of her posts, even though the number of them hasn't changed. I don't follow her anymore, either.

Which means only one thing:

Arden Blake just blocked me.

Chapter Fourteen

"Tell me again," I press Lea as we walk down the hallway. Her first-period class is near mine, so she's been meeting me in front of Eastwick's for the past two days so we can walk to Media Appreciation Club together. "You couldn't find anything about the number?"

"Correct," she says, shouldering her enamel-pin backpack as we stop in front of a vending machine and I feed it a crumpled dollar bill. "I mean, it doesn't have a Hillwood area code, but it's a burner phone. You can set it to say you're calling from anywhere. And unless you're with law enforcement, you can't exactly make companies tell you which burner number belongs to who."

The two of us reach Mr. Cooper's classroom and step inside, where Sammy enthusiastically waves to us from our usual seats. I drop into the one next to her, sliding her my newly acquired granola bar, and Lea plops her backpack next to Imani.

"Be careful," they warn us quietly, their gaze fixed on a series of fabric swatches. "We don't have the luxury of slipping under the radar today."

I look around Mr. Cooper's classroom for the first time and notice the four of us are the only ones in here. Sammy catches my confused expression and nods to the door. "The robotics coach finally got onto all those nerds for skipping practice, so they're working on fundraising today." She rolls her eyes, and I grin. Sammy used to be on the robotics team herself until she quit; she wanted to be a coder, but none of the guys took her seriously and shoehorned her into the role of social media manager instead. Which is very much their loss.

Mr. Cooper comes back into his classroom right as the bell rings. "Just you all today, huh?" he asks, balling up an old homecoming poster I recognize from the window in his door. When none of us respond, he raises an eyebrow. "Is everything okay?"

I stare at the poster and swallow.

"It's complicated," Sammy says. "Just...Heather."

Mr. Cooper seems to deflate. "I teach her," he says as he walks to his desk. "She's one of my best students, when she's also not forgetting to turn in her work." He glances at me, and I offer him a half-hearted smile. He's probably overheard enough of Ms. Eastwick's complaining about me to fill an entire textbook by now.

"Her disappearance has been hard on all of the faculty, especially since…" Another glance at me. "Well. You know."

I do.

Mr. Cooper taught Stella, too, back when she took his physics class as a junior. She'd always liked him. She said he was bright, which I always thought was funny because it seemed like something a teacher should say about their student, not the other way around—but either way, it doesn't matter now. Stella's gone.

I clench my teeth until the bell rings and pray they don't crack.

I'm scrolling through r/WithoutATrace as I walk through the halls on Thursday, trying my best to ignore the incessant gossip from the surrounding student body as I skim the newest posts. High school is difficult even when I'm not actively trying to solve two missing persons cases and being bombarded by literal death threats, but I don't really know why I'm going through Reddit, either; there haven't been any posts about Stella since she first went missing, and even though a couple about Heather have popped up in the past week, none of the comments on any of the threads have been helpful. What we really need is to find a way to get the recovery keys from Delphine Fontenot. Which we don't know how to do.

I exhale through my nose, my frustration threatening to boil over as the hallway empties around me. I'm late to class, but I don't have time for all these dead ends.

I switch gears, closing out of Reddit to open Sammy's list of leads. It's gotten a lot longer since the eighteenth, which also means we have a lot more people to investigate. The bell rings, and I chew my lip as I pore over each new bullet point. *heather was taking zoloft for depression. delphine might have the USB recovery keys. arden started abusing alcohol after heather went missing. nathan might not have a concrete alibi.*

I think back to confronting Nathan almost a week ago. The vehement way he slammed his hand against the locker next to him, and the quick way he closed his own. Out of all of Heather's close friends, I've already started digging into Delphine, and Arden blocked me.... But I've been hoping there's something I can dig up on Deveraux while I'm here.

Instead of continuing to AP Human Geography, I pivot to the locker wing. It doesn't take me long to find Nathan's, and it takes me even less time to dismantle it. Lucky for me, combination locks exist solely to deter people from trying to break into things. They don't do shit, however, against someone who knows what they're doing.

Someone like me.

I swing the latch open and pocket the shim I made thanks to a wikiHow article titled "How to Open Combination Locks Without a Code" three nights ago, ready to see whatever shady thing Heather's boyfriend has in here that he was so eager to hide from me earlier. But instead of being met with something that screams Deveraux is guilty, I find... nothing. Apart from a battered textbook about molecular biology and a hook holding Nathan's car keys, the locker is empty.

I'm just about to close the green metal door when something about the book strikes me. Molecular biology isn't a class that's offered at Hillwood, and Nathan sure as hell isn't the kind of guy to study protein synthesis for fun. I reach for the textbook and flip it open.

It's been hollowed out.

My breath catches as I scan the alcove. I thought I wanted to find something that proves Nathan Deveraux isn't the golden boy everyone says he is. I thought I was ready to find the truth. But I'm not ready, I realize as I lift out a stack of Polaroids from the thick book and sift through them one by one. Nothing in the world could have ever prepared me for this.

Most of the pictures are normal enough—Nathan and Heather, Heather with her friends, Heather alone—and even though they're not exactly the same, they're all strikingly similar to the ones Heather had up on the wall in her room, which makes me wonder why they're here. But none of that matters when I get to the last photo in the stack.

My mouth goes dry as I take it all in: her tumbling brown hair. Her sparkling crystal-blue eyes. Her freckled shoulders, clearly visible in the lingerie she's wearing.

This isn't Heather. It's my *sister*. Stella.

"What the fuck do you think you're doing?" a voice asks behind me, and I spin with my older sister's photograph still in my hand and come face-to-face with Nathan Deveraux.

He looks like he's going to murder me. But he won't be able to, because I'm going to kill him first.

"Where the hell did you get this?" I whisper, and I can hear how my voice shakes even when I'm trying to be calm. I am wrath personified. I am a monster contained.

"Where the hell did I get what?" Nathan snaps impatiently, not looking at the picture. "You're the one going through my locker, Blackthorn. How the hell did you even open it? I keep my car keys in here, and—"

"*This*," I interrupt, emphatically shoving the photo toward him. Making him *see*. "Where the *hell* is this from?"

Nathan blinks. "The fuck?" he says, finally registering it. "That's not mine." And then his expression changes, and he laughs. He *laughs*, and I see red.

I ram both my palms into Nathan's chest. Hard. He stumbles backward, and I have just enough time to see the bemused look on his face turn to rage before I shove him again.

There are no cameras within Hillwood High. There is no one in the halls. There will be no one here to see me rip him apart.

I reach forward one more time, but something twists before I can make contact, and then the world tilts and pain radiates through my entire body as Deveraux's fingers dig into my arm.

"Listen," Nathan spits. "Listen to me, Iris. That's not my photo, okay? Where would I even get a picture like that? Jesus."

He lets me go, and I stumble forward and whip around just in time to see his face.

He's telling the truth.

Dread settles deep into my bones, and I glance back at the photo in disbelief. I don't know where it came from. I don't know who could have taken it. But then I think about another Polaroid— the one Detective de Rosa slid toward me across a cold metal interrogation table—and refocus on Nathan, my anger renewed.

"Maybe you don't know where this one came from," I say

vehemently, pocketing the Polaroid of Stella. "But you definitely turned in one of me and Heather to the police." My voice rises, alongside the monster in my chest raring for Deveraux's head. "You tried to get me arrested. I had to go down to the station because of you."

Is he working with Delphine? Did she find the picture of me and Heather on one of her sweeps through Heather's house, decide that giving it to Nathan to hand over to the cops would be the best way to get back at me for asking her questions once her best friend disappeared?

Nathan's eyes flame. "I was just turning in evidence. If the cops are going to investigate me, they should look into you, too."

"You know damn well I didn't do anything to Heather," I growl. And then it hits me, sizzling into my veins as I stare into Nathan's dark eyes: Delphine wasn't Heather's only best friend.

I think about Arden's drinking. The way she blocked me after I reached out to her. Her stuttering outside Lucille's General Store: *Some people are saying Heather ran away just like Stella.... I'm w-worried it's my fault.*

The next words out of my mouth are fierce and biting. "But I bet you and Arden Blake did."

I'm not sure what flits over Nathan's face—shock, disgust, fury—but it's clear I've hit a nerve. His face contorts as he grabs my shoulder, pulling me into the nearest doorway, and I have just enough time to register we're now inside a girls' bathroom before my temple connects with a stall and I see stars. I blink, disoriented, as his hot breath ghosts my cheek. "You don't know what the hell you're talking about."

"What?" I mock, struggling against his grip even as a bolt of fear shoots down my spine. I may outmatch him mentally, but I can't throw football quarterback Nathan Deveraux off of me in the position I'm currently in without breaking at least six of my bones. "Worried I'm going to find out whatever you and Arden are hiding? Or maybe Delphine is in on it, too. I swear to God, Nathan, the second I figure out how the three of you did it—"

Except the rest of the words die in my throat, because my vision's finally cleared up enough for me to notice what's off about our surroundings.

Blood trickles down the smooth reflective surface of the mirror in front of us, framing a blown-up photograph above which someone's scrawled the word *CHEATER*. And below it, in the same lettering, is another word.

MURDERER.

I gasp, and Nathan releases me. If we were anywhere else, it would be hard to know for certain, but here, under the harsh light of the bathroom fluorescents, I have a clear view as his face drains into a sickly, ghostly white.

"Did you do this?" Nathan whispers. "Did you...?"

"No! No, Deveraux, I was with you this whole time, I—"

But I stop, because I've just registered the rest of the display. It's my photo. The one I took with my camera—the perfect shot of Nathan mid-kiss with Mystery Girl.

Chapter Fifteen

Thursday, October 28, 9:50 AM

My mind spins as I stare at the fake blood dripping from the bathroom mirror. Stalls get vandalized all the time in Hillwood—when Stella was a freshman, someone found a scrawled bomb threat while they were trying to pee and the entire school had to evacuate to the football field—but I've never seen anything like this.

At least, I think I haven't. Until my stomach twists with recognition.

This is Lea's handwriting.

"Shit," Nathan whispers behind me, his eyes locked on the bleeding words. *"Shit."*

Now that I've placed its writer, my eyes can't stop traveling over the word. *CHEATER*, in the exact same careful, precise lettering it was in when Lea keyed the word into Kevin Wu's car. *CHEATER*, outlined with red. *CHEATER*, exposing Nathan Deveraux. And below it, the accusation. The deadly one.

MURDERER.

I take out my phone with trembling hands and almost drop it on the disgusting, grimy floor. When I finally get it steady, though, I take a picture. And then I scroll back through my camera roll to find the Snapchat post Sammy sent me back when The Wu Incident occurred. I screenshot it, and then I swipe back and forth between the two until my vision blurs.

They're the same.

Behind me, Nathan lets out a choked whisper. He looks completely different from the guy who was just threatening me, and I realize I've never seen him look this...defeated. He slides onto the floor, and I keep looking at my phone, staring at it hollowly. I can't believe Lea would do something this dramatic. I can't believe she would make such a public display without putting it in an article first.

Doubt trickles into my mind. This isn't like her.

Behind me, Nathan raises his equally empty, unseeing eyes to meet mine in the mirror. "I knew it," he whispers, his voice ragged. "You were there that night, weren't you? You took that photo. God, Blackthorn. Why? Why are you so obsessed with ruining my life? Why did you do this? Why couldn't you stop meddling after I sent you that text?"

I glance back down at my phone, half expecting to find a death threat from Deveraux mixed in with all the other hateful messages I've been receiving since Delphine leaked my number, but then I realize there's only one he could mean.

GIVE UP THE SEARCH, IRIS.
YOU'RE NEVER GOING TO FIND HER.

The bathroom pitches, and I reach out a hand to steady myself against the stall. *Flashing lights. Low whispers. Running the tap in the gym bathroom while I desperately tried to breathe, to get everything under control.*

"That text," I repeat, blinking as Nathan comes back into focus in front of me. "GIVE UP THE SEARCH, IRIS. That was you?"

He moans in response, but I can see it on his face. It was him.

"I'm fucked," Nathan whispers, tilting his head back as he closes his eyes. "Everyone's going to think I killed her, aren't they? They're going to think I killed Heather to get her out of the way."

I return my gaze to the bloodied wall, my heart rabbiting in my chest. Nathan wrote the text. Nathan told me to give up the search. Nathan said I was never going to find her. Was that a dig at my detective skills, or something more? What does he know? What did he do?

Without thinking, I glance over at the taped-up photo. In it, Mystery Girl's pin-straight honeyed hair falls over her face in a way that makes her only partly visible—but in this blown-up version, I notice something I've never recognized before. She's wearing a necklace. Half of a miniature golden heart.

"That's looking pretty plausible right now, yeah," I tell Nathan softly. "Either you or your little girlfriend."

"Fuck," Nathan repeats. "They're going to—*fuck*, I have to call her." He shoots to his feet, and I freeze for a half second before I come to my senses.

"You can't leave. And you can't call her, either. Do you know how suspicious that'll look?"

As soon as the words leave my lips, I bite my tongue. I don't know why I just said that. I don't want to help Deveraux. But seeing him here, like this, my perception is realigning. I really have no idea how he could be involved in Heather's disappearance now—his reactions are too emotional, too worried. About the wrong things, maybe, but being an asshole doesn't mean he's a murderer.

Nathan's eyes lock on mine, desperate and a little unhinged, and I frown as I find a glimmer of understanding: He sent me the text because he wanted to scare me off. Because he was worried about people finding out about this. Finding out about *her*.

"Deveraux," I say, and my voice is as calm as I can make it. "You have to tell me who she is."

"Not until we scrub it clean," Nathan whispers. "You have to help me. We . . . we need to get rid of this. Before anyone else sees."

I shake my head. "We have no idea whether it's already been seen. Besides, the actual words are in permanent marker, and we can't risk getting our fingerprints all over the mirror." I take a breath, forcing myself to focus on this moment instead of who could have written this message or why. "The best thing we can do is act like we never saw this. Go to class. Be normal."

Find Lea.

I'm not sure if Nathan hears me. He slumps back onto the floor, his eyes as glazed as before, and I take the moment to glance at the door behind us.

I've never liked Heather's boyfriend. He's a cheater and a douchebag, and he definitely doesn't like me. But I can't trust him not to try and get rid of the bloody display as soon as I go, and I definitely can't leave him here. Not when there's someone out to get him, too.

"Come on Nathan," I say. "Get up."

And that's the moment the door to the bathroom opens and a gaggle of giggling freshman girls with vape pens walk in.

My combat boots pound against the linoleum floor as I skid past the mural of the Hillwood school crest, desperately searching for Lea's second-period classroom. The spectacle in the bathroom is probably on its way to reaching Principal Phillips by now, who'll no doubt be phoning the police immediately afterward. Which means I have to talk to Lea right now.

Luckily, it doesn't take long to get to her class.

I burst through the door, breathless, and startle when Jasmine de Costa, the editor in chief of the *Magnolia*, blinks at me. "Lea isn't here," she says, returning her attention to her computer. "She's in the lobby taking photos for the yearbook profile on members of the Media Appreciation Club. She was looking for you earlier."

I curse and whirl around, barely remembering to mutter a thank-you to Jasmine before making my way back through Buildings B and A. When I finally get to the lobby, I spot Lea instantly. She's standing in front of the trophy case, positioning Sammy and Imani for photos.

"El?" I say as I skid to a stop in front of her. My voice comes out strangled. "We need to talk."

Imani and Sammy exchange a look.

"What's going on, Iris?" Lea says. "I tried to come to your second period earlier, but you weren't in class."

I ignore her question. "How long have you been here?"

She throws a glance over her shoulder at our friends. "I don't know, since second period started. Why?"

Wordlessly, I take out my phone and swipe to the last picture I took. I hold it out to her, and Lea gasps when she takes it in. "What...how...?"

"Did you write this?" I ask.

"No," Lea says, her eyes wide as she glances from my phone screen to my face. "I didn't."

"It looks like your handwriting."

I swipe to the screenshot from when Lea keyed Kevin's car, and her face falls. "Yeah," she whispers, her voice hoarse. "It does."

Behind us, the front doors open. The air in the lobby changes, and I don't even have to turn to know that the police just arrived. Principal Phillips acted even quicker than I expected.

Lea swallows, her gaze flitting over my shoulder and then back to my face. "I know this looks bad, Iris, but I swear I didn't write those messages." She lifts her hand in a limp three-finger salute. "Scout's honor."

I put my phone down. I look at Lea—really look at her—and think about how she used to be my best friend. About how she's the person I cut out of my life, the one who hurt me, the girl who made it hard for me to trust people after she turned me in to the police last year. But I also think about how she's been consistently showing up for me and the rest of the agency ever since we all started working together. I think about how she apologized. About how she's helping me. About the fact she's being honest now.

"Okay."

Lea frowns as she scrutinizes my expression. "Okay?" she repeats uncertainly.

"I believe you," I tell her. And I do. "If you didn't do this, then we have to figure out who did and why."

"But we can't do it here," Imani says, throwing a glance at the small crowd that's started to form in the lobby. Sammy nods, the motion sending her oversize lollipop earrings swaying, and I feel a flood of overwhelming gratitude for my friends. We have one another's backs. We believe one another. We're stronger together. And that's why we're going to make it out of this mess unscathed.

One of the police officers glances over us in passing, and then he stops. I can tell he's trying to place me, and that's not a good sign.

"Come on," I tell Lea, ignoring the hushed whispers and overt stares as Imani digs out their car keys. "Let's bail before Principal Phillips can take you in for questioning."

As soon as the four of us step over the threshold of Joan's Diner, my stomach growls at the barrage of smells we're assaulted with. Cinnamon and sweet pickle relish, sizzling sausages and boiling shrimp, powdered sugar and frying okra.

I'm home.

"I'll be right with y'all," Joan calls over her shoulder as she makes her way to the back of the diner with two baskets of po'boys and fries. "Just seat yourselves."

If she's surprised we're here when her sons are still in school, she doesn't show it. That's one of the things I love about Joan: She doesn't ask questions.

Lea looks like she's going to pass out on our way to our regular booth, and I let out a sigh of relief when she manages to collapse next to me on the red-hot leather seat. But then she checks her phone, and her face goes sheet-white. "It's Jim," she whispers. "Someone sent him a photo of the mirror for a story and said I wrote it, and now he wants... he wants to..." She swallows, suddenly blinking back tears. "He's giving my article to someone else. And he wants to talk about terminating my internship."

Sammy, Imani, and I all make identical noises of outrage and disbelief. "What?"

Lea shoves aside her phone and drops her head onto the chrome diner table, rattling the napkin dispenser. "I hate this," she says, her voice muffled by her snow-white hair. "I did so much to get that position."

"We'll figure out who did this, El," I tell her, squeezing her

207

hand. My nerves flutter, and I swallow against the emotion building at the back of my throat. "No one's firing you yet."

"Right. In fact, the best thing we can do right now is figure out who else would have access to that photo," Sammy says. She drums her pastel nails against the back of her WORLD'S OKAYEST LESBIAN phone case—the one that's identical to Imani's—and frowns at Lea. "Or a motive to frame you," she adds.

I let go of Lea's hand to trace the edge of the Stella Polaroid in my cardigan. "I think…" I start, and everyone turns to look at me. "I think Lea isn't the only one being framed." I frown. "Nathan was, too. Someone planted…someone put a picture of Stella in his locker."

Sammy's eyebrows furrow. "Stella?" she asks, her voice soft. And then her eyes narrow. "What kind of picture?"

My voice is steady. "A bad one."

I've been thinking about it ever since I found the photo: Heather is gone. Stella is gone. But now this Polaroid I've never seen before appears in the newest missing girl's boyfriend's locker, and all I can think of is Detective de Rosa sitting across from me almost two weeks ago, talking to me about Heather's podcast. About the links between my sister and my ex-girlfriend.

"Do you think this happened because I'm working for the *Herald*?" Lea mumbles, her face still solidly planted on the sticky chrome tabletop.

"Potentially," Imani says. "But it could also be because someone's trying to take down Nathan and knew how to copy your handwriting. Or because you helped produce Heather's podcast.

Or because you were interviewed in it," they add, "during the last episode Heather was ever supposed to make."

I glance at them. I knew Lea helped produce Heather's podcast, but I didn't know she was *on* it. No matter how much I want to, it seems like I can't escape *How to Find a Missing Girl*. Or people's ideas about Stella. Or their opinions of me.

"I didn't help Heather with the last one, though," Lea says, shaking her head. "And I only appeared in the fifth episode so she'd help me land my *Herald* interview in the first place. As it turns out, having the mayor's daughter put a good word in for you with a local business makes your application shoot straight to the top of the slush pile."

"How could someone have even gotten the photo of Nathan and Mystery Girl?" Sammy muses. "We only distributed one copy."

"That's not true," I say quietly. "There's at least two. One is the original file on my camera, which I turned in to the police a few days ago." I swallow, looking up. "But the other one is on the USB we gave Heather on October fifteenth, which means someone must have gotten ahold of that drive. And we know that after we gave her the drive, Heather came here with Delphine and Arden for lunch."

Imani meets my eyes meaningfully, and I think they're about to say something when the bell of the diner chimes and a boy with messy blond hair and sunken eyes shuffles in.

"Shit," I whisper. "That's Jackson Criswell."

Sammy and Imani don't move. "Behind us?" Imani asks.

I nod, forcing myself to pick up the diner's breakfast menu as Jackson approaches the bar. I watch him over the description for Joan's Blueberry Beignets as he slides onto a red leather stool, his expression bored and his eyes clear. He's sober, then. That's good for us.

"We have to go talk to him," I whisper, remembering the conversation the four of us had earlier about him and his connection to Delphine. "He might be able to tell us something that can lead us to the recovery keys."

Imani nods. "Good idea, but let's wait until he starts eating. He's less likely to run out on us if he hasn't finished his food."

Waiting for Carrie to finish taking Criswell's order is excruciating, but the four of us stand up when she finally sets a crispy shrimp po'boy in front of him. But Jackson doesn't even look away from the bar's TV when we approach.

"Nah," he says before I can even open my mouth, a smile sliding over his face as lazily as dripping honey.

"Nah?" Sammy echoes disbelievingly. "You haven't even heard what we're here for yet."

"Don't need to," Jackson says. "It's the same as everyone else, right?" He blinks. "Get lost."

"Whatever happened to 'Hey, neighbor'?" I ask lightly, digging into the other pocket of my cardigan for my wallet. "We're not here for the Criswell Special. We just want information."

Jackson lifts an eyebrow as he takes a bite out of his sandwich. "Yeah?"

"Yeah," I repeat, taking out a twenty and sliding it over to him. "Anything you can tell us about Delphine Fontenot."

Jackson assesses me for a moment, and then he bursts out laughing. I wait, and when my expression doesn't falter, he clears his throat. "Damn, y'all are serious. Okay, then. Delphine, huh?" He strokes his wispy beard, and I hope that whatever comes out of his mouth next is worth dipping into my forensics kit fund for. "Bitchy, controlling, used to buy Adderall off of me when she was studying for the SATs. Her dad's a legacy, so odds are she's Yale-bound next August even though she scored a 1290." Jackson flashes a crooked grin my way. "The world's a bitch, huh?"

My eyes narrow. "I didn't pay you for a personality assessment. I need a way to get in with her."

Jackson stretches. Yawns. Looks up at the Mardi Gras beads hanging off of the silver chrome ceiling, and then back down at me. "She's having a Halloween party," he offers offhandedly. "At her McMansion, even with Heather gone. If you want to talk to her, you can probably do it then. It starts at 8:00 PM on the thirty-first."

Imani catches my gaze, and I nod. If Delphine really does have the recovery keys, there's no better opportunity for us to find them.

Jackson notices. "Y'all want the address?" he asks, another lazy grin flitting over his face. "I've honestly been waiting to give it out."

I give him my phone, and he types something into it. "There," he says, handing it back. "Now you can leave me alone."

"Just one more thing," I say smoothly. "Does Delphine have any hiding places in her house you know about? Anywhere she could be storing something important?"

Jackson rubs his chin. "I don't know, Iris. That's kind of a tall order. My memory's pretty hazy...."

I roll my eyes and hand him another twenty.

Criswell snaps his fingers. "You know what? I just remembered—there's a safe in the second-floor home theater. I don't know the code, but the Fontenot family jewels are probably stashed away in there." Jackson smirks. "What, are you four planning to rob her?"

Lea tilts her head. "Something like that," she says mildly.

"Good." Jackson returns to his sandwich, his eyes back on the bar's mounted TV. It's tuned to *Channel Six News*, where Claudia Garrett is discussing the ongoing construction of Deveraux Industries' new west wing. "It's what she deserves for stringing me along for months while she was pining over this town's golden boy."

Imani glances at me, and I inhale. *Nathan.*

"You know," Jackson continues thoughtfully, "the last time we got high together and I finally told her to let it go, that Deveraux was never going to love her back, she said she was going to find a way to *make* him." His gaze flicks back to us. "Messed up, huh?"

I remember Delphine's cold green eyes as she mutilated her salad: *You shouldn't be asking me questions.* Her caption when she leaked my phone number on her Snapchat story: *forget the real cops trying to figure out what happened to heather.* Her deadly quiet voice in the middle of the locker room: *Get the fuck out of here, Iris.*

Messed up is putting it lightly.

I frown, my mind trying to fit together everything old with

everything new: Delphine's in love with Nathan. Delphine broke into Heather's house. Delphine has a burner phone.

What if the flash drives Heather left me implicate Nathan in her disappearance? Could Delphine be looking for the USBs to protect him, or did she break into my ex-girlfriend's house to protect herself? Because the truth is, before the whole school knew about the cheating scandal, Heather was just dating Nathan. Dating someone Delphine wanted to have.

And whatever Delphine Fontenot wants, she usually gets.

Giving us a motive.

HOW TO FIND A
MISSING GIRL PODCAST

Episode Five

HEATHER NASATO: Hey-o, lovely people of Hillwood, Louisiana. If you don't already know, I'm Heather Nasato. And this is the fifth, and final, episode of *How to Find a Missing Girl.*
[THEME MUSIC PLAYS]

GIRL #1: Stella Blackthorn obviously doesn't want to be found....I think we should all leave her alone.
[THEME MUSIC FADES]

HEATHER NASATO: As you, my dear listeners, should all know by now, eighteen-year-old Stella Blackthorn went missing from Hillwood, Louisiana, on September nineteenth of last year. She reportedly left her house around 7:30 PM to go to the annual Hillwood High School homecoming dance; however, she didn't show, nor did she come back to her house the next day, leading her mother to file a missing persons report with the Hillwood PD. Although they originally treated Stella's case as high risk, the police later believed Stella was a runaway—a conclusion forced by the fact the only key witness in her case, a worker from Deveraux Industries, ran out of town—and the investigation into her case went cold. Over the course of this podcast, I've interviewed people Stella was close to and people who only knew her vaguely; I've talked to those who played major roles in her case, such as Detective Maria de Rosa, and those who didn't, such as Arden Blake. But today, I have only one interview. I hope it's enough for you, listeners.

GIRL #1: Honestly? I think people are ready to move on. You know...the podcast, the papers...everyone is tired. It's emotionally exhausting to keep up with something that, uh, doesn't seem to be going anywhere. That isn't turning up any new leads. And I think you're just beating a dead horse at this point. Stella Blackthorn obviously doesn't want to be found, so I think we should all have enough respect to leave her alone. Because I don't think there's a story here, Heather. Maybe there was one in the beginning, but no one's reached out to the tip line in a while...and I don't think there's more evidence to uncover regarding Stella's case. Not...not at this present moment.

HEATHER NASATO: I see. And can you introduce yourself to our listeners, please?

<u>**GIRL #1:**</u> Uh, yeah. I'm Lea Li Zhang. I'm an editor for the
Magnolia, which is the school newspaper at Hillwood High,
and I'm also technically a co-producer of *How to Find a
Missing Girl*.

<u>**HEATHER NASATO:**</u> So, Lea. You knew Stella personally?

<u>**LEA LI ZHANG:**</u> Yeah. We didn't run in the same circles, but I
used to be close with her younger sister, Iris. We're the
same age, but Stella's a year older than both of us.

<u>**HEATHER NASATO:**</u> Hm. So your journalistic perspective, if
I understand it correctly, is that you don't think there's
anything left to uncover regarding Stella's case. You believe
the police, and you agree with the consensus that Stella
Blackthorn ran away. Is that right?

<u>**LEA LI ZHANG:**</u> I mean, everyone has their own theories. But
personally, I...I don't really have a good angle on Stella's
case. I do think it's strange that if she ran away, she did it
without graduating. But maybe her...home situation...
maybe she just couldn't take it anymore. And the other
things people get hung up on...her not taking her credit
card or having money saved or packing clothes...we can
speculate, but it ultimately gets us nowhere. If Stella did
decide to run away, that was a decision that happened in
the heat of the moment. It was clearly...impulsive and...
not thought-out. She, um, wouldn't have told anyone she
was leaving because she wouldn't have known, and she
wouldn't have wanted to be traced through her card. We
don't know how much money she had saved. She could
have...she could have even stolen from Lucille's General

Store before she left, because she was still here around the time of the break-in. There's a lot of speculation about Stella Blackthorn—a lot of people like to imagine the worst— but we know her plates were sighted in Kentucky. And, um, given the weight of the grief her disappearance left on the Hillwood community, even with a lack of public pressure, I...uh, I don't really see how the police could have stopped investigating the case otherwise.

HEATHER NASATO: But what about the police witness? The worker from Deveraux Industries, who claimed to have seen something the night that Stella Blackthorn disappeared but was never interrogated?

LEA LI ZHANG: Yeah, I think that's the only real...loose end. The flaw in the story.

HEATHER NASATO: Can you elaborate on what happened? I understand you have a unique perspective on the circumstances behind the situation.

LEA LI ZHANG: Right. Well, Heather, after Stella went missing in late September and the lead detective in her case first indicated they were looking at the case as a potential runaway situation, Iris...didn't take it well. She thought the detectives weren't investigating Stella's case hard enough, so she—allegedly—launched an amateur investigation into her sister's disappearance that involved hacking into the Hillwood police database, obtaining their classified case files, and attempting to...interrogate the witness herself.

HEATHER NASATO: And?

LEA LI ZHANG: And she was...caught.

216

HEATHER NASATO: Keep going. This is some really important stuff, Lea.

LEA LI ZHANG: [*sighs*] In the process, the witness who supposedly had information related to Stella was scared off. Iris was detained, but she was ultimately released without any charges on her permanent record. Her aunt came to pick her up, and then they just went home.

HEATHER NASATO: I see. And can you tell our audience how you know all this? Just so they know they're hearing it from a . . . credible source?

LEA LI ZHANG: I don't know, Heather. How *do* I know this information?

HEATHER NASATO: Lea.

LEA LI ZHANG: I'm done talking.

HEATHER NASATO: Fine. Either way, Hillwood, Iris acted extremely poorly. She was impulsive, and she let her closeness to her sister blind her. As much as she hates to admit it, Iris Blackthorn isn't suited to real investigative work. But then again, neither am I.

[OUTRO MUSIC PLAYS]

HEATHER NASATO: Well, listeners . . . I wish I had more information for you. I wish I knew where the Deveraux Industries witness went or what he saw that night, but he left town before the police could get that information. I also wish I knew more about who reported Stella's plates in Kentucky, but no one's been in touch with me regarding that for the podcast. So I'm afraid that with all of that, and after all this time, the final episode of *How to Find a Missing Girl* has come to a close. I broke my promise: I wasn't able to figure out what happened to Stella Blackthorn, and I'm no longer going to try. I'm sorry.

[OUTRO MUSIC ENDS]

HEATHER NASATO: Now. For what I guess is the last time—wow, it really is, huh?—I'm Heather Nasato. Thanks for tuning in this long, Hillwood. And, Iris, if you're listening: I hope you know I miss her just as much as you do. I thought I could do more.

Chapter Sixteen

It's Halloween night.

Technically, it's Halloween afternoon, but I can't stop thinking about Delphine's party. I've been looking up how to open safes ever since our talk with Jackson Criswell, but I don't think even I can suddenly become an amateur safecracker from wikiHow alone.

I sigh, rubbing my temples as I swivel my chair away from my laptop. This is pointless. Short of literally taking explosives into Delphine's house, I have no idea how we're going to get the recovery keys—if they're even in the safe to begin with.

We have to try, though. I didn't give Jackson Criswell forty dollars just to give up on opening the USBs Heather left for me now.

Before I can dwell on the subject any longer, though, the door-bell rings.

My blood chills. I'm not expecting anyone, and my mind instantly jumps to the threatening texts I've received. The car that watched me from the end of the street earlier this month. The empty eyes of Assistant Detective Hunt.

I grab my pocketknife from my desk and stand up, unease swirling in my gut as I slowly walk into the hallway. I get to the front door and peer through the peephole, and the relief I feel when Lea's smug face blinks back at me hits me like a tidal wave.

"Hey," I say breathlessly, dizzy with dissipating anxiety as I open the door. "What are you doing here?"

I listened to the fifth episode of *How to Find a Missing Girl* yesterday. It was pretty obvious to me that Lea was coerced into saying most of what she did to Heather, which makes sense in the context of my ex-girlfriend helping her land the internship at the *Herald*. But still, the dichotomy between the closed-off version of Lea featured on the podcast and the one in front of me wearing a pumpkin sweater is almost incomprehensible.

Lea blows past me immediately, a smile tugging at the corner of her mouth. "When's the last time you checked your phone, Iris? Imani's sewing machine broke, so I'm taking you to the Southland Mall for last-minute emergency wardrobe replacements, like, right now."

Scooby-Doo costumes: Imani's idea of a joke *and* an easily put together ensemble of Halloween disguises. We're all infiltrating Delphine's party dressed as a member of Mystery Incorporated—Sammy is Daphne, Lea is Fred, Imani is Shaggy ("his clothes are the most androgynous," they'd pointed out after our collective eyebrow-raising), and I'm Velma. I wanted to take Succulent Velma with me as part of my costume, but quickly dropped the idea after Sammy said someone would probably just try to water her with beer.

Lea's voice gets farther away, and I scowl as she unabashedly sticks her head inside my bedroom door. "Of course you're still a plant girl," she calls from down the hall.

"Can you stop snooping for one second?" I ask exasperatedly, following her into my room. I watch her take it all in—Jacques Clouseau and my collection of succulents, the increasingly Xed-out kitten calendar counting down the days to November 14, my hastily made bed.

"I'm a journalist," Lea says, and when she turns back to glance at me I feel the force of her grin near the bottom of my throat. "And it's a nice setup. Very you."

"Are you going to put this in your article?" I ask as she moves to peer at the various objects piled on my desk—printed copies of first drafts of terrible college essays, and chemistry homework about dissolving organic compounds from at least three weeks ago that I still haven't done, and a fidget cube Sammy got me that's only slightly helpful in the moments I feel like I'm losing my mind. " 'The first thing you notice about my anonymous source is that her room is severely lacking thousands of newspapers.' "

"You could definitely use more newspapers," Lea says, nodding sagely, and I smile.

"Try not to look around too much, okay? I'd hate for you to find something that'll ruin your opinion of me forever—"

"It's too late," Lea interrupts. "Do you seriously sleep with a *221b Baker Street* pillow?"

"—while I let Megan know you're kidnapping me," I finish, ducking as Lea throws the pillow in my direction.

Her grin widens, and as I grab my bag, my pulse flutters with something that we've quietly built back up over the past few weeks of sliced persimmons and neon tabs and YouTube playlists. A feeling like quiet and warmth and home.

Oh, and Iris? I do think we're friends.

I force myself to swallow and step into the hallway. To mechanically climb the stairs to my aunt's room. To try and ignore the fact that Lea is back in my life and I'm happy about it.

I pick up my hand to knock on Megan's door, but she opens it right before my fist connects with the wood. She stumbles backward and puts a hand to her chest. "God, Iris, you scared me."

I blink at her. She's wearing a full face of makeup and a short black dress, and her hair is curled and sprayed with product. "Do you have…a date?"

"It's not a date," Megan says, fiddling with an earring. "It's more like…a drink. With a friend."

I can feel the soft smile on my face before I've even realized it's there. "You look nice, Megs."

"Yeah?"

"Yeah."

Megan finishes clasping her earring and zeroes in on my messenger bag. "And where are *you* going?"

"Lea's taking us costume shopping because Imani's sewing machine broke. We're going to the Southland Mall. Is that okay?"

Megan's eyebrows furrow, but I can tell she's going to let me go. She thinks Lea is a good influence on me. Besides, she has her not-date. "Sure, as long as you're back in time for dinner."

"Aren't you going *out*?"

"Oh. Um, midnight, then."

The corners of my lips tilt upward. "Deal."

It takes a half hour to drive to Houma. Lea and I pass the time by insulting each other's music taste each time we switch the aux, arguing over which iteration of *Scooby-Doo* has the most merit (it's obviously *Mystery Incorporated*), and devouring just about every Hot Kid Shelly Senbei rice cracker she has hidden in the glove compartment of her car. We pull into the Southland Mall parking lot after only three near-miss accidents ("A new record," Lea tells me smugly as she's reparking for the second time) and then head for the Halloween store.

On our way there, Lea pulls us into a photo booth and pays for a cheesy strip of pictures of the two of us. We cycle through a series of increasingly bizarre poses, and something sparks in my chest every time her skin brushes mine. "For the collage wall," she says when we finish, tucking her copy of the strip into her pocket, and I don't even try to hold back my smile as I slip my matching half into my bag.

When we're finally done finding enough ascots and makeup kits for Imani to be satisfied with our low-budget cosplays, my phone buzzes with a text from Megs. *Drinks are going well. I'm staying the night, OK? I hope u have ur keys, but you know where the spare is if you don't. Luv u.*

Lea reads the text over my shoulder as the bored cashier hands her back her electric-blue polo and snickers. "Nice to see your aunt isn't letting you hold her back."

"Shut up," I say, ignoring her half smirk as we walk out of the sliding glass doors and into the rest of the mall. "We have to get going anyway—the party starts soon."

Lea glances at her own phone. "We still have a little bit of time. Do you want to grab something to eat before we leave? I know this super-authentic nearby Cajun place, and..."

I raise an eyebrow before I can stop myself. "Are you asking me out to dinner?"

Lea smirks for real this time, and my stomach flips. "If I admitted that, I would have to kill you."

"I don't know," I say, unable to tear my eyes away from her face. "I mean, you're no William Randolph Hearst, but if it meant I got to tell people I dined by the side of future Pulitzer Prize–winning journalist Lea Li Zhang..."

Lea bats her eyes at me. "I'm flattered you think I'm going to win a Pulitzer, but you wouldn't be able to tell anyone. You'd be dead," she points out, but by then our pinkies are already brushing as we walk farther into the mall.

Thirty minutes later, Lea is wearing the smuggest expression in existence as I finish the last of my spicy chicken sandwich.

Around us, the rest of the people in the Southland food court—which means a woman with a very distressed baby, a gaggle of tween girls who look like they just held up the nearest Hot Topic, and an older couple with matching scowls on their faces—are immune to my pain.

"Well?" Lea says, leaning back in her chair and gesturing to the table between us. "Excellent Cajun cuisine, as promised."

"It's food from Popeyes," I tell her dryly, crumpling up my empty bag of LOUISIANA KITCHEN fries.

"Which you ate," Lea counters. "In its entirety."

I throw the bag at her head, and as she ducks with a dazzling grin before lobbing the wrapper back at me, it hits me, both literally and figuratively: It's so *easy* to spend time with Lea. If I thought we were just falling back into our old patterns before, today it feels like we're fully in them. And even if she still has the power to turn me in if she wanted...I don't think she will.

My ex-best-friend's phone lights up, and she glances at it for only a second before her sparkling eyes lock back on mine. "This has been an excellently terrible date, but now I'm taking you back to Hillwood. Imani wants to meet us at Delphine's, so we're getting ready at your aunt's house and then I'm driving us to the party."

"Sounds good," I say, trying not to spiral over the fact Lea just called this a *date*. I don't know how I feel about that, but I can figure it out once I have more time to examine my feelings. Or never.

Never is good, too.

Lea and I throw our trash away, and then the two of us leave the Southland food court and all its patrons behind. On the drive back, though, as we continue to argue and laugh and tease each other, all I can think about is how much I've missed her. And, strangely, how glad I am she decided to blackmail me.

When we finally pull into my aunt's driveway and I take out my house key, Lea scrolls through the dozens of texts Imani's sent us both about hair and makeup. "Do you have an eyelash curler?" she asks as I unlock the door, and I stare back at her blankly until she sighs. "Thought so. I'll just do your whole look for you."

"Yeah?"

"Yeah." She grins as we step over the threshold. "Consider it a social service. But I'm going to give you brown eyeliner—despite the flawed line of reasoning you laid out in the car, it's much more flattering for your skin tone."

I roll my eyes, trying to ignore the way my lips are curving up again. "I'm not even going to get started on how wrong you are— black eyeliner is a staple for a reason." I hold up my bag from the Halloween store. "But if you insist, you can totally mutilate my face—and incur Imani's wrath—after I go get changed."

Lea's grin widens. "Can I get that on the record?"

"I hate you."

"Even though we make such a good team?" she asks, brushing her white bangs out of her face, and I get that fluttering feeling again.

"Even though—and I hate to admit this—we make such a good team."

Lea looks at me. I look back at her. Something changes in the air between us, and I swallow. And then I force myself to turn

226

away, walking down the hall that leads to my room while decidedly ignoring the burn in my cheeks.

It's true. I forgot how well Lea and I work together, but spending time with her again is making me remember. And it's also reminding me how I can't help feeling like a lighter version of myself when I'm with her. That she brings out the best side of me, the part that knows how to do things other than investigate people and ruin lives. That I love her ambition when it isn't being used against me. And she makes me feel...

She makes me feel like I'm more than who I think I have to be.

I reach the end of the hallway and pause. Even though I don't want to, I still can't help thinking about Heather. About how it feels wrong to spend so much time with Lea when Heather still hasn't been found. When she left the flash drives to me. When I still don't entirely feel like we got closure for the intense way things between us fell apart.

But then I open the door, and all my thoughts of the girls I've cared about instantly disappear.

My bookshelves are toppled. Papers are strewn across the floor, and Jacques Clouseau is lying on his side, spilling soil like blood onto my carpet. My desk drawers are open and rifled through, and even my mattress has been moved, the sheets I haphazardly tucked in this morning crumpled and discarded like candy wrappers.

Someone was here. They were in my room.

I'm still processing the sheer arrogance of it all when I notice the folded white envelope on my pillow and my heart rate spikes. Hands shaking, I reach into my messenger bag and slide out a pair of latex gloves. Try and steady my breathing as I pull them on. Stride across the room—my room—and pick up the envelope. Fail to keep my body from trembling as I open it.

There are only three words on the folded paper inside, printed in a careful black font. Three thick bold words, the weight behind them burning into my eyelids as I read them over. And over. And over.

WATCH OUT TONIGHT.

Chapter Seventeen

Sunday, October 31, 7:48 pm

My heartbeat pounds in my temples, blocking out all other sound, crashing over me in waves of increasing terror. Outside, the cicadas pick up the rhythm, resolving it into words: *Watch out tonight. Watch out tonight. Watch out tonight.*

I don't know who did this. I don't know when they broke in or if they're still in the house or what this note means.

But I know what they were looking for.

Take a breath, Iris. Breathe.

I inhale, forcing myself to focus on the weight of the paper in my fingers. The earthy scent of my overturned plants, the chaos of the haphazard mess around me. But it doesn't help.

Someone really is watching me.

And they want Heather's flash drives.

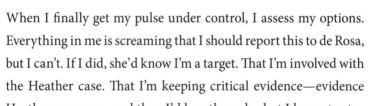

When I finally get my pulse under control, I assess my options. Everything in me is screaming that I should report this to de Rosa, but I can't. If I did, she'd know I'm a target. That I'm involved with the Heather case. That I'm keeping critical evidence—evidence Heather gave me—and then I'd lose the only shot I have at actually figuring out what happened to my missing ex-girlfriend.

Thank God the USBs are still with Sammy.

Hyperaware of how long I've kept Lea waiting, I change into my Halloween costume as quickly as I can with trembling fingers and then collect the gutted contents of my makeup bag from the floor—lip gloss, mascara, eyeliner. There used to be more, but I'll find the rest later. I don't want El to come looking for me. I don't want her to see what happened here.

I go back to the living room, masking the sick feeling in my stomach with another actual smile. I overdo it—Lea's eyes immediately latch on to me and narrow. She knows something's wrong.

"It's too much, isn't it?" I ask before she can say something, looking down at my red miniskirt and orange turtleneck sweater with exaggerated embarrassment. "I like the fake glasses, though. And the magnifying glass, obviously."

Lea frowns. "Are you okay? You're pale."

I wave her off. "I'm fine," I say as I crouch down and set my magnifying glass next to me, pretending to be preoccupied with pulling up my itchy knee-high socks. "I'm naturally pasty."

Except my face *is* drained of color, because I thought I had figured out the sources of the threatening messages. Nathan had sent that ominous text, and the rest were random threats from Delphine's brainwashed posse. But this note is different. Because someone went through my room. They know where Megan and I live.

My sweaty fingers slip as I pick my magnifying glass back up, and the lens cracks on the floor.

Lea's frown deepens. "Iris," she says.

They rifled through my things. They toppled my plants. They broke into my house.

"I'm just stressed about the party," I tell Lea, abandoning my Mystery Incorporated prop and turning to her with what I hope is an endearing, exasperated expression. "Do you think I can call in that social service now? I looked at Imani's texts, but I honestly have no idea what a...dewy base foundation with a Winehouse wing is."

Lea takes the makeup bag from me before I can disastrously attempt either of those things myself and directs me to sit on the living room couch. "You're not being honest with me."

Damn it.

"It's..." I start, and then stop. Because I want to say I'm fine. I want to tell her things are okay. But those would both be lies, and I don't want to lie to Lea. Not anymore.

She sits next to me, and her dark eyes pierce mine before I

have a chance to figure out what I'm going to say. "Iris," she says softly, "you know you can trust me, right?"

"I do trust you," I breathe before I can stop myself, and it's only as the words leave my lips that I realize just how true they are.

I don't know exactly how that happened. I don't know when I went from thinking Lea sold me out to de Rosa to believing in her like we were kids sneaking around the Chevalier Trailer Park again, but I did.

"Okay," my former ex-best-friend says quietly, taking out a couple of things from my makeup bag. "Then close your eyes."

I swallow as I comply, and a muscle jumps in my throat as Lea brushes something soft and cool over my lids. She's doing my makeup, like I asked, but all I can think about is how close she is. I can feel every feather-light touch, every spark, every new sensation as she tilts my chin with her six-fingered hand. I can smell her green tea shampoo, and hear her soft inhalations, and taste the flavored balm she sweeps over my lips.

"There," she whispers, her breath ghosting my face. "All done."

I open my eyes, and the hint of a smirk tugs at Lea's mouth as she twirls an eyeliner pen between her fingers. "I used brown," she says quietly, her eyes searching mine in that determined way that always makes me feel like she sees every part of me, every dark and twisted and bitter and broken thing, and the fluttering in my stomach suddenly explodes into bright and desperate need.

I want to kiss her. I want to lean in, to slide my hand into her white hair, to feel her mouth crash against mine. I am gasoline, and Lea is a flame waiting to ignite me. But even as my heartbeat stutters, there's an undercurrent of warning in this moment, too.

I think of the flash drives. Of my room just a few feet away, torn apart and thoroughly searched. Of all the people I love that I've put in danger—first Stella, then Heather, and now my aunt. I won't let the same thing happen to Lea.

I pull away just before her lips touch mine, and something wrenches in my chest at the hurt and confusion that flickers over her face. "I'm sorry," I whisper. "But I . . . I can't do this. *We* can't—"

"Do what?" Lea asks. Her voice is nonchalant, and something about her flippant tone splits my sternum more than if she sounded pained. "Us? Or me?"

"Both," I tell her softly. "I'm sorry. I'm sorry, El."

She stands up, her almost-smile still playing on her lips, but there's no humor in her it anymore. "Don't be sorry, Iris. I should have known. You don't get close to anyone, right?"

"That's not how it is," I tell her, and my voice breaks.

"Really?" Lea asks. "Because all I've done since you started acting like a teen detective is show up for you, Iris, and all you've done is push me away." She swallows, and there's a quiet fury in the way her eyes flame as she says it. "I want to be here. Not just because I want to get a piece in the *Herald*, but because you need someone in your life who makes sure you occasionally ingest something besides hazelnut iced coffee, and don't land in jail for obstructing justice, and stop to think about window blinds before breaking into the mayor's house in broad daylight." Lea takes a shaky breath. "What I *want* is for you to want me here."

My thoughts race as I stare at her. *She's protecting you, just like you're protecting the agency. She's here for you. Let her be here for you.*

"Well, I don't," I say flatly instead.

There's a beat of silence, and I can see the anguish in Lea's face for only a split second before she looks away, her short hair shielding her expression like a curtain. "Is that true, Iris? Or are you just saying that because I'm actually becoming something to you again, and it's scaring you?"

I swallow. "I'm saying it because I need space," I tell Lea, and my voice hitches in the middle of the sentence, snags right on my destroyed room and the death threats and the car that followed me home. *Protect her. Protect her. Protect her.* "Because I hurt everyone around me, and I don't want to hurt you, too."

Lea looks up at me. "It's too late for that," she says softly, and something about the sadness in her dark eyes makes me want to undo everything that just happened. All the things I just said.

But I don't. And when my best friend realizes I'm not going to, when she nods tightly and collects her keys and turns on her heel without looking back, the whole house fills with the weight of her absence.

Imani scrutinizes me from the driver's seat. "And Lea couldn't take you because...?"

"I told you," I say, adjusting the temperature in the Homicide Honda even though it was perfect before. "We had a disagreement."

Imani side-eyes me as they pull out of my driveway. "Uh-huh," they say, sounding equal parts convinced and unimpressed. I don't want to feel the weight of their silent judgment right now, though, so I just slouch farther in the passenger seat and try not to think about how the only person I want to talk to about the fight I just had with Lea is Lea herself.

By the time Imani parks in front of the mansion that can only be Delphine Fontenot's house, my stomach is in knots. It's no secret that the Fontenots are loaded. Still, though, there's a difference between knowing Delphine's family is rich and pulling up to what's basically a castle with a goddamn *fountain* in front of it. I don't know why I thought coming here for information would be a good idea. I'm completely out of my element.

Imani catches my panicked gaze. "Look, Iris. I don't know what's going on with you and Lea, but I didn't design all these costumes just for you to not be on top of your game tonight."

I set my jaw. "I'm always on top of my game."

They sigh. "This isn't...okay. I'm not the best at these types of conversations, and I get that you and Lea don't always get along. I understand she sold you out last year with your sister, and I know you're worried about that article she's working on. But she cares about you, Iris. And it's okay if you care about her, too."

My fingers drift to Stella's necklace, tucked away underneath my turtleneck. "It's...things are complicated."

"Can I ask you something?" Imani says, glancing over at me. I nod, and they look back at the fountain in front of us. Jack-o'-lanterns decorate its perimeter, their flickering smiles ominous in the half dark. "Are you still in love with Heather?"

"No," I say easily.

Imani smiles. "Do you regret dating her?"

"No."

"Do you think you deserve to be happy without her?"

I sigh. "Imani…" They raise an eyebrow, and I cross my arms. "Yes."

"Then stop punishing yourself."

I manage a smile as we get out of the car. "I'll think about it."

They nod. "For now, that's good enough for me."

Loud music pounds as the two of us make our way across a manicured lawn Aunt Megan would kill for, and it gets worse as soon as we step through the entryway. "Okay," Imani adds, surveying the drunken sophomores stumbling in front of us with distaste. "Let's find Sammy, and then we'll see if we can crack that safe."

We drift into the kitchen, which is filled with considerably more people: There's a couple of giggling zombified cheerleaders playing beer pong on a ridiculously long kitchen island, a junior I vaguely recognize from the football team and Sammy's screenshots of his #FreeNathanDeveraux Snapchats absolutely chugging a screwdriver while a wide-eyed brunette girl tugs on his arm, and a whole table set up with various drinks, cups, pretzel sticks, and the desiccated remnants of what must have at one point been Halloween cupcakes. I make eye contact with Kevin Wu, who's swiping handfuls out of the candy corn bowl, and grimace as I awkwardly finish pouring two Solo cups for Imani and me. They're just filled with water, but they'll help us blend in with the crowd.

"Yo, Iris!" Kevin says, pointing to my costume. "*Scooby-Doo*, right?"

I nod and hand a cup to Imani just as one of the zombie cheerleaders lands a perfect bounce shot.

Stella and I used to watch *Scooby-Doo* when I was younger. It wasn't my favorite show or anything—it didn't provide me with any career epiphanies any more than it made me want a talking dog—but she loved it, so I did, too. We would curl up together on our old beat-up couch after mutually bad school days, a bowl of microwaved popcorn balanced between us, and take bets on who the ghost or ghoul the gang was chasing would actually turn out to be.

"No way you actually think it's the nice old man in the beginning."

"It's always the nice old man in the beginning, Stell. Just wait—it'll turn out he's losing money or his daughter is sick, and he's relying on the ghost tourism industry to turn his life around."

"Funny. You should be a criminal psychologist."

"Ten bucks says I'm right."

"Ten bucks and a strawberry milkshake from Joan's Diner."

"You're on."

Something about those moments was always strangely comforting. Somehow, I think even back then, a part of me always relished the big unmasking. The idea that monsters weren't things to fear—people were.

Speak of the devil.

The crowd parts, and almost as if he can sense my presence, Nathan Deveraux turns around. He smirks and raises his cup in my direction, and only then do I register that he's dressed like a stereotypical cartoon detective, trench coat and all, because of course he fucking is.

"Imani," I warn, but it's too late. He's already coming over here.

"Well, well, well," Nathan sneers, taking in our outfits with a look of unstable derision. "I've heard a lot about your sewing skills, Turner, but this looks a little...sad. Are you losing your touch?"

Imani blinks coolly. "No, just my respect for whichever maid dressed you this morning. Are the seams of your Party City costume supposed to be that frayed?"

Nathan shrugs. "I'm wearing it in honor of Blackthorn," he says, tipping his cup in my direction. "Thought I'd pay homage to Hillwood's best and brightest."

Imani and I try to step around him, but a dark look crosses Nathan's face before we can. He grabs my arm, and every hair on the back of my neck stands on end as his grip tightens around me.

Imani's face hardens. "Let her go."

"Hang on, hang on," Nathan says, and I finally notice how unfocused his eyes are. How he's slurring his words. "We're all friends here, aren't we?" He glances around the room, and panic flutters against my rib cage as I realize just how many eyes are on the three of us. "And to be completely honest with you, Turner, *I don't remember either of you being invited.*"

Deveraux wrenches me even closer to him, and suddenly his lips are right against my ear. "Listen to me closely, you little bitch," he whispers. "I know you took that picture. I know you still think I made Heather disappear. But I also know you're a little shot in the head, so I'll say this one last time, real nice and slow for you: The police haven't arrested me. *So you're wasting your time.*"

Nathan lets me go roughly, shoving me forward so I stumble

into the crowd. Someone next to me giggles a drunken laugh, and rage and humiliation sweep through me in equal measure. I thought Nathan was innocent. I thought the worst thing he did to me was send the GIVE UP THE SEARCH text.

But I'm not so sure anymore.

I don't see who I take the drink from. I don't care. All I know is that one second, the cup is in my hand; the next, its contents are all over Deveraux, dripping to the bottom of his fake leather shoes.

"Don't fucking touch me again," I tell Nathan coolly. "You're a dirty cheater, and Heather deserved so much better than you."

I drop the cup and stalk away, Imani at my heels.

"You know what everybody's saying about you, Iris?" Nathan calls after me. "That you're the one who killed her! That you snapped and killed her, just like you snapped when you had your fucking breakdown at homecoming last month!"

I don't turn around, even though every bone in my body is aching to pummel Nathan into a pulp. "Ignore him," Imani murmurs next to me. "We have more important things to deal with right now."

"Yeah, like getting to the second floor," I mutter. "Where the hell are Delphine's stairs?"

"Probably over there," a girl dressed in a green scarf and a short purple dress says next to me, and I grin as Sammy pulls Imani and me into a hug that smells like bubble-gum perfume. "About time," she says, pulling away with a grimace. "Everyone keeps asking me who I'm supposed to be, because it turns out ensemble costumes only work well if you're not missing your ensemble." She raises an eyebrow, her glitzy headband sliding down her curls. "Where's Lea?"

"I told her to leave me alone," I say, and Sammy's eyebrow inches farther up her face.

"Are all pansexuals this bad at communicating their feelings? Or is it just you?" She shakes her head. "You know, you'd think you have it easier with the whole *falling for people based on how they act regardless of their gender* thing, but you really need to work on how you talk to people you clearly like."

I flush. "Can we talk about my personal life later?" I ask, glancing desperately at Imani for some kind of backup. In response, their unimpressed stare slides between the two of us.

"Stairs?" they prompt, and Sammy concedes with one final eyebrow waggle in my direction as we push through the crowd and toward the roped-off stairwell. Stairs.

The second floor of Delphine's house is much more subdued than the first. There's almost no one up here, probably because there's no alcohol or music, either. It's just a sprawling maze of hallways and rooms, though it doesn't take us long to find the empty home theater (which is playing *Scream* on a TV that's taller than I am) or the safe hidden behind an impressively large collection of DVD movies. Looks like Jackson Criswell knows his shit.

"I'm gonna try to crack this," Sammy says, inclining her head to the safe. "Four of the numbers are worn away, so I'm hopeful it won't take too long. Imani, take lookout. Iris, see if you can find Delphine's room—maybe she's keeping the recovery keys there instead."

I nod, grateful for Sammy's quick thinking. There's no way I'm going to be any help if I just stand around and watch her mess around with keypad codes, but I can definitely do a quick sweep through Delphine's room. At least, I think I can, until I open Door No. 5 to what must be her bedroom and realize it's crammed with *things*: shelves sagging under the weight of myriad cheerleading trophies, a vanity overflowing with hair products, a queen-size bed with countless National Honor Society volunteer forms snaking out from under the ivory bed skirt. I have no idea where to even start looking for the recovery keys.

But that doesn't mean I'm not going to try.

I slide on a fresh pair of latex gloves and gravitate toward the vanity, hoping to find a fake bottom. Zilch. Inside the cup of every pristine FIGHTING GATORS cheer award. Zip. Underneath the NHS volunteer forms. Nada.

I'm just putting the papers back into place when a familiar voice floats down the hallway, and I freeze. I need to hide.

I slide underneath the bed and reposition the ivory bed skirt just as the door opens. "I already told you, you can't be here," Delphine hisses, slamming it behind her.

"Del, baby, believe me, this visit is as unwanted for me as it is for you," a second voice drawls lazily, and I suppress a breath as Jackson Criswell keeps talking. "But it's like I told you—my supplier doesn't want to do business with me ever since you painted a big red fuckin' target on my back, so now I want in with yours."

Delphine scoffs. "Get your head out of your ass, Jackson. You can't really think I'm dealing. I mean, come on. *Look at me.*"

Criswell laughs, and the sound is soft and low and dangerous. "I am."

Jackson shifts his weight. The floorboards creak with his adjustment, and the top of the wooden panel nearest to my right arm lifts slightly. There's a loose floorboard underneath Delphine's bed.

"You're really not going to tell me who you're working with?" Jackson asks softly, drawing my attention back to their feet. Shit—I missed part of their conversation. "I know you, Del. You think you can keep Deveraux around by selling to him, but he's just using you."

"Get out," Delphine says coldly. "Or I'm calling the cops again, Jackson. I swear to God."

He scoffs. "At your own party? With Arden drinking herself to death downstairs?"

"Get. Out."

"Fine, fine. You win, baby." There's a beat, and my heart jumps into my throat as Jackson slowly pivots. "I'll leave. Just as soon as you tell me where you're keeping your stash."

I think back to Heather's fourth podcast episode, the one where she interviewed an anonymous Hillwood dealer: *I'm saying there's a market. I'm saying if someone wanted to connect with a supplier, it probably wouldn't be too hard to do that.*

It looks like whoever she was, Heather's informant was right.

I glance at the loose floorboard. If Delphine *is* dealing, it's not for the money—she must be doing it to impress Nathan. She wants him badly enough that she's willing to stake her reputation on it, willing to throw everything else away for a chance at his heart. Briefly, for a flickering second, I wonder if Heather found out. I wonder if that's what's on the seven USBs, if that's why Delphine broke into her house to look for them. Even with all her privilege, she doesn't want to get caught. Which means the burner phone—and the number—must be from her supplier.

"You have three seconds," Delphine says coldly.

"So demanding," Jackson drawls. "You know, you can't keep everyone in Hillwood under your thumb." He pauses, and I can almost hear the gears in his head as he pivots. *Under.*

He's looking at Delphine's bed.

I hold my breath, my eyes shut tight, willing Jackson to turn away. Willing Delphine to shove him out, willing my hiding spot to stay undetected.

But Jackson takes a step closer. Closer. Closer still.

And then, from down the hallway, someone lets out a blood-curdling scream.

Chapter Eighteen

SUNDAY, OCTOBER 31, 9:44 PM

Jackson stills. "What the hell?" he says, and then he and Delphine both run out. I wait one beat, two, three, and then I take out my phone and lift the loose floorboard next to me.

Sure enough, there's an entire collection of pills stashed away underneath. Zoloft—what Heather was taking for her depression before she went missing. Adderall. Xanax.

My stomach sinks. Drugs, but no recovery keys.

I snap a few pictures, and then I wriggle out from under Delphine's bed and slip out into the hallway.

be gay solve crime
9:44 PM

wedoalittlehacking:

okay so three things: i cracked the safe, safes are full of boring old rich people stuff, and there are screams in scream

imaniturnnerr:

Sammy and I heard Delphine coming up the stairs and figured you could use a distraction. Did we time it right?

I grin.

perfectly.

are you okay?

wedoalittlehacking:

yeah, we bolted as soon as we pumped up the movie volume

we are now babysitting arden blake downstairs xx

imaniturnnerr:

Did you have any better luck?

not unless finding out delphine deals drugs counts as luck

imaniturnnerr:

WHAT

yeah. hang on, i'm coming to find you

I close out of the group chat and put my phone away, heading back to the first floor to regroup with Imani and Sammy. A girl in a glittery short red dress slams into me as soon as I step off the stairs, and I stumble at the unexpected contact. She reaches a hand out to steady me, her sequined red horns sliding down her sleek curls, and I flinch at the clamminess of her skin. "Sorry!" she slurs, her crystal-blue eyes wide with guilt, and I barely have enough time to register Arden's face before she turns and stumbles away.

As I blink the stars out of my eyes and move past more drunk cowboys and hipsters and fuzzy animals, I can't resist scanning the crowd for a flash of white hair. I know it's hopeless. I know Lea didn't come. But even if she isn't here, that doesn't change the fact I want her to be. That I wish—

"Where did she go?" Sammy shouts, barging through the costumed mob with Imani close behind. She grabs my sweater, and I furrow my eyebrows. "Iris, have you see her?"

"What are you talking about?" I ask. "Seen who?"

"Arden!" Sammy insists, scanning the crowd. "We have to go after her—she stole my phone!"

Imani nods, their demeanor slightly more frazzled than usual, and I manage to gesture in the general direction Arden disappeared before Sammy grabs me again and we barrel forward.

"What even happened?" I ask as we emerge onto Delphine's lawn. I spot Arden's car reversing out of the driveway as Imani unlocks their own, and Sammy shakes her head.

"The two of us were watching her so she wouldn't chug an entire bottle of vodka, and we turned our backs for, like, *two seconds* to get her a glass of water"—Sammy pushes me into the Homicide Honda and slams the door, and we all buckle our seat belts—"and she just grabbed my phone and bolted!" She scoffs as the engine starts, and then we're swerving past Delphine's fountain and onto the main road. Ahead of us, Arden's taillights are barely visible as she jerkily whips around a bend of gnarled trees. My stomach clenches. She's so drunk, she definitely shouldn't be driving. But we're going to stop her. I hope.

Imani's hands flex on the steering wheel. "Never really been in a car chase before," they muse, switching gears. "This should be fun."

The car accelerates, and I squeeze my eyes shut as Imani expertly weaves through pothole-ridden bayou country back-roads. We're flying at fifty, sixty, seventy miles per hour, and we still haven't caught up with Arden. She's heading to the edge of town, toward the cypress swamp. She's leaving Hillwood.

She knows we're following her.

"Damn it," Imani hisses, gunning the engine past a swath of run-down trailers. Chevalier. "Sammy, can you grab my phone? The password's 5-2-5-6-0-0."

Sammy takes the phone and unlocks it, and Imani tells her to navigate to their contacts and call a number. It rings on the Homicide Honda's speaker, and my eyebrows furrow. "Who are you calling? What's going on?"

The person on the other end picks up, and Imani's eyes narrow. "I'm only going to tell you this once, Blake. You took the wrong phone, and I'll leak the photos if you don't pull over right now."

In front of us, Arden's car slows. Imani slowly brakes, and then they ease to the curb behind her. My eyes dart to them as Sammy gapes at Imani's phone. "What the hell was that? What photos?"

"Just get out of the car," Imani says, already opening their door.

I follow suit, and so does Sammy. Every nerve in my body hums like a live wire as I step out of the Homicide Honda and into the pitch-black night, humid heat rising off the cracked asphalt road and sticking to my clothes even under a cool and starless October sky. I don't know what's happening, but I don't like being in the dark.

Arden gets out of her car in front of us, her face ashen. Stella's face.

Imani's voice is cold. "Give Sammy back her phone."

Heather's best friend blinks and hands it over. WORLD'S OKAY-EST LESBIAN. "I'm sorry...this was stupid. I don't even know what I was planning to do with it. Toss it in the swamp, maybe." She attempts a smile, but it doesn't reach her eyes. "All I wanted was to erase the screenshots."

"What screenshots?"

Arden swallows, and Imani's gaze flicks to me. "Arden has the flash drive we gave Heather on the day she went missing," they say, and my entire world realigns.

"What?" I ask. Arden shifts her weight, and I raise an incredulous eyebrow as I reassess her. "You're the one who put up the photo in the bathroom? *You* framed Lea?"

"Yeah," she says, her voice raspy.

"Why?" I demand. "I mean, how did you even get the drive?"

"She took it from Heather," Imani says levelly. "Right before she went missing."

Arden bites her lip, her glittery red devil horns backlit by the deeper red of her car's taillights. "I know it looks bad. I just needed a USB for ph-physics, and Heather had one with her when we went out for lunch...so I b-borrowed it. But then she disappeared, and..." Her expression darkens. "I saw the photo of Nathan and that *girl*."

The picture I took at Bellevue Estates. The one of Nathan and his secret girlfriend.

Imani glances at me. "Arden DMed me to ask about it," they continue, crossing their arms, "but she must have realized stealing from Heather right before she disappeared wasn't a good look, because she blocked me before I could respond. She blocked all of us, actually."

Arden blinks again. "I panicked. I made a m-mistake....I've made a lot of m-mistakes lately. But not this time."

I don't miss the change in her voice. Sammy glances at me, and I know she didn't, either.

My voice is soft. "You think Nathan killed her."

Arden's bottom lip trembles. "I didn't want to b-believe it. When you asked me all those questions right after Heather went m-missing, Iris, I didn't take you seriously. But it's been a while now, right? And...and everyone in this town knows what happens when missing girls don't come b-back right away."

Next to me, Imani inhales. I ignore them.

"The cops believed Deveraux was innocent," I tell her. "Or at the very least, they didn't arrest him. Why risk so much by printing the photo and taping it to the mirror?"

Arden wrings her hands together. "I mean, Heather is my f-friend. Nathan was, too, but not anymore." Her eyes flash. "And his f-family..." She shakes her head. "I couldn't go to the p-police without him knowing, and everyone remembers what happened with Kevin and Lea when he asked me to the homecoming dance this year, so I copied her h-handwriting on the mirror. But I haven't done anything else. Delphine had a f-fight with Heather right before she went missing about the new episode of *How to Find a Missing Girl* when we went out for lunch at Joan's on the d-day she disappeared. Nathan was cheating on h-her. But I've only ever been caught in the crossfire, Iris. And it's…it's killing me."

I search her face. Her smudged makeup, her unfocused, sliding eyes. "I can see that," I say softly.

"My grades in Collin's—in Mr. Cooper's c-class—are dropping. My stepdad thinks Heather and her f-friends are a bad influence on me. Coach Hannequart is being harsher than ever, and everyone keeps treating me like some kind of s-suspect. But I'm not, because Nathan did it, Iris." Arden's expression rearranges itself into something cold, reminding me of every time Stella knew she had just won an argument. "I'm sure of it."

I scrutinize her posture. The set of her jaw, the way her hands lie at her sides. Arden is telling the truth—or at least she thinks she is.

Sammy gasps. "Oh my god," she whispers, and then she glances down at her phone. It takes me a second to understand what she's looking at, but then I know.

It's her tracking app.

I want to smack myself for not thinking of it earlier. Imani's eyes dart to her, and I know they're wondering the same thing I am. "Sammy," I say, and my voice comes out strangled, "please tell me you coded the app to keep historical data."

She nods, frantically swiping at her phone. "I did. I just need to…oh my god."

"What?" I ask, not knowing what I'll do if she's found something. Not knowing what I'll do if she hasn't.

"It's his car," she whispers, her voice shaking. "Nathan Deveraux left the school parking lot from 12:47 to 1:32 PM on October fifteenth." Her brown eyes flick up to mine, as big and round as saucers. "The day Heather Nasato went missing."

Our flashlights bob like fireflies in the darkness, illuminating downed conifers and marshy plant life as the four of us trudge through the murky swampland. I keep holding my breath as I sweep my phone over the water, terrified I'll light up a pair of glowing red eyes right before I'm snapped up and dragged under by a particularly pissed-off alligator, but so far it's been nothing but frogs, a single rat snake, and dozens and dozens of blackened bald cypress branches holding wispy, ghost-gray tendrils of Spanish moss. The swamps on the edge of Hillwood are limitless— even when the police swept through them after Heather first went missing, they didn't find anything.

But then again, they didn't have the information we do.

"This place is so creepy," Arden whispers as we wade through the stagnant water, her hushed voice joining the crickets, frogs, and buzzing mosquitoes making noise around us. "Isn't there supposed to be, like…a werewolf in here, or something?"

"The rougarou," Imani answers, flicking a gnat out of their

face. "Though I think we should be more worried about the Hill-wood High Fighting Gators."

My stomach lurches. Heather.

"Okay," Sammy says softly, squinting at the little red dot on her phone. She turns in a slow circle, and dark brackish water ripples out from her ankles. "According to the historical data, whatever we're looking for—if we're looking for something—should be somewhere around . . . here." She glances up, and the four of us stare at one another. Unease prickles the back of my neck, and I gulp in a breath of thick, hot air. Suddenly, being out here in the middle of a starless Halloween night feels like a very bad idea. No one knows where we are. For all we know, Arden could be a murderer.

"Let's split up," Imani suggests lightly.

I manage a hollow smile. "And search for clues, right?"

They nod, and so do Sammy and Arden.

All right. I guess we're really doing this.

The four of us splash off in an X shape from where Sammy's tracker stopped, and as I wade through the murky water, my flashlight beam illuminating hulking trees and the glowing green eyes of frogs who hop away mid-croak around me, I feel guilt as thick as the dead air around us settle onto my shoulders. Guilt for snapping at Lea, for losing my cool with Arden, for believing that lying to my friends would be the best way to protect them. Because now that someone broke into my house, it's clear to me we're all in real danger. And I need to tell everyone the truth before something happens. Before I lose the agency's trust for good. Before they realize I'm completely useless, and that everything bad is always my fault.

"Hey, y'all?" Imani's voice pierces my thoughts, odd and strangled and high. "Over here. I think...I think I might've found something."

I double back instantly, my flashlight swinging as I tear through the swamp. Mud sucks at my boots, and algae sticks to my skin, and nothing else matters. Nothing except for Imani and this moment and what comes next.

"Look," they whisper as Arden, Sammy, and I reach them, breathless, pointing to something in the marsh a few feet ahead. I follow their pained expression, terror shooting through me as I squint in the half dark, and my heart flatlines.

"Oh my god," Arden whispers. "Oh my god."

It's a body.

Part Three

Chapter Nineteen

Sammy turns away, gagging, and the sound of her retching echoes in my ears. I want to throw up, too, but I can't. I can't do anything. Because it's Heather. Beautiful, complicated, shining Heather, cheerleader and podcaster and my first love, shiny ponytail floating behind her in the brackish water, one pale, bloated arm outstretched. Reaching.

Almost involuntarily, my eyes track the path of her rigid fingers. And there, half-submerged in the shallow marsh, lies something sleek and black and unmistakable.

My breath catches in my throat.

It's a pistol.

"No," I whisper, struggling to comprehend the scene in front of me. The frogs take up the mantra, echoing my only thought. *No. No. No.*

"You don't think she...," Arden whispers, but it's too late. Already, my brain is spinning, locking puzzle pieces into place: Heather and Nathan had a fight. Heather was on antidepressants. Heather uploaded one final podcast episode before she went missing.

Something warm and soft on my shoulder. Imani's hand.

"Iris," they say, and their voice isn't here with me. It's from somewhere deeper, somewhere dark. My heart clenches, and the nausea finally overwhelms my body. Heather is dead. Has been dead for weeks. Lying here like this, waiting for someone to find her. Thinking that nobody cared.

I can't take it anymore—I drop to my knees and finally empty the contents of my stomach, the sour smell mixing with the stench of decaying plants and rot and death. I don't want to be here. I don't want to see her like this. I don't want to have to go through this again.

The glazed surface of the school gym floor. Shimmering dresses. My knees on the ground, trembling. Claustrophobic. Sweaty. Inhaling without any air. The panic and the crowding and the breaking down.

My fingers twitch, bringing me back to the duckweed seeping into my clothes. To the terrible, crushing reality of this moment.

We found Heather.

I didn't think it was going to be like this.

"Iris," Imani says softly. "We have to go."

"No." My voice is eerily calm. "We have to call Detective de Rosa. We need to call the police."

"Iris—"

"WE'RE NOT REAL DETECTIVES, IMANI!" They step back, eyes wide at my outburst, and my entire body shakes. "We're not real detectives," I say again, breathing hard. "We can't do this. I can't...." I shake my head. "We have to call de Rosa."

She'll put me in jail, but it doesn't matter. Everyone in my life told me not to investigate, told me I would get in over my head, but right now I'm drowning. I'm drowning, and I'll suffocate unless I come up for air.

I take out my phone with shaking fingers and make the call.

The déjà vu is nauseating. Someone's put a space blanket around my shoulders, and I stare at the reflective silver fabric with dead eyes. I don't feel. I am a reflection.

Memories flash through my mind, years and months and weeks that I want to forget: Heather's hard expression as she kissed me for the first time in the Hillwood locker room, Heather's soft lips brushing against mine in the summer, Heather's pretty doodles of butterflies all over the margins of my notebooks because that's what she said I gave her. Heather, Heather, Heather. Missing. Dead. Gone.

Time passes, or it doesn't. People try to ask me questions, but I can't answer them, and eventually they move on to someone who can. Imani. Sammy. Anyone but me.

Arden isn't here. She slipped away at some point in the chaos, sobered up and drove off before the police came. I would have left, too, if my legs could support my weight through the tall reeds and scummy water. If I could do anything other than shiver in my red miniskirt in the chilly October air.

"Iris?"

I glance up, and Detective de Rosa's sharp features swim into view. She looks aggravated, but something in her expression softens when my eyes meet hers.

The swamp falls away, and suddenly I'm back in the Hillwood Police Station, staring at the DET. MARIA DE ROSA nameplate fixed to her desk as she lectures me. *Iris, you can't keep doing this. Iris, you'll never be a real detective. Iris—*

"Iris, I need to take your statement."

The vision ends, and then I'm back in the swamp. Back with the swarming police and the flashing lights and the countless questions. But I'm not a determined sixteen-year-old girl anymore. And de Rosa was right—I can't keep doing this.

I nod numbly in response to the detective, but even sitting in the trunk of a police vehicle with my stupid blanket wrapped around me, covered in swamp water and trailing ferns as I give her my statement with the rest of the agency, I know nothing is ever going to be the same. Because I can't be a detective anymore. I never should have tried to be one in the first place. All of this, everything I believed I knew, was for nothing.

I thought this was my second chance. I thought I could find Heather to make up for how badly I messed up with Stella. But I couldn't save her. She was right in front of me, and I didn't see how much she was fucking struggling.

I'm just as useless as my sister always thought.

"Are we free to go?" Sammy asks from somewhere beyond me, after my voice is hoarse and the frogs are silent.

"Yes," de Rosa says.

It's the only word I hear for a long time.

TRANSCRIPT OF A VOICE MAIL FROM HILLWOOD HIGH:

Good afternoon. This is Principal Phillips at Hillwood High School.

We regret to inform you of a loss in our Hillwood family. Heather Nasato, a senior at Hillwood High School, has passed away.

Heather was a pillar of light in our small community, as well as an incredible student and varsity cheerleader, and we all will mourn her passing. There will be grief counselors available for students in the upcoming days.

We are unaware of any arrangements at this time.

Thank you for your support.

Goodbye.

Chapter Twenty

We're sitting at the diner. The detective asked to meet us here. Somewhere public, she'd said. Somewhere we could just *talk*.

Sammy and Imani sit across from me, the whipped cream atop their untouched milkshakes long deflated, avoiding my gaze. Neither of them said anything when they sat down, and the past fifteen minutes have passed between us in agonizing silence. I wish the detective weren't running late. I wish Lea's section of our regular corner booth weren't empty next to me. I wish Heather weren't dead.

Behind the agency, I catch a glimpse of myself in the fleur-de-lis mirror: blank expression, tight bun, and Stella's necklace tucked into the collar of my HWHS MEDIA APPRECIATION CLUB T-shirt.

I'm dressed in normal clothes today—no black longcoat. No plaid pants. Nothing that makes me look like an amateur sleuth, like someone who spends her free time finding dead bodies.

Because that's what Heather is now. A dead body.

I inhale and move to slide out from our booth just as the bell of the diner jingles and a woman steps through the entryway. She's not wearing her uniform today, either. But then her eyes meet mine, unsmiling, and I know.

Detective de Rosa comes to a stop in front of us. "Hello," she says calmly. "May I join you?"

"Yes," Sammy says after a beat of silence. Silence I'm usually supposed to fill.

The detective takes Lea's seat.

Carrie sidles up and asks if she can get us anything. To my surprise, de Rosa nods. "A cup of coffee, please," she says. "Black."

Of course.

Carrie nods, and I fidget with a loose thread on the side of my jeans as she leaves and comes back with de Rosa's order. I wish the detective would just get on with it already. Would tell us, officially, what I already heard last night in the swamp: Heather was holding the weapon when she died. She was on medication. There's no letter, but I forgot to tell the police about the flash drives. My mouth fills with a bitter taste. *Suicide notes.*

The detective takes a sip of her coffee. "I'm very sorry about what happened to Heather," she finally says. "I know last night must have been incredibly traumatic for the three of you, and I'd like to start things off by making sure you know that."

Sammy swallows. Next to her, Imani takes her hand.

"But," de Rosa says, turning my blood cold, "I also want to remind you that we discussed the consequences of interfering with this investigation, Iris. And as much as I understand that you want to get justice, I'm afraid you obstructed it. Again." De Rosa sighs. "That swamp was a crime scene. And last night, you contaminated critical evidence." Her steely eyes flick to Imani and Sammy. "Though it wasn't just you this time, was it?"

Imani levels their gaze at the detective. "I'm sorry," they tell her, their tone cool. "But what do you mean, Iris knew the consequences of interfering?"

For the first time since she got here, Detective de Rosa actually looks surprised. "I warned Iris on the very first day I was assigned to this case that if I found out she was meddling with my witnesses and evidence, I would have her—and anyone else doing the same—charged for obstruction of justice."

"Like, criminal obstruction?" Sammy asks, her voice barely audible. "Like, jail time?"

The tips of my ears burn. Every other part of my body feels numb, but dread seeps into my skin as the implications of what de Rosa's saying finally hit my friends. They had plausible deniability up until this moment, but they don't anymore. And maybe it was naïve of me to think they could keep it. But they didn't find out the truth from me, and now it's too late.

"We didn't interfere with your case," I say quietly. "We were just in the wrong place at the wrong time."

De Rosa's steel eyes spark. "I don't appreciate you lying to me, Iris," she says, her voice just as soft. Dangerously so. "And I don't appreciate you turning in anonymous tips about my officers, either."

"Did you look into him?" I demand, not even pretending I didn't do it. I lean forward. "What he said in that Facebook post—"

"Was inexcusable and well deserving of a reprimand," de Rosa says, holding up a hand. "But Assistant Detective Hunt had nothing to do with this."

I sit back down, the hollow pang in my chest resounding. Because she's right. Heather killed herself.

De Rosa regards me over the top of her steaming mug. "You didn't pass on my warning to your friends," she says simply, and her words twist like a knife in my chest. The detective turns her attention to Sammy and Imani. "In that case, I apologize. But it's something you both should have been aware of nevertheless."

I rip the loose thread free from my jeans and immediately shift my focus to the napkin dispenser in front of me. It has a photo of Joan's Diner on the front, all silver chrome train-car exterior and neon-red accents in a haze of swirling gray fog, and staring at it is much better than having to confront Sammy's hurt gaze or Imani's narrowed eyes.

"Now. The three of you are obviously smart, and undoubtedly capable," Detective de Rosa continues. "I'd be remiss not to mention the fact you all managed to locate Heather's body when my own team couldn't. But even with all of that being said, I'm afraid I still need to know exactly why the three of you were in the swamp last night in the first place."

Sammy's eyes drop to a sticky spot on the table, and I don't have to be a detective to know that she's thinking about her tracking app. About the fact it's highly illegal in the state of Louisiana to monitor someone's movements without their consent.

Detective de Rosa's eyes narrow, and Imani's eyes meet mine across the table in a silent demand. *Do something.*

"We already gave our statements," I tell the detective, forcing myself to take a casual sip of my strawberry milkshake. "On Halloween night, and earlier this morning. What more could you possibly want to know?"

"The reports were...conflicting," de Rosa says, setting down her mug. "I simply wanted to give you all this chance to change your stories while you still had the time."

I think back to the statements. To how much we had to omit, to how we collectively lied about Sammy's app and the GPS signal we used to locate where Nathan's truck had been. How we just said we stumbled upon the body while trying to scare one another. That we were hunting for the rougarou on Halloween night.

"It would help," de Rosa urges, sensing our hesitancy. Imani remains stoic and impassive, but Sammy fidgets across from me. "If we had the truth, if I could tell the rest of my department you three were cooperative...."

I set my jaw. I may have betrayed the agency once already. But I'll be damned if I rat them out to save myself.

"I'm sorry," I tell de Rosa coolly, forcing myself to meet her gaze. "But we have nothing left to add."

De Rosa's eyes are unreadable as she considers us. "I see. Well, in that case, I should get going." She stands up, her dark eyes boring into me one final time. "I have a lot of paperwork to go through."

Her words hang in the air, an unspoken threat, and I vaguely wonder how long it takes to charge a minor with criminal obstruction. Not that I'll legally be recognized as one in thirteen days.

As the detective leaves, I realize she'll probably have to collect concrete, damning evidence against us first. But she's out for us. All of us—I know that now.

And so does the rest of the agency.

As soon as the door of the diner closes after her, Sammy's eyes fill with tears. "How could you?" she whispers, her voice wobbling. "We're supposed to be a *team*, Iris. The Blackthorn Agency. We're supposed to *talk to each other*—"

"Right," I interrupt, my blood flashing hot. "Just like how Imani talked to us about Arden stealing the flash drive we gave Heather?"

Sammy blinks, her breath hitching, and the tears pooling under her lashes start to slide down her face.

"Oh," I say softly, finally realizing what I should have known all along. "You knew."

"Not at first," Sammy whispers. "Imani told me when they drove me to Delphine's party before they picked you up. And I swear we were going to tell you. We just...wanted to focus on looking for the recovery keys first, and Imani knew if we told you about Arden you'd freak out and go after her right away."

"So what? You two were just going to let Lea take the fall for everything?"

"Iris, that's not—"

"No, I get it," I snap. "I understand *exactly* how much of a team you both think we are."

Imani glares at me. "Look, Iris, we both messed up. I should have told you about Arden as soon as I found out, and that's on me. But me withholding information from you for the sake of

Heather's case and you willingly endangering us by not telling us about de Rosa's threat are two wildly different things."

I open my mouth, but Imani narrows their eyes. "Actually, were you ever going to tell us?" they ask. "Or were you just going to let everything play out and hope for the best? Keep being as selfish and narrow-minded as you always are? Keep using the two of us?"

That hits me like a punch to the gut. "What?"

"You heard me," Imani says, and their composure slips a little as Sammy looks from them to me. "You knew we could all get into trouble—serious trouble—and you strung us along anyway. And you can say it's for the case. You can say it's for Heather. You can say it's because you want justice for Stella. But let's be honest, Iris—we all know who you're really doing this for. And it definitely isn't your sister or the ex-girlfriend whose podcast sensationalized her disappearance."

My breath catches. "I don't...I didn't..." My voice breaks. "I really thought we would find her alive, Imani."

"Yeah," they say softly, their gaze flicking to Sammy. "So did we."

There's a beat of silence, and none of us fill it. I focus on the sticky diner table and feel the knife in my chest twist deeper. It's like there's a rift growing wider and wider between us with every passing second, but I don't know how to close it.

I don't think I deserve to.

Eventually, Sammy shakes her head. "Detective de Rosa is right—it's over, Iris. We can't...We have to disband. The agency was a mistake. It's over."

It's the same conclusion I came to in the swamp last night.

But for some reason, the words hit differently when Sammy says them. Because she doesn't mean we're done investigating. She means we're done being friends.

This is it. This is where we end. In the diner, with its neon lights and tinny jukebox music and mouthwatering food, where all those months ago I got the call from Megan telling me my mom was killed in a car crash. Where Joan gave me a lagniappe of milkshakes alongside my blueberry beignets for as long as it took me to start pushing through the dark cloud that hung over me afterward. Where I finally found my purpose again, learning about volunteer-run online databases for missing people and subreddits devoted to identifying bodies and people who solve cold cases through the National Missing and Unidentified Persons System in their free time. People who do the jobs the police won't do. People who make themselves useful.

And now, after all this time, it's where the agency is disbanding.

Sammy blinks at me, tears still tracking down her face, and reaches into the backpack by her side. "Here," she says, pulling out the plastic bag with the seven flash drives labeled FOR IRIS. "You should turn these in to the police. Now that the detective knows about us investigating—now that we know what really happened to Heather—there's no point in you keeping them."

I swallow. I don't want to turn in the drives. All de Rosa knows is that we found Heather's body—right now, we at least seem helpful. But if I hand over the USBs...if I let her know I've been hiding evidence and truly obstructing justice...

Not to mention that Heather left them to me. And I still want to know what's on them, even if it is just her note.

"Yeah," I tell Sammy, lying through my teeth. "I will."

There's another beat, and then Imani and Sammy both stand up. A bolt of anger courses through me at the motion, but Imani turns their eyes on me before I can act on it.

"Save it, Iris," they say, their voice devoid of all emotion. "I think you've done enough."

Chapter Twenty-One

It's been six days since we found Heather's body. I've been staying home from school, partly because the death threats have amped up and partly because I don't need anyone whispering about me as I walk through the halls of Hillwood High, which means I mostly stare at walls until Megan returns from the Hillwood Assisted Living Community at odd hours and I make a phantom appearance at dinner. The police didn't release my name to the public, but enough people saw me leaving Delphine's party on Halloween—and remembered her Snapchat story—to conflate Heather's death with my investigation anyway. I think Imani and Sammy are getting the same treatment, but I haven't asked. I'm pretty sure both of them have blocked me on every social media platform—not that I've mustered the courage to look.

The only information I get through my self-imposed isolation is from the *Hillwood Herald* Twitter, which I have notifications on for, and Lea's frantic texts, which I've been consistently ignoring. But none of that matters. Either way, knowing Heather's dead makes things worse now than they were before. Because before, at least we had hope. Now, we have nothing except the burden of knowing.

I clench my teeth, digging my nails into the soft wooden underside of my desk at the new message on my computer: *Incorrect password; please enter the password again.* I've been at it for hours now, trying to crack even a single one of the USBs Heather left for me, but it's hopeless.

Drives from a dead girl. The whole thing makes me so sick.

I swallow the bile in my throat and glance up at my calendar, at the red Xs that constantly serve to remind me that this is the second time I've failed to get justice. The second time I've had to see the lifeless body of someone I loved up close, all pale blue lips and glassy eyes and parchment-paper skin. Because I did love my mom, even if living with her was hard. Even if she was an alcoholic. Even if she never acted like the mother my older sister stepped up to be.

I swallow and input another string into my laptop. *Incorrect password; please enter the password again.* Another. *Incorrect password; please enter the password again.* Another and another and another, each failed input letting me know that no matter how hard I try to distract myself, I fucked up on a massive scale. My only friends hate me. Aunt Megan and I can't hold a substantial conversation for longer than a minute.

I failed to solve Heather's case.

A bitter laugh rises in my throat, bubbling like thick black oil from some dark and twisted part of me. Heather's case. I was so desperate to find her, so desperate to redeem myself after Stella, that I refused to look at the evidence. That I refused to believe that she...that she...

But the notes, another part of me insists. *The threats, the evidence. Deveraux cheating.* Though that had been explained away, too—the GIVE UP THE SEARCH text had been from Nathan, who felt guilty about cheating on Heather. Nathan, who thought he had something to do with her disappearance. Nathan, who wanted to dissuade us from implicating him in our investigation. Nathan, who had been questioned and cleared and released.

Nathan, whose car we traced to the swamp during the afternoon Heather supposedly died by suicide.

I force myself to take a deep, steadying breath. And then I start to think.

To really think.

The police—the police who think Heather killed herself—don't know we only found her because we tracked Deveraux's car. But if they *did*, that little fact wouldn't line up with the rest of the story. Because even if Heather drove herself to the swamp in her boyfriend's truck, if she had stolen his easily accessible keys out of his easily openable locker, there would be no one to return the car to school after she died. If she took herself to the swamp, *Nathan's car would still be there.*

I inhale, unable to believe I didn't get it before. Heather and her boyfriend argued about *How to Find a Missing Girl* before she died. Nathan was cheating on her, and he knew where she lived, and he definitely could have accessed the pistol in her family's gun cabinet. But still, there are things that don't make sense even if I want to connect everything to him: the Polaroid of Stella in lingerie inside his locker. The fact someone's been following me. The WATCH OUT TONIGHT note and Delphine dealing and Arden's reckless behavior.

Does all of that tie back to Deveraux, too?

I shake my head. Everything is blurring together, and I can't see the forest for the trees. There are connections here, intricate little webs woven between everything I know and all the things I don't, and there are still stones I've left unturned. Evidence I haven't figured out how to slot perfectly into place. Podcast episodes I haven't listened to.

I move to pick up my phone, seconds away from reaching back out to Lea and asking for her help—and her journalistic eye—but it pings with a notification before I can. Frowning, I scan the top banner. It's for the *Hillwood Herald* Twitter. There's been a breakthrough in Heather's case.

And Nathan Deveraux has just been arrested for the murder of Heather Nasato.

THE HILLWOOD HERALD

Home > Top Stories > Arrests & Crimes

By Gavin Cormier

On October 15, Hillwood High School senior Heather Nasato went missing during the middle of the school day. A little over half a month later, her body was recovered on Halloween night from a swamp right on the outskirts of Hillwood. And now, on November 6, police are wrapping up the 17-year-old's high-profile missing persons case by charging her boyfriend, fellow Hillwood High senior Nathan Deveraux, with second-degree murder. Deveraux's arrest was made possible through a key witness who came forward with relevant information in the past few days.

"We're very grateful to finally be able to bring justice to Hillwood and the rest of the Nasato family," Detective Maria de Rosa, the lead detective in the Heather Nasato case, said in a statement. "Thankfully, our witness was very cooperative. Without them, I doubt our department would have been able to make this arrest."

Heather Nasato's death was originally speculated to be a suicide; she is the second person in a little over a year to go missing from the Lafourche Parish town of Hillwood, Louisiana. The first was Stella Blackthorn, another senior at Hillwood High, who vanished last year on September 19.

This story is ongoing.

I can't believe it. Sammy must have come forward about the app and Nathan's car—that's the only way the police could have gotten enough evidence to arrest Deveraux. That's the only way de Rosa could have been confident enough to make that statement. They think they got it right this time.

I shake my head, my hands trembling as I scroll past another headline announcing the date and time of a candlelit vigil meant to honor my ex-girlfriend, and then I open a different app. I type in the name so familiar to me now, the one that never quite panned out for Heather, and click on her sixth and final podcast episode. And then, for the last time, I hit play on *How to Find a Missing Girl.*

HOW TO FIND A
MISSING GIRL PODCAST

Episode Six

HEATHER NASATO: Hey-o, Hillwood. Did you miss me? I've certainly missed you. I'll be honest—I thought I was finished with this podcast. But I have one more episode left in me. I hope it was worth the wait.

[THEME MUSIC PLAYS]

HEATHER NASATO: Up until now, I've been entirely focused on Stella Blackthorn. I've delved into who she was, what she meant to the people in Hillwood, and the circumstances behind her disappearance. I've talked to health professionals and teachers and the people who loved her about how she went missing, but back in July, I decided I was done. You might be wondering what's changed. Why I decided there's more to the story, why I decided to upload one final episode. Well, Hillwood, it's because when I finally stopped focusing on Stella...she came into focus for me.

[THEME MUSIC FADES]

HEATHER NASATO: Consider today's episode a warning. There will be no interviews. There will be no speculation. There doesn't have to be, because I believe I know what happened to her. That's right—I've finally found out the truth behind Stella Blackthorn's disappearance. And right after I upload this episode, I'm going to go to the police and tell them everything I know.

[SILENCE]

HEATHER NASATO: But before that happens, I wanted to take a step back and give you all one final update. Because this podcast is fully my space. And because, Hillwood, I feel like you deserve it.

[SILENCE]

HEATHER NASATO: First: Nathan Deveraux, you're a self-centered asshole. Your family may be rich and powerful, but you'll never live up to their expectations. I started dating you because I thought it was what I was supposed to do—I thought we would be the golden couple, the star football player and his perfect cheerleader girlfriend—but I've never been more unhappy. I don't like pretending to be something I'm not...even if you've always been great at it.

[SILENCE]

HEATHER NASATO: Second: Arden Blake, you're a mediocre cheerleader with sloppy tendencies and daddy issues. You shouldn't have encouraged Kevin Wu while he was still with Lea—it was wrong, and so was the fact you dumped him not even a week later. But he still cares about you. You should try to make it work. Not just for him, but for yourself, too. Because you should know—having someone's face doesn't give you permission to try and act like them. And even though I get moving to a new town your junior year is hard, you're never going to be Stella Blackthorn.

[SILENCE]

HEATHER NASATO: Third: Delphine Fontenot, the reigning queen of Hillwood High. You've done a good job taking up Stella's mantle—maybe too good, even. You're ruthless, cutthroat, and used to getting what you want. But I hope you know doxxing your friends has consequences. And getting involved with people like Jackson Criswell—in more ways than one—is never a good idea.

[SILENCE]

HEATHER NASATO: Fourth: Iris Blackthorn, I'm sorry I didn't live up to your expectations. I'm sorry I wasn't good enough for you, sorry I didn't devote as much time as I should have to helping you look for Stella, sorry that things between us ended because you thought I wasn't on your side. I hope, somehow, this podcast makes up for some of that. I did it for you. I did so much for you, Butterfly. All this time, I've just been trying to protect you. It's why I told de Rosa to keep an eye on you after you started closing yourself off when Stella went missing, and it's why I told her you were going to interrogate the only witness in Stella's case after I overheard you telling Lea your plan last year. This case deserves to be handled responsibly, and it deserves to be solved. Maybe that's part of the reason I started *How to Find a Missing Girl*, too.

[SILENCE]

HEATHER NASATO: I was going to say more here. I wanted to say more, but I think...I think I'll leave off with this: I know who you are. I know you're listening. I know what you did. And soon, all of Hillwood will, too.

[OUTRO MUSIC PLAYS]

I stop the episode before the outro music finishes, breathing hard, because Heather—not Lea—turned me in to de Rosa when I was looking for my sister last year. But my chest is also heaving because I finished the podcast. And the police are wrong.

They've written off Heather's death as a murder by her cheating boyfriend. Scandalously framed as a suicide, thwarted by our agency's tracker on his truck. From my conversation with Hunt at the station, it even seems like they've mostly categorized her podcast as a bid for attention—after all, they never found the evidence Heather talked about gathering.

But there is evidence. The flash drives Heather left me. The fact that the police have been wrong before. The way Nathan reacted in the bathroom, his sheet-white face when he saw the picture of him and Mystery Girl. How he wasn't lying when he said he'd never seen the photo of Stella that was left in his locker before.

I shake my head, my eyes traveling over the collection of potted plants in my room. I don't think Nathan killed Heather. I don't think he did anything to her besides be a shitty boyfriend, and I don't think he's stupid enough to keep Polaroids of missing girls in his locker, either. Someone is framing him. Someone bold enough to break into my room, someone desperate enough to get the USBs, someone who wanted Heather gone. Someone who thought her boyfriend would make the perfect scapegoat.

I think back to Jackson Criswell in the diner. *You know, the last time we got high together and I finally told her to let it go, that Deveraux was never going to love her back, she said she was going to find a way to* make *him. Messed up, huh?*

I take down my loosening bun and pull my hair up tighter, my eyes flicking back to the other headline on my phone. Because I'm going to Heather's candlelight vigil.

I need to talk to the reigning queen of Hillwood High one last time.

Chapter Twenty-Two

SUNDAY, NOVEMBER 7, 4:39 PM

Lea has been trying to message me ever since Monday. I have a string of unanswered texts from her, laying out what happened from Halloween up until today:

Monday, November 1st, 9:42 am

Iris, please call me when you get the chance

I'm sorry about our fight

Please text me back

Monday, November 1st, 11:12 am

Oh my God I just saw the news

They found Heather

They're saying she killed herself and that other students phoned her body in???

Iris

Iris I know you're seeing these messages

Wednesday, November 3rd, 9:47 am

You're not here again today, huh

You can't hide from this forever

I picked up your missing assignments from Eastwick and I'll get the rest later

Can I stop by and drop them off?

Sammy and Imani are kind of ignoring me

Did something happen between the three of you?

Thursday, November 4th, 4:11 pm

I'm just about to go through some more articles

Jim decided not to fire me, which is the only good thing that's happened this week

You want to join me? I could really use your help

And Sin misses you

IMG_0876.PNG

Friday, November 5th, 2:01 am

Hey can you at least let me know you're alive, please

Thanks

Saturday, November 6th, 2:55 pm

Holy shit??? The police arrested Nathan Deveraux???

> They're saying he killed Heather and made it look like a suicide

> There's a rumor going around about the police tracking his car through GPS or something

> Iris, come on. Please talk to me

Saturday, November 6th, 4:01 pm

> I don't know... something isn't right about all of this

> You know it, don't you? That's why you're not here.

> You're still trying to figure out the truth. Like always.

> Iris, please let me help

I'm definitely an asshole for not responding. But I just can't handle Lea right now. I can't handle the way she sees right to my core, can't handle how much I actually care about her, can't handle the thought of putting her in danger. Because someone has been watching me, someone who wants me scared, someone who might be dangerous. And even though Imani and Sammy should be safe after our public agency breakup at Joan's Diner, Lea isn't.

Which means it's better for her—better for everyone—if I continue to push her away.

Outside my passenger window, Hillwood blurs into grays and blues as Megan rumbles down Sugar Boulevard. I don't exactly know what you're supposed to wear to a vigil, but I'm wearing dark plaid pants and a wool jacket. Imani would know what proper vigil attire is.

We all know who you're really doing this for.

I swallow and fidget with the hem of my sleeve, focusing on the coarse wool fibers to ground myself. I've never been to a vigil, but I have been to a couple of funerals.

As soon as my sister disappeared last year, my mom insisted Stella was dead. Despite the claims on *How to Find a Missing Girl*, my mom was never physically abusive to me or my sister—but after Stella vanished, she became many other things. Absent. Sick. Grieving. She drank more than ever, she snapped at the cops when they asked her questions, and she scoffed at me when I tried to pry answers out of Stella's friends, but she also said she knew. She said she felt it.

And even if my mom never put her hands on me, I still haven't forgiven her for the fact that after her oldest daughter went missing—during the time other parents might have been barging into police stations and making phone calls and pleading on the national news—Diane Blackthorn paid for a black granite headstone at the Hillwood cemetery and buried an empty casket.

My aunt's eyes meet mine in the rearview mirror, and for a moment I think she's going to say something. But then she closes her mouth and pulls into the senior parking lot, and my throat closes up, too.

Heather's vigil is being held on the Hillwood High football field. It feels cruelly full-circle—the place where I first found out she was missing, now a place where others will mourn her death—and as Megan and I get out of the car, the cool, cloudless November evening settling around us like an empty promise, I can't help feeling that coming here was a mistake.

284

I want to cry.

I swallow, and follow my aunt to the Alfred J. Deveraux Stadium, and Coach Hannequart hands us each a translucent plastic cup and a candle at the entrance. I can't believe we're really doing this. I can't believe Heather is really gone.

"We should go find somewhere to stand," my aunt murmurs, and I nod and shake off the way I'm feeling so I can follow her through the dewy synthetic grass.

There are more people here tonight than I expected. It seems like half of Hillwood turned up for this; I see Lea's moms—mingling with the reporters from the *Herald*—and my AP Literature teacher and even Arden Blake, sliding a glinting flask back into the pocket of her wool letterman near the home bleachers. But everyone else melts away the second I lock eyes with Imani and Sammy in the crowd.

They're both dressed in perfect vigil clothes—black business-casual pants, dark jackets, minimal accessories—and Sammy's wearing earrings that I'm almost 100 percent sure are miniature lighters. I want to go over to them so badly. I miss the agency more than anything—I miss Sammy's ridiculous quips and Imani's dry sarcasm and the way the three of us work so well together—and I know I need to apologize. But I force myself to look away, to keep moving through the crowd, and the moment passes. I have to keep them safe. I have to stay away. And I have to focus on what I'm really here for: talking to Delphine Fontenot.

She has to be here somewhere, and I have a hunch she knows more than she's letting on. About the flash drives, about Nathan's car, about everything. I know I have to tread lightly, though, I think as I step around an old man in a wheelchair. Delphine already tried to destroy me once. She won't hesitate to do it again. Only this time, the casualties will be much more serious than just leaking my phone number.

"Miss Blackthorn?" a voice says behind me, snapping me out of my thoughts, and I inwardly wince as I turn and come face-to-face with my chemistry teacher. She's standing behind the man in the wheelchair, but her sharp eyes are no less hawk-like as they fix on mine.

"Hello, Ms. Eastwick," I say politely, fisting my hands in the pockets of my jacket. "I didn't know you would be here. At the... school."

To her credit, my chemistry teacher offers me a tight-lipped smile. "Every Hillwood teacher—past and present—wanted to come out in honor of Heather tonight," she says, gesturing to the man in front of her. He blinks at me, and I frown. Something about him is vaguely familiar, and it takes me a second to realize why. He has Eastwick's eyes.

"How kind," Megan says, sticking out her hand for my chemistry teacher to shake. "I'm Megan Sanchez, Iris's legal guardian."

"We've met," Eastwick says simply, shaking it, "though it's always nice to be reintroduced." Her gaze flicks to me. "Iris's sister was one of my best students."

I swallow. The underlying meaning of her words is clear: I'm no Stella.

It's fine. It doesn't matter. We're here for Heather—not even Eastwick would be callous enough to bring up my grades to Megan tonight.

The man in the wheelchair coughs, and my chemistry teacher immediately drops Megan's hand. "Are you feeling okay, Dad?" Her eyes flicker over the field, her mind clearly elsewhere. "Excuse us," she tells my aunt, and I glance at Megan as she turns around. "You know Ms. Eastwick?"

"Everyone in Hillwood knows each other, Iris," my aunt says, watching them leave. Her eyebrows crease slightly. "It's a small town."

Principal Phillips takes the stage—the same temporary one Hillwood High uses for their outdoor graduation ceremonies—and taps the microphone. Megan lights our candles, and while the sky dims around us, we're all subject to a sanitized speech about light and life and joie de vivre. No one mentions Nathan Deveraux. No one mentions Heather Nasato was found dead in a swamp on Halloween night with a pistol just a few feet away from her.

"I'm proud of you for wanting to come tonight, Iris," Megan whispers as Principal Phillips finishes speaking. "I'm proud of you for letting go."

I grit my teeth, trying to ignore the guilt weighing on my shoulders as I meet my aunt's warm brown eyes. If she really knew what was going on—how I haven't been sleeping, how I spend every waking moment thinking about how Heather died—she wouldn't be proud. She'd be disappointed instead.

But I can't dwell on that now. I'm trying to figure out the truth, and I haven't failed yet. Because Heather might not be alive, but I am. And as long as that's the case, I'm going to keep looking for her murderer.

Which is exactly why I'm here.

A hush descends over the crowd as Principal Phillips leaves, and then the Nasatos get up onstage. Hordes of cameras swivel in their direction, and I do my best to look sorrowful for the mayor of Hillwood and his wife without compromising the way I'm surreptitiously scanning the gathered parishioners. Joan, with her sons and her husband. Carrie. Claudia Garrett, Coach Hannequart, Arden walking angrily away from Mr. Cooper...

My mind snags. Mr. Cooper. Something about Mr. Cooper, something important, something I've been overlooking. His interview on Heather's podcast. His timing at the diner, back when Sammy was hacking into the flash drives. The way Arden talked about him on Halloween.

She called him Collin.

I'm halfway through the crowd before I'm even conscious of moving, every nerve in my body humming as I push against the mourners. I don't need to talk to Delphine Fontenot after all.

I need to talk to Arden instead.

I weave through the vigil-goers, fighting to keep Arden in my eyeline as I follow her. She's making her way to the edge of the football field, her face eerie in the glow of her solitary flame, and then she slips underneath the closed-off section of the bleachers.

She's heading toward the concession stand. Toward the bathroom.

But I won't let her slip away so easily this time.

I break into a run, the wet grass whipping against my combat boots as I duck under a GEAUX, FIGHTING GATORS! banner someone undoubtedly forgot to remove from the student section after the makeup Senior Night game, and then I'm stepping over the home bleachers and racing up the stairs. I slow only when I reach the bathroom door, stilled by the sound of muffled sobs, and for a second I think twice about interrogating Heather's other best friend.

But then I push open the door, and Arden hastily wipes her bloodshot crystal-blue eyes before meeting my hazel ones in the grimy mirror. "Oh. It's y-you."

Her heart-shaped face is flushed, and her long hair is wilder than ever. I can smell the alcohol on her breath, but I nod and take a small step toward her anyway. "Yeah. It's just me."

Arden turns to look at me, and my breath catches. The deep rings under her bloodshot eyes are gray and ghostly, and her makeup is smeared all the way into the hairline of her disheveled brown waves, but she still looks so much like my sister.

And suddenly I'm not here anymore.

The sweltering crowd. My too-tight black suit constricting my throat. Watching Arden tearfully stumble out of the gym in a glitzy blue dress that looks just like the one my sister was wearing on the night she disappeared. Sammy and Imani kneeling by me on the gymnasium floor, whispering it's going to be all right.

Something builds up behind my chest, a kind of pressure behind my throat, and I fight to keep my fingers from twitching. Things I can see: Arden Blake's pale, freckled face. Things I can smell: lemon cleaner and ammonia. Things I can touch: the wool of my black longcoat.

I have to focus on this moment.

"Why are you here?" Arden rasps, her voice hoarse. "We're not going to...talk. We're not...friends, Iris."

"No," I agree softly. "But you lied to me, Arden. And you're lying to yourself. That's why you're drinking, isn't it?" I brace myself, clench my fists, and twist my fingernails into my palms. If I'm wrong about this...

I dig my nails deeper. I'm not.

"You're dating Mr. Cooper," I tell Arden, and her entire face collapses.

"I...," she whispers, and then she inhales painfully slowly and vomits all over the dirty bathroom floor.

"Jesus," I say, automatically stepping back from the puddle between us. I almost ask her if she's okay, but then I think about the strawberry vodka she tried to share with me in front of Lucille's General Store. About the fake ID she showed the cashier. About her drunk driving at Delphine's Halloween party.

She hasn't been okay for a while.

I shake my head. Things start slotting into place, things I didn't pay enough attention to until now: Arden's outburst in Media Appreciation Club right after Heather went missing. Her tears at Joan's. How she insisted Nathan killed my ex-girlfriend, how she disappeared from the swamp before the police got there on Halloween.

"It's...f-funny," Arden slurs darkly, turning back to grip the edge of the sink. "I thought I was being so...careful. But you found out...anyway, didn't you? Iris Blackthorn, amateur detective. Always in people's...b-business. Always sticking her nose where it doesn't...b-belong." Her mouth twists unpleasantly. "Heather was...the same way."

"Did you kill her?" I ask, and I'm astonished at how level my voice sounds. "Did you kill her because she found out about you and Mr. Cooper and threatened to turn you in?"

I was so sure Arden believed Nathan killed Heather, that she thought she was telling the truth when we cornered her on Halloween night, but maybe I was wrong. Maybe I'm not as good at reading people as I thought I was. Maybe Arden Blake fooled me.

I take a step forward, the soles of my shoes squelching into blood-tinged vomit. "Is Delphine in on it? Is that why she was looking for the flash drives?"

"You're so...stupid," Arden says. "I was in...c-class when Heather went...m-missing, and so...was...Delphine. You know who w-wasn't, though? *The person who's actually...in jail...for her m-murder.*" Arden scoffs. "I'm no killer...Iris. But you sure are...a bitch."

I shake my head. "There's something you're not telling me," I insist, taking another step forward. Her speech pattern, her erratic breathing, her bloodied throw-up...Arden's clearly drunk out of her mind. But in this moment, she's also vulnerable.

I can get her help. But first, I need to know what she's hiding.

"What's making you spiral like this, Arden?" I ask. "What are you trying to block out?" Another step. "You know, don't you? You know what really happened to Heather. You know Nathan didn't kill her."

As soon as the words leave my lips, I wish I could take them back. I have no evidence. It's a wild assumption, and it shows just how desperate I am. But then I see Arden's reaction, the pure, undiluted fear in her eyes, and I forget how to breathe.

It's true.

291

"Arden," I whisper, but it's too late. She reaches into the right pocket of her letterman, her eyes unfocused, and takes out the flask I saw her drinking from earlier. How much alcohol has she had? How much does it take her to forget?

I move toward her, needing to take it from her before she touches it, but she drains it before I can. "Stay out of this, Iris," she says darkly, her voice suddenly crystal clear. "You don't know who you're messing with."

"Neither do you," I say softly, and her bloodshot eyes flick back to me a split second before she slumps to the concrete floor.

Something is wrong.

"Arden?" I say, closing the distance between us and sinking beside her. Hot, rank throw-up seeps into my pants, but that doesn't matter. I don't know if she's breathing. I don't know what's going on.

I shake her shoulder, hard, and her eyes flutter open. "I drank... too... m-much."

"No shit," I say shakily, reaching for her phone and holding the power button long enough to dial 911. "You're going to be okay, all right? I'm going to call an ambulance, and you'll—"

"No!" Arden says. She takes a slow, shuddering, painful breath. "I need to... I don't have a lot of t-time...."

The call connects. My pants and shoes are covered in vomit, and I stumble over the address of the Alfred J. Deveraux Stadium so many times that the operator tells me to take a breath and slow down, but I can't focus on two things at once.

"Listen," Arden rasps, drawing my attention away from the phone. "Collin... never... loved me. He said he did, but he... lied. Heather... tried... s-stopping me. Told me to date someone...

else. So I went out with... Kev... but I never meant to h-hurt...
Lea. Didn't want... to h-hurt... anyone."

"It's okay, Arden," I say consolingly. "That's okay. Keep talking. The ambulance will be here soon."

She doesn't respond for over a full minute, and panic shoots
through me until she manages to shake her head a fraction of an
inch. "It's too... late. They wanted to get r-rid... of me. But they're
already... watching... you. And if you... don't stop... Iris, they'll
get to you... n-next."

The hair on the back of my neck prickles, and I think of the
car that followed me. The threatening note. My ransacked room.
"Who?" I ask Arden, taking her by the shoulders. "Who's watching me?"

Arden closes her eyes. Her head lolls to one side, and her pulse
is alarmingly slow. I shake her again, but she's getting weaker.
"My... jacket..." she breathes, and I glance at her letterman help-
lessly as she reaches into her left pocket herself, her hands slick
with sweat, and pulls something out.

"Hello?" the 911 operator says. "Hello, are you still there?"

"Please," Arden whispers, wrapping her icy fingers around
mine, "take it. Take it all. I couldn't fix it, but maybe you..."

She slips under. I try to shake her, try to keep her awake, tears
blurring my vision, but her eyes don't open again. Her chest rises
and falls impossibly slowly, her breathing raspy and shallow. And
then she stops moving.

No. No, no, no. Not Arden. Not her, too.

I scream. I scream, and people must hear, because suddenly
the door is opening and someone is pushing people back, telling

people to get out, and I feel a twinge of something that could almost be gratitude if rage and sorrow weren't consuming me alive.

First Stella. Then Heather. And now this.

My head is pounding. The concrete around me blurs, and then someone is crouching in front of me, the faint smell of green tea shampoo cutting through lemon-scented cleaner and vomit.

"Iris," Lea says, and I have no idea how long she's been saying my name when I finally blink her into focus, her fierce face blazing back at me, "we need to get you out of here. Do you understand? Megan and de Rosa are on their way, but the media—" She stops, her eyebrows furrowed. "Where did you get that?"

I look down numbly at the glittery purple object in my hands, the one Arden handed me, and finally register it for the first time.

It's Heather's diary.

Chapter Twenty-Three

Megan is a statue of cold rage. Her knuckles are bone white from her death grip on the steering wheel, and her normally full lips are drawn into a pin-straight line. I look away from her, my chin in my hand, and resume staring out the window. Outside, the world passes in a rush of muted color. Inside, my dark plaid pants seep Arden's bloody vomit into the beige upholstery of the car.

Arden.

My stomach twists, and I fight against the bile threatening to rise in my own throat. Everything from the vigil blurs together just as much as the crooked magnolia trees we speed past—I remember the diary, and I remember the smell of Arden's vomit, but everything else is snippets of sirens and lights and my aunt's hard face, all sharp angles and barely concealed worry.

I saw a girl die today.

We pull into the driveway, and Megan kills the engine. I reach for the door handle, but a loud click stops me. I would be indignant if I weren't so goddamn tired. "Did you just use the child lock on me?"

"We need to talk," my aunt says in response. Her voice is tight, like she might shatter to pieces at any second. I don't blame her for wanting answers, but this isn't the time.

"We do," I say softly. "But I need to take a shower first, Megs. I need to change my clothes. I—" My voice catches in my throat. "Just...can we do this later? Please?"

There's a beat as Megan considers me. I know how I must look—sunken eyes, yellowed skin, crusted vomit drying into my combat boots—and I fight to meet her gaze. I'm just so tired. I've never been more exhausted in my life.

Eventually, she nods. "Fine. Later."

The car unlocks, and I practically trip my way through the front door and into the bathroom.

The shower doesn't help. Every time I close my eyes, I see Arden's face. I see Stella's. I see myself frozen, letting Heather's best friend slump to the floor, letting my sister leave, letting myself be useless.

It's not until I'm toweling off my hair that I finally feel brave enough to look at my phone. I want to know what the police said.

I want to know what the rest of Hillwood thinks of this—another teenage girl, gone.

But the headline I see when I check the *Herald*'s Twitter feed doesn't tell me either of those things. "Nathan Deveraux Released on Bail—Awaiting Trial," it reads instead.

And when I turn and finally empty the contents of my own stomach into the toilet behind me, it almost feels like relief.

It's been nearly a week since Heather's vigil, and they're already planning Arden's. It seems there's no rest for the weary. Not in Hillwood, at least.

I'm not going. I'm not doing anything, in fact, except for what I should have done a long time ago—researching my college choices. I don't have a lot of options, especially since I'm closer to the bottom ten percent of the senior class than the top of it, but I have to figure out something. Because I can't be a private investigator, and I can't solicit my friends for help now that I don't have any.

Megan is concerned about me. There was a story on the news the other day about Arden, but I turned it off right after Claudia Garrett said the words *alcohol poisoning* with a sad expression on her bottle-blonde face. My aunt should be happy, though. I'm finally doing what she wanted all along: I'm not looking into Heather's case.

My fingers fly over my keyboard, looking up statistics for another university on my tentative list. I have to keep busy. If I'm not busy, I think too much. Bad thoughts. Thoughts about how if I had done something differently, Arden might still be alive. Heather might still be alive. My sister might still be... here.

I don't know how much time passes—A few minutes? Hours?—but eventually, Megan knocks on my door. "Can I come in?"

I don't answer. The door creaks open on its own, and Megan's expression tightens as she finds me on my unmade bed, sitting in a maelstrom of clothes, empty water bottles, and baby succulents. C. Auguste Dupin and a few of my other plants have been browning lately, and I've taken it upon myself to fix them. They're currently recovering from leaf surgery on my wrinkled bedspread, but that also means there's soil all over the place I'm supposed to sleep. Not that I've been doing much of that anyway.

"You have a visitor," Megan says flatly, eyeing my trashed room with distaste.

I snap my computer shut and scramble to sit up. "What?" I say, just as Megan steps to the side and Lea appears in the entryway.

I gape at her. She looks exactly like she did at Heather's vigil— short snow-white hair, black knit sweater, blazing expression— but the moments between then and now are so disconnected, for a moment I think I'm seeing a ghost.

"Hey," Lea says softly. Decidedly not a ghost, then.

There are so many things I want to say to her. So many words, perched on the tip of my tongue and waiting to be unfurled. *I'm sorry. I'm happy you're here. Arden Blake is dead.*

Instead, I throw my bedsheet over the cesspool I was just sitting in, desperately scanning my room for anything that'll make Lea walk right back out of it. "Hey," I say back, my ragged voice operating on autopilot, and Megan takes one look between the two of us and closes my door.

Lea doesn't look at me. Her eyes travel over the empty space where my general store calendar used to be, my collection of surviving plants, and my torn-open box of latex gloves. She trails a hand over my cluttered desk, filling every pore of my room until the entire place pulses with the life of her. *Lea.* My heart beats softly. *Lea is here.*

I clear my throat, and her eyes meet mine. I want to ask her why she came, but she beats me to speaking. "How are you?"

Everything flashes through my mind: sink. Vomit. Diary. Arden, gurgling, telling me she failed. *If you... don't stop... Iris, they'll get to you... n-next.*

"Managing," I say out loud, forcing myself to snap out of it. To feign nonchalance, to swallow against the acrid taste building in the back of my throat. To shrug. "It wasn't my first dead body."

It's true. But that doesn't make it better.

"Iris," Lea says, and her tone is hard. "I'm here because I care about you, and because you can't scare me away. But you've been ignoring all my texts. You completely ditched me at the vigil. And now you're acting like you're totally fine, even though anyone with half a brain cell can put together why you're not."

Tell her the truth. Tell her you're glad she came.

I shake my head. "I just...," I start, but my voice catches before I can get out the rest of the words. Lea sinks down on the bed next to me.

"It's not your fault, Iris. She was drinking. A lot."

"I didn't think it was that bad," I whisper, thinking back to the bathroom. Arden's gaunt face. Her wrist, beating sluggishly against mine. "I didn't…"

"It's okay," Lea says. "It's all right."

And it's not. Nothing about this is okay, except for Lea. Lea, next to me. Lea, who came back.

"I'm sorry I didn't answer your texts," I tell her softly. "I'm sorry about our fight. I'm sorry I keep pushing you away. But I can't do it anymore, El." I exhale shakily. "I'm done investigating."

Lea almost smiles. "You're never done investigating," she says, and something twists in my stomach.

"I want to be," I say softly, meeting my best friend's gaze. "It's like you said on Halloween—I'm not a real detective." Lea opens her mouth, but I hold a hand up to stop her. "And you're right." I take a deep breath, steadying myself. I want to be vulnerable. I don't want to keep everything bottled inside of me forever, and I don't want to lose Lea again. She's my best friend, and I know her through and through. The least I can do is be honest.

"I haven't told anyone else this—but the night I pushed you away, someone broke into my house," I tell Lea softly. "They left a note telling me to watch out, and I…panicked. I never meant to hurt you, but…this investigation is getting dangerous. Nathan was arrested, but I think the police made a mistake with him. Delphine is dealing drugs. Arden was romantically involved with Mr. Cooper. I can't shake the feeling that there's something else going on, and I'm getting too close to it. *We're* getting too close to it. That's why I'm finished. It'll be better if I stay out of this. It's what I should have done from the beginning."

Even as I say the words, though, I don't wholly believe them.

300

The truth is, Lea is right. If I were done, I would turn the drives in to the police. If I were done, I'd report my room being rifled through. If I were done, I would let the so-called professionals finish tying up the loose threads in Heather's case.

"Hey," Lea says, snapping me out of my thoughts. "I hate to break it to you, Iris, but if someone really broke into your house, I don't think there's any way you *can* stay out of this." She shakes her head. "Besides, Heather left the flash drives for you. Arden wanted you to have the diary. *How to Find a Missing Girl* is about your sister. You're entwined in this case in more ways than one, and I don't think you can untangle yourself from it so easily. If anyone has a right to find out what really happened—and you *will* find out what really happened, because you're smart and talented—it's you." Her eyes blaze. "But I'm not going to let you do it alone."

I blink at her. It's the only thing I can do, because I don't have anything to say. Because she's Lea. Because she's still here.

"So stop lying to yourself," she finishes, standing up to retrieve the diary from my overly cluttered desk. "You're going to keep looking into what happened to Heather, and you're not going to stop until you find the truth. But from now on, we're doing this together, all right? The two of us. You and me."

I nod. "You and me," I repeat softly, and then I run a hand over the sequined cover and open my dead ex-girlfriend's diary.

Chapter Twenty-Four

My breath catches in my throat as I stare at the title page. I haven't seen anything besides the words FOR IRIS written in Heather's handwriting since the police showed me the Polaroid of the two of us, but her loopy script still manages to sear through my heart: *Property of Heather Rose Nasato. If found, please email howtofindamissinggirlpodcast@gmail.com.*

"That email," Lea says softly as I turn the page to a list inked in bubble calligraphy. *Research podcasters. Ask Mr. Cooper about microphones. Look into royalty-free music.* "Do you think…?"

Our eyes meet, and I swallow. This isn't just Heather's diary.

It's where she compiled all her notes for *How to Find a Missing Girl.*

More pages. Heather jotting down lines of script for her podcast trailer. Scribbling notes to herself in the margins: *Interview cheerleaders. Follow up with Noémie Charmant. Check out the Chevalier Trailer Park.* Her writing out how much time she has to study, practice cheer, and line up interviews in order to meet her self-imposed *every first Monday of the month!* deadline. Asides about audio-editing software and police procedures and Louisiana state laws, and an entire page that's just filled with the words *FIND OUT WHAT HAPPENED TO STELLA BLACKTHORN* in giant letters. Taped-in photographs of text exchanges with Heather and the people on her podcast. And then, eventually, a diary entry.

My mouth goes dry.

September 18

> *Homecoming was tonight, and it was fucking awful.*
>
> *I thought Arden was dating Kevin Wu. She was being all coy about it when we went dress shopping together earlier this month, but she's not. She's dating a goddamn <u>teacher</u>.*
>
> *I saw them together in the hallway. I think I have to confront Arden about it.... Maybe I'll even find a way to get <u>him</u> fired. I don't have enough evidence yet, though. So I'm going to try and get some.*

"Holy shit," Lea says. "Are you seeing this?"

Blood. Vomit. Vodka. Arden's voice: *Collin... never... loved me. He said he did, but he... lied. Heather... tried... s-stopping me. Told me to date someone... else.*

I force myself to nod. "Yeah," I say, swallowing. "I'm seeing this."

Lea flips the page, and I clench my teeth. Another one.

October 1

I don't think I'm making as much progress as I'd like.

As it turns out, gathering evidence is hard. I think I'd have to find a way to get into Arden's messages in order to even have a shot at something concrete, but that also means stealing her phone, and I don't know how to do that. I'm just... argh, I'm so frustrated. I feel like Iris would know what to do, but the last thing I want is to drag more people into this. And I think my boyfriend is cheating on me, which is just the cherry on top of the shitshow my life's become in the past few weeks.

I'm going to ask the Blackthorn Agency to investigate him at some point. Right now, though, I'm still focused on Arden. I'm giving myself one more week to keep looking for something concrete, and then I'm going to talk to her. If she can break things off herself, things would be easier. But then again, I want to make him pay....

Lea flips the page again, revealing one more diary entry. The last one, from the looks of it.

October 14

I'm worried something bad is going to happen to me.

I finally pushed too hard. I got too obsessed with looking for evidence to protect Arden, and then I uploaded that podcast episode. It was rash and stupid. But it doesn't matter. I still have everything I found. And now, so do the USBs.

"Iris?" Lea says again. But I can barely hear her, barely register her voice.

Heather wrote about the flash drives one day before she went missing. Delphine and Arden were the last two people to see Heather alive. Arden gave me Heather's diary right before she died.

"This is how Delphine found out about the drives," I say, glancing up at Lea. "She and Arden must have taken the diary from Heather when they all went out to lunch right before Heaths went missing, and then Delphine broke into her house—twice—to try and destroy them."

Lea frowns. "But why would she care? If Heather was trying to expose Arden's relationship, it doesn't make sense for Delphine to be involved."

"It does if Heather found out she was dealing," I tell her,

thinking back to the sixth podcast episode. *Getting involved with people like Jackson Criswell—in more ways than one—is never a good idea.* "If Delphine thought Heather had evidence against her on the flash drives, too—evidence that risked her reputation— she would have risked burglary to stop it from getting out."

Still, that doesn't explain everything. And there's something else, something at the edge of my memory. Something taunting me. Something I should know, something I can't quite remember.

"Wait," Lea says, pointing to something at the bottom of the final diary entry. "Iris, look at this."

My brows furrow as I follow one of her six fingers. Heather's handwriting: *They're keeping evidence.* And below it, a string of cramped numbers that's barely legible.

"See this?" Lea asks, pointing to a tiny scribble to the right of one of the strings. "These are prime marks. And this," she adds, pointing to another squiggle, "looks like an *N*. And maybe a *W*, too."

She glances up at me, and sparks fire in the cylinders of my brain.

"Coordinates," Lea and I say at the same time.

"Decipher this," I tell Lea, sliding the notebook toward her. I open my laptop back up, and Lea rattles off a string of numbers. I type them in, click the little magnifying glass at the corner of my search bar, and forget how to breathe. *They're keeping evidence.*

"Did you get something?" Lea asks. I turn my laptop to her, and she frowns. There's no mistaking it: Even with the smudged coordinates, there are only a few locations in Hillwood worth seeing, and even fewer that match the scrawled numbers in Heather's journal perfectly. Only one, in fact.

I watch Lea as she takes it in, her eyes traveling over the named location above my dropped map pin.

"Oh my god," she whispers, glancing up at me.

The coordinates in Heather's journal lead to Deveraux Industries.

Chapter Twenty-Five

"We have to go," I say, standing up so fast that my vision spots over. "We have to go right now."

Lea glances out of my window to the street, where it's started to rain, and bites her bottom lip. "Iris, I don't know if that's a good idea. I heard a flash-flood warning on the drive over, and we don't even know what we're looking for."

"I still want to check it out," I say, my voice radiating certainty. "Heather dug up a lot of secrets before she disappeared. She knew about Arden and Collin Cooper. She had dirt on Delphine. But if she knew something about the Deveraux...if she found out something that would bring them down..." I meet Lea's eyes firmly. "We need to figure out how all the pieces fall into place. How everything connects. And if we retrace Heather's footsteps, I'm sure we can find out what she knew."

Lea nods. "I think so, too," she says softly. "Those articles we spent so long poring over...the only throughline was rumors about the Deveraux. Human-interest stories about a disabled worker who was illegally laid off after Hurricane Dexter, a letter to the editor about wrongfully cut wages...I wonder if there was some truth to them. I wonder if Heather knew. But driving out in this storm..."

Rain taps against my window, and my gaze drifts to the discarded kitten calendar in my trash can. To the sea of red Xs, taunting me still.

I think about Stella. I think about justice. I think about how I've failed before, how I promised myself on the night Heather went missing that I wouldn't fail again.

"We don't have a choice," I tell Lea quietly. "I have less than eight hours until I legally turn eighteen. This is our last lead. Our final chance to find out what Heather knew...what she died for." My eyes seek hers, imploring. "Help me take it."

There's a beat as Lea assesses me, and then she blows out a breath. "Okay," she relents, shooting one last apprehensive look outside my window. "But only because amateur teenage journalists don't let amateur teenage detectives solve murders alone."

I nod and shove Heather's journal into my messenger bag. "Okay. Let's go."

The light drizzle Lea and I observed from my bedroom turns into a torrential downpour by the time we inch out of my driveway. My knuckles are pale and bloodless from where I clench my fists on the tops of my knees, and I try to still my breathing as Lea hunches forward, her windshield wipers working furiously against the rain. *This is our last chance*, I think to myself as the car crawls along. *Suck it up.*

We drive in silence for a while, Lea focused on navigation and me lost in my thoughts. Wispy clouds envelop us as we snake through Sugar Boulevard and stop at the intersection in front of Lucille's General Store; through the dense fog ahead of us, the red stoplights blur into a hazy oblivion.

Lea glances over at me. "Do you want to talk about it?"

I let out a long breath. "I don't know, El. What can I even say? That in the past few weeks, I've watched a girl die right in front of me, found the decomposing body of my ex-girlfriend in a swamp, and gotten more death threats than mail from colleges? That the police are looking for any excuse to throw me in jail, I managed to fuck up badly enough to lose two of my closest friends at the same time, and worst of all, I feel like a failure?" I blink, trying to shove down the lump in my throat that's forming against my best intentions. "Ever since Stella's case went cold because of me, I've been waiting for something like this. To avenge her. To prove to myself I have what it takes to not mess up again. But the truth is, I don't. I don't, El, and now it's too late."

Lea brushes her snow-white bangs out of her eyes. "It's not too late. Hey, look at me." I turn to her, and her expression softens. "You're doing the best you can, Iris. And no matter what happens with this case, I'm proud of you for that. I'm always going to be proud of you for that."

I swallow. "It's just... hard. You know?"

"Yeah," Lea says softly, flicking her turn signal on. "I know."

The conversation stills to a gentle thrum, but I keep studying Lea. She's here. She's taking this seriously. She didn't have to come back.

Lea frowns. "What?"

I blink, realizing I said the last part out loud. "You didn't have to come back," I repeat softly. "After our fight, when I stopped going to help you look through the articles." I frown. "I honestly didn't think you would."

"Then you don't know me very well," Lea says simply. "You deserved an apology, Iris. It wasn't right of me to expect more than you're willing to give, and I get that you need space and time." The light turns green, and the paved road narrows as we leave Sugar Boulevard and its collection of mom-and-pop shops behind. "And it wasn't right of me to give up on the investigation because of my own personal feelings. To give up on you."

I bite my lip, hating myself for what I'm about to ask. For refusing to overlook Lea and her determination, Lea and her exposés. But because I'm me, I ask anyway. "So you didn't come back just for your article? Because you got reinstated at the *Herald* and wanted content for your story?"

"No," Lea says quietly. Rain pounds around us, and her

windshield wipers pound back to stop it. She glances over at me. "I actually came back for you."

"Lea," I whisper, and something in me unravels. Feelings that flutter against my ribs like wings. Like butterflies.

She shakes her head. "I know—you don't have to say anything, and you don't have to like me the way I like you. But even if you don't reciprocate my feelings, Iris, I'm still your friend. I'm not going away. And I'm not going to betray you."

Reciprocate my feelings. The way I like you. I'm not going to betray you.

I did so much for you, Butterfly.

"I know," I tell my former ex-best-friend, swallowing past the lump in my throat. "I listened to Heather's last podcast episode. You weren't the one who turned me in to de Rosa."

Lea nods.

"Why didn't you tell me? You let me think it was you."

"You hadn't listened to it yet, and I didn't want you to find out from me." Lea shakes her head. "And honestly, Iris, I didn't think you'd believe me, either. It had to be from her. All great journalists know the sources you're most likely to believe are the ones you interrogate yourself."

I smile softly. "All great detectives know that, too."

Lea turns again, and suddenly we're approaching Le Pont de Fer Bridge. "Hey," she murmurs, glancing over at me for a split second. "You're okay. We're okay, Iris."

But something doesn't feel right.

On impulse, I lean forward and peer into the mist. The hairs on the back of my neck rise, and I frown. I can barely see ahead of us, but the distant twin glow is instantly recognizable even through the fog. Headlights.

"Lea," I say warningly, my tone sharper than usual. "There's a car coming straight toward us."

"I see it. They're going too fast, but they're not going to hit us. We're going to be fine."

I squint at the headlights in the fog. "Are you sure? Because it kind of looks like they're—"

Time slows down. I can feel the sickening crunch even though it hasn't happened yet, but I can't do anything except feel the swirl of tamped-down memories come undone around me.

Stella.

The diner.

Detective de Rosa: "We're doing our best."

She was my sister.

Megan's call: *They found your mom's car, Iris. At the bottom of the Bayou Lafourche.*

The sound bites from the December evening news after the machines pulled up her car dripping with brackish water: *The crash claimed the life of forty-two-year-old Diane Blackthorn, a lifelong resident of Hillwood, Louisiana.*

Time speeds up as the car in front of us races forward, headlights too bright and too close. Lea whips the wheel sideways, and then metal crumples around us, and I float for a single blissful second before my temple slams against the passenger window and blood fills my ears.

I draw in a ragged gasp. I'm breathing. I'm still conscious. I survived.

Next to me, Lea says something, but I lose the words. Everything sounds muted, as if we're underwater. And then I follow Lea's panicked gaze, my sluggish eyes drifting in and out of focus, and frown at the murky landscape outside my cracked window. We *are* underwater.

I laugh.

I can see what Lea is so worried about now—my window is spiderwebbed, the cracks in the glass starting to let the river water through. I want to tell her that's a good thing, that at least this way the water pressure will equalize and we'll be able to get out, but my mouth won't move. My tongue feels like rubber. I laugh again.

No. Laughing is bad. I need to focus.

I turn my attention to the footwell. I need to find…something. Something important. My messenger bag. The one with Heather's journal, yes, and the bag of USBs. Miraculously, I manage to grab the drives and secure them in my coat—thank God there's a plastic bag protecting them—and I grab the diary a few dizzying moments after. Something falls out from the pages as I lift it, and my heart drops as I scan the heptad of unintelligible papers. Unreadable, except for the only words I recognize on the top of every page. *RECOVERY KEY.*

The glass shatters.

The river rushes up, filling the car entirely before I even have time to suck in a breath. Heather's diary turns to mush in my hands, and so do the recovery keys.

No.

I open my eyes in the churning water. Lea floats next to me, her white hair forming an angelic halo around her head, her own eyes wide as she gestures for me to do...something. The water buffets her sweater sleeves with the motion, distorts her until she looks like a shadow of a girl. I wish I knew what she wanted me to do. I wish I could think clearly. But I can't, because my head is splitting. Because my limbs don't feel like they're attached to my body, and because my lungs are already starting to burn for want of air.

In the precious few seconds I have left, I think about my mom. About how she was still alive when she drove off this bridge... about how it was the water that did her in. I've always wondered if she was scared. Whether it was peaceful. How it felt, to drown in this very river.

And now I know.

My air runs out. I breathe in, involuntarily, my brain carrying out a function designed to keep me alive that will kill me instead. Fire burns in my lungs. I am going to die here.

It's the last thing I manage to think before I drop into nothing.

"IRIS!" Lea screams, shaking me, and I'm stunned by the raw emotion in her voice. I can hear now, can feel the sky break around us. "Iris, stay with me. IS ANYONE OUT THERE? CALL 911!"

I lurch forward and gag, a forceful wave of nausea sweeping through me as I cough up water onto the sludgy bank of the

Bayou Lafourche. I'm soaked and shivering, my clothes plastered to my body like a second skin, but I'm still alive. I didn't drown.

I inhale raggedly. Dark, blurry shapes swim at the edge of my vision and blur into the glass embedded in my fingers. There is so much pain in my head.

With all the strength I can muster, I lift my face in the rain and squint against the downpour. I can focus on only a few things at a time:

Far above us, on the bridge, something distant and flickering.

Lea, screaming beside me. My vision, swimming and darkening like I'm still underwater.

Are those people?

The pain swells, threatening to swallow me whole. Static and choking and fog. Water droplets sliding down the bridge of my nose. Headlights. Silhouettes. Everything woozy, light and dark at the same time.

And then darkness again.

Chapter Twenty-Six

Megan is glaring at me in the glow of the bright fluorescents. I can't tell what's more piercing—her gaze or the harsh white lights above me. My head is throbbing. I try to sit up, but the motion makes me wince and I abandon the effort almost immediately.

"You're up," my aunt says flatly. She's wearing her nursing home scrubs, though a beige overcoat is draped over the back of the chair she's sitting in, and her voice has an edge to it that makes me squirm. She sounds exhausted. Concerned. Angry. Her expression sharpens, and panic rises in the back of my throat as the night comes back to me in fragments: reading Heather's diary, finding the recovery keys, losing them in the river. The crash.

My voice is hoarse. "How long was I out?"

"Over three hours. They brought you here in an ambulance—thought it would be a good idea to let you sleep." Megan blinks, and I notice her own eyes are red-rimmed and bleary, her makeup is smudged on her lower eyelids, and there are twin lines of runny mascara on her neck that she only half-succeeded in wiping away. "It's 8:37 PM."

Which means I have a little over four hours to get to Deveraux Industries with Lea before I turn eighteen and legally have to stop looking into Heather's case for good.

Lea.

I bolt upright, and this time the bright room tilts sideways. My vision explodes with stars, and Megan shoots to her feet. "Iris! You have to take it easy."

I nod. And when the dizziness passes and Megan seems convinced I'm not going to immediately pass out again, I assess my surroundings for the first time.

I'm in a small room in Hillwood Regional Hospital. The walls and floors are both a sickly shade of white, and there's a smiley-face balloon tied to the post of my bedside table. On top of that, Megan's keys sit next to my phone, my pocketknife, and the bag of flash drives.

My phone.

I reach for it out of habit, suddenly equally grateful that I forgot to take it with me when I left the house and that Megan thought to bring it, but then I stop. Lea's is at the bottom of the Bayou Lafourche. The only way I'll be able to talk to her is if I go to her hospital room.

"She's not here," my aunt says, reading my mind. Nothing

escapes her sharp stare. "Her moms took her back home a while ago. She managed to get the two of you out of the river, and some people passing by saw the accident and pulled over to call for help." Megan shakes her head, some of the tightness in her jaw softening. "You were both incredibly lucky."

Guilt floods me, and I nod again.

The door to my room opens, and the tension between Megs and me washes over the entering doctor immediately. His brow furrows as he assesses us—Megan's pitch-black, heat-straightened hair and my limp brown strands. Her full lashes and brown skin and my watery eyes and paper-white face. He glances down at his chart again, and I know he's hesitating on our last names.

"Ms.…Sanchez?" the doctor asks skeptically, addressing Megan. "You are…?"

"Iris's legal guardian, yes," my aunt says, clenching her teeth. She looks like if someone asks her that question one more time, she's going to explode.

"Ah," the doctor says, finally turning to look at me. "Well, you were in quite a spill, young lady. How are you feeling?"

I set my jaw and cross my freckled arms. "Fine."

As it turns out, I am not fine. After a few minutes of examination, the doctor concludes I have a concussion. He makes a few notes and purses his lips. "We'll want to keep you overnight to monitor your vitals. Considering everything you've gone through today, it seems only fair we do all we can to alleviate your pain."

He gives me what I'm pretty sure is supposed to be a sympathetic smile, but it comes out as more of a grimace. Keep me overnight? No. I legally turn eighteen at midnight. If I stay here,

I won't be able to bring justice to another missing girl. I'll fail again.

"What if I want to leave?"

The doctor turns back to me with a quizzical expression, and pure panic fills my veins. This is it: I need to make my case. I need to convince him to let me go.

But when he raises an eyebrow, my mouth won't let me say the words.

"Legally, that decision lies with your guardian while you're still a minor."

I glance at Megan, his unspoken chastisement hanging in the air between us: A few extra hours won't hurt you.

Except they will.

My aunt presses her lips together, and the doctor nods. The door closes behind him as he leaves, and my shoulders slump. I'm staying. It's too late. I ruined it. Fighting the tears threatening to pool in my throat, I turn away from my aunt as a disappointed sigh hisses its way out of her mouth. And I'm preparing myself for it. I know what she's going to say, and I'm ready.

"Iris," Megan says, "when are you finally going to let this detective act go?"

But that doesn't keep it from stinging.

"It's not an act, Megs," I tell her. "This is my life." My voice hardens, and I force myself to meet her gaze. Set my jaw. "This is what I'm *good* at."

"Good at?" Megan repeats. "Look at you, Iris. You're in the hospital. You have a concussion, and Lea—"

"She knew what she was getting into."

There's a beat of silence. My words hang between us, and an unreadable expression settles onto Megan's face. "Do you really believe that?" she asks, her voice dangerously soft. "Do you really think endangering people—endangering yourself—is okay if it makes you feel like you're doing something with your life?"

I swallow. My mouth is paper-dry, and underneath the thin sheet of my hospital bedding, my hands are trembling. I don't want to do this. But every second I argue with Megan is one less second I have to figure out the truth. To put all the pieces together. And if I want the time I desperately need, I need to get my aunt to leave.

"Does it matter what I believe?" I ask Megan quietly, making my voice as flat and emotionless as possible. The vapid smile of the bobbing yellow balloon in front of me. The smell of over-bleached sheets. The cool metal of Stella's necklace against my skin. "It never has before."

My aunt's voice gets even softer. "Iris, that's not fair."

"It isn't? Because I think it's completely fair, Megan." I dig my nails into the plastic mattress cover of my hospital bed. "You want us to have The Conversation again. You want to tell me that I can't be a detective, that I shouldn't be trying to figure out what happened to Heather, a girl I once loved who's now *dead*, and just go get a job at the diner instead. That's what you want, right?" I laugh flatly. "To tell me I should stay away from the house all day like you do. That I should be scared off by police charges and my record and just let the police—*the police*—handle Heather's case." My voice rises. "Just like they handled my sister's, right?"

"Iris," Megan says again. The word is sharp—it's meant to be cutting—but my knife goes deeper.

"No. *No*. You want me to stop investigating, but she disappeared without a trace and we never talk about her. We never talk about Stella."

Megan's face crumples. "I didn't think you wanted to. You're always so closed off, Iris. You make it so hard for people to get through to you."

I close my eyes against the pain of the words I'm about to say next. "Well, you know what, Megs? Maybe it would be easier to get through to me if you talked to me half as much as the people you're paid to take care of, but you don't. And that's okay, because I know you never wanted kids. I know I'm nothing but a burden to you. But you don't actually care about me, so *stop fucking pretending to be my mom*."

It's the final nail in the coffin—Megan inhales, but there's no indication of the true impact of my words until I open my eyes and notice hers are glittering with tears.

Instantly, the overwhelming urge to apologize takes me over—to hug her, to tell her I didn't mean it, to make her pain go away. But I can't.

So I don't. For Heather, for Stella, for Arden, I stay silent and stony-faced until Megan finally blinks away the silent tears tracking down her cheeks and walks out of the door.

Something in my chest cracks as the room empties, but I shove the feeling away. As much as it hurts, now I'm free to focus on what matters most: trying to solve this case. Because even though the police think Nathan staged Heather's suicide, and that Arden drank herself to death, I think the girls are connected. I think their *deaths* are connected.

Now, I just have to figure out how.

Mentally, I go over my notes. The evidence the agency collected, the confession I got from Arden Blake. Mr. Cooper on Heather's podcast. Stella's disappearance. The threatening messages, the warnings from my classmates. Delphine and Jackson Criswell at her Halloween party. YOU'RE NEVER GOING TO FIND HER. The Deveraux at the center of everything, controlling this town from the inside out.

I'm so close—I can feel it. I have bread crumbs, scattered bits of evidence, individual pieces I need to find a way to link together.

But I'm also running out of time.

Silently, I swing myself over my cot and start lacing up my combat boots. Megan's given me some space, but there's no telling for how long. I need to change locations. Be stealthy. Get out.

I straighten up, wasting no time in taking the overcoat my aunt left behind. I pick up my pocketknife. I grab my phone.

And then my eyes land on the bag of flash drives. The one clue that eludes me—the one thing I still haven't cracked. The objects whoever tried to kill Lea and me today thought were worth dying for.

I need to open the damn USBs.

My mind races as I snatch the bag off the nightstand. I thought if Sammy couldn't crack them, if the recovery keys were gone, then no one could. But Heather left them for me. And even if the two of us didn't ultimately pan out, at least I can say this for my ex-girlfriend: She always believed in me.

That decides it. I slip my phone and my pocketknife into the front pocket of my aunt's coat and fix my hair, pulling it back into an even tighter bun at the nape of my neck. Because Lea was right: Iris Blackthorn isn't fucking done investigating.

I pull open the door and step out into the hallway.

I don't know how long I have before my aunt comes back to my hospital room and realizes that I'm not in it, so I try to walk with as much purpose as possible. There's no way I could evade detection by the dozens of harried night-shift nurses who pass me in the halls if I were still visibly wearing my hospital gown, but no one even spares me a second glance in Megan's large beige overcoat. As long as I don't run into my doctor, I'm exactly what the sticker on the front pocket of my borrowed outwear says: a visitor.

I swallow a grin as I turn down another corridor, past an out-of-order vending machine and a man holding a GET WELL SOON, DICKHEAD! balloon. It seems like I've managed to learn a thing or two from Imani's knack for disguises after all.

Through a set of double doors. Farther away from the wing I was just in, farther away from my aunt, until I reach the front reception desk.

By some miracle, it's empty.

I slide into the swivel chair in front of the missing receptionist's computer and set the bag of flash drives next to me, minimizing various hospital records windows in the process. I may be a criminal, but at least I respect patient confidentiality.

My vision swims, and my knees buckle. If I weren't sitting down, I would've collapsed.

I need to hurry.

Okay. I scan the monitor base hungrily, searching for the place to plug in a USB stick—how does Sammy do this so quickly?—and finally locate the port. I open Heather's plastic bag, and then I stare at the seven flash drives. At the scrawled words on the front of the plastic. FOR IRIS.

For a second, I let myself think about Heather and how methodical she was. About how much she cared about her podcast. About the real reason I now think she might have started it...that she was trying to get *my* attention, because she felt guilty about sabotaging our relationship and my sister's investigation by turning me in to de Rosa. That she thought publicly digging into Stella's life might get me back into hers.

And then I pick up the first USB stick, the drive studded with pink rhinestones, and turn it over in my palm. Number one.

I hold my breath and stick it into the monitor. A pop-up window appears, and the cursor blinks patiently.

I take a deep breath. I think about all the passwords Sammy tried that failed: podcast, secret, Hillwood, hey-o, pages and pages of countless words in hundreds of different combinations. I think of Delphine Fontenot rifling through Heather's room. Her, on the phone: *I know her better than anyone.*

The pain swells again, and I close my eyes against it. There are more images playing on the backs of my eyelids, snippets of words blurring together:

Look, kid—

need to pull it together

—never be a real detective

This case deserves to be handled responsibly, and it deserves to be solved.

My eyes snap open. The cursor keeps blinking, but I feel strangely calm. Because mixed in with all the memories, one stands out to me in particular. Something I can't believe I didn't think of earlier.

The final clue she chose to leave me.

<3 u butterfly, I type.

My pulse stutters as the pop-up mulls my response over. And then the drive loads, and every nerve in my body ignites.

Holy shit. I fucking did it.

There are only two files in the drive. I load the one with a .MOV ending, and a soft gasp escapes my lips as Heather's face fills the screen.

Tears fill the back of my throat.

"Hello," my ex-girlfriend says softly, and something in me wrenches apart. Because this is the Heather I knew—shiny pony-tail cascading past her shoulders, perfect matte makeup, a determined expression that could level the whole parish—and she's so alive in this video, I feel like if I reach out for her my fingers will meet skin.

My hand drifts to the computer, but it's cold under my touch.

"If you're watching this, that means I'm dead." Heather swallows, and I swallow with her. "But don't misconstrue me—this is not a suicide note." She lets out a quiet, shaky laugh. "No. If you're watching this, and I hope you are, Iris, then that means I was murdered." Heather Nasato stares straight into the camera, and my breath catches in my throat. "And this is why."

Chapter Twenty-Seven

Heather takes a breath. And even now, even here after everything, she still manages to steal mine from my lungs. She looks hauntingly beautiful, but she's clearly not okay.

"Mr. Cooper is Nathan's half brother," Heather whispers, twisting her manicured hands together, and the entire world slots into place. "I'm not supposed to know. It's a huge secret, but Edward Deveraux really did have an affair." She laughs softly. Darkly. "I only found out because I wanted to start the podcast back up again. I felt bad about how I left things, and I thought I could do better. Investigate harder. Pursue the truth." She blinks. Swallows. "I didn't...I didn't think anything bad could happen, you know? I mean, I'm the mayor's daughter. I'm friends with a Fontenot. I'm dating a Deveraux. But once I started poking around again, I realized that none of that matters, because this town is hiding something much more sinister."

My ex-girlfriend inhales, her lower lip trembling. "And so are the Deveraux. Because I don't think Mr. Cooper is just their dirty little secret. I think...I think he was dating Stella. Last year, before she disappeared. And I think he killed her, Iris." She blinks, and tears spill from under her dark lashes. "I think he killed her, too."

No. No, no, no. Heather is wrong. Stella would never date a teacher. She's not like Arden—she watches *Scooby-Doo* and listens to the Rolling Stones and refuses to drink alcohol because she saw what it did to our mom. She's clever. Bright.

I love Eastwick, but Mr. Cooper is bright.

"No," I say softly.

The video keeps playing. "I know you never liked my podcast," Heather continues. "But I really do listen when people talk, you know?" A rueful smile ghosts her lips, and something in my heart shatters into a million pieces. "And at homecoming last month, when I was coming to check on you...do you even know about that, actually? When you broke down at the dance, I followed you to the bathroom."

The foggy memories of that night come swirling back to me: breaking down. Wanting fresh air. Leaving, pushing my way through the sweaty bodies. Finding a bathroom. Voices, in the hallway.

"I saw them there. Arden and Mr. Cooper. Talking. They were just talking, but I'm not an idiot." Heather swallows. "I was going to put it in the last podcast episode. Put him on blast for it, try to get him fired, but Arden convinced me not to. She said it was a mistake and promised she'd break it off." My ex-girlfriend laughs, her voice breaking in the middle of the sound, and my sternum splits with it. "And I believed her. She was my friend, so I believed her, and..." Her voice softens. "I think...I think he was with Stella first. They look almost exactly the same....I think Arden reminds him of her. I think, at some point last year, your sister decided she didn't want to date him anymore, Iris." Heather's eyes blaze, and my throat goes dry. "And I think he murdered her because of it."

I think of Heather's voice, angry and hard in the final podcast episode she ever made: *Having someone's face doesn't give you permission to try and act like them.* About Arden, her expression crumpling as she left Mr. Cooper's classroom in the very beginning after my ex-girlfriend went missing. About the fact I saw the same look on my sister's heart-shaped face before she slammed the door of our trailer in her homecoming dress late last year.

Arden and Mr. Cooper. Mr. Cooper and Stella. And Mr. Cooper silencing Heather for good. This is how they all connect.

"He kept finding ways to flatter her," Heather continues, and my attention flicks back to the screen. "Extra credit assignments, bonus points on tests...I kept trying to catch him in something, to get hard evidence, to get someone to believe me....I knew the police—or my dad—wouldn't do anything if I didn't have proof." She laughs hollowly. "But I talked to Nathan about it. I was so stupid—I didn't know Mr. Cooper was his half brother, and he just went *apeshit*. 'Collin would never do that,' I'm *insane*, I *don't know what I'm talking about…*" Heather's expression darkens. "In short, I fucked up. And now Mr. Cooper knows that I know, and he's going to find a way to make me disappear, too, Iris. I'm almost sure of it."

She shakes her head. "Either way… I know it's not all ironclad, but I've compiled everything I've managed to find up to this point on these drives for you. They're a failsafe, and I hope you never have to look at them. But if you do… know I did my best, yeah? I tried to make you proud. I tried to… I tried to help." She leans forward, and her dark hair ghosts the screen. "Okay." Heather laughs nervously, and emotion wells up in my chest. "God, I don't even know why I'm doing this. It's fine. I'll be fine." She laughs again. "All right. Be safe out there."

The screen goes black.

I blink at it numbly, trying to comprehend everything I just heard. Everything I just saw. Wishing for a universe where I never had to watch these, one where Heather is alive and Stella is safe and Arden is happy.

But that's not the universe I'm living in. So instead, I tamp down my emotions and get to work.

I comb through the rest of the files in Heather's numbered flash drives by first inputting our anniversary PIN date and then cracking their passwords, following the rabbit trail of clues inside each USB's sole .docx file. *what you take in your coffee—2* leads to my correct input of "fourpacketsofsugar" for a teal drive; *your favorite food—3* lets me crack a USB with "muffulettas." Each piece of plastic holds a single piece of evidence Heather's collected—the audio file of an interview with a lady from Lexington, Kentucky, recorded one day before Heather went missing, that implies someone paid her to report seeing Stella's plates; screenshots of dozens of emails between howtofindamissinggirlpodcast@gmail .com and someone named woodhill47564 claiming they consistently bought drugs from Stella beginning a year before she went missing; photos of newspaper clippings related to Stella's disappearance from a desk labeled as Collin Cooper's; a blurry photo of Arden in her glitzy blue dress at homecoming talking to someone tall and brown-haired from behind; an audio file from the fight between Heather and Nathan, where Nathan tells her Collin is his half brother; secretly taped conversations between Heather and Arden, where Arden tearfully confesses she doesn't want to break things off with Mr. Cooper. When I've finished going through everything, cold dread settles in the pit of my stomach. Some of what Heather theorized about is impossible—Stella isn't someone who would ever date a teacher or deal drugs. But there's something else there, too. Adrenaline. Satisfaction.

Hope.

Because now we have proof. I'm convinced whoever ran me and Lea off the road is the same person who killed Heather. Who orchestrated Stella's disappearance. And, according to these flash drives, who may have driven Arden to overdose, too.

Collin Cooper did this. And he's going to eliminate everyone in this town who knows the truth in order to make sure his secret stays six feet under. Unless I can finish what Heather started.

I eject the last USB and slip it back into Heather's plastic bag. FOR IRIS, her scrawled Sharpie handwriting says. I'm the only one she trusted with this information.

Which makes what I'm about to do with it even worse.

After I finish doing what I need to do, I snatch the drive bag and spin around in my chair. Now all that's left is to—

"Hey," the receptionist says. His voice is gruff from what sounds like years of chain-smoking. I can sympathize. "You're not supposed to be in here."

No shit, Sherlock.

I'm out of his chair and running before he even has a chance to register I moved.

Door. Hallway. Lights. Pounding head. Pounding footsteps. The man behind me: "Hey! Get back here!"

I'm concussed. I probably shouldn't be running. Parts of my hair are still damp, and I can barely see where I'm going. But I'm breaking out of this hospital anyway. So.

I burst through the nearest exit doors, blinking at the sudden switch from fluorescent lights to murky darkness as I stumble through the parking lot and sluggishly duck behind the nearest car. It's still raining, and dark clouds swirl around a sliver of the bright moon overhead. But I'm outside the hospital. A grin finds its way onto my face as the doors slam once. Twice. Open and shut: The receptionist decided I'm not worth it. I made it out.

I take in the cars in front of me, and my smile suddenly disappears. I came here in an ambulance. Sammy and Imani aren't speaking to me. Lea's phone is at the bottom of the river.

I don't have a ride.

I stand up, assessing the dark pickup I just used for cover. On closer inspection, it's clear the truck is falling apart—the body is corroded with rust, the right taillight is broken, and one of the rear side windows is covered in silver duct tape—but when I peer into the cracking windshield, keys blink up at me from the center console.

I laugh. There's a touch of hysteria in my voice as I take out my pocketknife, but I can't think about that now. All that matters is getting out of here.

I flick open the blade and methodically start working away at the tape covering the rear side window, sawing and hacking until the material comes away in small, sticky clumps that gradually leave a hole big enough to snake my arm through. I reach into it and curl my fingertips around the manual lock.

It lifts, and the door pops open.

I slip my pocketknife back into Megan's overcoat, glance up at the moonlit clouds, and step inside the car. The light green seats of the truck are cracked and peeling, and the inside smells like ash and booze. A single fleur-de-lis air freshener hangs from the rearview mirror, but it's clear that whatever scent it used to emanate stopped working long ago.

I maneuver myself into the driver's seat and pull out my phone before I can think too much about the fact I'm behind the wheel. Still, images flash through my mind as I navigate to my web browser with trembling fingers: Heather's blanched body in the swamp. Arden's vacant, glassy eyes. My mother's closed casket.

I swallow as the article I need loads. I can do this. This is nothing.

HOW TO DRIVE STICK-SHIFT (WITH PICTURES)

There are fourteen steps in total. I skim them quickly, then I go back to the beginning and press the clutch, shift gears, and twist the key in the ignition.

The engine turns over.

A strangled cry erupts from me, something between a whoop and a scream, and I catch a glimpse of my reflection in my phone's darkened glass as I take my foot off the clutch and move to shift gears again. For one disorienting second, I don't recognize myself. My hair is thin and stringy, and the purple bags under my sunken, feral eyes are heavy and deep-set.

I clear my throat, my grin gone, and tap my phone to get it to turn back on.

The tutorial's last few steps talk about gradually shifting into higher gears, and as I stall out the engine and restart the car, it finally sinks in: I'm committing grand theft auto. Even though I'm going to return the pickup, I've definitely crossed a line this time. And even worse: I still don't have my license.

Already, the anxiety is building. Visions of crashing, of drowning in the Bayou Lafourche, of cracking my head on spider-webbing glass...they all overwhelm me, and I have to shut my eyes against the pain and breathe to keep from spiraling out of control. I can't let it get to me.

The cracking leather of the wheel under my fingers. The smell of cigarettes and stale beer. The open road, dark and wide and beckoning.

So I don't. With all my senses screaming, with the oppressive weight of every fear I've ever felt on my chest—watching Stella slam the door of our trailer, seeing Heather's outstretched body in the bog, gasping in a crowd of sweaty bodies as Arden laughs in a sparkling blue dress that perfectly matches my missing sister's—I shift gears and lurch out of the parking lot.

For once, I'm actually listening to my ex-girlfriend.

And now, I have a little over two hours to prove myself useful by proving her right.

Lea's street is quiet as I pull into her driveway and kill the engine. I get out of the truck and consider her house, the hem of my white hospital gown fluttering around my kneecaps. I need to make sure she's okay. To check on her after our accident. To tell her everything I've figured out.

For a second, though, I'm stuck. I can't ring Lea's doorbell without having to explain myself to her moms, and she lost her phone in the river. But then a memory flickers in the back of my mind, and I find myself moving before I'm even fully aware of it.

Lea and I used to sneak into each other's houses constantly when we were kids. She would bike all the way to the Chevalier Trailer Park to visit me, and I'd return the favor by sneaking into her second-floor bedroom by climbing...

Ha. Mrs. Zhang's rose trellis.

It's rickety, and the roses aren't blooming in the middle of

November, but the structure is standing. I shake it, testing if it'll still hold my weight, and then decide I don't really care and start climbing anyway. The muscle memory makes it easier: hook my fingers over the edges to steady the wood so it doesn't rattle. Put my left foot up first, to gain more momentum for the larger foothold on the upper right.

I reach the window and open it, the overhead moon lighting my way as I clamber over the sill and onto Lea's padded carpet. Something mewls at my heels, startling me, but it's just Upton Sinclair. I pick him up and stroke him, letting my eyes adjust to Lea's room.

Her bed is empty.

Don't freak out, Iris, I tell myself, even though I feel like I'm already spinning out of control. *She's not here right now, so think. What would Lea have you do?*

I close my eyes and pretend she's here, making fun of my hospital gown. Guiding me through this. Helping me find her.

"*Check the bathroom*," the fake Lea I've invented in her absence says. But the bathroom is empty, too. Panic rises in me as I let the shower curtain fall limp and retreat back to the bedroom, Sin purring contentedly in my arms. And then I see it. On the bed. A note.

Oh God. No, no, no. Please, no.

I set Sin down and step forward, my heartbeat pounding in my ears, until the note is right in front of me. Part of me doesn't want to pick it up. If I pick it up, it'll be real.

But this is real. I know that now.

I grasp the piece of paper and unfold it, and my heart flatlines.

DEVERAUX INDUSTRIES, WEST WING, BACK ENTRANCE. 10:00 PM.

YOU KNOW WHAT TO BRING.

COME ALONE. TELL NO ONE.

COMPLY, AND YOU'LL SEE HER AGAIN.

Chapter Twenty-Eight

My hands won't stop shaking.

I force myself to slow down. To stop, to breathe, to think. To latch onto things I can see, things I can smell, things I can touch. *Think.* I cannot let myself be caught off guard.

I look around Lea's room. At her collage wall, at the precarious stacks of old and thoroughly tabbed newspapers, at her unmade bed. At the unbroken window.

There are no signs of a struggle. So maybe this note wasn't meant for me.

I curse, and Sin bolts out of the room. Lea got here first. Lea is at Deveraux Industries, trying to get Heather's evidence, and she doesn't even have the flash drives. I do.

Blood rushes to my temples as I glance from Megan's overcoat to Lea's open closet. I change into a pair of Lea's jeans and the midnight-blue star sweater she wore on the day I broke into the Nasato house, leaving my aunt's outerwear and my hospital gown behind. I stuff the note into Lea's deep front pocket. And then I unlatch the window and step out into the cool November night.

The chemical plant looks sinister in the moonlight, all sharp edges and reflective windows. The headlights of my stolen truck illuminate the dark pavement as I roar toward it, one hand gripping the wheel while my other messes with my phone. Texting and driving is dangerous, but it's already almost 10 PM—and if I don't send this message, more people might die soon.

be gay solve crime
9:57 PM

> I'm sorry about not telling you both the truth about de rosa earlier. i thought i was protecting you, but i was wrong. this time, though, i'm not shutting you out: heather was murdered, and collin cooper killed her. don't come after me. stay inside. keep your doors locked. if anything happens, tell the cops that heather was right.

My heart pounds in my ears as I hit SEND and drop the phone into my coat pocket, the soles of my combat boots scraping against the truck's rusty footwell as I brake into a hard turn. Next to me, Heather's seven flash drives clatter. The only pieces of real evidence I have, and I'm about to hand them over to save a girl I despised only a month ago. A girl who used to be my best friend. A girl I'm still willing to throw everything else away for.

From somewhere deep inside me, the younger version of Iris Blackthorn chides me. *This is why we don't forge connections,* she whispers. *This is why we don't let people in.*

It's a good thing I'm not listening to her anymore. My friends are the only reason I'm still alive—my relationships with them kept me going after my mom's accident and Stella's disappearance, and through finding Heather's body, and even after Arden's death. It took me too long to realize it, to understand that I truly can't do any of this alone, but I hope I'm making up for it now. I have their backs. I am going to atone for all of my mistakes.

And I'm going to save Lea, even if it kills me.

I pull into the parking lot of Deveraux Industries and slowly shift into lower and lower gears. Take a shuddering breath. Grab the USB bag and my phone and leave my stolen truck behind the back entrance, just like the note to Lea instructed. I don't see any other cars, but hers is at the bottom of the Bayou Lafourche. Maybe she hitchhiked here.

There's a bad feeling in the pit of my stomach as I approach the newly constructed west wing, but I push it away. It'll be fine. I'm going to get her. Everything's going to work out.

I swallow and step inside the belly of the beast.

My footsteps echo as I walk through the cold, construction-wrap-covered halls. The very air around me seems to hold its breath as I press forward, the flashlight on my phone illuminating the path ahead. With each step, I keep looking for something out of place. For something that'll lead me to Lea.

And then I find it—a light, coming from underneath a sleek silver door. My pulse pounds as I walk toward it, my boots thumping in time with the beat. Collin Cooper is behind that door. I'm going to see his face, going to have to confront him. He'll probably try to kill me.

I have to make sure I survive.

I take a steadying breath. Things I can see: the walls of Deveraux Industries. Things I can smell: cleaner and soap. Things I can touch: the star patches sewn on Lea's sweater.

It's 10:08 PM. Enough stalling: I have to go inside.

I take another breath, press a few buttons on my phone and shove it into my back pocket, and push open the door.

A pair of hawklike eyes behind horn-rimmed glasses greets me.

I startle. "Ms. Eastwick?"

My chemistry teacher looks from her watch to me. "You're late, Miss Blackthorn," she says softly.

No. This doesn't make sense. Eastwick shouldn't be here. I glance around the room, barely registering shelves of labeled solutions and dark lab tables that look like more expensive versions of the stations in my AP Chem classroom as I search for Mr. Cooper. But there's no one else here.

"Just the two of us, I'm afraid," Ms. Eastwick says, following my distracted gaze. Her sharp eyes lock on mine, and I desperately try to push down the panic rising in my throat. Did I get it all wrong? No, I couldn't have. The note said to meet here. Eastwick's eyes flick to the bag I'm still clutching, and my heart drops. Heather was wrong. Nathan's half brother isn't the killer.

"It's you," I breathe.

A wry smile flits over Ms. Eastwick's face, but it doesn't reach her eyes. "Give me the drives."

"Where's Lea?" I whisper, barely able to keep myself standing.

"That's what I'm here for. It's supposed to be an equal exchange."

Eastwick tilts her head, like I've failed at balancing yet another crucial chemical equation. "That's right," she says, stretching out her hand. "So exchange."

She must see the rage on my face, because her eyes narrow. "Save your strength. You have no power to negotiate in this situation."

No. I have no power at all, except for the weight of the plastic USBs at my side. And I don't intend to relinquish those without a fight.

"I cracked them," I blurt, glancing at the plastic bag. FOR IRIS. "I know everything Heather knew." *Keep her talking. Appeal to her ego. Make her feel smart.* "But I didn't...I didn't suspect you at all," I continue, forcing myself to look Ms. Eastwick in the face. "You weren't...connected to anything. I thought the murderer was Mr. Cooper." I swallow, weighing my next words carefully. "And so did Heather."

Eastwick's eyes flash. "Wrong again, Miss Blackthorn," she

says coldly. "I'm not a murderer—I've never killed anyone, and I never will."

My stomach clenches. She's telling the truth.

"You're confused," Eastwick says. "You don't quite understand. But you will, because the two of us aren't so different." She closes her eyes, and when she opens them again, her expression is emotionless. "We're both willing to do anything to protect the people we love."

I have no idea what she's talking about. My brain keeps spinning, trying to latch onto a single coherent thought, but I come up with nothing. I didn't think there was anyone on the planet my chemistry teacher cared about. Unless...

My mind snags. I think back to the old man in the wheelchair at Heather's vigil, the one with Eastwick's eyes. I think about my chemistry teacher holding me after class, her vulnerable voice: *I almost lost my father a few years ago. He was diagnosed with lung cancer, which was treatable, but the treatments themselves were so expensive, I thought he wouldn't be able to survive.*

But he did.

"Your father," I tell Eastwick, feeling like I'm starting to understand. "You love him, but you couldn't afford to save him. Not on your teacher's salary."

Eastwick nods, looking beyond me. "I didn't have a lot of people in my corner growing up, but my father always believed in me. He's the reason I stayed in Hillwood—he taught, and I figured I could do the same thing and stay close to him. But then he got sick, and nothing I did was enough.... In the end, there was

343

only one way for me to make sure I would have the money to help him stay alive."

"Drugs," I whisper, remembering the anonymous man on Heather's podcast. *If you're dirt-poor in Hillwood, you stay dirt-poor in Hillwood. You live in Chevalier or another white-trash trailer park, and you get mixed up in drugs tryin' to get out.*

Eastwick looks at me, and another piece slots into place. "You're the 0141 number. You're Delphine's dealer."

Shit.

"It paid for the treatments," Eastwick says slowly. "It took a long time, but my father is still alive."

"And all you had to do to save him was rope in Hillwood students to deal with you as their supplier," I breathe. A mistake—Eastwick fully refocuses on me, and I clench my teeth so hard it's a wonder they don't break. *Don't hurt me. Please don't hurt me yet.*

"It might be hard to hear this, Iris, but Stella approached me," Eastwick says. "She needed the money, and I didn't ask too many questions. But she was planning to run. They didn't pay her enough at Lucille's General Store, and she didn't want to be traceable once she left, so she needed cash." Eastwick frowns. "Smart girl."

The words hit me like a brick to the chest. My sister really *was* planning to skip town. And she was dealing drugs to do it. To get away from us.

To get away from me.

"She made a mistake, though," Eastwick continues. "She planned to leave after she saved up enough money, but something happened on homecoming night to make her decide to do things early."

My heart wrenches. The fight.

"Instead of skipping town right away, she stopped to see Collin first," Eastwick says. Her voice lowers, and a chill goes through me. "And he got angry."

I bite my lip so hard I taste blood, thinking back to the Polaroid picture in Nathan's locker. The one of my sister in lingerie. There's no reason Stella would go see Mr. Cooper on homecoming night unless I was wrong about her. Unless Heather was right.

"He didn't want her to leave, did he?" I ask through the metallic taste in my mouth, looking up at my chemistry teacher.

Eastwick nods. "They had a huge argument, and Stella...fell. Over the banister, while they were arguing." Her lips twist, but the world is exploding around me.

Stella fell.

Stella fell.

Stella...fell.

Something in me breaks. I can feel it, like my heart splits in two. My face crumples, and my knees almost give out. No. I can't.

Stella is dead.

My sister is gone.

"One of the workers from Deveraux Industries was there that night," Eastwick goes on, but the words are coming from underwater. I can't listen, can't hear. I'm drowning, being suffocated by the same thought washing over me, pulling me under. *My sister is dead. My sister is dead. My sister is dead.*

"The witness, the one who you thought you scared off? He went to Collin's house before homecoming last year to deliver a message from the Deveraux, and he saw Stella's car in the driveway.

Mentioned something at Joan's Diner, got on de Rosa's radar, got paid off by the family after you showed up to his house. And once he left, there was nothing else the police could do. They'd exhausted all their leads. They had to say Stella ran away, just like she was supposed to, and that was that." Eastwick frowns. "She's a runaway now."

I am shattered. I am broken. But I have to keep going, have to understand. I inhale. "How did you get involved?" I ask Eastwick, my voice cracking. "Why help Mr. Cooper cover up the death of your best student?"

Ms. Eastwick waits, and the gears in my head spin.

"Unless Stella told him," I say slowly. "She told him where she got the money from, didn't she? My sister ratted you out."

Eastwick nods. "And afterward, Collin blackmailed me," she says simply. "He said if I disposed of her body, he wouldn't go to the police about my operation." She tilts her head, and her expression is almost...regretful. "He said if I dealt with everything else, he would get rid of the car and I could keep my father alive."

That's what she says—"dealt with." Like covering up who murdered my sister was just a chemical equation to balance. Like it was just another problem to solve.

"How could you?" I whisper, a crushing weight settling on me at the same time red-hot rage courses through my blood. "How could you do that to someone you cared about? I know you don't like me, Ms. Eastwick, but my sister *loved* you. She cared about you. You were her favorite teacher." Tears swim in my eyes, and I fight to remain rooted to the spot. To prevent them from falling.

"And instead of bringing her killer to light, you worked with him. You're the reason he's free. You're the reason he was able to keep harming people. Keep hurting other girls."

Eastwick doesn't say anything, and I force myself to refrain from lunging for her throat like a feral animal. "You were going to keep quiet forever," I whisper, disgust radiating from my voice. "You got Delphine to take over for my sister as your Hillwood High dealer, and you thought everything would be fine. But then Heather found out about Mr. Cooper and Arden, and she eventually pieced everything together about Stella, too, so you...what, killed her to keep her quiet?"

Ms. Eastwick's eerie detachment returns. "I already told you; I've never killed anyone. All I've ever done is clean up Collin's messes." She closes her eyes and takes a breath, and I take advantage of the second she's distracted to scan the room more critically: zero windows, a single buzzing fluorescent light, another sleek silver door. No sign of Lea.

"Was it Mr. Cooper, then?" I ask, glancing back at my chemistry teacher. "Did he kill Heather? Is he the one who framed Nathan for her murder?"

Ms. Eastwick sighs. "Collin has his third period free to plan lessons, so no one suspected anything when he intercepted Miss Nasato at school. Principal Phillips has always been too much of a cheapskate to invest in security cameras, and I covered for Collin while he took her to the swamp. He was certain Heather would go to the police after she threatened him in the final podcast episode, so he...took measures to prevent it.

"Heather had a gun with her that day. She'd taken it to school,

maybe for self-defense—she did seem paranoid—and things…
escalated. I wanted to dispose of her the way I normally would,
but Collin thought the Nasatos would be too desperate to uncover
the truth without a body. He said he would handle it. And he did,
although you weren't satisfied with the police's conclusion. We
underestimated you." Ms. Eastwick's eyes glint. "But we won't be
making that mistake again."

A hand clamps over my mouth. My eyes widen, but I don't
have time to think past that—I react. My teeth sink into clothed
flesh, and there's a loud grunt in my ear as my assailant kicks the
backs of my knees, forcing me to the ground.

"How spirited," a familiar voice drones above me, and I grit
my teeth in response. He's here. Of course he's fucking here.

Collin Cooper yanks my hair back, his expression a mask of
complete calm. His gray eyes betray no emotion as they stare into
mine, and my stomach curdles.

"No more games, Iris. Give me the drives."

I want to strangle him. I want to wrap my fingers around his
throat and squeeze until I crush his trachea. Instead, I mutely
hold out the plastic bag. Heather's multicolored flash drives—my
evidence—clatters around inside. Collin Cooper takes it wordlessly, his half smirk gloating. "Is this all of them?"

I nod as much as I can with my hair in his fist. If I start
talking again, I won't be able to stop myself. Control myself, like
I am now.

Collin lets me go, and my neck tenses with the motion as he
steps around me and into the light. He nods at Eastwick, and she
reaches into her pants pocket and takes out a single key. I barely

breathe as she strides over to the only other door in the room and unlocks it. I bite the inside of my cheek to keep from crying out, but something low and strangled manages to erupt from me anyway.

Lea.

She fought—I can see it in the bruises that bloom on her face, in the way blood trickles slowly out of the corner of her mouth. She's breathing, but barely. Unconscious. Battered. Bloody.

Fury unfurls in my chest.

"You bastard," I whisper, getting to my feet. The word seems to echo through the room.

Collin looks up. "Excuse me?"

"I said," I whisper, my voice ragged and dark and poisonous, "you *goddamn* bastard."

The slap is instantaneous. Dark shadows blur at the edge of my vision, taunting me. *Look*, they whisper. *Look what you did.*

My knees buckle. I stagger sideways, unable to see. There's a sick crunching sound, and when my eyesight swims back into focus, I see what's left of the flash drives. They've been mangled, splintered into bits of plastic.

Heather's evidence—my evidence—is gone.

Collin smiles. "There," he says, extracting his shiny black shoe from the pile. "That wasn't so hard, was it?" His cold gray gaze turns on me, and my stomach sinks at the finality in his eyes. He looks at me like I'm expendable. Disposable. A problem that needs to be dealt with.

My head throbs. No matter what happens tonight, I am going to die here. Luring me here with Lea—letting me see her—all of that was just a formality. There's no way Collin will let either of us go now that I've figured out the truth. Now that I'm following in Heather's footsteps.

The monster in my chest—the one desperate for revenge, the one keeping me alive—roars. I need a confession from Collin before I die. I need to get him to talk.

"That car that almost ran Lea and me over," I say softly. Raspily. "Was that yours? Or did you get Ms. Eastwick to do that for you, too?"

"Does it matter?" he asks lightly, gesturing for Eastwick to clean up the remains of the drives. She moves to handle it, her motions stilted and disdainful, and a wave of contempt sweeps through me at how she's letting herself be used. At how she lets Collin's threat hang over her when what she knows about him is so much worse.

If she really wanted to turn him in, she would. But then she would go to jail, too, and there'd be no one left to take care of her father.

"I guess not," I tell Collin, my attention turning back to him. "Though you murdered Heather Nasato to prevent her from coming forward about how you killed Stella Blackthorn"—I pause, swallowing the bile that rises in my throat as I speak aloud my own last name— "and slept with Arden Blake. So I was just wondering. Naturally."

More, Iris. We need more.

"That wasn't enough, though, was it? You learned Heather made encrypted flash drives exposing all the secrets she'd collected— about Delphine, about Arden, about you—and it wasn't too far of a leap to conclude they might incriminate you in Stella's death. You set out to destroy them before they could destroy you, using Eastwick and Delphine as pawns. You wanted them to fix things for you. But by then it was too late—our agency got to them first."

"I am aware," Collin says slowly, "of my own motives, Iris. I do not need you to reiterate every single second of the last month just so you can fulfill your fantasy of solving crime."

I force myself to keep going. "Arden didn't know you were responsible for Heather's death, but she started to suspect Nathan—and then you—after the two of you stopped seeing each other. On Halloween, she helped us to trace the car you used— a car you had access to without Nathan's knowledge, because he always keeps his keys in his easily accessible locker—to take Heather to the swamp, knowing if anyone saw the truck, they would blame your half brother—"

Something has materialized in Collin's hand—something sleek and black and solid. My vision swims, and I fight to remain conscious. Between the slap and my concussion, I'm missing things, losing pieces of both auditory and visual input. I'm not at the top of my game.

But still, I'm aware enough to recognize a gun when I see one.

"God, Iris," Collin says lazily, pointing the barrel in my direction. "Will you just shut up already?"

"You could kill me now," I whisper, my voice hoarse as I stare at my Media Appreciation Club teacher. "Right here, in this very room. You could get Eastwick to clean up for you and stage my suicide just like you framed Nathan for Heather's death—it would definitely be an easy way to get back at me for interfering, just like you got back at Heather. Just like you got back at your father when you decided to destroy his 'pristine family reputation' by making Nathan look guilty." I lick my lips. "Everyone knows I had a breakdown at homecoming. It would be believable."

Collin's face doesn't change. But I can see the shift in his shoulders, read the signs in his stance. He's intrigued.

"But." I pause, taking a breath. "As Stella's sister, don't you think I deserve an explanation before you kill me, too?"

Collin sneers. "What do you want from me, Iris? Do you want me to tell you that you're right? That even though I'm Edward Deveraux's son, I'm not in his will? That I wanted Nathan to go down for his girlfriend's death so I could finally take my place as the rightful heir of Deveraux Industries?" Collin smiles. "That's what you want, isn't it?"

I suck my teeth, remembering all the papers I looked through with Lea. The sketchy business practices. The letter to the editor.

The love child rumors.

"You're not the rightful heir."

Collin's voice is deadly quiet. "What?"

I've hit a nerve. "You're not the heir of Deveraux Industries," I repeat, and my voice is stronger now. Ms. Eastwick glances between us nervously. "You won't inherit the company. You're an illegitimate son, and you're not entitled to anything."

The safety clicks. I register a sound, half-real and half-imagined. And then there's fire.

Flames. Agony. Pain.

I'm screaming. I'm screaming, but I can't hear any sound. Blood pours out of me, soaking through Lea's sweater. My hands go to the wound and come away covered in red. *Fuck, Iris, focus.* My shoulder. He shot my fucking shoulder.

"That was a warning," Collin says coldly. The black shadows swell, threatening to overtake me. To pull me under, if only to escape the inferno spreading through my veins.

I fight them off. Blacking out now will only mean death—it won't help Lea. *Get up, Iris. Get up.*

"You idiot," Eastwick growls, rounding on him. "Control your temper."

I struggle to my feet, still clutching my shoulder. There's blood everywhere. Collin Cooper watches me lazily, sees me hiss in pain. Ms. Eastwick won't look at me.

Confession. Confession. Confession.

"All this trouble," I say, the words oozing from my mouth like sludge, "just for a heptad of flash drives?"

"You're a detective," Collin says, his voice dripping with condescension. "You know how important evidence is."

"Evidence that marks you as a pedophile and a killer," I whisper.

Collin's smile chills every cell in my body. "Not anymore."

He aims the gun at my head, and I notice how his hand doesn't shake—his arm is as still as ever. Practiced.

But so am I.

Collin's finger twitches toward the trigger, and I dive behind the nearest lab station a millisecond before the bullet explodes above me. My shoulder screams, and I whimper.

"Collin!" Ms. Eastwick snaps. "We agreed to be more careful about this. We still have the other girl."

But it doesn't seem like he's listening anymore. I can hear it in the way he laughs; he's enjoying this.

"Playing games with me, Iris?" Collin purrs. "How interesting. You're less like Stella than I thought. You know, she was still alive after she fell over that banister. She begged me to call an ambulance, but of course I couldn't do that, because then I'd have had to explain what she was doing at my house in the first place. So I put her out of her misery instead."

I bite down on my tongue to keep from crying out. I am fire and rage, but I can't hide here forever. Collin is going to come around that station, and he is going to finish what he started.

But I'm not going to wait for him. I came here so that I wouldn't be useless; I came here to avenge my sister. To carry out Heather's wishes. To save Lea.

I wrap my hand around my pocketknife and move to stand up, some dim part of me registering that I'm literally bringing a knife to a gunfight, when I stop. Ms. Eastwick inhales, and hope flutters in my rib cage. She heard it, too.

Voices. In the hallway. They're far off, but it's only a matter of time until they find us.

I struggle to my feet. Collin stares at me, and there's something dark and hard in his expression now. He's not amused anymore—he's done underestimating me. I'm facing the real Collin Cooper, and he wants to kill me. Is about to kill me. Has killed others just like me.

"Fucking bitch," he snarls. "I told you to come alone."

His gun pivots, and he's not aiming at me anymore.

No.

Without thinking, I launch myself at him. It's a stupid move—a desperate one. One meant to save Lea, even if it means I die in the process.

But Ms. Eastwick reaches him first.

Another bullet discharges, and I hear it explode in the wall somewhere behind me as Collin whips around, his eyes wild. The fury radiating from him is so palpable that I lose my breath for a second, but it doesn't have the same effect on my chemistry teacher.

"Enough, Collin," she says, struggling to restrain him. "I'm not going to keep doing this."

Collin grunts. Eastwick shoves. And then something gives, and the firearm skitters across the floor.

I pick it up.

"It's all over, Mr. Cooper," I say softly, turning to point the weapon at him. My arms do not shake, and even though my shoulder burns, I keep the gun steady. Some dim part of me realizes this is the first time I have ever held a gun in my life, and that I am pointing it at another human being. The thought makes me want to throw the weapon as far away as I can.

Another part of me wants to squeeze the trigger.

I do not do either of those things. I focus on breathing. The voices grow louder, and the lights grow brighter—whoever's coming can't be far off now. The gunshots gave us away.

Collin raises his hands, his face expressionless. "What are you going to do, Iris?" he says. "You don't even know how to fire that gun."

My lip quivers, but my hands stay steady. "Try me," I whisper.

The door bursts open. Light floods the room, and I blink at the swarm of paramedics and police officers that suddenly seem to be everywhere at once—Detective de Rosa and Assistant Detective Hunt. Woodsy deodorant and bubble-gum perfume.

I do not lower the gun.

There are words being spoken around me, people shouting harsh and loud, and someone restrains Collin Cooper.

I do not lower the gun.

I hear the click of handcuffs. There is garbled noise as what sounds like thousands of walkie-talkies go off in thousands of hands.

I do not lower the gun.

Somewhere from deep inside myself, I become dimly aware my arms are trembling. My shoulder feels like it's on fire. People sweep out of the room, and more come in. But the cool weapon in my hands is a lifeline in the chaos. So I stand there. Frozen. Immobile. Pointing at nothing, eyes hollow, until someone is finally brave enough to try and coax the firearm from my grip.

Once it's out of my hands, the spell breaks. I take in a gulp of fresh air, chest heaving, and fall to the ground.

Imani and Sammy catch me before I sink completely, one of them supporting me on either side. They're here even when the whole world feels like it's falling apart. They're both here.

"I thought I told you two to stay inside and lock your doors," I rasp, and Sammy laughs even though her eyes are brimming with tears.

"Are you kidding? You said there was a m-murderer. Of

c-course we weren't going to sit around and do n-nothing." She sniffs, her eyes flicking to the blood on my hands. To the red soaking through Lea's sweater. To the sanguine streaks behind us on the cold concrete floor.

"Sam," I say softly, drawing her gaze away from the violence. "Don't worry about me. I'm fine."

"You got shot, Iris," Imani says flatly, their eyebrows drawing together as they survey my bloodied shoulder.

"I know," I whisper. "I'm going to have the coolest scar."

Sammy sob-laughs and crushes me, her arms squeezing all the air out of my chest, and Imani does the same. "We've m-missed you so much, Iris. When we got your sh-shitty little apology, we were already g-going to forgive you. But then we saw your Instagram...."

"Which we still have notifications on for, by the way," Imani adds as we break apart, plucking my phone from my back pocket and turning it toward me.

I stare numbly at the glass screen, the live video feed I started recording before I stepped foot into this room blinking back at me. "You watched it?" I ask softly. "The whole thing?"

"Yeah," Sammy says, tapping to end the stream. A message pops up asking if I want to save the video, and Sammy says yes and tries to title it "murderers get asses kicked by local seventeen-year-old," even though she runs out of characters halfway through. She beams. "Voilà! Confessions saved."

I sag against my friends, knowing they'll hold me up. We did it. We fucking got them. It's over, and Lea and I are safe.

I bolt up so quickly that Imani almost falls. *Lea.*

I extract myself from the smart and resourceful friends I'm incredibly lucky to have and stagger across the room, stumbling forward until I sink to my knees in front of her. There are paramedics tending to her, and someone's removed her duct-taped bonds, and as I stare at her bloodied face emotion wells up in me, filling the back of my throat.

Sitting here with my best friend, with the girl who clearly fought tooth and nail for the truth, all of it hits me at once, like I can't accept one emotion without the rest: Collin pointing his gun at me, Heather's lifeless body, Arden's sluggish pulse. My mother's empty, unseeing eyes. The euphoria of finally solving a case. El, unconscious in front of me.

And through all of tonight, I haven't cried. I didn't cry when I stole the car I couldn't drive. I didn't cry when Collin pointed the gun at me. I didn't cry when the bullet went into my shoulder. But I'm crying now.

"It's okay, El," I whisper, stroking my red hands through her hair. "It's all okay. I'm here."

Her eyelids flutter open. She takes a ragged breath.

"Iris," Lea breathes, and I sob with relief.

Chapter Twenty-Nine

I don't know how much time passes in the Deveraux Industries west wing, and I don't care. I don't, because paramedics flit between us and cops shout in unintelligible voices and nothing matters except for Lea, Imani, Sammy, and me.

Safe. The word feels almost too good to be true, and I want to scream it until my throat is raw. We're safe.

"Iris," Sammy says, snapping me out of my reverie. I meet her eyes; I don't know if it's the dim light or the fire in her features, but tonight, Sammy looks older than all of us. She glances over my shoulder, where a lab table is being prepped for me. "You're hurt," she continues matter-of-factly. "And if you don't let the paramedics take care of the bullet here, they're going to tranquilize you and do it at the hospital."

"Is that even legal?"

She raises an eyebrow, and I relent. "Fine." My gaze drifts back to Lea.

My best friend nods, her dark eyes fierce. "Go," she says hoarsely, that determined expression back on her face. "We're all going to be fine. You better be, too."

I swallow and stand up, thankful for my friends. Thankful for my family. Without them, I would be dead right now. And so would El.

The thought makes bile rise in the back of my throat.

Dead, like the other girls who got trapped in Collin and Eastwick's web. Dead, like Heather and Arden. Dead, like Stella.

My sister isn't alive.

I stagger to the lab table, trying to force the unwelcome thoughts out of my head. People are waiting for me, but I can't register their faces. The adrenaline rush from facing my sister's killer is wearing off, and now the only thing left behind is the truth: Stella was seeing her teacher. Stella did leave me that night. But she didn't come back, because she was murdered. The last thing she said to me was that I'm useless, and now I know she'll never get to speak again.

Someone cuts away the fabric of Lea's beautiful sweater and inspects my wound, and someone else tells me to look away while they sterilize it, and around me police tape winds and cameras flash and my shoulder is searing and none of it matters. My sister is gone. Heather is gone.

A light shines in my eyes, and I realize too late that my movements are sluggish. "We need to get her back to the hospital," one of the paramedics says. "She's concussed, too."

Stella. Podcast. Heather. My ringing ears and brackish-water stomach. Lurching forward and vomiting right onto a paramedic's shoes.

"Wrap her shoulder," Vomit Shoes instructs. "The stretcher's outside."

I want to protest that I don't need a stretcher, but I can feel consciousness slipping out from under me. My brain is shutting down, telling me this is too much. And I guess it is, because I think I hear a voice telling me it's okay, that I've held out for so long, that I can rest now. And I don't know if the voice is real or not. But I want to rest.

So I do.

When I wake up, sunlight streams through the soft curtains of my familiar sickly white hospital room. I'm back in a gown, and tubes run along the length of my entire body this time. My shoulder is bandaged, and as I sit up and push my hair out of my face, I'm finally able to take in the people in front of me.

"Thank God," Sammy says with a soft smile. "How do you feel?"

"Tired," I rasp, my eyes traveling to the chair in the corner of the room and the figure slumped in it. My two friends must have gone home to change, because Sammy has her lion's mane of curls wrangled into half-up space buns and Imani's wearing a fresh set of gold jewelry and a *The Lion King: The Broadway Musical* shirt that isn't covered in blood. "How's Lea?"

"Stable," Imani says. "We actually think she's going to get released before you—from what we've been able to gather, she was admitted with internal bleeding, but it stopped on its own."

"She's okay, though," Sammy adds quickly. "A little confused, but—according to some very confidential hospital records that I totally did not find a way to access—the doctors say she'll have no long-term problems."

I smile weakly. "Look at you two. You're proper sleuths."

"Well, duh." Sammy lowers her pink heart-shaped sunglasses and winks at me. "We learned from the best."

My heart aches, and my bones with it. I feel a thousand pounds heavier than I did yesterday. Than I did before I went into that dark lab room. Than I did before I learned about Stella's death.

Behind the agency, Megan, sleeping, stirs in her chair.

"She was here the whole night," Sammy says, lowering her voice as she glances over her shoulder. "Don't be too hard on her, okay? She was worried sick." There's a pause, and her voice softens even more. "We all were."

Imani squeezes my good shoulder gently before I have a chance to respond, the faint scent of their woodsy deodorant floating over me. "We'll let you rest, but we're taking you out to eat once you're out of here and in much less ugly clothes. Joan's Diner, okay? On us."

Sammy bobs her head. "So hurry up and get better already," she adds. "Unless you'd rather celebrate your eighteenth birthday with more hospital Jell-O." She pulls a face, and I force myself to laugh past the lump in my throat. That's right. I guess I'm a legal adult now.

Sammy swoops down to kiss my forehead and Imani waves goodbye, and then my two friends leave, and Megan lifts her head right as the door shuts behind them. She blinks, her eyes meeting mine, and then she promptly stumbles to her feet. "Iris. Oh my god."

"Hi, Megs," I say softly.

I brace myself for the onslaught of her accusations, for the same anger she had for me after Lea and I first landed in the hospital, but it never comes. Instead, she crosses the room and pulls me into a fiercely gentle hug, like she can't believe I'm real without touching me. "I thought I lost you," she whispers into my scraggly hair.

Tears fill the back of my throat. "You almost did," I whisper.

In response, Megs just hugs me tighter. Like she's letting her arms fill in the cracks of all the words we can't say, like she's regretting not holding me after Lea and I got into our car crash. This hug lets me know she's thankful she didn't lose me. That she's right here. That even though I'm not okay, I will be.

"You're not going to yell at me?" I whisper as she pulls back to stroke my hair.

"You're safe," my aunt murmurs. "That's all I care about."

And that, if nothing else, breaks me.

The tears spill over, and Aunt Megan looks at me like she's seeing me for the first time as she wipes them away. "Don't cry, Iris," she says softly. "You solved the case. You did so well, and I'm so proud of you."

I laugh, but the tears garble the sound. "What?"

"I'm so proud," Megan repeats. "You didn't give up. You put your life at risk to save your friend. You kept going, even after everything you've been through. After everything you've seen."

I don't know how to respond. This is the sincerest conversation Megan and I have ever had—this is uncharted territory for both of us. She seems to realize it, too, because she takes a step back from me and clears her throat. "I, uh, just want you to know I think you're a remarkable person. And from now on, I'm planning to support you more." Megan swallows. "I...I saw the note. Detective de Rosa spoke with me this morning—she said you've been having a hard time at school, that kids have been sending you death threats—and I don't want you to feel like you can't talk to me, Iris. Or like you have to keep secrets."

Secrets. I think of all the ones I've collected over the past month: Delphine dealing, Nathan cheating, Arden drinking. Heather's USBs. The break-in. Being followed. I think of the countless anonymous messages on my phone, the hate emails, the vandalized bathroom. I think of how lies can worm under your skin and eat you alive before you've even realized they're there, and I make a decision.

"No more secrets," I tell Megan, shifting on my bed to extend my pinky finger to her.

I'm not sure if I can do it. But I sure would like to try.

Megan reaches forward and entwines her little finger with mine, and something soft floods me. The feelings I've tamped down for so long are slowly loosening up.

She smiles. "No more secrets."

The door opens, and a frazzled nurse bursts in behind my aunt. "I'm sorry," he says as Megan turns around, "but Detective de Rosa wants to see you, Iris. She's in the conference room on the first floor."

I inhale. The monitor to my right starts beeping, and the nurse shakes his head. "I told her to come back later. You're in no condition—"

"I need to talk to her." I appeal to the nurse first, and then to Megan. "Please."

The nurse consults his clipboard. "Ms. Sanchez, I—"

Megan glances at me. Her dark eyes assess me, scour my greasy hair and the wires coming out of me, and I wiggle my pinky finger at her. *You promised.*

She sighs. "Have her come in."

"If you don't, I'll just break out of here again to talk to her anyway," I add.

The nurse looks between the two of us, and then he nods stiffly. "Fine. But make it quick—you really do have to take it easy."

The door shuts again, and my aunt stares at me. "Are you sure you want to see her? You can wait, you know."

I nod. "I know," I say, and Megan nods back.

She turns to leave—to let me have this space with the detective to myself—and as she does, I realize that this is it. Megan Sanchez is always going to be there for me, regardless of whether or not I appreciate the way she shows her care. She respects me, and I understand her. We've been forced to learn how to grow together.

"I love you, Megs," I say before she steps into the hallway.
She nods, and tears prick the corners of my eyes again.
"Yeah, Iris," she says softly. "I love you, too."

As soon as I glimpse the detective through the top window of my
hospital room door, my throat closes up. This was a terrible idea,
but it might not be too late. I could probably still try to unhook
myself from all these tubes and make a run for it—I got shot in
the shoulder, not the leg. I would probably be fine.

But then the detective looks up and catches my eye, and all my
well-laid escape plans evaporate as she opens the door.

"Hello, Iris," Detective de Rosa says as she enters my sickly
hospital room. With her in it, the whole space seems smaller.
She points to the chair Megan slept in, silently asking if she can
move it, and I shrug as she drags it closer to me. I know I must
not look the best. The new paper-thin hospital gown I'm wearing definitely seems like it's weathered more than its fair share of
Louisiana hurricanes—and honestly, I feel like I have, too.

My gaze flits to the detective. She doesn't seem to have brushed
her hair, either, and the bags on her ashen face are a shade of deep
gray. There's an empty to-go cup from Joan's Diner in her right
hand, accompanied by the distinct scent of black coffee, and a
battered-looking manila envelope in her left.

I stare at her. "You look like hell."

"Thank you," Detective de Rosa says sarcastically. "Can I take
a seat?"

I manage a wry smile as she remains standing. "Will I get a lesser sentence if I say yes?"

I'm not naïve. Even in the chaos of last night, I know I broke the law. I kept looking for Heather's killer. I ran out of the hospital. I kept evidence from the police, and I almost shot Collin Cooper.

I stole a fucking car.

Detective de Rosa sighs, but she doesn't look like she's going to put me in handcuffs just yet. A wave of exhaustion suddenly hits me. If she looks like hell, I must look a hundred times worse.

"Yeah," I say softly, and she sinks into the yellowed chair.

"I looked at the content of the flash drives," de Rosa says.

I raise an eyebrow, savoring my last little bit of freedom. "Oh yeah?"

"It was a bit hard not to, considering you tweeted the link to the Dropbox through the official *Hillwood Herald* account and tagged our police department in it."

I allow myself a small grin. Turns out all that time watching Lea log into Twitter to post news articles paid off.

De Rosa takes a minute to phrase her next sentence. She's being careful, more careful than she usually is, but I don't feel like I'm playing right into her trap this time. I'm heading for the slammer anyway. It doesn't matter what I say anymore.

Finally, she looks up at me. "The physical copies of the drives are no longer available, correct?"

I nod. "I had to give them to Collin Cooper. He destroyed them, but the files are all still on the cloud."

De Rosa nods. "Like I said, the department has reviewed

them." She looks down at the manila envelope in her lap and then back up at me. "Heather showed an incredible amount of foresight in creating the USBs, although I understand her choice of encryption posed somewhat of a...challenge."

I swallow. "She was the bravest person I've ever met."

Detective de Rosa dips her head. "I believe there are a lot of people who would say the same thing about you."

The weight of the words washes over me slowly, and it takes me a second to fully comprehend them. But then I do: Detective de Rosa is *complimenting* me.

Something wells up in the back of my throat, something I can't place or name, and I bite my lip to stop myself from bursting into tears. I have to keep the conversation moving, to ask the one question that's more important than my future behind bars or de Rosa's praise: "Is it enough to convict?"

"Normally, it wouldn't be," the detective says evenly. "But Eastwick and Cooper confessed. There's still a lot of paperwork we'll have to go through, but I'm hopeful. If everything goes as it should, they'll be in prison for a long time."

I say the words without thinking. "How much time?"

Detective de Rosa's eyes are hard. "Enough."

I nod. Collin Cooper is dangerous, and there will still be hurdles to making sure he and Eastwick both get what they deserve. My chemistry teacher's father will probably have to be moved to the Hillwood Assisted Living Community, and the media is going to have a field day over Principal Phillips having a murderer in his employ. Delphine and Jackson will likely face consequences. The Deveraux might lose credibility once the story breaks, regardless of how many NYC bigwigs they can hire, and there might be walkouts staged at Hillwood High and policy changes regarding school surveillance thanks to Mayor Nasato. But it's about time that some serious change started happening in Hillwood. And Detective de Rosa is right—it will be enough.

It has to be.

The detective taps the manila folder in front of her—the one containing the warrant for my arrest, no doubt—and snaps me out of my thoughts. Ah, here it is. Show's over.

Although I dutifully hold out my wrists, I can't help the grimace that finds its way onto my face. "Can't you wait until I'm officially released from the hospital to take me into the station, at least?"

"What? I'm not taking you into the station," de Rosa says. "This is Heather's case file. Part of Stella's, too." She flips open the manila folder and shows me the first page of my sister's official police report, and I do an extremely poor job of acting like I've never seen it before. "Look."

She points to the bottom. Somehow, the police have gotten a copy of my most recent school photo and affixed it to the sheet, along with a bar of text underneath it that reads THIS INVESTIGATION WAS ASSISTED BY AND CLOSED WITH THE HELP OF LOCAL HIGH SCHOOL STUDENT IRIS BLACKTHORN.

My brow furrows as I read the box once. Twice. Three times. I look back up at de Rosa. "It doesn't say I'm being charged with criminal obstruction of justice anywhere."

"No," the detective says, her brown eyes locked on mine. "It doesn't."

I inhale, hardly daring to believe my own ears. "I'm not going to jail?"

Detective de Rosa smiles. "Not today, Iris."

"You're going to let me go? Just like that?"

The detective's smile disappears. "Don't make me regret my decision." She stands, picking up her empty cup of soulless black coffee, and I lurch upright, too. "Now, you've had a traumatic night. After the doctors say you can leave—through the front door this time—you should go home. Rest, recuperate, maybe call up a therapist." She raises an eyebrow. "I've heard Dr. Brenda Miller does great work with private investigators."

A phantom grin flits across my face, and de Rosa switches how she's holding her empty coffee cup so she can extend her right hand to me. "Thank you, Detective," I say, taking it. "It's been an honor to unofficially work by your side."

She rolls her eyes and drops my hand. "I'm going to get another cup of coffee from the third-floor vending machine, which should take me no less than three minutes," she says. "I expect that file to be exactly where I left it once I get back," she adds, pointing to the folder still sitting on the yellowed chair, and then she opens the door and closes it behind her.

A real grin spreads across my face this time.

I lean over and grab the folder—de Rosa's three minutes are a gift to me. A sign of trust. But just as I brush my fingers over the cover of the first police report, I glance up to see a girl with chin-length snow-white hair in the door window, and time stops entirely.

"Do you know how hard it was to find you in this place?" Lea asks as she steps into my hospital room. "I swear, it's like a goddamn maze." She looks me up and down, a smirk tugging at the corner of her mouth. "Nice dress."

A laugh bubbles up in my throat, and before I know it, I'm hugging her. I'm broken and battered and scarred, but here, with Lea's beating heart pressed against mine, with her twelve fingers digging into my freckled skin like she can't believe we're both alive and here together, it hits me: I love her. I love her, and even though I've tried to push down this quiet, unfurling thing between us, I can't lie to myself any longer: I would die and kill for El. And after everything we've been through, the idea of keeping her at a distance any longer seems absurd.

Even for three more minutes.

She pulls out of our embrace, her sparkling eyes dancing, her lips slightly parted from her being out of breath. "I ran down here to find you because they said you'd be here. And that apparently, you solved the case. Both of them, actually." I nod, and Lea mimes holding out a microphone. "I was wondering if I could be the first to get an official statement?"

I shake my head, trying and failing to hold back my smile. "Of course you would use our near-death experience to extract a story from me for the *Herald*."

El grins, and then her gaze drops to the manila folder in front of me. "What's that?"

But suddenly the file isn't important, because Lea Li Zhang is in front of me. She's alive and we're safe and we're thirteen again, eating sno-balls and skinning our knees in the backwoods bayou.

"I'll tell you all about it later," I whisper, and then I tilt her chin up with my thumb and capture her lips with mine.

Chapter Thirty

The diner is completely packed. It's drizzling outside, tiny raindrops splattering the glass block inlaid at the front of Joan's Diner, but I still don't think I've ever seen *this* many people here before. I squint at the crowd as Andre and Damon escort the four of us past a barrier of tables outlined with Mardi Gras beads—a lot of them are locals, but even more are reporters.

"National news," Lea whispers, tipping her head to a huge camera pressed all the way up against the makeshift barricade. A smirk ghosts her face, and something in my stomach flips as her teasing eyes meet mine. "It looks like we're stars."

"Y'all sure are," Andre agrees brightly. The agency and I slide into our regular booth, and lights flash behind us. "Moms is losing her mind trying to keep up with all our broiled crawfish orders—the media's been camping out here for hours. Who knew all we needed to put Joan's Diner on the map was a couple of local celebrities?"

Damon glares at him. "They solved a murder, dickwad."

"Actually," Lea says, picking up her menu nonchalantly, "we solved two murders. I'll take the usual, please."

Imani and Sammy snort-laugh, and I blink at my girlfriend. She beams back, the blazing intensity in her face now simmering soft and low, and my heart aches with how much I love the four of us. How much love I have to give.

If any of us are stars, it's El. She finally published her article for Jim—a tell-all exclusive about the sapphic teenage detective agency that solved both Heather's murder and Stella's disappearance before I legally turned eighteen—and it included an incredible call to action regarding missing at-risk women and the importance of amateur sleuths that's already been cited in everything from the *Huffington Post* to the *New York Times*. To be honest, I've never been prouder of anyone in my life—or more ready to recruit them into the agency, if Lea decides to accept my offer to officially join. But that comes later. First, the four of us are here to celebrate: solving the case; bringing the agency back together; getting justice for Stella and Heather; and my birthday, since I never got to have a proper party in the aftermath of what happened at Deveraux Industries.

As Joan's twins walk away with our orders, Imani leans forward. Their expression is fiercely protective, and something sparks in my chest at the sight of it. "I hate to say it, but the

Hardy Boys are right, Iris. There are a lot of eyes on us in this place."

"So?" Sammy counters, gathering her curls into a high ponytail. "Let them look." She bats her lashes in the direction of the cameras, and Lea hides a smile behind her menu as Imani rolls their eyes.

Hillwood's newfound notoriety hasn't been too bad for the agency, either. Tickets to the fall production of *Grease* are completely sold out, and Mrs. Landry told Imani she's going to put in a good word for them with some big-shot designer who holds a lot of sway with the admissions board of the best costume design school in New York. The FIRST Robotics club asked Sammy if she'd be interested in coming back to code for the district competition after Lea's article went wide, and even though Sammy had to pay a fine for using her GPS-based app to track Nathan, she's currently working on improving it—along with her skills as an ethical hacker.

And I no longer feel like I'm useless. After all, I got justice. I solved a case. And it looks like I might be able to keep solving them, seeing as I finally finished all my college applications. I applied to every state school with a good undergraduate criminology program, and I'm excited to go somewhere next fall that won't make me pay for my own forensics kit.

A loud bang echoes through the diner, and the four of us whip around. A few feet away, Carrie and another server are struggling to restrain the media—some of the more enthusiastic journalists have broken through the tables, and one of the women even manages to make it halfway to us before a familiar figure steps in front of her.

"I'm sorry," Joan says, not sounding sorry at all as she holds her arm out like a guardrail. "They're not taking any questions tonight."

I frown. The blonde, curly-haired woman attempting to get a good glimpse of us is instantly familiar, but I'm more concerned with the necklace she's wearing. The golden charm hanging from it is shaped like half of a heart. Like it's part of a set.

Imani catches my eye, and I know they're thinking the same thing I am. There's still one mystery we haven't solved.

"It's okay, Joan. Let her through."

Joan turns around, the skirt of her baby-pink dress swishing. "You sure, cher? You know who she is, right?"

I grin. "I know."

Joan throws the woman one last nasty look before withdrawing her arm, muttering something that sounds like "too nice for their own good" and "eat them up alive." The woman beams, fixing her megawatt smile into place, and then the four of us are face-to-face with her.

"Claudia Garrett, *Channel Six News*," Claudia says, stretching out her hand. I don't take it, and her smile wobbles for only a fraction of a second before she amps it up even more. "Would you be willing to answer a few questions for me? I'm looking for a fresh angle on the Heather case, and I think a lot of people would be very interested to hear your side of the story. I mean, it's incredible what you all managed to accomplish. Livestreaming a murder confession? Uncovering a secret drug ring? Getting evidence that'll put Collin Cooper behind bars? That's one way to really stick it to the patriarchy, isn't it?"

Across the table, Sammy kicks my leg. *Patriarchy?* she mouths, her nose wrinkled in disgust. She turns to Claudia, decidedly not mouthing anymore. "People *died.*"

Claudia ignores her. "Or," she says eagerly, considering me alone now, "maybe you could tell me what drove you to investigate Heather's disappearance in the first place, Iris? I'm sure—"

I hold up a finger, and Claudia startles. "Just one second," I tell her. "I actually have a question for you first." I smile sweetly, taking out my phone and swiping through my camera roll until I find the picture I'm looking for. It's a big risk, but if I've learned anything during the past month I've been investigating Heather's case, it's to trust my gut.

I slide my phone across the table to Claudia and steeple my fingers. "Do you know this girl?"

The reporter's saccharine simper drops off her face. "Where did you get this?"

"I took it," I say plainly, staring at the photo of Nathan kissing Mystery Girl. "In October." When Claudia continues staring at me, I offer her an apologetic shrug. "I have a Nikon."

"That's my daughter, Lauren," Claudia says slowly. "But how…?"

Sammy blinks at her, wide-eyed, and I nod. "Well, your daughter is currently dating the ex-boyfriend of Heather Nasato and the half brother of Collin Cooper, the man who killed Heather and my sister. So if you're looking for a fresh angle"—I tilt my head, my eyes locking on Claudia's—"you might want to start your story there."

As the dazed *Channel Six News* reporter stumbles away from our booth, Imani shakes their head. "I should have known," they murmur, staring at the photo. "It was the necklace, wasn't it? They have matching ones."

"Not to mention the family resemblance," Sammy adds, watching Claudia go. "Or the fact we couldn't figure out who lives in Mystery Girl's house because Claudia Garrett is practically a local celebrity—they live in Bellevue Estates for protection. To be untraceable." Sammy sighs. "God. Nice one, Iris," she adds, punching me on the arm lightly. "I actually thought we were going to sell out for a minute there."

The corners of my lips twitch, and Imani stares at her. "Weren't you the first to volunteer to be deanonymized when Lea finally let us read the first draft of her article?"

"What does that have to do with anything?" Sammy retorts. "Lea's article was good, and we trust her. The story worked better when we made ourselves known." Her eyes glitter. "Besides, your recorded interview was *sixteen minutes long*, Imani. That's, like, a fourth of my entire stakeout playlist."

"And yet you called me to complain about only being quoted twice when it actually came out," Imani replies smugly.

Lea snickers and leans her head on my good shoulder, and as my friends descend into another one of their lighthearted sparring matches, I close my eyes and let the current of their conversation wash over me. I breathe in the scent of the diner, the grease and cinnamon and green tea shampoo mixing into one, and I think about how far I've come. About how this town is filled with broken girls. About how I'm one of them and know that now. But I'm also beginning to pick up my pieces and put them back together. For Stella. For Arden. For Heather. For Lea. For myself.

Next to me, my girlfriend squeezes my hand. I breathe out. I open my eyes.

The world has changed around us. It's visible in the sheer number of people here tonight, in the bags under Lea's eyes, in the exhaustion in Sammy's body, in the caution in Imani's expression. But it's okay, because I have the agency. It's okay, because we have one another.

"You know what? This place *is* too crowded," Sammy decides as another camera flashes behind us. "Carrie, can you make our order to-go?"

And as Carrie nods when she passes our table, the neon glow of the diner catching her tri-eyebrow piercing and faded green hair, my heart swells with gratitude.

After Carrie brings us a couple of foam containers filled with po'boys and Joan's Blueberry Beignets, the four of us head to the back exit. But before I step through the silver chrome door, I glance over my shoulder for one last look at the diner's patrons and see someone. Like the shadow of a ghost.

"Iris, you coming?" Imani asks, holding the door open for me with one hand while shielding their face with the other. It's a cloudy, muggy night in Hillwood; it's started to drizzle, and it looks like we're in for another Lafourche Parish storm.

"Go on without me," I say slowly, turning back to the diner. "I'll catch up in a bit."

Nathan Deveraux doesn't notice me until I'm right next to him. His skin is pale, almost translucent, and there's a line of uneven stubble on his chin. He looks up at me, his eyes red and watery, and a scowl settles over his face.

I gesture to the empty barstool next to him. "Mind if I sit?"

His scowl deepens, but he doesn't object when I slide onto the red leather seat. Instead, he keeps his eyes trained on the small TV above the bar, and I pretend to busy myself with the laminated menu in front of me—*Joan's Diner: The Best Cajun & Creole Breakfast in Town!*—until he finally speaks.

"If you want a thank-you, you're not going to get one."

I put down the menu. "I don't want you to thank me," I say softly. "I'd rather have an apology."

Nathan turns to me, his face completely hollow. "An apology? I didn't kill her, Iris. I didn't kill either of them."

"No," I agree. "But you suspected."

Something in Nathan's expression cracks. "What?"

"During the fight," I say simply. "The one you had with Heather in the parking lot just outside before she went missing. She told you, didn't she? About Arden and your half brother."

Nathan lets out a shaky breath. He looks absolutely miserable, and for a second I think he's not going to tell me the truth.

"She was looking into things for the final podcast episode," Nathan finally says. His voice is so quiet, I have to strain to hear him over the sounds of the kitchen and Andre taking the order of a nearby regular. "Trying to tie up loose ends, and she…she saw the two of them together. At homecoming."

"Did you confront him?" I ask quietly. "Mr. Cooper. That same night?"

Nathan runs a hand over his worn face. Nods. "I never talk to Collin. But I wanted…I wanted to be sure. Heather was making all of these accusations, and…Arden was my friend, too, you know? I needed to hear it from him. That he was innocent. That he wasn't involved with her." He shakes his head. "I didn't mention Heather, but it didn't matter. He figured it out."

"And then Heather went missing," I continue as an old rock-and-roll song starts playing faintly from the table jukebox behind us, "and that's when you knew something was wrong."

"I…I got worried." Nathan swallows. "Collin got into my head.…He made me think Heather skipped town because she found out about Lauren, and I was desperate. I didn't want other people to know. I didn't want them to find out the truth."

"He made you erratic and reckless. He turned you into the perfect scapegoat. And then he tried to take what he always wanted from you—your prestige, your power, your family legacy—by framing you for Heather's death."

Nathan laughs, but the sound is false and hollow. "They planned the whole thing out.…I got a note in my locker saying Principal Phillips needed to talk to me about some award I was going to hand out at Senior Night, but then he never showed. I was in the office the whole time, but there are no cameras anywhere in that goddamn school, and no one saw me come in, so how could I prove I was actually there?" He shakes his head. "And then they found her body, and Collin made me think I killed her." He looks up, his eyes dark. "But it wasn't me. It wasn't me, Iris."

I inhale, and my nails cut crescents against my palms. "Your half brother killed my sister, Nathan. He killed my sister, and he nearly killed me, and you knew about Arden and Collin and still didn't say shit to anyone."

"I didn't know for sure," Nathan whispers, and his walls break down. He swallows, his Adam's apple bobbing. "I wanted to be, but I wasn't, and Collin was so convincing...."

I remain silent. On the bar TV above us, an old photograph of Principal Phillips appears beside a somber newscaster's face, the words HILLWOOD HIGH SCHOOL PRINCIPAL PUT ON ADMINISTRA-TIVE LEAVE IN THE WAKE OF THREE STUDENT DEATHS, ILLICIT DRUG DEALS taking over the screen.

"Over the past month, I found out some things," I tell Nathan softly, not taking my eyes off the TV. "About my family and my friends. About my sister. And those things were hard to learn. They were hard to live with.... They still are."

I exhale, and this time I turn my full attention to him: Nathan Deveraux, Heather Nasato's cheating douchebag ex-boyfriend. "I want you to know I'm not here to forgive you for what you did to Heather or me or anyone else. I don't think I'm ever going to. But Nathan...I understand what you're going through. I've lived through it—thinking I was useless, being blamed for crimes I didn't commit, wanting justice without knowing how to get it— so if you want to talk to anyone about how you feel, you can talk to me." I slide off the red leather barstool, tilting my head to the phone in front of him before I can change my mind. "After all, you already have my number."

I turn around without waiting for a response, ready to rejoin the agency outside. But Nathan's voice stops me before I can. "Iris?"

I look back at him. "Yes?"

"I'm sorry."

I blink, and then I nod curtly. "See you around, Deveraux."

"Yeah," he says, and there's a note of something new in his voice as I leave. Regret. Understanding. Respect, maybe. "Yeah, Blackthorn. I'll see you around."

"All good?" Lea asks as I step out of the diner. "Ready to go back to your place and eat all this food? Maybe take a few minutes to figure out why most of the blueberry beignets are already missing?"

I can feel myself smile, and I don't try to stop it this time. "I would love that," I say, glancing at Imani just as Sammy finishes licking powdered sugar off of her fingers with a sheepish grin. "But can we make a quick stop first? There's something I still need to do."

Chapter Thirty-One

It's raining. Mud sticks to the soles of my worn combat boots and dots the edges of my favorite black longcoat, but the umbrella in my messenger bag stays unopened. I'm holding a fistful of saggy white roses—Lucille's General Store had only one bouquet left— but I'm here. And that's what matters.

I squelch forward in the muck and approach the wrought-iron gates. Imani's headlights illuminate the glistening metalwork of the definitive words above me: HILLWOOD CEMETERY. But the rest of the agency isn't coming in. They all know I have to do this part alone.

I push open the gates. Rows of headstones greet me, damp

and glittering in the drizzle, and I take a deep breath. There's no turning back now.

Thorns dig into my palm as I push forward, searching for Stella's name in the misty haze. I haven't visited my sister's grave since my mom buried her empty casket in a desperate bid for closure over a year ago, and I don't remember where her plot is. I don't remember much about that day.

But I don't want to forget. Not anymore, and not right now, and not ever again. Because Stella may be gone, but her memory lives on in the people who loved her. It lives on in the people who care. And because I owe it to my sister to honor her life. The kind of person she was, the kind of *sister* she was, even if that makes it harder to ignore the kind of person she could have been with more time.

Water droplets cling to my cuffed pants as I pass slabs upon slabs of gray markers, memories of my sister running through my mind with every step: Stella throwing popcorn at my head during the night we tried to stay up for a twenty-five-hour *Scooby-Doo* movie marathon. Stella lip-synching to old rock songs every time she took me to Joan's Diner because she knew watching her head-bang to the tinny jukebox music never failed to make me laugh. Stella smuggling me saltwater taffy after coming back from long shifts on Sugar Boulevard, Stella helping me with my junior year chemistry homework until we both fell asleep at the kitchen table, Stella coaxing me to help her feed the white Great Danes in our neighbor's backyard in Chevalier because she worried about them going hungry. Stella insisting there wasn't a single thing a person couldn't learn how to do from shitty wikiHow tutorials alone.

I still can't believe she's really gone. That after this long, my journey ends here, on a cloudy November night at the Hillwood cemetery. In the place where Heather and Arden will be buried soon. But even though there's still so much to go through—the funerals, the paperwork, the trials—I also know our community will get through it together.

I weave my way through the stones.

Above me, a crow caws. And then I see it. One of the newer headstones, with a white inscription and a printed portrait.

My breath catches. "Found you," I whisper.

I pick my way across the graves until I'm standing directly in front of my sister's, and then I collapse. Mud seeps into my clothes, but I can't move. I just kneel there, clutching my flowers, seized with a quiet unfurling. Grief and hope rolled into one.

In the photo etched into the black granite, Stella is stoic and pale. Dark hair sweeps across her shoulders in a pretty wave, but her lips are tight and drawn. I don't know when the photo was taken. There are so many things I'll never know.

My eyes drop to the inscription below her:

STELLA MIRANDA BLACKTHORN

AN ANGEL ON EARTH AND IN HEAVEN

AND FOREVER IN OUR HEARTS

And maybe the police couldn't save Stella. Maybe I couldn't save her, and maybe I'll have to live with that weight for the rest of my life. But tonight, I'm not here as a mourner. Tonight, I'm here to pay my respects.

I lay the fragile white roses on her headstone. There are five in total—one for every girl that Collin and Eastwick hurt. One for every girl we'll remember.

The petals are limp, but they do not fall.

And neither will we.

Acknowledgments

It truly does take a village to raise a book—I've always wanted to say that!—and here is mine.

First, thank you, Reader, for picking up *How to Find a Missing Girl* and giving Iris and her sapphic detective agency a chance. It's an honor you chose to spend your time with the characters I created. I hope you enjoyed the ride.

Writing this book as a high school senior was one of the best things I've ever done, but getting it published at twenty is a very close second. Thank you to my amazing literary agent, Jessica Errera, for championing my work and guiding me through the turbulent waters of publishing. I am so appreciative of you and all the work you do.

Thank you also to my spectacular editor, Alexandra Hightower, for your keen eye and inimitable insight. You brought out the heart of this story in a way I didn't even think was possible, and I cannot wait to work with you again.

Thank you to Georgina Mitchell, my lovely UK editor, for taking *HtFaMG* across the pond. Thank you also to Dan

Letchworth, my incredible copyeditor, and Lindsay Walter-Greaney, my fantastic production editor, for making me sound smarter than I may deserve; to Crystal Castro and Brittany Groves, for keeping things running behind the scenes; to my entire NOVL squad, including Mara Brashem, Andie Divelbiss, Alice Gelber, Bill Grace, Stef Hoffman, Savannah Kennelly, and Emilie Polster, for the warmest welcome; to Hannah Klein, for spreading the hype; and to the rest of the team behind Little, Brown Books for Young Readers, including Patricia Alvarado, Michelle Figueroa, Hannah Koerner, Amber Mercado, Christie Michel, and Victoria Stapleton. As a voracious young reader, I used to dream about one day being on shelves with my favorite books. Now I share a publisher with some of them, and I could not be more grateful.

A giant thank-you to my cover designer, Karina Granda, for the pink, bloody YA thriller cover of my dreams. The milkshake splatter! The title font! The blood on the spine! I could scream about (and stare at) it forever—thank you for turning my words into a stunning work of art.

Thank you also to Allison Hufford, Jack McIntyre, Madeleine McGrath, Chris Prestia, Julianne Tinari, and everyone else at Jane Rotrosen Agency. I am indebted to your expertise.

To Becca Rodriguez—thank you for believing in *HtFaMG* enough to try to take her to the screen.

To my friends in publishing, for their wonderful words of encouragement: Ananya, Birdie, Birukti, Chelsea, Casey, Elle, Erin, Kalie, Kamilah, Kyla, Mackenzie, Nancy, Ryan, Sarah, and so many more. This would all feel a lot scarier without you. Thank you for being here, even if I can't name you all.

A huge thank-you to my friends outside publishing, who keep me sane through the ups-and-downs the industry entails. You know who you are. And thank you to everyone who took the time to read an ARC of this book and leave a review or blurb. Your early support is so appreciated.

Amias, thank you for being the World's Best Beta Reader. You've read every one of my NaNoWriMo first drafts, dignified each of my incoherent 3:00 AM dialogue snippets, and supported me unconditionally through my entire publishing journey. I am incredibly lucky to have you in my life. We made it this far.

Ann, Layla, Sydney, and Famke, thank you for the group FaceTime calls, holiday cards, and general commiserating. I can't even describe how much it has meant to have the four of you by my side throughout every step of this process, and I can't wait to buy a bajillion copies of all your books in the upcoming year(s). Big Five forever. And to the fellow young writers in my circles who have advised me, connected with me, and encouraged me along the way, however briefly—thank you. I see you. We exist.

To my fellow pansexuals: This one is for us. And to every LGBTQ+ author who had the courage to write their truths before I wrote mine: It is because of your strength that there is a place in the industry for authors like me. Thank you for paving the way.

My most sincere appreciation to WMC and all its members for being there for me before I even started drafting *HtFaMG*. Your collective knowledge and concentrated effort to share information has opened countless doors, and I am proud to stand among your ranks.

To the authors of the 2023 Debut Slack, for holding my hand throughout one of the most nerve-wracking years of my life. And to every other writing group I've ever been in, for however long: Thank you for your love and counsel.

Special thanks to Mr. Alexander for giving me a safe haven within the Creative Writing Club in high school. It is my belief that every queer writer needs an emotional support English teacher—thank you for being mine.

Thank you to Jacque Jacobs for always being willing to chat with me about writing. You inspire me every day.

Děkuji také mé rodině v Čechách: Elišce, Valtrovi, Ivetě, Tomášovi, Ivetce, Nikolce, Heleně, Vladkovi, Radkovi, Dáši, Silvince, Tomovi, Danečkovi a Tomáškovi. Všech si vás vážím, mám vás velmi ráda a vaši lásku a podporu cítím i přes oceán!

Thank you also to my two amazing younger sisters, Natalia and Karolina, for always having my back. I can't wait to see the incredible people you both grow up to be.

I am endlessly grateful to my parents, to whom this book is dedicated, for encouraging me to pursue my dreams with fervor and passion. I couldn't have done any of this without you. I hope I made you proud.

And lastly, thank you to my partner, Elijah, for always picking me up on my bad days, giving me the space to create, and accepting me just as I am. I love you. Here's to the rest of our story.

Resources

Resources for families of missing persons under the age of eighteen, including abducted children and endangered runaways:
National Center for Missing and Exploited Children (NCMEC)
https://www.missingkids.org/MissingChild
1-800-THE-LOST (843-5678)

United States national database and resource center for missing, unidentified, and unclaimed person cases:
National Missing and Unidentified Persons System (NamUs)
https://namus.nij.ojp.gov/

Resources for young people in abusive relationships, households, or situations:
National Resource Center on Domestic Violence
https://www.nrcdv.org/rhydvtoolkit/teens/
1-800-799-7233

24/7 crisis intervention and suicide prevention for LGBTQ+ individuals under the age of twenty-five:
The Trevor Project
https://www.thetrevorproject.org/resources/
1-866-488-7386 or text START to 678-678

Mental health support for teens and young adults:
National Alliance on Mental Illness (NAMI)
https://www.nami.org/Your-Journey/Kids-Teens-and-Young -Adults